❧

The Sugar Maple Grove

John E. Espy

OPEN BOOKS

Dedication

The Sugar Maple Grove has two dedications, the first is to my wife of now many years, Treasa Glinnwater. Each day, from the moment we first laid eyes on each other, has been a love story that I had only imagined could have come true.

The second dedication is to Mr. Robert Lewis Yoakum, which requires a bit of an explanation. A character in *The Sugar Maple Grove* is Robert Lewis. This character is based on my friend of the same name. Robert Lewis was seventeen years older than I was. I had just turned six and my family moved into the house where our property bordered Robert's, whom we called Bob. Bob, how I knew him, was "retarded"—a term used in those days to describe the developmentally disabled. He was also a *caulbearer*. I remember a time shortly after my father suffered a near fatal electrocution, Bob's mother called out of the blue to tell us, "Robert Lewis said I should call you right away, that something bad has happened?" This wasn't an isolated event and his mother, when these *knowings* happened, would just say, "well, you know he was born with a veil."

All in all Bob was one of the finest human beings I have ever known. He wasn't black, as Robert Lewis is in *The Sugar Maple Grove*, but he did in fact eat onions like apples and whenever he could helped himself to hunks of butter from his mother's table, who would chastise him by yelling "...Robert Lewis!" Bob was my best friend for many years, I taught him to write his name and to read some. Bob taught me the meaning of kindness and an *unflinching* commitment to friendship.

He suffered all of the indignities that one suffers being different. And yet, he never lost his dignity or his ability to express forgiveness to those who treated him less than they imagined themselves to be. Often saying, "Dey don't know what der doing, I'm gonna pray for um." Bob died in 2007 and is buried next to his mother and father. Yet few will remember to recall his name or who he was in this world and that to my mind would be a tragedy. His decency as a human being could offer much to many. Bob was someone who should not be forgotten to the knowledge of man. I hope in this small way that those reading *The Sugar Maple Grove* will remember that Robert Lewis in fact inhabited a place in this world and for that all too brief time, this earth was a better place for it.

A special thank you to Mr. Richard Plank, who was an early and ongoing reader. Rick offered much support, kind criticism and research material along the way.

Author's Note

The Sugar Maple Grove is not about what we have lost. Rather, it is about what we are returning to: Those times when slavery of many forms was not only tolerated but promoted. A time when thugs of one kind or another were not tolerated but considered *De Rigueur*. A time when workers were considered nothing more than expendable chattel. A time when deeply derogatory representations for human beings was considered common place and in explanatory form, "… Just being descriptive." A time when courts were little more than legitimized sanctuaries for the corrupt. And, in many ways, a time when revenge was the only redress to set something right.

By the rivers of Babylon,
There we sat down, yea, we wept
When we remembered Zion.
We hung our harps
Upon the willows in the midst of it.
For there those who carried us away captive asked of us a song,
And those who plundered us requested mirth,
Saying, "Sing us one of the songs of Zion!"
How shall we sing the Lord's song
In a foreign land?
If I forget you, O Jerusalem,
Let my right hand forget its skill!
If I do not remember you,
Let my tongue cling to the roof of my mouth—
If I do not exalt Jerusalem
Above my chief joy.
Remember, O Lord, against the sons of Edom
The day of Jerusalem,
Who said, "Raze it, raze it,
To its very foundation!"
O daughter of Babylon, who are to be destroyed,
Happy the one who repays you as you have served us!
Happy the one who takes and dashes
Your little ones against the rock!

Psalm 137
KJV

Part One

Van Lear, Kentucky

Chapter 1

AND THEN, THERE WAS Flem. Flem Lemaster'd had three brothers, who now are long at rest. And always when he was tossin' and turnin' this way and that, the same distressin' dream would come to haunt him and he'd see them after the blast, layin' there boxed-up with their arms forever folded across their breasts. On that airish fall morning about 6:00 or so, he awoke to a thick hoary fog covering the holler. So thick it was that Flem couldn't even see the cornfield across the way, where, when he was just a youngin' he and his granddaddy had seen one of Van Lear's white frocked lost spirits, with her coal black hair being caught up in such a state of frenzy that it looked like it was trying to escape from the top of her head. "There she is boy," Flem remembered his granddaddy whispering. "That ain't a sight that you'll ever be likely to forget." And, right after Flem's eyes took sight of the wandering soul, he tried like the dickens to push his chin into his chest, for it was said that your life is cut short by the amount of time that you cast your sight on an itinerate one that had been ill fated to a vaporous eternity. But, being the way his granddaddy was, he grabbed a handful of Flem's hair, jerked the boy's head back and made him stare until she disappeared into the stripped corn stalks just as though she'd never been there in the first place. Flem also remembered that he wet the bed that night, soaking the straw. The next morning he got a lickin' from his momma who said he was too big a boy to be pissin' hisself. Weather had beginning to turn now, it wouldn't be long before the snow started up and he'd have to be trudging his way back up to the mine.

Flem had been laid off for a few months because he'd blown his thumb and forefinger off while testing a fuse to open a coal vein.

He'd peeled back the fuse and struck down on it with a piece of glass when it jumped right to the shot and exploded in his hand. Took his thumb and finger clean off. Flem had already lost two of his fingers on that hand years before, when his old man, figurin' it was about time to admit him into manhood, had takin' Flem down to the muddy banks of the Ohio snappin turtle huntin. No boy, having heard tell the stories from the other finger-missing older boys, ever looked forward to it but if you were going to prove yourself worthy in the eyes of your daddy it was just something you had to do.

"There weren't no choice about it," Flem could remember his daddy saying about when he'd lost a couple of his own fingers. First you find a turtle hole in the thick bank muck, shove your hand deep into the turtle nest and pull that snapper out by its head before your hand got tore off. If that turtle's beak gotchur hand first he sure wudn't about to let go before hearing a clap of thunder. Most all of the boys brought up from that part of West Virginia were missing fingers and some even whole hands.

The day Flem 'd blown his thumb off, a couple of the other miners took him down to the Golden Rule hospital.

Dr. Ernest Elmo Archer, who founded the hospital and had come back from the war with surgical experience, said that Flem's one remaining finger on that hand was just too mangled from the blast, it was gonna have to go. Dr. Archer'd knew what he was talking about, he'd seen a lot of soldiers overseas who'd been blown up in one way or another. The doctor joked that there wasn't even enough finger left for Flem to pick his nose with. After the amputation, Flem was left with a finger-less palm sticking out of his shirt sleeve that he could barely squeeze tight enough to cup a spoon when eating Nora's mashed potatoes. He'd never be able to swing a pickaxe again, but since he knew mine work better than most anyone else the boss man said he wanted to move Flem up to the top, working the tipple.

Nora, Flem's wife, was one of the Prater girls, having been born and bred in Van Lear. Said it was that her great granddaddy had helped to make that part of Kentucky safe from the Shawnee. Hell, her daddy had said the Shawnee even tried to scalp Daniel Boone up around the late 1700s. Nora never met her great granddaddy though 'cause he'd been killed by a fur trapper who said he was poaching his prey, long before she'd even been thought of being born. Nora was a plain girl, thinking to herself just like her momma 'd say that she'd never find a good-for-something husband. So when Flem came along and asked her to marry him, right just before Nora came into her sixteenth year, she said yes almighty for sure. Flem was about twenty years older or thereabouts, they figured. They'd had seven children but only four were living. Two had died, right about the same time when a fever came through the junction and their oldest had been swept into a swell fishing in the Levisa Fork. It had been flooding pretty bad that year and the river was mighty and muddy. They looked long and hard for days but never found Flem Jr's body.

Flem, still in his nightshirt, stepped out the backdoor and felt the wet dirt sticking to his leather-soled feet. He swung open the door to the outhouse. Too cold now for flies, Flem thought. In the muggy heat of the Kentucky summers the flies in the outhouses were just about unbearable. Sometimes, being blocked up didn't seem nearly as bad as having hundreds of frenzied flies buzzing around your ass.

He spit his morning hock of thick black phlegm. Even though he'd not been down in the mine for a while, Flem was still coughing up coal-laced phlegm. He knew he was coming down with the black lung. Didn't make no matter how old or young you were. If you went down into the hole for long at all the black lung'd end up getting you. "Breathe that coal dust in, it's good for you," the company doctor used to say when Flem complained he was having trouble catching his breath. The doc just wrote in his records that Flem was coming down with the asthma. Probably'd had it since he was a boy. According to the doc, just about every one of the miners had asthma when they were youngins. Best thing Flem could do, the doctor said, was to smoke as many cigarettes as his coal scrip would buy him at the company store. "The smoke'l keep your lungs clear," the doctor had told him.

After pissing, Flem thought it'd be good to get his blood circulating so he walked down the grassy embankment to the front of the white frame house. When he rounded the corner Flem froze right in his stride. There, standing on the slats of the porch, were dozens of switches stacked and bound tight waisted, like Devil's Night corn stalks.

They'd been so careful, he and Runa. Neither one of them had intended for things to get out of hand and now they'd been found out. It didn't matter by whom. But if they'd didn't stop the men who'd left the switches on his porch would take him out to the woods, tie him to a tree and switch him to within an inch of his life. If he still didn't stop cavorting with another man's wife, the men in white hoods would snatch him out of his bed right as he lay sleeping next to Nora, strip him butt naked, just like the way God had brought him into this world, and then shoot him dead, avenging Nora's honor.

Just as quick as he could Flem gathered up the bundle and tucked the switch stalks under his arm. He walked back up the muddy hill around behind the outhouse, bent down and undid the baler twine that held the switches tightly together and then scattered them about the field. Then he tossed the twine into one of the outhouse privy holes. It was the same kind of twine that'd get mixed in with the hay during harvesting. The kind the cattle'd eat along with the feed hay. It'd bind the cows guts up to the point where they'd have to be shot, they'd be hurting so bad. Flem had told Runa that he'd be coming over her way later that afternoon after Obadiah had left for the mine. Even though it was gonna to break his heart, Flem knew he'd never again be spending time alone with Runa Whitt.

Nora started stirring awake about an hour or so after Flem had scattered the switches. Her dressing gown was still hiked up above her waist from the night before. Nora took no pleasure from intimate relations with Flem. It had always bothered her that it didn't hurt when Flem was going in and out of her. There'd been whispers about that it was supposed to be real painful but Nora'd never known that. An older God-fearing woman that Nora sometime confided in had told her that some good women had to contend with the Devil temptin' them by making it wet between their legs to take the pain away. Sometimes right when she climbed into bed, Nora would tuck her dressing gown up between her legs to wick up the wetness that always made her thick red public hair sticky. She could never figure on a good answer as to why it was called public hair, it being hidden away and all.

Every night, Nora 'd silently pray up to God to make it stop, but she'd get so flushed with embarrassment trying to talk to the Lord about such intimate matters, that she always stopped right in mid prayer. She guessed that was why God had never really run the Devil out from between her legs. Maybe someday she'd be able to finish her prayers and God would make her dry up like a droughted out creek bed. Sometimes Nora'd even tried to fool God and Flem too, by acting like she was sleeping when he rolled her over on her back and pushed the dressing gown up around her waist. She did her best to live by the Word of the Lord. It was fact that intimate relations were not a favor to your husband, no matter what, but were an obligation, even if you were tired and worn out from taking care of the children and tending to the chores around the homeplace. Even though she'd never had any experience with another man, Flem, it seemed to Nora, had a powerful need, turning her over several times a week. As Nora wiped her eyes of sleep and lifted her legs off the side of the bed, some of Flem from the night before dropped out of her and fell into a puddle onto the floor.

Nora reached between her legs and cleaned herself to the wafting smell of Kentucky scramble. It wasn't Sunday, so she couldn't figure out why Flem'd be cooking up breakfast. One thing for sure, the bacon that Flem was creaming into the eggs was sure waking up her belly.

"Flem LeMaster," Nora said, appearing at the kitchen door, "… what are you doing cookin' up breakfast?" Flem, thankful that Nora hadn't seen the switch stack on the porch, laid the spatula down beside the well-seasoned cast iron skillet, walked over to her and gave her some sugar, right there in front of their two oldest living children. Nora put her hand right up to Flem's flannel-covered chest and pushed him back hard away, as the jowl bacon crackled behind them in the skillet.

It was hard to tell whose eyes had seen them, things'd been changing in the Junction. Everybody it seemed was on edge about being watched by somebody. There seemed to be more looker on'ers now that the White Knights had taken root in Van Lear. The Night Riders, as the Knights sometimes called themselves, had to come a long ways over from Powderly, 'cause the niggers had figured out how to slick up over the Tennessee-Georgia line by taking a more eastern route and then doubling back up over the Appalachians. They'd come up through the woods from West Virginia, cut up over to Butcher Holler and then try and lay low in the hills around Van Lear 'til night fell. No doubt about it, it was hard to see a nigger at night. Rumor said there was a nigger lover over the ridge from Butcher Holler who'd cut a path up through the woods that led right up over to Van Lear.

If the nigger lived to make it over the Appalachians, he'd work his way west to the tributary of the Ohio. It was a mighty trudge then all the way up the Ohio to Ripley. Mostly they'd stay in the water right along the bank so the dogs guarding nearby houses didn't catch their scent. It was said too that niggers carried a powerful scent.

When a jig was caught sneaking around in the woods the Knights would strap him to a tree and whip his back with barbed wire, with a promise after each lash of just going ahead and hanging him, if the boy'd just say who was still part of the railroad that helped the niggers make their way north. But they'd not been told much of anything, just pretty much to go here and there, so there wasn't much left to hang once the beating did stop.

If a colored made it through the morass of the dense forest to Ripley, which was known to be real nigger friendly, they'd buy their way across the Ohio by loading pork barrels onto the broad horns.

Once the Night Riders got word that any boys were slickin around in the woods, they'd hide out and either shoot them on sight or leave them strung up off the long arm of a white birch. That way other nigger boys'd see them swingin' neck stretched from the tree. Here tell their peckers got hard when they got lynched up too. It didn't make no mind too much to Flem about the niggers though. When he'd been back in the fifth grade, Flem'd been taught that the war between the North and the South was fought because of niggers. Just didn't make no sense to Flem, why do all that killing just over a bunch of niggers? Plus, at least down south, even though the north had won, it didn't make no difference no how. Now the White Knights had their eyes set on Flem because he'd been having unnatural relations with Runa. If they didn't stop now, Flem knew they'd kill him and pour hot tar on Runa's privates. He couldn't even tell her why he'd not have anything more to do with her, no matter how he felt.

Runa flitted more than usual that morning waiting for Obadiah to leave for the mine. She'd just begun to wake up their slow-eyed boy, Ned, from a deep sleep, shaking his shoulder trying her best to make him get his self moving. Not that he did much when he was awake. When Cora Pelphrey had helped deliver the boy, fifteen years ago now, she snarled up her lip and shook her head when she saw Ned's misshapen head come pushing out of Runa. "He's got the slow eyes, this boy, he ain't gonna be good for much, that's for sure."

Cora'd delivered so many youngins in her day that even the doctors would call on her for help if they had a baby leanin abouts this way or that. Cora'd been a big girl all her life. Her momma had said that of all the thirteen children she had beared, Cora'd been the one that almost tore her apart. And, once Cora got the sugar, she bloomed up to more than five hundred pounds, being forced to stay right around her homeplace, rocking her way through the rest of her life, spending most of her time trying her best to swat away the horse flies that'd lay their eggs in the well of ulcers that were all over her legs. When the day of Cora's passing finally came, the undertaker had to nail two coffins together just to make one big enough to hold her. He said to the relatives that it was best if they didn't show poor Cora at her funeral not giving any particular reason. But, truth be told, the undertaker had to take Cora's body out to his farm and use a horse sling to get her into the coffin he'd pounded together, dropping her when the block and tackle came busting apart right when she was about five feet or so shy of the box. The undertaker told his wife later that night that when Cora fell into the coffin she split open like a rotten peach, making a mess like he'd never seen before.

Runa and Flem usually met in the plow shed up behind the house amidst the mule collar, halter and a couple of dusty straw bales that Runa had covered up nice and soft with a patch quilt. Flem could come back over the ridge just behind Obadiah's homeplace without anyone seeing him, or so he'd thought. Obadiah always left for the mine at 7:00. Runa tried her best to always have Ned up and about before Obadiah walked out the door, lunch pail and pickaxe in hand in case Ned needed a swattin. He was gettin' to be so big now that Runa couldn't handle him like she used to be able to. She and Obadiah got into some awful arguments when Obadiah'd say that Ned was so good for nothing that if he were a dog he'd take him out and shoot him. If he weren't gonna do his part what was the use in keeping him around having to put hard worked for food in his mouth? Often, right before Runa dreamed herself off to sleep, she wondered if the Lord had gone ahead and put Ned, broken beyond fixing, inside her belly because He knew she was going to be up and breaking His seventh commandment. Later in her life, Runa figured that He'd just gone ahead and punished her for what He knew she was going to up and do anyhow. Preacher said that the Lord knew his plan for us from the second a woman was with child. It didn't make no sense to Runa though why the Lord would make someone sin to go against His ways. Although Runa never uttered a word out loud, she felt guilty for thinking that the Lord used His people to do his dirty work. She was sure she was going to burn in Hell for thinking that way but the more of life's bark that grew on her, the more Runa suffered her doubting thoughts.

Flem'd never known a woman like Runa before. When he and Nora had intimate relations, she'd just lay there, not moving a muscle. He just thought that was the way it was supposed to be. Then when he and Runa started committing adulterated relations he'd been surprised how worked up Runa got. It didn't seem natural to him at first, especially when she'd start breathing real hard and whispering in his ear for him to go faster and then push her private part right up against his. But he'd say to himself that Runa was like white lightning was when he was a younger man. When no matter what, he couldn't stop himself from calling on the moonshiners atop Turkey Knob. Before Obadiah left that morning he gave Runa some sugar on her cheek and hugged her close. Other than suffering the embarrassment of their slow-eyed boy, Obadiah was a satisfied man. He had a good, faithful, church-going woman, who was one of only a few redheads in the junction. Obadiah had already been made a crew boss and was sitting next in line to take over handling loading the coal cars when the #1 rolled under the slat loader coming off the tipple. The paymaster never made a mistake in putting the right amount of scrip on Obadiah's pay slip the way he did with so many of the other miners. Obadiah also worked his men harder and made them pick deeper than any of the other crew bosses.

Before he left for work, he turned around and took one last look at Runa, standing on the unleveled porch waving him on his way. Right then, Obadiah heard the first whistle call of Mine 151 giving the junction miners a thirty-minute warning to report for work. If they weren't on time they wouldn't be able to go down into the hole and if they didn't go down into the hole they wouldn't get their scrip for the day. Obadiah was the only crew boss that had a one hundred percent production for the whole year.

Truth be told, the men knew it was best not to cross Obadiah. He was a quiet man who didn't have no qualms about letting his scarred-up fists do his talking when he got riled. It was once said that a panhandler who'd come around got real ornery with Runa one day just a few years back, not taking no for an answer. Obadiah heard the ruckus and came out from inside the house and told him he'd better be on his way. The panhandler thought better of it and was insistin' that Runa pay him fifteen cents for wastin' his time by havin' him show her the newest pots and pans straight over from Lexington. Right in between his insistins' the panhandler stood stunned, like he'd just been hit by lightning. He staggered sideways drunk like and then fell backwards off the porch. He was dead from Obadiah's right hand to the side of his head before he ever hit the ground. Jiles Ratliff, Obadiah's neighbor across the way, saw the panhandler die and sauntered over to help Obadiah drag the body up the road for the constable to figure out where he'd come from. He'd have a hard time of it though 'cause no one talked to the constable no how, troublemaker that he was. The folks in the junction knew what had to be done and took care of it accordin'. They didn't need no law coming around stickin' its nose in their business. That night Obadiah and Jiles' families had supper together. Runa and Esther Ratliff cooked up a big mess of white beans and ham hocks in the new pots and pans that they'd divided up between them.

The entrance to the shaft Obadiah and his men worked was off to the back of Mine 151, cut into one of hillsides. The timber framing the entrance looked like a midget's railroad tunnel with a set of vanishing rails that led deep into the unforgiving darkness of the earth's core. There was no cage at this hole to take the men down into the mine, only the hopper car where all eight miners on Obadiah's crew had to crowd right up next to one another.

The miners preparing for their shift could be seen trudging up the rails, pickaxes over their shoulders, wearing their leather hats with carbide lanterns attached to a bent metal plate riveted to the front right over top of the bill. The miners took turns lighting each other's lanterns as they descended into the hole. They all knew the mine was a dangerous place, not a one of them didn't know someone who hadn't been killed in the mine one way or another. What would scare them the most was if the canary stopped singing its song. If the bird song stopped for more than a few seconds the miners knew they had precious few minutes to get up outta the darkness. If they didn't, the coal bed gas that'd killed the canary would reach a point where they'd all either die of gas poisoning or their carbide lanterns would ignite the methane and incinerate them alive.

As Obadiah's men crowded into the hopper, Jacob, Obadiah's first cousin by marriage, checked the hand brake, which was nothing more than a forged handle pinned to the side of the hopper. When the miner manning the brake pulled the arm bar hard back against the steel wheels, it would start slowing the car. The drop to the bottom was about a forty-five degree downward slope. It sometimes took upwards of half an hour for them to get all their hearing back once they got down into the hole. The brake lever grinding against a steel wheel, with the hopper traveling about twenty miles an hours, was deafening to the men.

The ride down took about fifteen minutes or so and the ride up took about thirty because the winding gear at the top on the hole always seemed to groan the most after having hauled up load after load of coal rock all day long. Also, the CONSOL foreman who ran the hoist despised Obadiah. After ten hours down in the hole, the miners were especially stiffed up from being bent over in a space barely four feet tall, swinging pickaxes while resting their bleeding knees on knife-sharp rocks, breathing coal dust and shitting and pissing in a vein that'd been stripped bare.

The foreman had been brought down by CONSOL from Chillicothe. Said they needed a man who wasn't from around the area to manage the mine. One of the miners overheard the big bosses talking, saying that the foreman had worked the steel mills up the Ohio way and would beat his men senseless if they got out of line. The bosses thought that was the kind of man they needed down Van Lear way to take care of the 151, especially with the whisperin' going on amongst the miners about bringing in the union and all. Given that the foreman hated Obadiah for commanding a respect with the men that he'd never have, he always made the ride back up out of the hole twice as long as it needed to be. Seemed like the foreman always had some kind of excuse about the winding gear getting jammed up or some other such lying bullshit. Once the men caught onto what he was up to, they saved their moanin' and groanin' about being stiff and sore until they got out of earshot of him. For whatever reason the foreman never was known to pull out his leather sap and threaten any of the miners. As a matter of fact, it was him who seemed like he was intimidated by the miners. Obadiah guessed that the steel workers up north didn't carry pick axes.

The talk going down the hole that morning was all about Lon Lynch having been arrested by the constable for raping his neighbor girl, Belinda Blevens. She was only nine years old and he hurt her real bad, Jacob said. Lon'd been broken up from his wife going on three years now and used to talk about how lonely a man got not having anyone to come home to after being underground all night long. Lon worked one of the holes higher up on the back ridge. Jacob thought they should get a posse together and make justice their own way. The way justice used to be: drag Lon out of jail and hang him from the Miller Creek water tower. This way everyone'd see him hanging there, knowing what they'd get if they hurt any of the youngins the way Lon had. When the men in the junction were still able to handle their own affairs, there weren't so much of this kind of nonsense goin' on. But Jacob'd heard it was now happening a lot in Van Lear but it seemed like no one ever spoke up much about it. He swore though that if any man ever hurt one of his girls, he'd kill him with his bare hands. Jacob and Cissy, his wife of more than ten years now, had two daughters, Ruby and Della.

Jacob said he was surprised that the constable had gotten to Lon before the Knights had. They'd a killed him for sure. He must've been awful secret in his dealings, what he could figure. Obadiah shook his head in disgust and changed the conversation saying that it had sure been a busy night at the jail. He'd heard that the constable shot and killed the no account Lee Dollarhide, who was already sitting in a cell, waiting to be transferred up to the state prison for beating his daddy to death with a shovel. When Dollarhide pushed past the constable while he was trying to put Lon in the cell, the constable turned around, pulled his 32-20 Colt, and dropped him dead with a shot right smack to the back of his head. Once the undertaker got there, he said he was surprised that there wasn't much blood oozing out of the bullet hole. The constable pushed on ol' Dollarhide with his muddy boot and said that was because there wasn't much between Dollarhide's ears to bleed out.

The engineer bringing in the #1 that day had actuated the whistle right at the time that the constable's revolver delivered the cartridge that'd killed ol' Dollarhide. Being as loud as it was, the whistle'd drowned out the sound of the shot, making it seem like Dollarhide'd been killed by the blast of the whistle instead of the blast of the constable's gun.

The undertaker'd got a couple of the Irish Micks who'd rode in on one of the #1's flatbeds to help him put Dollarhide's body in the back of his draft horse drawn hearse. Usually the stiffs from the state didn't have any relatives that wanted to claim them so the undertaker didn't have to do much to fix them up to make them look presentable. He could just wipe the body down with lye soap and water, have the constable officially say that was who he was burying and haul them in a pine box up to Cumbo mountain cemetery. Then he'd put them in a grave marked with their names painted across as flat a rock as he could find. No one knew it but if the man he was burying was particularly despicable, the undertaker'd always piss on his grave before he came back down from Cumbo ridge.

The hole stunk particularly dank that morning when the miners caught the first draft of air coming back at them as the hopper started its roll. The rail-polished wheels of the car rattled against their axles as the weight shifted back and forth. The men always made sure they were up and eating breakfast at least an hour or so before they boarded the hopper so they didn't vomit over the side from being tousled around.

A heavily coiled cable unspooled like a taut snake behind the descending hopper, slipping here and there, causing the men's words to bounce off the shaft walls like they were being slung from a slingshot.

Rolling along a few hundred yards down the rails, the miners in unison ducked down to miss getting hit by Sammy Bickett's beam that stuck out from one of the timber braces. The men called it Sammy Bickett's beam because on his first day going down into the 151, Sammy had not ducked down far enough and the beam caught him right between the eyes. Knocked him right out of the hopper. Two of the miners had to pull themselves back up a couple a hundred yards once they got to the bottom and then drag Sammy back down in order to put him in the hopper to get him back up top. By the time they'd done all that Sammy's head was swollen as big as a springtime melon and his eyes were buggin' out something awful. There wasn't much anyone could do for him that they knew for sure. He'd pretty much never been the same after that. It seemed like when that beam hit him it had just knocked all the sense out of Sammy's head. Everybody in Van Lear knew what had happened to him and just made excuses for him, saying that he wasn't right in the head. A few months later, Sammy for some reason or other just started walking the tracks from the Junction down into Paintsville. The blow to Sammy's head had made him not only dumb but mostly deaf too. The constable guessed that's why he didn't hear the train coming around the rim of the Cumbo ridge before it hit him from behind.

Bickett's Beam also marked the spot where the men knew they had about two hundred more yards to go before they reached bottom. It was Jacob who usually began singing "Jesus Lover of My Soul" right about then as a way letting the Lord know to keep an eye out for them whilst they were underground.

> *Jesus, lover of my soul*
> *Jesus, I will never let You go*
> *You've taken me from the miry clay*
> *Set my feet upon the rock and now I know*
> *I love You, I need You*
> *Though my world may fall, I'll never let You go*
> *My Savior, my closest friend*
> *I will worship You until the very end*
> *Jesus, lover of my soul*
> *Jesus, I will never let you go*
> *You've taken me from the miry clay*
> *Set my feet upon the rock and now I know*
> *I love You, I need You*
> *Though my world may fall, I'll never let You go*
> *My Savior, my closest friend*
> *I will worship You until the very end*
> *I love You, I need You*
> *Though my world may fall, I'll never let You go*
> *My Savior, my closest friend*
> *I will worship You, until the very end*

As the hopper began to slow to a stop, the screeching of the brake bar grinding against the metal wheel made Jacob wonder if Jesus could even hear them praising His name, even though they were singing at the top of their lungs. Obadiah was the first to throw his leg over the side of the hopper and touch the ground with the thick cut waffle sole of his Viking boot.

Jacob followed right behind. Each man in turn of seniority climbed out of the car. The last man out was always the one carrying the canary who'd made the ride sitting on a mess of straw in a small screened-in wooden box.

Obadiah strode over and kicked the turnout switch, as Jacob and Samuel pushed the hopper over onto the second track that would take it down the horizontal shaft, where they'd set a fuse to blast out a new vein. Obadiah'd be the one to set the charge. He'd had to take it over after Flem had his accident a few months before.

The men had heard that Flem wouldn't be going back down in the hole since he'd blown his fingers off. Obadiah'd said that Flem was going to be working up top side.

Samuel looked like a wind-whipped white oak that'd weathered a lot of winters, standing some six feet five and weighing upwards of two hundred forty pounds. He seemed to be born with a special understanding about how big he was and always was willing to take an extra share of the work. Especially from some of the men who tended not to be on the big side. The first push to get the hopper rolling straightaways once it had set even for a few short minutes was the hardest. Especially if there was even the slightest incline in the flat track heading it back into the shaft. Once Obadiah had kicked the red topped turnout switch and pulled the track over, Samuel bent down like he was getting ready to pray, folded his arms back into his broad chest and set his fingers that were about as thick as grubs over the rim of the hopper. And with a mighty grunt the car began to move up the slight incline with Samuel's outstretching arms. Once it was over the bump in the track the other miners gathered around and pushed as though they were all one body. They'd left their drill, tamping rod, pickaxes, joints of dynamite, primers, batteries, glass igniters, jugs of water, pickles, and canvas bags of jerked meat in the hopper.

Each man always carried a Boker knife right beside his smokes. That a knife can save a man's life more than any other one thing on this earth was a truth the men lived by—from whittling, to maybe having to cut off a finger or two in case things turned bad before you could get over to see the doc.

The shaft was only dug about four feet from bottom to top. The miners had to bend in half to push the hopper blind toward the bumper posts at the end of the tunnel. Amber light from the carbide lanterns on the miners' hats followed the tip of their noses so they could see where they were stepping but not too much of where they were going.

The hopper settled itself into a cave about twenty feet around. A couple of the men had bent some roofing tin and tied it with twine around their knees. The pounded-out tin kept the jagged obsidian, hiding down in the dark murky wetness of the ground, from cutting into their kneecaps. Most of the men though thought it was just too much to bother with. They were the ones whose wives complained about the thick white calluses that had grown up like stalagmites on their knees from the years of cuts and bruises.

The vein the men had been working had been bleeding coal like a stuck pig. It hadn't even seemed like work to dig it out like the other veins they'd worked over the past few months. The rock holding the coal wasn't as disagreeable, makin' their jobs just a bit less difficult. But then, just like it'd become possessed by a demon, the vein had dried up. A new one would have to be opened.

Obadiah and Samuel lifted the drill from the hopper and hauled it toward the sweet spot Jacob had found where the sediment and the rock seemed to say that there'd be a good vein of coal buried beneath. The foreman every time would send Jacob down a shaft to find a fresh vein. Obadiah said Jacob was as divinin' at finding coal as a dowser was at finding water.

Samuel lifted the drill, set the augur against the damp rock face, and began a fast hand-over-hand twisting of the bit through the crust of the wall. After reaching the six-foot marker on the drill, Samuel began turning the bit back out of the hole. Flecks of fine black coal dust spinning off the augur muted the twinkling of the mist that was reflected in Samuel's carbide lamp. The tip of the heavy bit fell to the rock bed after its last flute cleared the hole. With Samuel holding onto the handle, Obadiah picked up the augur end of the drill and together they carried it back to the hopper. Obadiah lifted out the pine box with "DYNAMITE" stenciled on the side and set it gingerly onto the bed rock. He peeled off the paraffin paper from around six sticks of forty percent nitroglycerin-laced dynamite, tucked the explosives into the cargo pocket of his canvas jacket, and walked back to the hole. Samuel followed close behind with the detonators.

Obadiah began pushing sticks of dynamite into the hole, one after one, laying them head to toe, resting up against each other. Samuel pulled the igniter out of his pocket and handed it to Obadiah after the last stick was placed. The blasting cap slipped into the straw end of the last stick of nitro. Obadiah pulled the three-inch fuse free from the hole, reached down, and picked up a handful of muck and packed the mouth of the hole with the black clay. Looking back over his shoulder, he nodded for Jacob to get the men behind the hopper.

Obadiah moved his hands close to the fuse, pulled the glass striker out of its metal sleeve, and struck it against the knurled grip. A spark jumped from the tip of the striker to the flash powder infused wick. The moment the fuse began to hiss, Obadiah turned and took up with his men behind the hopper.

It was a thirty-second fuse. The men crouched down, bunched together, quiet, listening.

The second they stiffened themselves up for the blast, the hissing stopped. The only sound was the dripping of water from the ceiling of the cave. "Shit," Obadiah said. He and Jacob got up from behind the car, walked over to the hole, and began scrapping away the clay. Obadiah could see that the fuse had burnt itself all the way into the shot. The best thing to do Jacob knew was to drill another hole a foot or so from the first one and reset the first charge with a new stick. Then when the second stick blew it'd set off the first round of explosives.

Each man could load a ton of coal a day if he worked like a dog and for that ton he could earn himself and his family upwards of one dollar fifty seven cents worth of scrip. Eight men meant eight good tons of coal. Obadiah worked his men hard, his crew was almost always over that in tonnage. That was why the paymaster usually put a little something extra on Obadiah's pay slip each week. And now, as of late last week, Runa had surprised him and said she was pretty sure that she was with child, soon there'd be another mouth to feed. He'd need every penny of scrip he could earn. Obadiah hadn't had much of a need lately, so he was surprised that the Lord had blessed him so. He knew every Psalm by heart and when Runa had told him right after she had fixed him a special supper of pork ears and fried chicken feet with buttered hominy grits, Obadiah recalled part of Psalm 127, *Sons are a heritage from the LORD, children a reward from him. Like arrows in the hands of a warrior are sons born in one's youth. Blessed is the man whose quiver is full of them. They will not be put to shame when they contend with their enemies in the gate.* Obadiah was praying up to the Good Lord to give him a son that'd be worth keeping this time.

Drilling another hole was just time that'd be wasted, Obadiah told Jacob. Jacob argued that he'd done enough blasting and it just was too dangerous to try to reset another detonator on top of the first one. Obadiah, seeming not like himself, told Jacob to move on out of his way. Samuel and the rest of the miners listened and watched the goings-on between Obadiah and Jacob from behind the hopper. The more Jacob insisted, the more time got wasted and the less coal could be loaded and if less coal was drawn up out of the hole, the less scrip would go onto Obadiah's pay slip.

Obadiah pulled the Boker from his pants pocket, opened the long blade, and began carefully digging the black clay packing from around the hole. The blade of the knife slipped into the outer rim and began encircling the hole. The black clay coated the Boker's blade as Obadiah made careful, delicate in and out movements. Jacob stood beside Obadiah cocking his head in such a way to throw more light from his lamp onto the hole. He was pissed off but still appreciating the way Obadiah was digging the packing out of the shot hole. It took more than five minutes for the butt end of the first stick to start lookin' back at Obadiah. He could see the shiny end of the blasting cap sitting right where he'd put it in the first place. He looked as careful as he could to see if the fuse had burnt all the way to the end of the detonator. But even with the light from his and Jacob's lamps the blackness of the clay made it hard to know for sure. What had happened though was the most dangerous of all. Sometimes all of the sticks but one will explode. But this time none of the dynamite went off and the blasting cap was nestled live in the straw end of the stick. The only thing to do would be to push another blasting cap into the straw beside the first one, light the fuse, and blow the vein. Jacob handed Obadiah another detonator. His hand was trembling as he placed the igniter in Obadiah's hand. Obadiah's hand though was as still as a dead man's. He slipped the blade of the Boker into the straw end of the dynamite and delicately pressed the first blasting cap against the side while he laid the new blasting cap in beside it.

19

He wondered if the wet clay had killed the fuse right before it hit the igniter. Didn't matter, just as long as this one burned all the way down and set off the shot.

The rest of the miners crouched behind the hopper waiting for Obadiah to finish and light the fuse. And, in that moment, one of the men, right as the fuse began hissing and Obadiah and Jacob began running toward the hopper, noticed that the canary wasn't singing.

The miner known as Moses Kitchen, whose ears lost the sound of the canary's song, knew a split second before everyone else that he was, in a split second more, going to die. Moses, who wasn't a man for many words and known to nod when asked a question, said nothing, figuring that if there was nothing to do then there was nothing to say. And, in that next split second, the detonator that Obadiah had so carefully snugged up against the one that didn't ignite exploded, just the way God had meant for it to.

When the blast came, it obliterated the coal vein. Turning the coal deposits into a powder of fine dust mixing with the methane gas that only the canary had known was building up in the mine. Being the closest to the shot hole, Obadiah died first, having his spine blown mostly out of his back when the methane and coal dust came together. If any of the men had been alive to see Obadiah's body they might have thought his spine lying next to him looked like the tossed away backbone of a scrod. The blast had killed Obadiah instantly. Jacob was knocked down to his knees by the blast when the fireball that followed washed over top of him, burning him alive. Right before the fireball hit the hopper Moses remembered what every miner prayed would stay buried deep in his mind: "Down here in the mine, you have to be right with God all the time, 'cause if your time comes you ain't going to have the time to ask for your salvation."

The explosion hit the hopper so hard that it drove it right over top of three of the men. One of the miner's heads was taken off when the right back wheel of the hopper rolled back over his neck. The other two miners' legs were broken in about a dozen places when the hopper hit them like a runaway train. With useless limbs they lay crisscrossed in between the tracks waiting for the unstoppable hellfire roaring toward them. Samuel died when the blast made his pickaxe spin around like a top and one of the freshly sharpened tips opened his chest up like a can of dried meat. Moses' lungs caught fire from the inside out from breathing in the burning methane gas. In his final moment of being alive, Moses begged God with all of his might to kill him. Fifteen-year-old Oral Conley, Samuel's first cousin by marriage, had only been mining a month before the fiery explosion sent him onto his Lord. Just the Sunday before, the congregation of the Freewill Baptist Church had prayed over him as Pastor put his hand, held strong by Jesus' Love, behind Oral's back and lowered his head into the still water of Paint Creek. When Pastor pulled Oral's head from the blessed waters, he heard all of his church people screaming, "Hallelujah, Hallelujah." The rescue crew found Oral's body blown halfway up the mine shaft slung over the top a timber strut. His face hadn't been burnt up too bad so they were able to tell right away who he was.

When a miner showed up for his shift he pulled a wooden peg from a board with his name penciled beside it. Then he'd take the peg and push it into a dowel hole. Each miner would then take a metal medallion that had his name engraved on it and put it in his pocket. That way if he died in the mine, they'd find the medallion and be able to tell who he was. But with Obadiah's crew, most all of the men's pants were nothing more than piles of ash and for some reason or other, maybe they'd been melted, but the medallions were nowhere to be found.

Most of the blast was contained deep into the bowels of the mine. The shaft itself was mostly clear of debris. When the rescuers came across Oral slung over a timber strut they figured there wasn't much reason to be looking for any survivors. "If that boy Oral'd been blown that far out of the mine, there ain't no chance anything else is living down there," one of the rescuers looked up and said. After seeing Oral, the crew boss decided that if they ran into anything he considered too dangerous to go on they'd just blow the hole and seal the shaft up forever. The miners laying dead would do same thing if it was their decision to make. There was some rocks and timber strewn across the track but nowhere near what they'd been expecting.

When the rescuers climbed off the flatbed cart, they saw the hopper settled right over top of what was left of two of the miners. Their boot-covered feet were sticking out from under the hind end of the car. Lying upwards toward the front of the hopper was, as best as they could make out, a charred head. It looked like the rest of the body was wedged underneath the hopper. They figured the car must've cut his head clean off when it ran over top of him.

Mr. Harold LaViers, the CONSOL mining engineer over from Ashland, who was there on other business, went with the rescue crew to decide where the blame was going to be put. He looked over the hopper and decided that it hadn't been damaged too bad in the blast. "Mostly from the fire," he said, so it seemed. It'd be easy enough, once it was hauled back up top, to chip off the flesh and bones that'd been burnt into the dense coal dust that caked the outside of the car.

A blackened body with its chest splayed open, twisted in a way that a man wasn't meant to be, lay just a ways up in front of the hopper. From the look on what little was left of his face it didn't seem that God had snatched him soon enough from the door that led straight to Hell. Then again it seemed that God must've been busy elsewhere, because on that day he sure hadn't bothered to be anywhere near the 151. Right close to where the shot had been drilled laid Obadiah. A few feet away lay most of his backbone. Mr. LaViers stood in between Obadiah and his spine looking one way then the other, shaking his head. "Gentleman," he said, "pay close attention to how this man died. His spine was blown clean out of his back. This was a strong man," Mr. LaViers said, as he kicked at the backbone with his boot. "See how it doesn't fall apart even after exploding out of this man's backside." He turned around, took a few short steps, and bent down close to Obadiah's body. Mr. LaViers reached to the scabbard hanging off his side and slid out the Jigged Bone knife with a deep brown stag handle that he never went anywhere without. He'd got it straight from its maker in Boulder, Colorado.

Mr. LaViers took the tip of his blade and flipped out, as best he could, the burnt flaps of skin outlining the hole in Obadiah's back. His headlamp lighted the charred cavern where Obadiah's spine had once been. The rescuer standing closest to Mr. LaViers heard him mumbling to himself as he pushed around whatever was left inside of Obadiah. Then he lifted up Obadiah's body by the shoulder and saw a gaping hole in the front of his chest. "This man blew up twice," Mr. LaViers voiced echoed out in the cave. "He'd taken too much dynamite with him in the first place when he was going to blow the coal seam. Problem was gentleman he didn't bother to put back what he didn't need. When this man set off the shot he used a secondary charge and most likely used too short a fuse at that. Then he didn't bother to check see if the bird was still breathing before he lit the fuse. When the shot went off it ignited the methane that was hovering in the air, then the blast coming out of the hole hit this man," Mr. LaViers pointing down at Obadiah, "and set off the dynamite he'd left in his pocket. When that stick went off, it blew his spine right out of his back. Then the methane cooked in with the coal dust and it all went to hell. This man was dead before he even knew he was going to die."

The crew boss called out for the men to get the bodies loaded on the flatbed. Obadiah was the only one that needed two men to lift his body on the car. All the water in the other men's bodies had been vaporized by the inferno. With them there wasn't much weight left to lift. The only problem was being able to find all their parts and figuring out what part belonged to what miner. They also had to be careful to keep limbs and rib bones from snapping like burnt twigs as they moved them. It was certain that once the undertaker got their bodies up top, he'd have to put them back together with what they'd given him to work with.

In looking close, Mr. LaViers saw that the blast had in fact opened up one of the richest seams of coal he'd ever laid eyes on. Mr. LaViers heard that there was a man who'd been part of Obadiah's crew that had had a gift for finding rich veins. It was too bad the company had lost a man of that caliber, he thought. It was going to take a redig of the hole, firming up the timbers and clearing away some of the debris before the seamed could be mined.

Once the rescuers had loaded what they could find of Obadiah's men, they signaled with a yank on the tug line to the winding gear operator. When the loosened cable attached to the flatbed tauted up, the car began its roll. They'd be picking up Oral's body as they made their way back up. The men up top didn't know what to expect when that flatbed'd come up out of the hole, bodies that'd be sitting up waving hard or bodies that'd be laying down not waving at all.

Chapter 2

As soon as Obadiah had walked out of sight that morning, Runa got Ned settled in doing what little chores he'd do. She put on her best unmentionables underneath her best flowered feed sack dress and walked back up to the plow shed to wait for Flem. Runa brushed her hair back with her fingertips, flicked away the mouse droppings from the quilt covering the straw, stretched out, and began to imagine herself wrapped again in Flem's arms. They'd met with a formal nod at a company dance yonder a year ago. Obadiah wasn't much for dancing but Runa on the other hand certainly had a real flair about her, especially when the fiddlers'd kick up an Irish reel. Runa just seemed to have rhythm born in her bones.

Not quite dreaming, not quite awake, Runa pushed her body that'd been ready for loving up off the straw bale with her right elbow and looked around the shed. Seeing how much the sun had woken up, Runa realized that she'd been laying there coming up on an hour now and still Flem hadn't come like he'd said he would. Today was the day that Runa had planned to tell Flem that she was with child. She didn't know how he was going to take the news, given the circumstances of their lovin' and all. The last time they'd been together on the quilt, Runa thought it odd that she completely lost control of herself, shaking and trembling the way she had. When Flem loved her, she'd always got a feeling like electricity running up and down through her body that she'd never got even one time with Obadiah. It was like Runa had developed some kind of fever for Flem. But even with Flem she'd never embarrassed herself like she had that last time. It wasn't long after that when Runa stopped her monthly bleeding and realized that she had another youngin' growing inside her belly.

Right at the same time Runa came to the conclusion that Flem wasn't coming, the mine whistle started going off. Then the steady whine of the whistle began to warble. There'd been an accident.

Chapter 3

STILL ADORNED IN HER finest unmentionables secreted under her sack dress, Runa set off down the hill toward the road. Directly across the way was Cissy, Jacob's wife. They stopped and looked at each other only for a moment to gauge the worry in each other's eyes. Running past a few wandering head of cattle wading in the puddles from last night's rain, they met up with the five other wives who, like Runa and Cissy, were wondering if they'd been widowed.

A man driving a flatbed apple truck flagged his arm at the running wives. "There's been an awful accident at the 151," he yelled to them. The foreman hadn't said nothing else, he said, just to go on and collect up the women the miners belonged to. The wives pushed and pulled each other up onto the back of the flatbed as the driver, young Spencer Duty, ground the transmission into gear, jerking the truck when he popped the clutch.

Right as Spencer Duty made the turn around Oliver and Mandy Spradlin's homeplace, he saw Oral's mother, Margaret Jewel, standing barefoot in the road, praying up to God that he hadn't done her wrong by taking her boy. Spencer Duty slowed down to a crawl so that the hands reaching out could catch Margaret Jewel tight by the wrists and pull her up onto the back of the truck.

Squeezed in tight beside Margaret Jewel was Mary Mary, the mother of Samuel's children. Benumbed by heartache, Mary Mary sat stone still, her legs dangling over the edge of the truck bed, glaring off with eyes that looked like milk glass.

It wasn't long after Mary Mary had turned three when her momma was told by a preacher who'd looked deep into Mary Mary's blue eyes that her only living offspring and name sake, having been born a caulbearer, with a veil that wasn't pale, was cursed. Her momma knew that Mary Mary'd see things and know things that one wasn't meant to know or see before they happened. And because of her having brought about this burden upon her name sake, Mary Mary's momma defied what was believed to be true and took Mary Mary's dried up caul, neatly folded it over three times, tucked it into her apron pocket along with rock after rock after rock, and being unable to live with her blameworthiness, walked into the deep waters of the Green River, surely receiving redemption as she gasped her way to its dark silty bottom. And, just the night before the blast, while squatting over the slop pot, Mary Mary'd seen the shadow of death lurking, veiled in the blackest darkness. And so on that awful morning Mary Mary had gone to the road to wait for the others who she knew would be coming long before the mine whistle ever began warbling.

Chapter 4

Mr. John Gordon Smyth, General Manager of CONSOL, and Rev. J. W. Butcher met Spencer Duty when he pulled the women up to the mouth of the mine. Right as Mr. Smyth and Rev. Butcher helped each woman off the truck and told them they were waiting like everyone else to find out how bad it was, the winding gear tauted up and began coiling cable. Dozens of men and women from the hollers now stood around the lip of the ridge watching the women weeping and wringing their hands. Those who'd been close by heard the explosion. One miner up top said under his breath that he'd felt the burn from the fire when it came roaring up out of the hole. "There ain't no one alive down there," he said. About the time that Rev. Butcher told the women it'd be a good time to start praying, the cranking of the winding gear came to a halt.

From the shadow of the shaft, Mr. Harold LaViers came walking out of the tunnel. There was no ceremony in his voice, only a flat declaration. "They're all dead. They blew themselves to smithereens. If you all don't want to see what's left of them then you best be on your way, may want to get the women outa here too."

The women saw Mr. LaViers but they didn't hear what he was saying on account of the loudness with which they were praying. Runa rocked back and forth, first on her heels, then on the fat pads of her feet, smoothin' down the folds in her shift, even though she didn't need to. She worried about what she was wearing underneath and hoped no one looked too close. Runa felt her moral failing now in the presence of so many who were calling on the Lord to come close, herself included. She was promising God almighty that she'd repent if only He didn't punish her and all of the other wives for what were her misdeeds.

Mary Mary stood recollecting to herself that she'd known they were all dead about half an hour before the whistle had warbled. She'd just wrung the neck of a fryer hen and was getting ready to scald off the feathers when the blackness came back from the night before. And with that, she laid out the dead hen beside the stew pot, dampered down the cook stove, wiped the steam from her face with her apron, and walked on outside.

Old lady McCarty, whose name before marriage to Edger McCarty, who'd up and taken her hand in Holy matrimony in the old country right at the end of the Great War when he was just finishing up his service to his country, was Carmelita Balboni, and whose house was right across the way, had gotten worked up when she'd looked out her window to see Mary Mary standing in the road, looking like a statue. The old lady McCarty had known that it'd been rumored around the junction that Mary Mary'd been born with a caul. Then one day, and just right before old lady McCarty had all of a sudden lost the use of her right side and couldn't talk no more, Mary Mary had showed up on her porch knocking at the door. When old lady McCarty answered, Mary Mary just stood there looking at her, not saying so much as a word. The old lady's first thought was that she hadn't been born with no caul but that Mary Mary was a witch. When Carmelita had just been a girl in Triora her momma had told her about *il strega's* and how they'll just stand there lookin' at you all the while hexin' you. And then, just as old lady McCarty was startin' to scream "*la maledetta strega, la maledetta strega,*" her words stopped movin' from her mind to her mouth. As a matter of fact she couldn't even seem to get her mouth to move to be able to make the words she knew that she wanted to say. Then her whole right side just turned soft and right before she collapsed onto the porch Mary Mary caught her. Later on, Doctor Archer said that there wasn't nothing he or anyone else besides God could do. They'd just have to wait and see if she was ever able to walk or talk again. But since that day, old lady McCarty had always gotten frantic as could be whenever she even so much as laid her drooping eye on Mary Mary. For she didn't believe that Mary Mary holding her up had saved her from falling down hard onto the porch. No, old lady McCarty *knew* that Mary Mary had hexed her. That's what had robbed her of her voice and stolen her legs right out from underneath her. So when the old lady had looked out her window to see Mary Mary standing in the middle of the road, still in her apron, starin' off somewhere, she knew she was hexin' someone else. It wasn't but a short while later, right when the whistle began warbling, that old lady McCarty had some kind of fit, throwing herself out of her chair and swallowing her tongue. Edger, sittin' by the cook stove, drawing hard on a cigarette, heard a gurglin' sound coming from out by the front room window where he'd put the old lady, just like he did every morning about the same time. Had he not stubbed out his cigarette and gone lookin' when he did, she'd a surely gagged herself to death on her tongue.

Mr. LaViers waved his hand high in the air hailing the foreman to start up the winch. The sudden dry sound of the teeth of the winding gears meshing together brought on a silence of hope amongst the women that their men would be riding out of the hole in victory. When the flatbed was pulled from the tunnel and began to be lit up by the sunlight, the only color coming off the car other than charred black was Oral's red flannel shirt and matching bandana that he had tied around his neck wanting to feel some kind of kinship to West Virginia miners who were trying like hell to bring the unions down into the mines.

Margaret Jewel was the first from the circle of praying women to raise her head and begin looking upwards for Jesus. Her eyes moved from the coal-stippled dirt to the thickening clouds over the holler to the sight of a red neckerchief tied around the broken neck of a head protruding from atop of the pile of somber. Margaret Jewel's fervent praying stopped. Maybe she'd looked up and seen Jesus and that was why she'd gone silent, Runa thought. She lifted her own head to see the look of hideous terror on Margaret Jewel's face. Her eyes followed Margaret Jewel's and now she too, with the baby of another man living inside her belly, stood captured by the anguish emanating from the wagon of gloom. The other women snapped to when Margaret Jewel screamed and fell onto the ground consumed by the torrents of her dolor.

The women tried to run towards the flatbed but were stopped by some of the other miners who were now congregating after knowing for sure what had happened. "No one can tell one body from another yet," Rev. Butcher angrily yelled, also wondering to himself what had been so all fire important that God had saw fit not to be down in the mine that awful morning. Mr. LaViers in the meantime ordered some of the miners to pull the flatbed off the tracks and roll it over to the 151 bathhouse, which Mr. Smyth had cleared out to use as a makeshift morgue.

Spencer Duty grew nervous after being ordered by Mr. Smyth personally to go back down the hill and get the undertaker. He hoped he was still in Van Lear, as he did embalming in other counties besides Johnson. If he was anywhere he'd be sitting at the company store playing checkers waiting for someone to pass on. It didn't take Spencer Duty's apple truck long to get down the side of the hill and roll up in front of the company store. There was the undertaker already stacking up coffins on the back of a horse drawn cart, getting ready for the slow pull up the ridge. "Don't just be sittin' there in that jalopy, boy, get yourself over here and help me load up. How many we need?" The undertaker asked of Spencer Duty. He didn't rightfully know for sure, he answered back, but he was recollecting that Mr. Smyth had said for him to make sure that the undertaker brought back eight coffins.

Right before the undertaker snapped the reins against the back of the draft horse, the company store keep came running out the door wanting to know if he was going to be needing him to order up more Ozoform from Paintsville. "No," the undertaker yelled down off the black leather covered seat adding, "Ain't no reason to waste good embalming fluid now, don't you think?"

Margaret Jewel and the huddle of newly-widowed wives clumped together holding each other up as best they could. They seemed so slick with tears and grief that they were sliding down to the ground just as fast as they could pick one another back up. Rev. Butcher and some of the other miners had tried with all their might to keep the women back from the flatbed where their loved ones were stacked on top of each other. But no matter what trying they tried with, the women had managed to push by them. When Margaret Jewel reached up and grabbed at the red kerchief around Oral's neck, a burnt-up hand fell off a burnt-up arm bouncing off her bodice. When the hand landed on Cissy's foot, she screamed and kicked like it was a rattler coming at her, hurling it onto a pile of spilled coal. Runa leaned against the car, gripped by guilt, asking, like someone could know, which one of the burnt-up remains was Obadiah. Out of the blackness a gold tooth, pushing through what was left of a mottled pursed lip, caught the twinkle of a single beam of sunlight breaking through the clouds. The beam ricocheted off Obadiah's gold tooth and poked right into Runa's eye. It was then that Runa knew that Obadiah'd done sent her a sign, telling her that he was with his God. Early on when Obadiah had been courting Runa, she'd asked him how he'd ever been rich enough to buy himself a gold tooth. He said that it was the only nugget he'd ever found when he was panning and it took him a year to find that one. There was a tooth, just a rotted slither of a thing that had been right up in the front of his mouth. Obadiah one day decided to have a dentist yank it out, melt the nugget down, and shape it into a tooth. That way, no matter how broke he ever found himself to be, he'd know that he had that nugget of gold at the ready sitting right there in his mouth. Obadiah also told Runa one night right before he went off to sleep that he'd made a secret pact with God. If he never had to have that gold tooth pulled in order to provide for his family, he'd put that nugget right into God's hand when the time came for their meeting up. Runa guessed instead of God taking the gold tooth, He'd let Obadiah use it to send her a sign from the beyond.

If it weren't for Obadiah's gold tooth, Runa would not have had any idea about which pieces of flesh and bones belonged to her man. Other than Runa and Margaret Jewel, it was going to be mighty confounding to figure out what belonged to whom. Mr. Smyth and Rev. Butcher attempted to wedge their way in between the congregate of women flailing around and grieving something awful at the side of the flatbed. They tried their best to get them calmed down so some of the men could push the car over to the bathhouse and unload the bodies so when the undertaker got there he could go on about his work. Even though Rev. Butcher didn't understand why the miners had to die, he knew that it all figured into His greater plan that we just couldn't know nothing about. Rev. Butcher was also having trouble understanding why the Word of the Lord did not seem to bring comfort to the grieving women. The funeral, Rev. Butcher figured, would be the place to preach that death is only a loss for the living. The dead don't need us anymore, they have gone onto their greater glory. Right at this very moment they are being warmed by light of the Divine.

The miners pushing the wagon over to the bathhouse were

respectful of the women following their men. Mr. Smyth could be seen shaking his angry head, walking up the hill back to his office. Rev. Butcher was right behind the women, reading John 14 aloud from his tattered Bible, "*Let not your heart be troubled: ye believe in God, believe also in me. In my Father's house are many mansions: if it were not so, I would have told you. I go to prepare a place for you. And if I go and prepare a place for you, I will come again, and receive you unto myself; that where I am, there ye may be also.*"

The clacking of Spencer Duty's apple truck could be heard coming up the back side of the ridge before anyone actually saw him. Not too far behind was the undertaker's wagon loaded up with coffins. The flatbed carrying the remains of the miners, Spencer Duty, and the undertaker all converged on the bathhouse at just about the same time.

The women had seemed to change on their trudge up the hill to the make shift morgue. Smelling the acrid stench coming off their pile of men started them imagining the screams of the miners being burnt alive in the inferno. They now looked like they'd aged ten years, haggard and more weather-worn. At one point along the way Runa saw that Oral's arm had fallen off the side of the wagon. From best she could tell it was the only arm that was still pretty much attached to a body. Runa walked up to the side of the cart, lifted Oral's arm, and sat it back up beside him.

The folks in the junction all thought that Margaret Jewel, even as a little girl, should've been put in the lunatic asylum over in Lakeland. Almost nobody had let their children play with her because of her unpredictable fits, running around and screaming not to mention her trying to bite the other children. Even though she'd been baptized over and over again, it hadn't seemed to do any good. And now, with the death of Oral and after what seemed to be the forever walk up the hill to the bathhouse, Margaret Jewel up and lost what little wits she had. It wasn't that she was suffering different than the other women, it was more like there just wasn't anything left inside of her to suffer with. When Runa lifted Oral's arm back up on the flatbed, she'd caught sight of Margaret Jewel. And, in that moment, Runa witnessed the life disappear from Margaret Jewel's eyes. She thought to herself that maybe in some kind of odd way that Margaret Jewel may have it easier than the rest of them.

The undertaker had had to shift the position in his seat all the while that he was coming up the ridge. He figured that traveling all over the county, bouncing around on the bunk board of his buggy, had pretty much made his rheumatism about as bad as it could get. "Help me down, boy," he said to Spencer Duty when he stopped the horse in front of the Bathhouse. "Get on outta here," the undertaker scolded the women with his tone. "Get now, let me do my work." Rev. Butcher told Spencer Duty to pull his truck around and help the women onto the back. They were needin' to go on down to the church and let the undertaker tend to their dead.

Runa helped Spencer Duty get all of the women up on the back of his apple truck. It seemed natural for the women without speaking about it to put Margaret Jewel in the middle so she didn't go falling off on the way back down the hill. As Cissy sat on the edge, hanging her legs over the side, she looked down and saw the lace of Runa's pink fringe camisole peeking out the top of her dress when she lifted her arms to ease one of the women onto the truck. But on a chilly morning that didn't seem real no how, it didn't make any sense right then in Cissy's mind why Runa'd be wearing such fancies. "Get yourself on back up here after you drop them women off," the undertaker said to Spencer Duty.

Being it was a bathhouse the undertaker went in by himself to turn around any shaving mirrors hanging on the walls to keep any of the miners wandering spirits from being trapped inside of mirrors' reflections. Then he waved his arm out the door for the men who'd pushed the flatbed up the hill to begin bringing the remains into the bathhouse. A row of each was started for torsos, arms, legs, hands, feet and heads. Anything else they laid out to see who and what it would fit on. The men who'd accompanied Mr. LaViers had found a few ID medallions lying on the ground close to some of the bodies. They'd tried to keep track of what legs they'd found the coin right near but in the confusion it was more likely than not that they'd got things pretty mixed up.

It wasn't the first mine explosion that the undertaker had been called out on. The last one was across the river right outside of Williamson, West Virginia a few years back. Because he had had so much experience, he had a good idea about how to put bodies back together. He sat the heads on the wash basin, one right next to the other. From a distance and except for the occasional white tooth that hadn't blackened up in the fire, he thought that they looked like unbroken lumps of coal sitting there. Most of the hair had been burned off. The undertaker told one of the miners to round up as many of the other miners as he could and have them come on up to the bathhouse. While the miner was gone collectin' up the men, the undertaker walked around figuring over each part of each body. After he was done figuring, the undertaker drug the only set of legs with feet over to one of the torsos, pricked the bloated bowels to let the gas out, and then pushed them back into the body cavity with his boot before he slid the legs up against the jagged cut waistline. "Yep," he said to himself, "those seemed to go together just like they'd belonged to each other." He worked like this with each part until he had reassembled all of the miners across the floor of the bathhouse. Even if some of the parts didn't fit just right it wasn't going to make no matter because he was going to dress them up in at least something before he pounded the last nail into the lid of each coffin, never to be opened again by any man. He'd already told Spencer Duty not to come back until he'd got a pair of britches and shirt for each man. He said Spencer Duty oughta bring on up a few bails of straw too.

The undertaker stood proud, with his thumbs hooked in his suspenders, surveying how each man looked almost whole now, except for their heads. Oral had been laid out separate from the others because aside from not being burnt up too bad he had a chunk of his skull missing from the back of his head. The undertaker knew there was going to be some spare bone leftover that wasn't from no one in particular; he could chip a piece and fit it into the cavity with horse glue. Then he began walking around the bodies, figuring again. He walked over and picked up a head, rolled it over in his hands, and looked intensely at where the neck had been severed from the body. Carrying the first head over, he leaned down to one of the bodies and saw that the serrations on the neck matched up with the serrations on the torso. When he lifted the torso, the head in his hand slipped right into place, like two train cars coupling up, he thought. The undertaker did the same thing with each of the heads, smiling with pride when each one fit without him having to pull too many shenanigans. It was easy to tell which man the blown-out back bone belonged to so that wasn't of no concern.

An hour or so later, the man the undertaker had sent to round up some of the other miners arrived with about a dozen or so men. One of the men was carrying the hand that Cissy had kicked up onto the coal pile. The way he was holding it so casual like made it look like the body it should've been attached too had gotten lost somewhere along the way.

"Just walk on around and try to figure out who each man was," he said. Mr. Symth had put a list of the miners in the bathhouse so the undertaker would know who'd been working down the 151 that morning. The miners doing the identifyin' were to work from the list. One of the miners had been on Obadiah's crew before he'd been moved over to the 152. He'd known all of the men who'd been down the 151 that day. The undertaker handed him the list.

The miners walked in unison behind Hobart Cantrell, who'd finished the eighth grade before going to work in the mines, so he could read the names on the list. In front of each corpse they stood, bowing their heads for a few seconds to show their respect and to thank God that it wasn't them lying there. Most of the men's voices were muted as they talked because their elbows covered their mouths and noses. Mostly they agreed with Hobart Cantrell when he said who he thought each miner was, figuring he'd known the men the best, so why shouldn't they just go along with what he said. Even bent and broken, Samuel was the easiest to say who he was, "As big as an oak," Cantrell looked down and said. When they came upon a miner with an arm missing a hand, the man carrying the hand with no body leaned down and set the hand in place. Right as they started to walk away, one of the other miners spoke up and said, "It don't go there. You put a left hand on a right arm." The undertaker walked over and said they should go on about their work, he'd be double checking that everything fit up the way it was supposed to before he laid each man out proper.

Spencer Duty was a tall boy with hair that looked more like fur than hair. His face was off kilter just enough to notice, making him look cockeyed. He had a beard here and a beard there but didn't have a beard everywhere a beard should be. When folks looked at him they'd say that he had way too much face and not enough beard. But, truth be known, Spencer Duty had grown what beard he could to cover up the cockle-thick scars from where he'd fallen into a vat of stripping acid when he was just barely out of his boyhood years. Depending on how you looked at it, the doctors down at the Paintsville hospital had saved his life. Just laying eyes on Spencer Duty for some conjured up talk about hearing the screams tearing down the hospital corridor when the nurses held him down so that the Doc could change the bandages on his head. But aside from him being an ugly boy, Spencer Duty had done alright for himself. During the year or so he'd spent in the hospital, he had read somewhere about becoming a shoe salesman for the Mason Shoe Company. After he got out of the hospital, he waited some years until the scars healed as best they were going to and his eyes had settled down. Then he wrote the Mason Shoe Company a letter saying how much he'd like to start selling their shoes over and around Johnson County. He'd be the best darn shoe salesman they'd ever have, if they'd give him an opportunity to prove himself. It wasn't long before he got a letter back saying that they'd be proud to have a man like Spencer Duty represent them to the good people of Johnson County, Kentucky. They'd just need ten dollars for the shoe samples and order forms and then he could commence selling their product with pride. In even less time than it took for the Mason Shoe Company to write Spencer Duty back telling him how proud they'd be to have him representing them, he had raised that ten dollars digging out root cellars. In just a few short weeks after he'd sent off the money, a suitcase full of shiny Sunday church shoes and work boots, complete with a stack of order forms and an authentic Ritz Stick for measuring the size of customers' feet, arrived at the post office addressed in his name. They'd even sent an official identification card with "SPENCER DUTY, SHOE FITTING EXPERT" printed in bold black letters. Before long, he was traveling all over Johnson County, selling shoes right and left to whoever he could get to prop up their feet. It was said that if you sat down with the young shoe salesman and heard his pitch, it wouldn't be long before you'd be wearing a pair of his shoes. He liked to say that he sold shoes that worked as hard as the feet they were fittin'. If you heard Spencer Duty's name just about anywhere in Johnson County, you weren't likely to hear it mentioned without words being spoken about his shoemanship. It wasn't all that long after he got his reputation that he received a certificate signed by the president of the Mason Shoe Company congratulating him on being the number one salesman west of Lexington. It was an honor that Spencer Duty didn't take lightly. Wherever he went and whatever the occasion he always had the most handsome shoes of any man in all of Johnson County, maybe even some would say in all of Kentucky.

As Spencer Duty headed back up the hill from taking Rev. Butcher and the women down to the church, he saw that the undertaker's wagon now sat bare in front of the bathhouse, freed up of the load of coffins. Inside, a coffin sat alongside each put-back-together miner. Spencer Duty saw the undertaker holding a head in his hand when he pushed open the door and walked in. "Terrible thing this is Spencer Duty, terrible thing."

"Yes sir, it is," he answered more to no one than speaking to the undertaker directly.

"Gonna need help getting that boy over there in his box, he's the only one whose got anything left in him that's going to be too heavy for me to lift by myself, now that I'm gettin' up in years and all. Someone's gonna be putting us all in a box someday, boy, don't forget that, we're all gonna get our turn." Like the undertaker had asked, Spencer Duty'd brought back with him britches, shirts, and straw. "It's all out on the truck, sir," Spencer Duty said when asked.

"Go on and get those clothes in here, so these men can meet their maker with more dignity than when they came into this world."

Spencer Duty had driven by each widow's house on their way to the church and waited while each one went in and got a pair of pants and a shirt for their man. "Oral's clothes'd be just fine to send him along in," Margaret Jewel said. He didn't have much more than what he had on.

Spencer Duty rolled up each pair of dungarees and cotton shirt like a bed roll, one beside the other, right after he'd taken it from the widows. He remembered what clothes belonged to what miner when he brought them into the bathhouse. The undertaker read off the name of each miner while Spencer Duty sat the rolled-up pants and shirt beside the body. "Oral's mama said to go ahead and lay him out in what he's wearing," Spencer Duty said. "Margaret Jewel said he ain't got no clothes any better than what he's wearing, so may as well go ahead and bury him in those." Nodding his head, the undertaker mumbled something he couldn't quite make out.

The two men laid out each torso on top of a shirt with its sleeves draped over the side of the pine box. Then they filled up the chest cavities that had been blown empty with handfuls of straw and packed it as best they could into shape. The undertaker buttoned up the shirts, leaving the top buttons undone. Then Spencer Duty held up the sleeves while the undertaker slid the arms up to where the shoulders were supposed to be. All the better if the arm had hands. For those arms without hands, the undertaker laid the arms down alongside the torso and slipped the hands up the sleeves with as much of the wrist bones as was left. Then he tucked up the cuffs as snug as he could around the wrists.

The heads were burnt up so bad you couldn't tell one from the other, so figuring about it some more the undertaker thought it didn't matter much what body got what head. It was more important to get everything to fit together as good as could be. Samuel was the biggest one and he'd been the easiest to say who he was, Obadiah's gold tooth had been recognized right off by Hobart Cantrell. And Oral, well he wasn't burnt up, so you could look at him and tell who he was. The other bodies were good guesses at best, but they were just going to have to make do.

The undertaker took each head and slipped what was left of its neck down into the open shirt collar and buttoned it up just about as tight as he could get it. Then he packed more straw all around the bodies to hold them in place so they wouldn't jar around so much when got them loaded up and hauled down to the church. CONSOL was going to want funerals about as soon as could be so to get the grieving over with and the mines cranked back up to full production. Spencer Duty and the undertaker loaded each coffin on the back of the horse-drawn carriage. He offered to take some of the coffins on his apple truck but the undertaker thought better of it, saying, "that old rattletrap of yours'd jar all of my hard work right apart." Once they were all loaded up the undertaker told Spencer Duty to go on down and talk to each of the women, "Take Rev. Butcher with you if they ain't all still at the church," the undertaker added. "Find out if the women want to see their men one last time or if they want me to just go ahead and nail the coffins up. Let me know before too awful long."

Rev. Butcher had corralled the women into the basement of the church, preaching to them about heaven. "Right at this very second," he said, "they are walking on streets paved with gold." Runa sat right beside her guilt giving her the cold eye, feeling like that Hester Prynne woman she'd read about in school, getting ready to be led through the streets, tarred and feathered for bringing calamity on the town. One minute she couldn't seem to catch her breath, and the next she couldn't seem to get rid of it fast enough. Cissy rocked and rocked and rocked, back and forth, back and forth. Right now none of the children knew they were daddyless, she kept thinking over and over again as she rocked and rocked and rocked. Mary Mary just *knew*, she just didn't know how much longer she could go on with the burden of always knowing so much. Margaret Jewel sat, mostly ignored by the other women out of their own grief and helplessness, talking to someone who wasn't there, giggling as she said things that made no sense, making it impossible for anyone to think that she was anything other than mad, except for Rev. Butcher, who, as he listened carefully to Margaret Jewel, remembered up Mark 17, *These signs shall follow them that believe; In My name shall they cast out devils; they shall speak with new tongues.* And in that remembering he knew that the Lord God Almighty had descended down and given Margaret Jewel the sovereign gift of interpretating His ways by speaking in tongues. "What are we going to do," they asked of the air. There were no good answers that came back, only Rev. Butcher saying that the Lord will provide. A "Praise God," came from someone and Rev. Butcher thought it was good.

Spencer Duty walked head-strong into the room where the grieving women sat, like he was going to have them try on new shoes that'd just come over from Louisville, irritating the good Rev. Butcher. "The undertaker wants to know if y'all want him to go ahead and seal up the coffins, given the circumstances and all," he said. Runa and Cissy spoke over top of each other like they were singing in a round. If the undertaker nailed their mans' coffins shut before they got a chance to say goodbye, they'd make him pull out every nail he'd pounded into the lids with his teeth. Spencer Duty said he didn't mean no disrespect, he'd just been passing along a question because the undertaker was on his way down with the bodies right now. Just then the sound of clacking hooves followed by a "whoa… Bessie," came in from outside the church.

When he pushed open the sanctuary door, the undertaker hollered, "So boy, what do the widas want me to do with their loved ones, 'd ja find out, boy?" Pushing out right behind Spencer Duty was Runa, the draft from the opening doors blowing her loose dress back at the neck, briefly exposing the finery outlining the curve of her shoulder. Cissy, right behind her, saw it again and again her confusion momentarily burrowed through her grief. For that moment she was thankful that Runa had unknowingly given her a brief distraction from her agony.

"Get our men on in here," Cissy informed the undertaker. "Don't go gettin' your bowels in an uproar," the undertaker responded back. "Just didn't want to put y'all through any more than you'd already been through, that's all I'm a sayin'."

"We all appreciate your figurin' on it," one of the wives said, "but we got to see our men no matter."

"How much worse could it be than seeing them all burnt up on that wagon, you tell me," Runa said. By now everyone was outside and people from the junction were starting to congregate around. Miners not working shifts had showed up to help carry the coffins inside the church. Rev. Butcher directed them to take all the coffins inside and line them up east to west right at the Crossing. Each miner took special care in doing their part of the lifting just like they were carrying snowflakes, not wanting to do any disturbing to any of the precious crystals.

The undertaker followed the grieving women back into the church right behind Rev. Butcher. They all stood in front of the row of coffins waiting for the undertaker to tell them who was in what coffin. The smell of burnt flesh and the stench of what little fluids were left in the bodies, now draining out into the coffins, quickly permeated everywhere in the church.

The women's bones had seemed to turn to saplings since that morning had begun. Their swollen, reddened eyes looked oddly out of place set inside the hollows of their gaunt faces, dried up from the wringing out of tears and heartache. Now they weren't even walking right, more like scooting their feet along to get from one place to the other. Each of the wives wondered how they were going to make do without their men. CONSOL sure wouldn't take care of them and would be telling them to pack up quick and leave their homeplaces because they'd have new mining families coming in to replace the men who'd just been killed. They were going to be needing a place to put down their belongings, so the widows would have to up and go. Plus now that Mr. LaViers had officially announced that Obadiah'd caused the explosion, Runa knew that she'd be the first to be told to move on. Not to mention that she'd be treated like a leper once the idea caught up with the other women that her husband had been responsible for killing their men. Right now they were all in it together but that wasn't likely to last long once the men were lowered into the ground.

Margaret Jewel walked out from the rest of the women and went over to Oral, who was the only man who was fully stretched out. Even if the other miners hadn't been burnt up they just didn't look right, the way their bones were sticking this way and that pushing up against their shirts and pants. She reached out and began stroking Oral's hair. The undertaker, realizing that he'd forgotten to glue a piece of bone in the back of Oral's head, walked over and took Margaret Jewel's hand in his. "Just let him be for now," the undertaker said. He noticed that Margaret Jewel's hand was just as lifeless as her boy's. When the undertaker sat her arm on the edge of the coffin, it just slid right off and hung limp by her side. Rev. Butcher stood watching, rocking a bit in place, overtaken with the Mystery in the way the fruit of the spirit was still talking through Margaret Jewel, comforting her in this time of great need. He couldn't understand though, other than figuring it must have something to do with righteousness, why Margaret Jewel had been singled out amongst those suffering souls to receive the comfort of the Fruit. He knew though that his place was not to question but only to watch with reverence.

Mary Mary knew right off which corpse was Samuel. Even with the fire having drawn him up something awful, he was still the biggest of all the men. She stood looking down at the body, remembering about how much he had loved her biscuits and gravy. Every morning before he left for the mine, Mary Mary always had a skillet of gravy going on the stove with buttermilk biscuits baking in the oven, thinking that was the least she could do with him working in the mine and all. She smiled softly when she remembered Samuel's big body on top of hers when they were in the midst of loving one another. What she'd never talked about with anyone was how they both felt the need for each other. And that Samuel being the kind of man he was would never allow himself to have pleasure before she did. Out of all the wives, Mary Mary was the only one who didn't shed a tear. She'd always known because of her knowing that even though she and Samuel had a powerful love that she wouldn't have it for long—that the love would be taken away from her while she was still young.

But, like a powerful secret tied up with twine and kept hidden under the bed, her knowing, which seemingly could be as miserly as a banker at times, held onto the knowing that she would, after her sorrow had found its place in her life, have an even more powerful opportunity for love.

Before Runa looked for a gold tooth she noticed Obadiah's back, curled, coal-crusted toe nails from where he'd been blown right out of his boots. She used to get on him all the time about his toe nails, "Obadiah!" she'd say. "Now you've got to trim those back the way their growin' down into your toes like that." But he'd just shake his head, never telling her how much he'd hated having his toe nails cut back ever since he was a youngin'. His daddy used to have to hold him down while his mama'd grab hold of a foot and cut his nails back with his daddy's folding knife. It'd hurt like the dickens when he'd be jerkin around and the tip of the knife blade'd slip way down under the nail making it bleed, they'd be sore for weeks rubbing up against his shy-to-short hand-me-down boots. He'd never told Runa about that though, instead he'd just let them grow until they turned back around and dug into the right up top tip of his toes. The coal dust would get down in his boots and make some kind of coal cake all jelly rolled up in between the layers of his toe nails. Runa couldn't even remember how long it'd been since she'd seen Obadiah's nails trimmed up like every other man's was. There weren't toes like Obadiah's probably anywhere else in Kentucky, maybe even in the whole world, she thought. As Runa stood at the foot of the coffin looking down at Obadiah's feet, she began to lift her sad eyes. His knees looked all buckled up with his left one poking up at an unnatural angle through his pants leg. When her eyes got to Obadiah's chest she saw a piece of straw sticking out from between two buttons. As natural as could be, Runa reached out to pull on the straw twig. When she gave it a tug, the flannel shirt came open showing that most of his insides had been blown out and that he was filled with straw.

Runa's legs gave out and her body began twisting around like it was trying to drill itself down into the earth. In that brief second before she collapsed onto the church floor, Runa's eyes rolled upward catching sight of Obadiah's head; its gold tooth nowhere to be seen. In her faintliness, Runa wondered if between when she'd first seen Obadiah come out of the mine shaft and now, that he'd gone ahead and put his gold tooth into God's hand.

Mary Mary stopped in front of the body of the miner known as Moses Kitchen right before she turned around to walk out of the church. She and Moses had had a lot of talks together about right and wrong, God and the hereafter. Mary Mary felt a kin with Moses thinking that he was a caulbearer too but he'd always said that was nonsense. He didn't know any more about any more than any other man. They both figured that when God said your time was up there wasn't much that could be done. But, one thing was for certain, Moses always respected Mary Mary's caulings.

People didn't know much about Moses, except that he wasn't married and lived in a tin shack that he'd built up from scrap that he'd gathered up here and there. He'd found himself a spot up in the hills hidden by a grove of sugar maples. Folks around Van Lear said that he was the nigger lover but no one ever really talked about it, just pretty much under their breath if they were going to say anything. It was also said that the Knights didn't want nothing to do with him and left him to his self.

Supposed one of the knights had been rumored to have been patrolling up in the sugar maple grove when he came on Moses. The Knight, it'd been told, started demanding of Moses about niggers coming up over the ridge. Moses looked up at the Knight riding high in his saddle with a white bandana covering up everything except his uncaring eyes and said, "You better just get on outta the woods and be minding your own business about other people's troubles." The Knight was said to have laid down to Moses that if he didn't cooperate that he'd be coming back with others and they'd take him out and give him a good whippin'. What everyone did know best about Moses besides him being God-fearing was that he didn't hesitate. If you were going to call Moses out in a fight you'd better hit him hard before he ever figured out that you wanted to fight in the first place.

In that second right after the Knight looked down over the baccy-stained rim of his white bandana at Moses, he knew that he wasn't going to be leaving the woods under his own authority. Moses before he'd come up Van Lear way'd rode shotgun for a dozen or so years on the stagecoach run from Kansas City to Tulsa. He'd met up with bandits enough times to know that to hesitate most likely meant that you were going to die first.

As quick as a thought Moses drew up an L.C. Smith stub twist coach gun and pointed right up at the Knight's chest. As the gun swept up from Moses' side, the Knight made out the clicks of the hammers being cocked back. Right when Moses leveled the 10 gauge at the Knight's chest, his thumb rolled tightly around the grip of the buttstock. An explosion of blue smoke left the right barrel at the same time that the buckshot blew out most of the Knight's chest. Right then Moses wasn't sure if the blast had blown the Knight off his horse or if the horse rearing up had thrown him onto the ground. The Knight laid in the tall green grass with his legs pulled up to his bleeding chest. Moses guessed that the Knight's heavy canvas coat had given him a few more seconds of life. He sat the barrel of the 10 gauge right on top of the Knight's heart, looked squarely into the begging eyes of the trembling head, and pulled the other trigger. The body first bounced up hard against the barrel of the shotgun and then acted like it had been slammed into the ground by a boulder.

The next morning, a hundred yards or so down the mountain from the sugar maple grove, a couple of Knights found one of their own tied to a tree. His dark-stained bandana, now mostly red, had been cut from his neck and shoved in his mouth. In looking him over, they figured from his reputation that Moses Kitchen must've been the one who had killed him. The tall one jerked the reigns of his horse around, kicked his heels into its hind-quarters, and started it galloping up towards the sugar maple grove. The short one followed right behind. At the edge of the grove both Knights stopped, their horses rearing back a bit when they pulled hard up against their bits. "You know what they say 'bout Moses, now don't you?" The short Knight said to the tall Knight.

"I know," he said.

"They say he ain't even human."

"I said I know what they say."

"You goin' with me or am I gonna have to go in and get the nigger lover myself?"

Their debating and figuring was interrupted by the click of hammers being pulled back on Moses' shotgun. The tall one's hand slapped the top of his pistol but before he could wrap his finger around the grip he heard, "Don't. I ain't never shot no man in the back, don't make me make you the first."

The tall Knight extended his arm away from the Smith and Wesson and lifted his hand right high in the air. The short man just sat on his saddle and shook. Moses walked in between the two horses with his back to the Knights. The tall Knight knew that he couldn't draw faster than Moses could turn around and kill him so there was no point in going again for his pistol. When Moses stepped in between the heads of the two horses he turned around and said, "I reckon you came on up here to kill me." The tall one looked down and told Moses he'd best be heading on if he knew what was good for him 'cause one way or another he was going to be hanged for what he'd gone and done to the Knight. Moses pointed his 10 gauge up at the tall Knight, "Well then I guess it don't matter if I shoot one of you bastards or three of you, I can only be hung once." And on that Moses let loose the right barrel of the L.C. Smith. In that moment after the bleeding Knight cleared the haunches of his horse and in that other moment before he hit the dirt, the Knight took his last gasp of life. When Moses' shotgun leveled onto the short Knight, yellow piss started running down the sides of his saddle. "Guess now you know what it's like for those colored boys you all go chasing through these woods like they're some kind of game. Never seems like there's just one of you though when you up and go hanging a Negro. There's always a whole gang of you cowards, just never seemed quite fair to me." The short Knight tried to say something but he was shaking so much that his jaws just weren't working right. "Unlike you and your kind I'm not a cruel man, I ain't gonna let you sit there and shat on yourself too." The shoulders of the short Knight dropped and for a moment thinking that Moses was going to let him live. Then the short Knight heard the blast of the shotgun and he too was dead.

Moses threw the tall and short Knight over one of their horses and led it down the side of the ridge, right beside the tree where the first dead Knight sat propped up. Hating for the horse to have to bear the burden of the weight, Moses lifted the Knight and flung him atop the other two. Then he tied a rope around each of their wrists, looped it under the belly of the nag, and cinched it to their ankles. Before Moses pointed the nose of the horse toward Van Lear proper and swatted its rump to get it on its way, he took out his knife and cut out the eyes of the Knights and tossed them across the way.

The horse nibbled its way back into Van Lear, stopping here and there to enjoy the tall Timothy grass just off the side of the road. It wasn't long before a Knight, who was out looking for the Paddy Rollers who hadn't come back yet, found his empty socketed compatriots hogtied over the back of the grazing mare. The patroller took up the reigns and led the horse behind him back into Van Lear.

Word of the deed that Moses had done made its way down to Lawrenceburg, Tennessee, right to the founder of the Knights himself, Confederate Army Capt. John B. Kennedy (retired).

Said it was that his ranting and raving over Moses' crimes to three of his God-fearing Christian soldiers had provoked him so that his heart up and stopped. Not only did the Knights want to kill Moses for what he'd done to three of their own, but now he had a bounty on his head for having caused Capt. Kennedy such grief that it killed him. Supposed it was said that Capt. Kennedy spoke the words *Klu Klux Klan* for the first time in history right before he passed the death sentence on Moses and then died himself. Word came back fast to Van Lear that Moses Kitchen was to be taken out and hung where everyone could see him. He was to be made a public spectacle of what would happen if you went against the ways of the Knights. But even though they'd huff and puff about how they were going up to kill Moses, not a one of the Knights Paddy Rollers ever again ventured up into the sugar maple grove. Nor did anyone in Van Lear ever say a word to Moses about the deed, not even the constable. The Knights never so much as pestered Moses when he rode into town to get supplies or walked down the road going to the mine. They could have for sure rounded up enough men to kill Moses but fact was that the Knights were about as afraid of Moses as any man they'd ever had dealings with. They figured that if they didn't go up yonder to the sugar maple grove then there be no call for having any more problems with Moses Kitchen. Word was sent back down to Tennessee that as far as the bounty went Moses had up and left all of Kentucky, probably changed his name too, too afraid the Knights were going to hang him. It was all written up in a letter to Capt. Kennedy's widow along with a pledge that if Moses ever did come back down Van Lear way they'd kill him for sure.

The corridor that ran right through that part of the ridge was just about the only safe place for a colored slickin' over the river from West Virginia. Lots of Negroes over Ripley way held the burly man who lived in the tin shack hidden away in the sugar maple grove in high regard. Sometimes when Moses awoke he'd find a hoecake sitting on a stump right outside the door to his shack.

Chapter 5

MARGARET JEWEL STOOD LOOKING down at Runa's head lying on her foot. The others, Rev. Butcher, and the undertaker, encircled her, hands fanning in every direction. Cissy lifted Runa's head and cradled it in her hands. "Wake up darling," she said, jostling her. Cissy smoothed back the thin pink strap of peaking finery before anyone else likely took notice. Runa began to come back from nowhere, blinking her eyes and licking her dry lips. The sight of Obadiah stuffed with straw had just been too much for her, somehow even more horrific than the pile of bible-black men piled up on the hopper car. The straw had just made him seem like he'd not even been human. Runa's wondering why Flem hadn't come over that morning kept bumping up against the heart beatin' guilt she was carrying around inside her belly. Once she'd got up to her feet the women took her outside to let the breeze cool her flushed face. The undertaker took Rev. Butcher aside and said he'd better be pushing the women to get the funeral over with so he could get those men buried. Before too long the bodies were going to be in a state that the undertaker couldn't do nothing about. They were already bad but they were going to get a lot worse if he didn't get them in the ground.

The women stood leaning against Spencer Duty's apple truck talking amongst themselves, shaking their heads, crying on and off. Rev. Butcher, talking with his hands as much as with his mouth, tried to assure the grief-stricken widows that right when the body is about getting ready to die, Jesus snatches up the soul and takes it right on up to Heaven. Particularly when one is about to die in an unnatural and painful way. It was in the Bible too, Rev. Butcher went on saying, that when someone dies when they're young, like Oral,

49

hoping to soothe Margaret Jewel, it means that they were just *too* special for God to leave here on this earth and He wanted them for Himself, right then and there. The good Lord was selfish that way. Mary Mary right in the middle of Rev. Butcher talking thought he looked not like a man of the cloth preaching the Good book but like a man who had demons coming out of his eyes. It was the oddest thing, she thought to herself, not able to make any sense of it. Even as Rev. Butcher tried to comfort the women with the Word, the words were lost on Margaret Jewel whose lost mind wasn't nowhere to be found. Then Mary Mary surprised Rev. Butcher when she suddenly stepped close to him, resting her fingertips on his lips, and gazing for a moment into his eyes. And in that moment Rev. Butcher became afraid. He wasn't sure why he was afraid but Mary Mary was having a moment of knowing about him that she guessed, and rightly so, that he wouldn't want to know what it was she was knowing. For some odd reason, also in that moment, Rev. Butcher, for the first time that he could recall since becoming a Reverend, didn't believe a word he was saying.

———————

It was decided that the funeral for the miners would be that Sunday at a special service. Most likely all of Van Lear would come to pay their respects and a big carry-in supper'd be held at the church after the miners were laid to rest up in the cemetery on top of Cumbo Mountain. Mr. LaViers already had a crew down in the 151 beginning to clear out the debris from the blast, getting ready to mine the vein that had opened when Obadiah'd blown the hole. "It a rich sumbabitch," Mr. LaViers was heard saying over and over again, shaking his head in disbelief at his good fortune.

The undertaker went ahead and straightened the miners out as best he could after the jostling ride down the hill. The coffins were lined up one after another right up at the altar.

As the undertaker walked from coffin to coffin looking at how he'd laid the men out to the best of his ability, and especially given what he'd had to work with, it dawned on him that he wasn't getting any younger. Might say that going from town to town in his buggy'd helped keep him fit as a fiddle, but too it was wearing on a man, he felt that for sure. With the way Van Lear and Paintsville was growing and with the railroad running regular between the two, maybe he thought it was time to settle down and start undertaking in just one place. After he stopped figuring, he asked the women to come back in for one last look before he boarded up the coffins for good.

They all walked past the coffins of their men like soldiers parading in front of a general, not like the grieving mother and widows they were. Rev. Butcher walked behind them softly singing, "*On a hill far away, stood an old rugged cross, the emblem of suffering and shame... How I love that old cross where the dearest and best, for a world of lost sinners was slain.*"

The undertaker shooed everyone out telling them to go on home. It all seemed to go so fast. It'd just been morning, their men going off to the mine, the explosion, them all being taken up to the 151, the men being hauled out of the mine all burnt up. Runa said, "Time ran everything together so fast it's kept us from being able to make sense of it all." Margaret Jewel cocked her head when she heard Runa say what she did but just couldn't make sense of the words coming into her ears.

Spencer Duty had lifted each woman up onto the back of the apple truck one right after the other. He noticed that somehow, even though it didn't make no sense to him, that each one of the widows and even Margaret Jewel seemed lighter now. It was like some of their life had just evaporated right out of them. That's what made them lighter when he helped lift them up onto the truck, he figured. Those widows who had children all sat wondering if their kids knew yet about their dead fathers. The school had most likely gone ahead and shut down for the day, sending the youngins home to find out if their daddies had been one of the miners killed in the explosion. Runa wondered what she was going to do with Ned now that Obadiah was gone. The truth was that Obadiah couldn't believe that God had ever put something like Ned in her belly. Right when Cora Pelphrey'd said he had the slow eyes and that he was good for nothing, Obadiah decided he didn't want a thing to do with him except to help make him mind. It'd all been up to Runa, and now she just didn't know what she was going to do.

It seemed to Spencer Duty that the billow of grief had luffed a bit as he dropped each widow in front of their homeplaces. Looking down he saw wraps made from this and that covering their dusty feet.

51

He figured that maybe someday he'd try and sell those women some decent-looking shoes that they'd be proud to wear. When someone sees someone else in shoes that ain't just for work, they know right off that that person takes pride in every step they take in life. That's what he'd be telling them if the time was ever right. The widows weren't anywhere near ready to hear that right now but someday he'd stop by with his suitcase of samples. "Doing something right nice for yourself is what your man would have wanted you to do," he'd eventually want to say, while sitting in their front rooms having a cool glass of water drawn right up from the well.

He also knew that he wouldn't charge them a penny for the shoes, figurin' they'd be needin' something that'd lift them up a bit from the earth that now eternally had their men. Once a man gets put into the ground it ain't very often they get dug back up, Spencer Duty thought.

Runa went into the house calling for Ned. He was nowhere to be found. The house was quieter than it ever had been. It was like there wasn't even any air in the house to be moving around. Runa called out again for Ned before she went into her bedroom and dropped her dress to the floor. Then she took off her unmentionables, laid it across the bed, and carefully folded it over and over until it formed a neat square that she slipped into her dresser drawer under the towels she used when she had her time of the month. Runa closed the drawer and then sadly realized that there was no longer any reason to hide the camisole from Obadiah. He wouldn't be coming back home from the mine tonight.

Chapter 6

JACOB HAD BEEN A devout man, a follower of the Good book, and a man of what he knew to be right and wrong. He sang hymns around the house and taught them to Della and Ruby. They got to where they could sing them right along with him. Never missing a word and praising to high heaven the name of Jesus when He was mentioned in song.

Jacob was particularly partial to Leviticus and Revelation. He'd learned to read at his daddy's knee who would sit by a flickering candle reading him Bible passages and instilling the fear of God into him just like he was now doing with his youngins. "You ain't nothin on this earth without the Good Lord walking beside you," he'd say. Someday he'd hope to leave the mines, start a small church, and begin preaching himself like John Pelphrey had done a few years back.

Just like the Jacob of Genesis had a favorite son—Benjamin—the miner Jacob had a favorite daughter—Ruby. "You're the apple of my eye," Jacob always said right in ear shot of Della, hoping that some of Ruby would rub off on her. Even though they'd always sit at their daddy's feet listening to stories of God's retribution of sinners and his rewarding of those who lived by His Word, Della just never seem to take it to heart the way Ruby did. They could both quote the Bible sometimes better than preacher but Ruby had what Jacob called the "fire" that Della did not. "She's got herself a different kind of fire," Cissy would say back to Jacob. "That she does, that she does," Jacob would retort.

Della had reached the point where she'd try and fight back when Jacob gave her a lickin'. It was taking him having to hold her over his knee while Cissy would swat her bare behind until it turned red with welts just to get her to mind. Why just the night before the explosion

Jacob and Cissy had had to swat Della a good one for not doing her chores. Ruby though, being the kind soul she was, would always sit by and read out loud from the Bible when Della was getting a paddling. Jacob couldn't have been more proud. He'd always wanted a son and maybe someday the good Lord would've blessed them with one, but for Jacob, Ruby couldn't have filled a son's shoes better.

When Spencer Duty lifted Cissy down from his apple truck Della and Ruby came running up over the small hill in front of their house yelling for their mother to tell them that their daddy wasn't dead. Cissy, not speaking a word, tucked both of her girls under her arms and walked heavily back up the hill to the front door. Inside the three cried and cried. Cissy told them they'd have to be strong, that was what their daddy would have wanted. "The Lord certainly has our best men sittin' beside him, there ain't nothing uncertain about that," Cissy said. Ruby wanted to know if her daddy was going to be a miner up in Heaven too. "The Lord'l most likely make him a preacher of His Good Book, other than Jesus Himself, there ain't no one who knows the Good Book better than your daddy," Cissy answered back. "Daddy's going to look pretty silly with wings," Ruby imagined out loud. Della kept squirming around, finally settling on tucking her knees up under her so the wheals on her bottom weren't resting directly on the hard stool. Della knew in her heart that she'd loved her daddy more than Ruby. But it seemed like for reasons that she could never figure out, her daddy just had never been able to see it. And now she'd never be able to show him.

Chapter 7

FLEM HAD COME BACK up over the ridge behind Runa's house. He'd gone way far around the junction, careful to look like he was going somewhere else, and to be as sure as he could be that no one had been looking out for him on a day like this. Problem was he didn't know where Ned'd be. Runa usually had him occupied piddling around with a chore, likely making a mess of whatever he was doing. When Flem got down a ways from the plow shed he could see Runa walking around her kitchen through the back window overlooking the field behind the house. Best he could tell, Ned was nowhere to be seen. Flem had told Nora he was going down to the miners' hall. There be sure to be men congregating there right about now. She outta go on down to the church because there was probably going to be a supper sometime soon and the ladies would need help with the fixings.

Runa was pulling water out of the pump in the kitchen when she looked up and saw Flem peering in at her through the window right over the sink. She almost screamed his name but thought better of it not for sure if Ned was about. Flem motioned with his head for Runa to come up the hill, meaning up to the plow shed. He turned, not wanting to be out in the open any longer than was necessary, and walked crouched over back up to wait for Runa. It wasn't long before Runa came running up the hill, her apron coming untied as she ran. When she came through the door she grabbed onto Flem not ever wanting to let him go. If there was ever even a second's doubt that she would burn in hell, it went away the moment she pushed the yoke of her dress off her shoulders and let it fall to the floor. Flem, now sure that he too would burn in hell with Runa, pulled her down to the quilt. He never even had a chance to pull his pants all the way

55

down before he was inside of her. As God be his judge he'd never known anything like whatever it was between him and Runa. They both seemed to last for a long time, Runa breathing hard and pulling him against her over and over again until he was finally spent and let his seed flow into her. Then Runa began crying, her tears flowing down the furrows of confounded grief that she was sure were now etched forever into her face.

Chapter 8

Spencer Duty had picked up all of the women early for the service. The night before he'd cleaned off the bed of his apple truck so Margaret Jewel and the widows wouldn't soil their mourning clothes. When the women arrived at the church the coffins were arranged in order of seniority and a bouquet of fresh-cut flowers were laid on top of each pine box. Right after the women had left the day before, the undertaker had gone ahead and packed more straw around the sides of the men, mostly to soak up the fluids that'd likely still be leaking from their bodies. He also poured boiled cider around the coffins to ward off some of the burnt and decayed smell. It was a good thing it was coming into fall and times were cool, otherwise they'd have to have been packed in ice. For *one* man that takes time, especially having to do it overnight, but the undertaker doubted if there was enough ice for *eight* men in the whole junction.

Rev. Butcher had stayed up most of the night preparing his sermon. After he had figured on it long and hard, he was able to reconcile that God had taken the miners to bring the people of Van Lear closer to Him. He also figured that he was being tested by the Lord. How many souls could he bring to Christ in this time of need? It was both an awful burden and a divine privilege, Rev. Butcher figured, that Jesus loved him enough to test him in this way.

There was a lot of lawlessness beginning to happen because of the mine bringing in elements hell bent on tempting good God-fearing Christian's with the counterfeit ways of the Devil. Rev. Butcher had believed in the cause of good Christian soldiers like the Knights bringing God's law back into the land. And, he also believed, that if one did not heed the Word then one should die by the Word.

"*Within the Holy of Holies, in the sanctuary of heaven, the Divine Law is sacredly enshrined. It is the Law that was spoken by God Himself amid the thunders of Sinai and written with His own finger on the tables of stone,*" Rev. Butcher would always say as he offered the benediction at the end of every one of the special Knights' church services that he officiated.

Certainly Rev. Butcher had been told that a lot of moonshining had been going on and fornicating too. The Knight's had been keeping an eye in particular on two of the fornicators that they knew about. They'd made their presence known to one of them and if he didn't heed their warnings, then he'd have to suffer the consequences and be made an example of and several of Rev. Butcher's regular worshippers'd already gotten the Jake walk from partaking of bad liquor. Rev. Butcher told one of the Knights that the stink of sin permeated up the whole of Johnsons County.

The good Rev. Butcher, the undertaker, and Spencer Duty ushered what seemed like most of the whole junction into the church. On this day, however, there was as many worshipers congregating outside as there were inside. Right before 10:00, Mrs. Crowley, who'd played piano at the church long before her hair had turned white, began playing "O Love That Will Not Let Me Go." Then after Margaret Jewel and the widows stopped taking sympathies and were seated, Rev. Butcher began his sermon. He knew he was going to be longer than usual but the opportunity was ripe with desperate souls waiting to be found. Rev. Butcher stood at the pulpit, faced the living breathing spirits hungry for His Word, and remembered the Gospel of Mark, 4:29, "*But when the fruit is brought forth, immediately he putteth in the sickle, because the harvest is come.*"

"My friends, why does there have to be death? Why funerals? Why can't we live forever? Do you know the reason why? Because Margaret Jewel, widas, ladies and gentlemen, *Death* Comes From *Sin, But* Eternal Life Comes From *Christ!* Halleluiah!

"In the beginning, God didn't create Adam and Eve to *die*, but to live forever with Him in the Garden of Eden. They enjoyed *perfect* happiness living with God. God spoke to them, they heard His voice, and felt His peace and love.

"Life with God was perfect. There was no death, no sickness, no pain, no tears, and no hunger. *And* Adam and Eve had the perfect marriage, perfect love and peace, no disagreein'. Everyone was happy. Adam and Eve were happy, and *God was happy*. Praise the Lord!

"But then they lost their perfect life of peace and happiness. Do you know how they lost it? *Sin!* Sin not only brought down Adam and Eve, it brought the whole world down with it and now we have suffering and death because Eve up and *disobeyed* the Lord!

"God gave them only *one* command, only *one*, 'You are free to eat from any tree in the garden; but you *must not* eat from the tree of the knowledge of good and evil, for when you eat of it you will surely die.' But then they went ahead and disobeyed God and sin ruined their perfect lives. *Halleluiah!*

"How did sin ruin their lives? Their bodies grew old, their faces got wrinkles, their hair turned gray, they got tired, and then they finally died.

"But worse than that, they died of a broken spirit, separated from God when He cast them out of His presence in the garden. They no longer felt His peace and love. And people were unhappy, and *God was angry*! Halleluiah!

"The Apostle Paul tells us, 'Sin entered the world through *one* man, and death through sin, and in this way death came to *all* men, because all sinned.' And so, that's why we have to die, why we have to have funerals, and why we are having burials today, because Adam and Eve's *sin* brought *death* to us all.

"After their sin, people started getting sick with all kinds of plagues. And people started hating and murdering. Cain attacked his brother Abel and killed him. And husbands and wives started fornicating with others outside of Holy Matrimony. And men began partaking of liquor and doing shameful acts.

"But God saw how sin separated us from Him. He saw our lying, stealing, unforgiveness, idolatry, fornicating, and drunkenness. So He did something to remove sin and bring people back to Him.

"Jesus, the Son of God, came down from heaven to earth to take away our sins. He was born of a virgin. A woman so pure she had never even had relations in the marital bed with her husband Joseph. Jesus lived a perfect life. He was the only person who never sinned. And He performed many a powerful miracles. He calmed the storm winds, walked on the water, cast out demons, made the deaf to hear, made the blind to see, and *even* raised the dead! Halleluiah! Praise the Lord!

"But evil men murdered Jesus on the cross! Then three days later, God raised Him from the dead, proving that He *is* the Son of God! After that, Jesus went up to heaven, and sat down on the throne of God, where He reigns as King over all of earth and Heaven. Halleluiah!

"It is He who says who will live, who will die, and who will have eternal life! It is He who puts food on your table, *or* holds it back when we are being punished for your sinfulness. And it is *He* and only *He* who can forgive us our sins, or send you into the flames of hell for eternity. Praise Jesus!

"Listen, God did not send His Son the Lord Jesus Christ here to suffer and die so that we could continue living in sin like hypocrites. *No*, He did not! He tells us, 'Do you not know that evil people will not be received into the kingdom of heaven? Do not be deceived!' *Please*, ladies and gentlemen, don't be deceived by liars who tell you that you can continue sinning and still go to heaven because you were baptized. The Lord says, 'Neither idolaters, nor adulterers, nor men who lay with men, nor thieves, nor the greedy, nor men who partake of drink, nor liars, nor swindlers will be received into the kingdom of heaven!' And, that is what some of you were. But you were washed, you were set apart, you were judged not guilty in the name of the Lord Jesus Christ and by the Spirit of our God.

"Did you hear that! I ask you? It's impossible to know the great and Holy God without being changed by Him! Right *NOW,* ladies and gentlemen, accept the Lord Jesus Christ into your hearts and be changed forever. Take this solemn occasion to dedicate your life and your soul to the Holy Spirit! Halleluiah!

"The Good News is that no matter how many sins you've done, dozens of sins, hundreds of sins, thousands of sins, Jesus Christ is ready to forgive you *today!* Jesus the only True Priest, the only priest who *never* sinned, WILL wash away all these years of guilt and sin! Halleluiah! Halleluiah! Halleluiah!

"The Lord says, 'For the wages of sin is death, but the gift of God is eternal life in Christ Jesus our Lord.' God will give the free gift of eternal life to all who trust in Jesus Christ as Savior and Lord.

"Remember ladies and gentlemen I'm not just talking to Margaret Jewel and the widas', I am talking to each and everyone of you all. Adam and Eve enjoyed life with God in the Garden where there was no death, no sickness, no pain, and no crying. Well y'all, God is coming to recreate the Garden of Eden. He tells us this is so in the book of Revelation, 'Then I saw a new heaven and a new earth, for the first heaven and the first earth had passed away, and there was no longer any sea. I saw the Holy City, the new Jerusalem, coming down out of heaven from God, prepared as a bride beautifully dressed for her husband.' *I am coming soon!* My reward is with Me, and I will give to everyone according to what he has done. Blessed are those who have the right to enter into the city of heaven. Outside are the *dogs*, those who practice *magic*, the sexually *immoral*, the *murderers*, the *idolaters*, and everyone who loves and practices *lies*.

"Ladies and gentlemen our Lord promises us eternal life. *There is no grief allowed here today* for these men, what we need to be feeling is downright envy that the Lord God has taken these men to the Place of Places where the streets are paved with gold, the land of milk and honey. And now Margaret Jewel and you widas' like the rest of us have to wait our turn. We have to be like obedient children and be patient as we wait in the line of life to ultimately receive out eternal reward.

"I ask you: *If you or you or you or even you* died tonight, do you know for certain that you will enter the kingdom of heaven? When you kneel before God waiting to be touched by his scepter, if He asks you, 'Why should I welcome you into heaven,' what will you say?

"If the first words that come out of your mouth are, 'I did this, I did that, or I'm a good person,' then you will be cast to the waiting arms of the Devil himself. *For you have not chosen Christ as your personal savior!* Halleluiah! But if the first words that come out of your mouth are, 'Jesus Christ died to pay for my sins,' and you have proven your worthiness by following God's commandments, then God will touch you with his scepter, open His loving arms, and welcome you into His Kingdom.

"When the jailer asked the apostle Paul, 'What must I do to be saved?' He said, 'Believe in the Lord Jesus Christ and you *will* be saved.' You will receive salvation and have eternal life! Hallelujah! Hallelujah! Hallelujah! Hallelujah! It is sin that brought these deaths into our lives. But Jesus Christ is offering you eternal life. *Trust Him now and invite him into your life and he will grant you for free the gift of eternal life.* Oh Praise the Lord! Hallelujah! Hallelujah! Hallelujah!

The *longer* Rev. Butcher's sermon had gone on the more worked up he'd got. By the time he was finished he was crying and waving his battered Bible around in the air, shouting and screaming one 'Hallelujah' right after the other. Those there to mourn the miners seemed to forget about the dead's salvation and were now mostly wondering about their own. Most especially the drunkards and fornicators.

When Rev. Butcher announced that right after they buried the miners he was going to be having a special baptism at the Levisa Fork, shouts of elation erupted from the sanctuary. The good Rev. Butcher was going to reserve a seat for each and every man, woman, or child who'd pay their way into the Kingdom of Heaven with their souls. And then Margaret Jewel, with her eyes big and glassy, leapt from the pew and began screaming, "Jesus, Jesus, Jesus" on that Rev. Butcher ran from the pulpit and cradled her in his arms and felt the Holy Spirit at work inside of her, cleansing her soul of sin. He half-thought that a bolt of lightning would strike Oral's coffin and set it ablaze. And in that moment of fiery fury Oral would be raised from the dead. Rev. Butcher knew that he had done what the Lord had asked of him. "*Praise the Lord,*" he screamed as the congregation began singing "Hallelujah, Sing To Jesus" so loud and so filled with the Holy Spirit that a weeping Rev. Butcher was sure that no matter what else was happening in the world the good Lord was sitting right there in the front pew listening to His people sing His praise.

Chapter 9

SIX MINERS SERVED AS pallbearers for each coffin. The way the men were lined up by Rev. Butcher, Flem was on the left front of each box. When they were carrying Obadiah's coffin up the aisle to a resounding rendition of "Rock of Ages," one of the men right at the back of the church, who it was said was high up in the Knights, sat watching the goings-on. When Flem got right close to the man's elbow that was pushing out over the arm of the pew, the man looked stone cold at Flem and put a feather deep into his heart with his eyes. Flem felt his legs go so weak that he was for sure that they were going to fold up right underneath him. For a moment he lost pace with the other pallbearers as he felt the fire from the Knight's eyes setting his back ablaze with the sin he'd committed against what was left of the man he was carrying to bury.

The pallbearers slid Obadiah's pine box atop the last of the coffins and tied them to the apple truck bed with a mud-caked rope that Spencer Duty had used just last week to pull a calf out of a sludge pit. Margaret Jewel and the widows were escorted down the aisle mostly by the husbands of other wives. The wives were busy caring for any of the widows' children.

The husbands had been told to keep their eyes on the women in case one of them fainted and needed carried out of the church right quick to be fanned. When Runa walked past the man with the protruding elbow she too, confusing as it was, caught the feathers of an arrow from his cold eyes. Curtis Arms, who'd been escorting Runa, whispered for her not to pay attention to a no-count, who'd go and cast an evil eye at a just wida'd woman.

Once Margaret Jewel and the widows were all outside, the

procession up to Cumbo cemetery began. The church was just off to the left of the railroad tracks that led in and out of Van Lear. Once they crossed over the tracks the dirt road leading up Cumbo Mountain was just a few bends down. Spencer Duty led the procession with those stricken with the most grief following right close behind the apple truck. When they got to the turn off to head on up to the top of the mountain, he yelled out the window to make sure that the coffins were tied on tight because the road, or what little of it there was, was full of dips and holes. Flem gave a hard yank on the rope and it seemed to be about as tight as it was going to be so he waved Spencer Duty on. The apple truck bounced this way and that 'til it reached a point where the road was almost washed out. They'd have to carry the coffins up the rest of the way. The biggest and strongest men took Oral and Samuel's boxes and whoever was left grabbed hold of the other men. Someone yelled out that there were blackberries still bloomin' off to the side of the road. So every now and then folks would stop to rest, smoke a cigarette, and eat some blackberries. After the cigarettes had burned down and enough of the blackberries had been stripped off of the bushes to make them look bare, the pallbearers picked the coffins back up and made their way again.

At the top of Cumbo Mountain was Cumbo Cemetery. Probably in all of the time the cemetery had been there collecting up bodies it had never had so many mourners traipsing around all at once, walking over this grave and that. Some of the more respectful though looked like they were doing a gandy dance the way they'd try and avoid stepping right on top a grave and all. Margaret Jewel and the widows all took their places around their men's holes as Rev. Butcher said his piece and then read the 23rd Psalm, *The LORD is my shepherd; I shall not want. He maketh me to lie down in green pastures: he leadeth me beside the still waters. He restoreth my soul: he leadeth me in the paths of righteousness for his name's sake. Yea, though I walk through the valley of the shadow of death, I will fear no evil: for thou art with me; thy rod and thy staff they comfort me. Thou preparest a table before me in the presence of mine enemies: thou anointest my head with oil; my cup runneth over.*

Surely goodness and mercy shall follow me all the days of my life: and I will dwell in the house of the LORD forever. And at that, Rev. Butchered ordered the coffins, now sitting on ropes stretched tight across the mouth of each grave, lowered down into their forever resting place. Finally after a bowing of heads, Rev. Butcher said, "and now the earth shall be cast upon the body." Weeping, Margaret Jewel and the widows each reached down and picked up a handful of dirt and tossed it into the graves. In that moment all was silent except for the muffled sound of tear-soaked earth dropping onto the top of each woman's man's coffin.

As the last handfuls of dirt fell toward the graves, Rev. Butcher called forth his people to follow him down to the river. The time had come for soul-saving. Holding his Bible close to his heart, Rev. Butcher turned and began walking down the Cumbo road, singing thunderously, "*As I went down to the river to pray, Studying about those good old ways, When you shall wear the starry crown, Good Lord, show me the way. O mourners, let's go down, let's do down, let's go down, O mourners, let's go down, Down in the river to pray.*" Behind him, it seemed like all of Van Lear was following. Margaret Jewel turned away from the widows and began walking right beside Rev. Butcher. She gyrated and praised the Lord knowing that He had guided Oral just the prior Sunday to come to Him. When pastor had lifted Oral's head from the cool water of Paint Creek that day there were no louder "halleluiahs!" than Margaret Jewel. Jesus cleansed Oral, readying him to spend eternity in an amazingly glorious place of indescribable splendor, beauty, and joy in the presence of the Light.

The widows all climbed on the back of the apple truck, hooking their arms together so if one started to fall off the others could pull her on back up. Spencer Duty had thought about getting baptized by Rev. Butcher but he couldn't imagine being any more saved than when the good Lord made him a shoe dog. Once he'd found shoes, he knew he'd found his life's calling.

There weren't many blackberries to pick on the way back down, as most of them had already been eaten on the way up. But it wouldn't have mattered none because the followers, just like Jeremiah, had the fire of the Lord in their bellies. They were so worked up that they needed the cool water of Levisa Fork to cool them down. When Rev. Butcher turned around and looked at His followers he was so overwhelmed with Jesus' love that he began trembling. Why had the Lord Jesus chose him, him of all people, to lead so many to Him? he thought.

Once they got to the bottom of Cumbo Mountain, Rev. Butcher and his followers made their way through the woods to the bank of the Levisa Fork. There, standing on the bank, Rev. Butcher, encircled by his followers, looked out and saw swirling eddies and agitation everywhere. It made Rev. Butcher wonder for a moment why the river was so doggone boiling mad. He figured the Devil must be churning up the waters trying to scare the ravenous souls from receiving the Holy Spirit. But the men, women, and children were still singing, waiting to feel the cleansing waters rid them of their sin. Flem had come on down too thinking that any little bit sure couldn't hurt after what he'd done. None of the widows except Mary Mary, who'd gotten off the apple truck at the bottom of Cumbo ridge, had come over with everyone else. She'd worked her way up to where she was standing right beside Margaret Jewel but she wasn't holding hands with anyone. Rev. Butcher turned to his followers and raised his Bible into the air and called for quiet. "We are here to be made pure in the eyes of the Lord," he said. "After today you will be a different person, filled with Jesus' love." Margaret Jewel now was speaking directly to the Lord in Holy Words that only she and Jesus could understand. They'd said for a long time that she'd had the gift but no one until now had ever heard her speak so clearly in the language of the Lord. Mary Mary rocked on her heels, swaying with the wind that was now winding through the canyon like a snake through tall grass just yonder downstream.

"Bow your heads and prepare to be cleansed of your sins, as I read from the first chapter of the prophet John." Then Rev. Butcher began walking and reading aloud, trying to be heard above the increasingly stirred up waters. "*The next day John seeth Jesus coming unto him, and saith, Behold the Lamb of God, which taketh away the sin of the world. This is he of whom I said, After me cometh a man which is preferred before me: for he was before me. And I knew him not: but that he should be made manifest to Israel, therefore am I come baptizing with water.*"

Waist deep and wearing boots that he had bought a few months before from Spencer Duty, Rev. Butcher spun around, calling his devoted followers to come forth. For a moment time seemed to stop as he looked at the men, women, and children standing on the bank aching for him to lead them into salvation. A smile came over his face, a sense of serenity that he had never known before. "Oh sweet *Jesus*," he said, his thought drowned out by the raging waters. Then Rev. Butcher was blessed with a remembrance from Romans, "*I beseech you therefore, brethren, by the mercies of God, that ye present your bodies a living sacrifice.*"

And with that, Rev. Butcher was swept away into the raging Levisa, never to be found. By the time the followers had raised their heads from prayer, he'd long vanished. The only one not bowing in prayer when he was lost was Mary Mary, who stood unmoved as she watched him swept up by a swell, pulled under, and disappear, his arms aching for Jesus to grip his wrists and pluck him from the wrathful waters.

Chapter 10

Mr. LaViers knew that Obadiah had found a coal vein to beat all coal veins. Some of the old timers were calling it a Hades vein. It was rich with layer after layer of black gold. Damn shame they'd lost that miner who'd divined it. "Well hell," he said to himself, "it doesn't matter; it's opened up now and there for the picking."

After the dead miners had been laid down for their final rest, Mr. LaViers took charge of putting together a new crew to secure up the shaft so they could get back to mining the hole. Most likely he was going to be having the miner named Flem crew bossing. He'd been told that Flem was missing one of his hands but he didn't want him doing any digging anyway so it was of no concern. He just wanted Flem to work his men to the bone to get out every damn ounce of coal every damn day of the week.

Flem had heard from one of the bosses at the mine that he'd not be staying up top like he'd been promised. The vein that Obadiah had found was worth too much not to have one of their most senior men down in the hole calling the shots. He'd be paid a crew boss wage and get something extra depending upon how his men produced. But what Mr. LaViers wanted most was for the miners to get as much of the coal up top just as fast as they could.

After a night of discourse and spirits with Mr. John Gordon Smyth, Mr. LaViers appeared droopy-eyed and talked-out when he sat down on a hard-scarred oak bench to take the #1 from Van Lear to Paintsville. In about an hour or so after getting to Paintsville, Mr. LaViers leaned back on a "more civilized" leather-covered seat after he had boarded the C&O back to Ashland. The ride back would give him time to figure on the decisions that needed to be had about the new vein and all the clamoring about needing the union to come in.

The union people had already started gnawing on the deaths of the miners and raising Cain for all it was worth. Mr. LaViers was convinced though that there just wasn't enough discipline occurring right from the bottom on up. When he was walking the mine he'd watched the boss man running the breaker boys. It was obvious that the boss man wasn't using his whip enough to keep the little bastards in line. "I mean hell," Mr. LaViers said to himself, "it ain't like half of those damn imbeciles have enough sense to even come in out of the rain." And they sure couldn't do any organizing or even understand union talk, so why not give them a good whipping right from the start to let them know where things stood. Mr. LaViers often looked off in the distance and remembered his time as a boy on his family's Virginia plantation. His daddy had kept his slaves right up to the day Lincoln set the niggers free. It was clear from what he'd done that Lincoln never knew what it took to tend to coloreds. And they needed constant tending. Sometimes they needed a good whipping too. The most troublesome ones might even need to have part of an ear sliced off. You parade a few niggers around with welt marks as thick as a leech and missing part of an ear, and it sure makes the others work harder and think less about being trouble makers. Just like the miners, the worse troublemakers of all though were niggers that'd learned to read more than just a few words. Probably should have just gone ahead and shot them right when it was found out they understood the written word. It would have saved a lot of grief for everyone, he thought.

Over in Van Lear the rabble-rousers that'd hooked up with the union were using the working conditions of the breaker boys as a rallying call to get folks up in arms. If anyone had given a damn about the breaker boys before, they'd sure never said a goddamn word. Right when their sons turned nine, most every miner would have his boys climbing the grimy stairs up to the screen room. The boss man usually had so much coal to separate that he'd take all the boys he could get. The twelve and thirteen year olds could work the longest without getting tuckered out. The imbeciles that wanted work were the hardest to keep in line and had to be whipped the most always wantin' this and that.

All the breaker boys daydreamed about becoming door-boys, sitting there in the dim light of their small carbide lamp, whittling and whistling, not knowing if it was day or night and not caring much either. They had an important job being the ones who controlled the ventilation in and out of the shafts. And if you did a real good job as a door-boy you'd likely go on to become a mule boy, getting to be in charge of hooking up the mules to the coal carts and hauling the coal that'd been separated from the slate rock out of the mine. You had to be careful where you stood though because it seemed like every time you'd whoop the mule's ass to get it moving along, it'd go and shit right on you.

Right before the C&O pulled into Ashland, Mr. LaViers had fully figured that the situation developing in Van Lear needed to be tampered down before it became a powder keg and blew up like had happened in other places. Problem was that in those other places the bosses had waited too long before they'd gone and did what needed to be done and things had gotten too far out of hand. It'd be best to go ahead and bring in the Baldwin-Felts Detective Agency out of Bluefield, West Virginia. No one had more experience controlling these kind of people than they did, that was for sure. As sure as not, when a miner got killed his widow would think she was owed something. It was hard enough evicting one widow from company housing much less eight. The sooner they got that bunch of widows out over in Van Lear the less time they'd have to freeload. The detectives would be the ones to take care of that along with any other kind of enforcement that was needed to keep the mines productive.

When the Norfolk & Western railroad people had trouble with the loaders in their coal fields, they called in Baldwin-Felts. It wasn't long before the loaders were doing what they were told without belly aching. Aside from their .32 Smith and Wesson pocket pistols, the detectives carried what they called their "teaching sticks," made special for them from genuine Virginia pignut hickory. Giving a rowdy good beating always seemed to teach him a lesson he wasn't going to forget anytime soon. It was best they'd come to learn to make sure the enforcement was done with others looking on. This way there was no misunderstanding their intent. There just wasn't anymore figuring needed, it was time to bring in experts to set things right.

Chapter 11

THE DAYS PASSED LONG for Runa and the other widows. Cissy had packed up, getting ready to head over to Prestonsberg. Her momma and daddy were there and they'd take care of her and the children for a bit at least, and if the good Lord was willing, before too long she'd up and meet herself another good man. Cissy had proved herself to be of good breeding stock having had two fine children already so it weren't likely that she'd have trouble finding a man who may not have been blessed with a fertile woman, at least that was what her momma said. Cissy, right before she snapped the reigns against the back of the swayback horse that was hitched up to her wagon, looked down at Runa who'd been standing out in the road watching the goings-on, and announced that she thought that Runa had been up to no good on the morning of the explosion. That was why Obadiah had been so careless an up and killed all of his men. Cissy said she'd seen Runa's unmentionables slipping out from under her shift and knew they'd been meant for someone else other than Obadiah. She knew as sure as nothing they weren't meant for Obadiah because being the God-fearing man he was he wouldn't have put up with that kind of tomfoolery. Ruby, waiting for Cissy to pull her atop the wagon and clutching a cornhusk doll that her daddy had made her the night before Obadiah took him from her, looked Runa smack dab in the eye and said, "Momma says you're a strumpet and are going to burn in hell." Her butt plopped onto the bunk board right beside her mother and Della, and Cissy snapped the reigns and got them on their way. Runa thought that if Ruby was her flesh and blood she would have smacked her right across the mouth for talking like that. But Cissy hadn't said a word of discipline so she guessed that Ruby had spoke the truth about her.

Someone had already been around to Margaret Jewel's and the widows telling them they had to get gone. The mine was back in full production and they had folks coming in that needed to be put up. If the women weren't going to cooperate and move on, then they'd be made to. After settling up with the company store and paying for explosives, blacksmithing, and doctoring Obadiah usually had about six dollars and seventy-five cents of scrip left in a week's pay check. It had been just enough for them to get by and have a few cents extra to put away for a rainy day. Sometimes Runa would sneak to Paintsville and sell some eggs even though she knew if the mine found out she was taking their commodities out of the junction they'd give a talking to Obadiah and take whatever they thought she was stealing out of his pay. There'd been a couple of times when the #1 had jerked harder than usual when it was coupling up causing some of the eggs to break in the pocket of her shift. When that had happened it was too late to get off the train and she just had to stay sitting 'til they got down to Paintsville and turned around to come back to Van Lear. It was good fortune that both times the eggs broke she had had her shawl with her to cover up the mess Obadiah later say she'd gone and made. There was three dollars forty-five cents in the coffee can and that wasn't enough to get her too much of anywhere. So until they came to force her out of her house she was just going to stay put and take the time to figure on things.

Runa had been getting the heaves more each day now, barely able to get started in the morning without first having to vomit in the slop can. Flem had been trying to come over every chance he got since they laid Obadiah to rest but she still hadn't told him she was carrying his baby. She hadn't seen Ned for almost as long as Obadiah'd been dead. He'd just up and left. Someone said they thought they'd seen him hop a freight car that'd come through right after the funerals. Runa thought she should be more upset than she was having just lost her husband and all. Then her boy just up and leaves. But truth of the matter was that there just wasn't much to Ned to love on. Every boy, no matter how broken he is, has to make his own way in life, and she guessed that Ned's time had come to go and do just that. It'd been awful rainy and cold the past few days. But now the clouds were beginning to blow out so it was looking like maybe a good tomorrow was beginning to get setup today.

Chapter 12

THAT AFTERNOON, AFTER FLEM had finished crew bossing, he started walking around the back end of the junction. Runa had gotten in an awful state since Obadiah died and Ned had up and left. She'd also gotten stubborn refusing to pack up her belongings and move on. He'd been figuring with her after they finished loving about where to go and what to do. It was going to be best if she just got going sooner rather than later, Flem kept saying. Runa knew she was being talked about and got looks wherever she went. Her dead husband had gone from a being seen as a church going, hardworking man to a pariah. Runa being what was left of Obadiah's family was now being seen the same way. She knew she'd have to go, it was just that she didn't have any place or anyone to go to.

As Flem crossed over a drainage ditch and crouched down to go under a hanging tree branch to get to the path that would take him up over the hill to Runa's, he felt a blow to the back of his head, and then there was blackness. Runa was standing by the back window waiting for a sight of him coming down over the hill. After waiting for what seemed to her to be the longest time, she figured that he wasn't coming. Cloaked in her longing, Runa went on about doing her chores.

He came to blindfolded and bound by his wrists to a black oak tree that'd been standing in the forest for longer than Van Lear had been Van Lear. His arms were tied so tight that each fitful gasp scraped his bare chest against the jagged scabrous bark. "We sent you a warnin' Flem Lemaster. If you didn't stop adultorating you knowed what you were goin' to get." Flem began begging, he'd stop seeing Runa, never go back again, he said.

"By the authority granted under God and the Constitution of this great land, the Order of the White Knights sentences you to eighteen lashes for the crime of adultorating. The sentence is to be carried out immediately." And on the close of the decree Flem felt the first lash from a finger-thick hickory switch open up a salty fissure in his back. There were no more words spoken by the Knights during the whipping.

Flem was a hard man, tears were not of his nature, but as each lash scored a deeper furrow into his back he began sobbing. With lash after lash, he writhed in torment against the tree scraping his chest raw against the gnarly bark. By the time the tip of the switch had torn the last piece of flesh from Flem's back, his legs had buckled underneath him.

The last thing he remembered before he collapsed onto the pieces of bark and flesh strewn around the foot of the oak was his wrists being lifted by the blade of the knife cutting the binding.

The droplets of cool rain dripping from the leaves of the black oak fell onto Flem's bark-clawed face. He hadn't noticed that his back was on fire until he shifted his body trying to refigure where he was. It seemed like something had happened, he thought, as he blinked his eyes taking in the dark canopy of the tree, opening his mouth to catch a few beads of the gentle wetness falling seemingly in slow motion. Then Flem twisted his body and felt the skin of his back pull at the crevices opened up by the switching.

Flem lay shivering on the ground trying his best not to make his chest rise up and down any more than he had to. It occurred to him to hide up in the woods until his back healed up enough and then just up and take off for somewhere else. But even though he'd gone and sinned against everything he knew was right he couldn't leave Nora alone with his youngins. Flem pushed himself up with his elbows and clung to the tree clinching his teeth trying to figure on where he even was.

Nora had been worried sick he knew but once she saw his back she'd know for sure that he'd gotten a whippin'. It wasn't that long ago that Cyrus Stamper, who'd even been a Kentucky Colonel, had been taken out and whipped. Cyrus'd been cavorting with Georgie H. Pepper's wife while he was working over on the Port of Wheeling as a Riverman on the steamboat the *Old Brilliant*. Cyrus, not being a smart man, had thumbed up his nose at the Knights even after he'd almost died from the whipping. It wasn't more than a month of Sundays that he was right back up fornicating with Georgie H. Pepper's wife. Said it was that he'd been just ready to snap the suspender strap of his overalls right after he'd fornicated with her, when a Knight stepped out from behind a long hanging willow and shot him dead as could be. There weren't no other reason for a man to be shot dead like that, so when Georgie H. Pepper got back to his homeplace after a long run down the Ohio to the Mississippi, the mother of his children confessed her sinning ways to him. It broke Georgie H. Pepper's heart into so many pieces that he came down with some kind of fever and was dead six days later. The Knights pretty much ran Georgie H. Pepper's wife out of town on a rail with her youngins dragging behind. Added to his obituary by one who remained unnamed read: "He was universally esteemed wherever known, high minded, honorable and generous to a fault. He leaves to the world a rich heritage which thousands living might envy and emulate—an untarnished, wholesome and God-fearing character."

There wasn't much left to do but for Flem to make his way on home. It took more than two hours to come down from the hillside, having to stop every few steps to catch the wind that was being sucked out of his chest by the pain riding hard on his back. Day was just beginning to snuggle up to night when Flem pulled open the front door and stumbled in. Nora, who was just sick as could be with worry, came running up and caught him just before he fell to the floor. When her arms wrapped around his back he made a cry she'd only heard out of a rabbit being torn apart by a coyote. As Flem rolled himself around in Nora's arms she saw the dried blood on the back of his shirt. Only a whipping would cause that kind of bleeding and if you weren't a nigger then there was only one reason for getting a whipping in those parts.

The children watched their daddy walk bent-over behind Nora toward the kitchen. "You want something to eat I suppose," she said shortly. Flem said he would mightily appreciate it. Nora had a pot of white beans and ham hocks on the stove that'd been there since early morning. She spooned a bowlful out for Flem and sat it down in front of him. "Nora," he began to say with a shameful slouch to his head. "Flem Lemaster, I'm not wantin' to hear anything, not a word from you. But I'll tell you this much, I'm guessing no one else knows about your whipping and it's going to stay that way. You ain't going to humiliate me. Whatevers the reasons don't make no matter to me. I don't want you leaving the homeplace 'til you're healed up and well enough to walk without looking like you're all crippled up. Then you can go on back down to the mine. Now as far as anyone's going to know, you've just gone and got yourself a case of the rheumatism and are going to stay right back there in bed."

Flem right then, taking his first spoonful of soup, knew it would never be talked about again. It took upwards of a week of Nora salving up his back before he could walk upright and another until he could get on back to work. Whatever money had been in the cookie jar was gone by the time Flem went back to the mine after his bout with rheumatism.

Chapter 13

IT WAS HALF-PAST TWO when Runa felt the judder of leather on wood vibrating up her legs and then came the rap on the door. A man with the thickest mustache she'd ever seen hanging down over his upper lip stood outside with his thumbs tucked up into the lapels of his heavy wool suit coat. He also had the coldest right eye Runa had ever encountered. She was sure his left eye was just as cold but she couldn't see much of it due to the fact it was so lazy that it looked like the tippy-top of the bald head of a drowning man bobbing up and down in a choppy lake. He also had a revolver of some sorts with fancy-cut grips tucked into the waistband of his pants, a gold badge pinned to his coat that best she could make out said something about "Baldwin" and a hickory stick in his left hand. Funny though, Runa thought, how smooth the lazy-eyed mustached man's hands looked, especially when compared to the gnarled hands of the miners.

He hadn't bothered to even introduce himself before he said, "It's time for you to be moving on. You've been freeloadin', waiting around for I don't know what and now the time has come for you to get on."

Runa said she didn't have nowhere to go but it didn't make no matter as he lifted his hickory stick and pushed one end right in between her breasts. "You're gonna be long gone by sundown. If I find you here when I come back I'll shoot you dead, it's just that plain and that simple."

Frightened to death, she ran like a moth to a light gathering as much of her things as she could after the some-kind-of detective turned and walked back out the door. She was down on her knees putting what few clothes she had in a pile beside her and Obadiah's bed. Lying on the top of the pile was the finery that Runa had worn just the day before when Flem hadn't bothered to come over like he'd said he was going to. She'd felt so brazen that she hadn't even worn her shift over top of her unmentionables. She'd waited for what seemed to be forever before changing into her shift and started doing the chores that Ned had left her with once he'd up and left. Once she had her necessities all ready for moving on Runa went out into the kitchen figuring about how to take with her half of the pots left over from the panhandler Obadiah had killed back when. Cast iron was heavy and she'd sure to be walking where ever she ended up.

The lid to the Dutch oven slid off the pot and fell to the floor, rolling like an out of balance top, *bthump, bthump, bthump,* over and over and over again until it all of a sudden came to a rest seemingly being sucked right down onto the floor. Runa would figure right before she took her last breath, that the sound of the lid encircling the floor was the reason she didn't hear the front door hinges squeak. No matter how many times Obadiah'd done oiled the hinges the squeak never went away. She'd always heard it no matter what she was doing but on that afternoon either the sound of the spinning lid drowned out the squeak or the squeak just decided to go ahead and finally be quiet. When Runa looked up from the floor, the cold-eyed mustached man stood above her holding a revolver pointed right down at her.

"You told me I had 'til later on," she protested. "I'm a getting my things together to get gone, I'll be long gone by sundown."

The lazy-eyed man cocked the hammer on the Smith and Wesson and leveled the barrel at Runa's chest. The .32 cracked right at the split second that the bullet blew a hole in her heart. She fell back, her eyes rolling up in her head, twitched a few times, stretched out tight as a drum for a second or so and then, relaxing in death, she was gone. For those few seconds, before her heart stopped fluttering, rich red blood pumped out the smooth hole right between the breasts that Flem had loved looking at so much. For just a moment, the man appeared confused when he looked down and also saw blood pouring out from between Runa's legs, pooling underneath her. He walked into the bedroom and gathered up the clothes he saw piled up next to the bed, went out the front door and flung them into the street. Then he went back inside and dragged Runa through the house, out the front door, down the slight hill and rolled her with his boot right out into the middle of the road. He'd gotten some blood on his hands from Runa's feet so he walked back up to the house, raised the pump handle a few times and washed himself clean. Before he left he tucked up his tie, crimped the front and back brim of his derby and then mounted his horse. He didn't bother looking down at her laying twisted up in the bloody muck as he and his horse trotted away.

Chapter 14

THE WIDOWS THAT WERE still left lived close enough by to hear the shot when the detective from Baldwin-Felts killed Runa. It weren't a loud gun being just a small revolver, certainly not like the blast coming out the end of a shotgun. More like a fire cracker going off come the fourth of July. As a matter of fact Florence Pelphrey, when she was just a young girl, had walked out onto the porch one day when her daddy, John Pelphrey, stood talking to a neighbor about forging out a new blade for his scythe. It must've been close to around the time of the celebration of our country coming into being because John Pelphrey for some reason or other had a fat old fire cracker in his palm with the fuse hanging down. Florence, being an ornery one, dashed back into the house, got a match from the cook stove, ran back out the door, struck the match off the head of a rusty nail, and lit the dangling fuse. The fuse ran fast. In the split of a second that fire cracker blew John Pelphrey's little finger clean off. Being cupped in his hand the way it was the blast barely made more than a soft crack. Blood went every which way and Rose, John Pelphrey's wife, chased Florence around the house three times before she caught her and gave her the licking she'd still be telling her children about some fifty years later.

The constable nodded docilely to the Baldwin-Felts detective as they rode past each other about half a mile down from where Runa lay dead in the road. A few minutes after passing the detective, the constable looked down from his horse at the crumpled, blood-sodden body of a woman. He lifted his head, turned in the saddle, and saw the fading silhouette of the black-wool coated derby-hatted rider he'd passed just a bit before. His wasn't even close to a gallop trying to get away from what he'd done, more like he was out for a Sunday ride, just giving his horse some stretchin' time.

Flem was still at the homeplace tending to his lashes when he heard Spencer Duty's apple truck putter up. In but a few moments Spencer Duty's clenched fist was pounding on Flem's door. It was Sunday morning and Nora and the children had gone onto church.

"Flem, something awful's done gone and happened, Runa's up and been killed. The constable found her shot deader than a door nail, lying right out in the middle of the road." Flem stood out of step with time, looking at Spencer Duty through pained eyes, beginning to drown in a sea of cravenness.

Word spread quick about Runa. Some wondered if there was going to be a service at the church while others didn't want to speak any at all of what had happened. Word too was that she'd been with child. So happened that Margaret Jewel right as she was making her way out of the junction had come upon the constable, holding the reins of his horse standing over top of Runa laying dead in the road. Now that Oral was dead, Margaret Jewel's life had become nothing more than time devoid of substance. In her dreams by day and dreams by night she was always with Oral. They weren't hungry anymore and they didn't have to set pans around the house to catch the water when it rained. Oral, being the good boy he'd been, had a special place with the Lord, she was sure because Oral told her so over and over again when he came to her.

Standing beside the constable shaking her head, "Terrible, terrible, terrible," Margaret Jewel said over and over again. Then she stepped over top of the body, lifted Runa's shift to the aghast of the constable and there, laying in the dark blood pooled between her legs, was what looked like a just born possum still in the sack. Margaret Jewel figured, as she poked the pinkish half-moon unborn youngin' with a stick, that it would have been just a few short months before it had turned into a baby boy. "Terrible, terrible, terrible," she kept saying as she turned and continued to walk down the road, pulling the small wagon of belongings behind her.

It was cold-blooded murder, the constable knew that without much figuring. There was also no doubt in his mind who'd done it. He'd been hearing that CONSOL was saying they weren't going to be putting up with this talk going around about unions and what not. He knew that Runa had been the last holdout when the mine boss had told her it was time to move on. All the other widows and Margaret Jewel had been working hard to get on but she'd been the stubborn one. Mary Mary and her youngins had got on board the #1 right early the next morning after Rev. Butcher disappeared, each one carrying a carpetbag, making their way first to Paintsville and then onto Louisville, where her sister had settled down. Mary Mary figured they'd do some reconnoitering and then decide where they'd end up settling down. Maybe start figuring on how to get an education and go about homesteading out west.

Now, as Margaret Jewel pulled her wagon down the road, Cissy gone, Mary Mary gone, Runa dead, and the other couple of widows gone who no one ever knew or cared much about anyway, there weren't anyone left to raise Cain about anything that had gone on in the past couple of weeks. It wasn't but a short while until the constable heard the undertaker's shodded horses clip-clopping down the road. He'd list "gunshot" as the official cause of Runa's death but the constable didn't hold any hope of ever bringing the culprit who'd shot her to justice.

Runa was hauled up to Cumbo Mountain and buried right atop a bump in the earth. The undertaker thought about putting her right next to Obadiah but being the adulterator that she was he'd thought better of it. He chipped her name into a rock then pushed it down into the dirt with his boot 'til it felt like it wasn't going anywhere. A few days later a big rain came causing the dirt to swell and send Runa's rock rolling down the hill. In but a few short seconds it came to rest in a deep dent under the canopy of a tall black walnut. Until the fall foliage fell and covered Runa's rock, the chiseled out "RUNA" would sometimes catch the dappled light of God twisting this way and that through the limbs of the tree. After not too many winters had come and gone the fallen leaves covering Runa's rock had turned into thick mulch. Once those folks who'd kept Runa alive with their whispered rumors of her fornicating ways had passed on themselves, the morass that had covered up Runa's rock over time also covered up any trace that she'd ever even walked the face of the earth.

A few months later it was heard that Margaret Jewel had found her way over to Louisville and got work as a domestic, cooking and ironing for a highfalutin'. Someone said it wasn't long after that Margaret Jewel began coughing up blood and having bad pains in her chest with every breath she took.

That went on for a while until her neck swelled up so big that she looked like a bull frog. The doctors there in Louisville said she'd come down with the King's Evil kind of the white plague. Likely they said she'd given it or maybe been given it, to or from the highfalutins'. The whole highfalutin' family, it was reported, had to go to the Waverly Hills Sanitarium right alongside Margaret Jewel.

The worse the plague spread throughout her body, the more Margaret Jewel called for Oral, demanding to know why he wasn't coming to see her when she was so sick. She always took care of him, and when a boy's momma came down with sickness he should be there to take care of her back, she'd say to the nurses over and over again. No one knew how long for sure it had been, because by the time the news reached back to Van Lear it was close to a year that Margaret Jewel had sneaked off up to the bell tower of the Sanitarium and thrown herself off. One of the Sanitarium nurses, it was reported back, was rumored to have come right up behind Margaret Jewel and heard her speaking the language of the Lord right before she leapt over the wall. Said it was that the nurse being devout herself knew not to interfere with one's intentions when one was being summoned by Eloha Himself.

Chapter 15

THE COLD-EYED MUSTACHED MAN could be seen riding slow around the junction now, never nodding or tipping his hat to anyone. One afternoon right before the first snow a truck wrapped up like a tin can rolled over the railroad tracks and pulled up in front of the company store. The way the steel plates wrapped around the outside of the truck made the five derby-wearing men look like they were missing their legs. Tied to the hitching rail, out in front of the company store, was the detective's horse. The driver of the armor plate wrapped truck recognized the "B-F" stitched into the black saddle right away.

The man closest to the back of the truck was the first to lift his leg over one of thick steel plates and hook the heel of his boot into a foot hold that was welded strong to what there was of a bumper. Each man in unison followed suit, hanging their shotguns or rifles in the crook of their elbows. The fancy ivory grips of their .32 Smith and Wesson's peaked out from under their gussied-up suits that conferred on them a sense of dangerous righteousness. Sherman Pelphrey, who'd been playing checkers with Elmer Picklesimer when the armor car pulled up, nodded to each of the detectives as they made their way up the steps to the company store. Elmer Picklesimer, now about seventy or so, recognized what looked like a spanking new Colt M-1895 machine gun mounted on a polished brass tripod sitting up tall in the back of the armored truck. He'd done faced those unholy beasts when he'd fought in the Spanish-American war. In those days they'd been nicknamed "potato diggers," because sometimes if the soldier manning the Colt was stupid, he'd set the tripod too low and the operating lever would dig itself right into the ground. That didn't bode well for combat when your weapon would end up burying itself instead of the enemy.

The cold-eyed mustached man stepped out of the store as soon as the first detective's boot heel let it be known that someone had just jarred a loose porch board. Handshakes and nods went all around ignoring anyone else who might have been buying goods or relaxing for a spell. The detectives walked out to the armored car pridefully patting the plates, stopping and staring up at the polished potato-digger like she was a bespangled ten cent taxi-dancer or the Egyptian Dread Lord of Darkness. Most of the detectives were drawing hard on cigars brought back all the way from J.J. Russell's Cigar shop in San Francisco.

A wide-eyed breaker boy just done from his time in the screen room came out of the company store sucking on a piece of penny candy. Right as he pushed open the door with his sticky fingers he raised his head from sucking and saw something like he'd never even seen before. It wasn't something that he could have even conjured up to see in his imagination. He wasn't sure if it was the armored truck adorned with its fancy gun or the six dandies standing there with their thumbs hooked into the waist of their suspender held wool pants talking to each other under the brims of their dusty derby's that bowled him over the most. One of the detectives glanced up and saw the breaker boy looking stupefied and told him to come over to him. Like all of the breaker boys, it took a bit before their hearing came all the way back after the banging of hammers and grinding of conveyor belts up in the screen room. The detective, thinking he was being ignored by the filthy little anklebiter, walked up to the bottom step of the porch, reached up, took the breaker boys ear in between his thumb and forefinger, and twisted. Then he threw the breaker boy onto the ground. Sherman Pelphrey stood up like he was going to do something when one of the detectives unholstered his pistol. The two men gave each other a hard look but the eyes of the man with the gun won as Sherman Pelphrey sat right back down.

The breaker boy tried to stand back up but the detective pushed him back down and told him to clean off his boots. Some other folks had heard the commotion and had come out of the company store watching the goings-on. The breaker boy began to pull himself over to the feet of the detective when the detective kicked the boy in the face, sending him rolling butt overhead two or three times before he stopped. He sat himself up and spit out a mouthful of blood and what was left of the few teeth he'd had. "I told you boy, to clean my boots," the detective said, lifting his boot to within inches of the breaker boy's fractured face. The breaker boy reached out with his coal-blackened fingernails and began picking away at the gravel and dirt caked into the sole of the detective's boots. With the quickness of a viper the man brought his boot down onto the breaker boy's hand, grinding the young bones in his fingers into splinters. The screaming breaker boy twisted and turned every which way trying to get his hand from underneath the detective's boot. But it was no use. "Let's get on," one of the other detectives said under his brim. Right as Elmer Picklesimer pushed a red checker to the Kings Row and said "Crown me," Sherman Pelphrey looked up from the board and said, "I quit." Several of the women who'd been buying dry goods were carryin' the broken breaker boy to somewhere they could get some whiskey into him and damper the pain. Then a couple of the ladies would hold him down while whoever was the strongest would straighten out what was left of the bones in his fingers.

Chapter 16

Talk now was about nothing but what had happened down at the company store. Even the Knights were becoming disconcerting in their figuring about what was going on. The men dressed in black and their steel plated truck seemed to up and disappear right after they'd left the company store. One of the church women, just coming into Van Lear, said she'd seen a vehicle of some sorts making the bend around Cumbo Mountain right short after the detective had crushed the breaker boy's fingers.

Right after the explosion some of the rabble-rousing transient miners who were behind the union talk catching fire put the word out that they were going to have an organizing meeting. The meeting was mostly to work the men up with strike talk and shut the mine down. There wasn't a one of them that hadn't been poorer than they were right now, so going out on strike wasn't going to be nearly as much of a hardship for them as it'd be for the mine bosses. Maybe it'd even bring some of the regular miners around more to their way of thinking. One of the old men listening to the goings-on had been at the Ludlow, Colorado mine in 1914 when the mine bosses had the tent town soaked in kerosene and set on fire. Along with a dozen or so miners, they'd also burned up thirteen children and pregnant women that night. "They'll kill us all, wait and see," the old man said shaking his finger.

Two nights later, word was put out that a union organizing meeting was going to take place in the tent town set up for the transient miners just below the main tipple. On that night most of the lanterns were dim and few tents glowed yellow except the cook tent that sat right at the edge of the shanty. Even from far away, the cook tent looked like it was on fire with the bright yellow glow from all the lanterns scattered about. More than two dozen miners and a couple of their wives crowded around the cook stove to be inspired by Merle Ratliff talking about John L. Lewis. The way he spoke of John L. it sounded like he knew him first hand. "*No black-hatted brigades of heavy stepping thugs or bibble-babbling blackguarding scoundrels will prevent the onward march of labor. The only way to protect the rights of the worker is to unionize. We miners, like the Israelites, are faced with many sorrows. But like Moses led the Israelites out of bondage, John L. was put on this earth to lead each and every one of you out of bondage.*" And right when Merle Ratliff uttered the last syllable of "*bondage*" the men and women hunkered around the cook stove, threw up their fists, and stomped their feet to the chant of "*Union, Union, Union.*" Their cry was so loud it could be heard throughout the entire tent town. And then, for just an odd moment, all fists went down, all stomping feet went still, and all voices went mute.

There was no ceremony, there was no trumpet call or ballyhoo, the only thing heard before the repeated rips of the potato digger tearing apart the cook tent and the people inside was the detective who manned the digger cycling the first round into the chamber. After the last round left the smoking barrel the detective threw up the breech cover and tossed the empty oily cloth cartridge belt over the side of the truck. No one was left alive inside the shredded tent to hear the armored truck slowly driving away.

There was no money to pay for funerals for the migrating miners. The undertaker didn't even show up and the constable just road his horse around the cook tent not even bothering to dismount and go inside. The day-to-day miners and their families looked down pretty hard on the transients, thinking they were taking food right out of their mouths with their always comings and goings. It wasn't that the junction gave much of a damn about the transients being shot up; they weren't no one to anyone anyways. What rattled up the miners in Van Lear was that the transients getting killed sent out an earful that no union organizing had better be going on. There most likely now wasn't a soul who didn't know about the breaker boy's hand being made useless by a derby topped detective and now back fence talk was saying that Runa had been shot by the cold-eyed mustached man.

It wasn't long before the armored truck was making regular patrols around Van Lear. Sometimes it'd even be seen down Paintsville way. Other than the cold-eyed mustached man who always rode by himself, the other detectives though were never seen less than two-by-two. No one seemed to know where the detectives stayed when they weren't out and about.

A few months after the cook tent killings, habits mostly seemed to be getting back to what they'd been before all the commotion'd got stirred up. A fight here, a company dance there, church goings-on and bean suppers, some niggers who'd been caught slicking over the mountain from Butcher Holler'd been hung by patrollers, and still, no one would go up near Moses Kitchen's sugar maple grove believing it was haunted.

Chapter 17

FLEM AND NORA NEVER spoke of Runa being killed. As a matter of fact they didn't talk about much of anything most especially those things which were best left unspoken. Flem went to the mine and did his crew bossing, got off work, came home, shook off the coal dust as best he could on the porch, went on inside to a big plate of ham hocks and beans that Nora had ready each and every day when he walked in the door, pushed back his chair from the table after his belly was full, nodded to his youngins, walked on out to the outhouse, came back inside, sat down in front of the radio, and listened to Ray Barger and the Roanoke Jug Band with Mahon Overstreet on guitar and Big Clyde Dooley on Banjo. Ray played mouth harp and Flem would play right along with him. It'd taken him and Nora more than a year to save up enough to buy the radio. They had to trade coal scrip for real dollars which never yielded an even trade. But Nora had insisted on wanting to learn more about the goings-on in the world, said she didn't want their youngins only knowing about the little bit they were learning in school. They'd be grown soon enough and it wasn't enough if you were going to get ahead. Each night the Roanoke Jug Band would close their show with Ray blowing a sorrowful, "Let Me Call You Sweetheart." And each night Flem would blow sorrowfully right along with Ray, longing for Runa. Word had it that the cold-eyed mustached man had put a bullet in her though no one was saying for sure and just as for sure no one was accusing him of doing so. Said it was that the constable knew for certain but he was being tight-lipped on the matter. There wasn't really no more law now only what the detectives let happen and what they didn't. It didn't matter to no one that the Knights would find them a nigger or two to hang sometimes. But the real goings-on was run by the detectives and they did what the mine bosses told them they wanted done.

One afternoon round about when spring was coming in and the air was just beginning to get sultry, Elmer Picklesimer sat on the porch of the company store waiting for a worthy opponent to play checkers. He sat with a cool glass of fresh-pumped water sitting right beside the checker board atop a drained whiskey cask. Just right when he was about to crown himself the most feared checker player in all of Kentucky the steel plated truck rolled up in front of the company store.

The tops of the detectives' derbies all cocked back and forth at the same time when the armored truck came to a stop then they just sat there not moving, looking like mole mounds in a field. It wasn't long before the clip-clop of horse hooves could be heard coming up the road, the silhouette of a black domed rider moving up and down in time with each four-beat gait. In a few minutes the cold-eyed mustache man dismounted and tied his horse to the hitching post right outside the company store. Each derby-topped detective followed his dismount. They mingled around talking under their breaths, nodding this way and that. Shortly the constable rode up, tipping his hat, staying astride his mount, leaning against the saddle horn.

Elmer Picklesimer had been a hard worker all his life expecting a handout from no one. Said it was that he'd laid track to open up the Deadwood Central Railroad back in '88 before coming east, somewhere around when the century turned over. He was known around Van Lear as a man who didn't bother no one and for the most part no one bothered him. It was also said about that Elmer Picklesimer was the silent voice of the union rabble-rousers, offering advice about how to go about causing trouble from his days back in Deadwood. The miners had been getting stirred up again but not like before the detectives had showed up. Now it was more like the miners were realigning their backbones after all those people had been gunned down in the tent town. To just look at the busted-up old man who spent his days sitting on the porch of the company store waiting to shark another checker player, you'd never know that Elmer Picklesimer was the fire behind the slow burning fuse of the union voice. It was also on the porch where he heard things, important things that were whispered here and there about this and that.

The cold-eyed mustached man was the first to look over his well-tended lip whiskers at Elmer Picklesimer from under the shadow of his derby. There was a lot of slow head nodding going on amongst the detectives seeming to imply a collective agreement in their thoughts. Like a pebble dropped into a still pond the detectives began to disperse in a perfect circle with only the lead detective breaking away being tethered by the threat imposed by the others. The comings and goings in and out of the company store stopped, the door slowly closed, a dozen or so pairs of hand-cupped eyes, like parentheses, now peered from the coal-dust caked windows at the cold-eyed mustache man approaching Elmer Picklesimer who still sat waiting to be kinged.

One collective gasp could be heard from the sets of peering eyes when he dropped a lead filled blackjack from under his right coat sleeve and began beating Elmer Picklesimer to death. He was a tough ole bird and was able to take many blows from the sap about his head before he finally up and died. The other detectives stood at the ready with shotguns cradled in the crotch of their elbows waiting for someone to be stupid.

⤜⤛

Chapter 18

NORA HAD BEEN ONE of the sets of peering eyes looking out from the window when the lead detective had murdered Elmer Picklesimer. It'd seemed like the poor man hadn't even raised his arms to defend himself. Truth be known though, the first blow to his head robbed the checker-playing man of his volition to even lift his arms. All he could do was sit there, let himself get beat, and then die. What struck Nora the most was that the cold-eyed mustache man's face didn't change from the first swing of the blackjack to the last. Even when Elmer Picklesimer's head lolled back on his shoulders and his eyes rolled up in their sockets, looking about as dead as a man can look, the man didn't stop swinging that awful sap. And like Nora thought, the hoarfrost that was his face didn't so much as quiver.

All who'd witnessed Elmer Picklesimer's killin' wordlessly swore themselves to silence. When that night Flem said Nora was being particularly quiet, she lowered her chin to her chest and modestly said that time of the month was starting earlier than expected. With that Flem said no more and Nora knew she wouldn't have to be bothered for the next few days with being turned over in the middle of the night.

Elmer Picklesimer's funeral wasn't much to be talked about either. The good Rev. S.C Honeycutt who'd come to serve as pulpiteer since Reverend Butcher had been washed away had been brought in by CONSOL to bring comfort and salvation to the wayward. His sermons talked about the sin of rebellion and the promise of eternal life for the faithful. The good Rev. S.C. Honeycutt preached a wholesome service for Elmer Picklesimer speaking of his many "virtues as a family man, a hard worker, and Kentucky's answer to the greatest checker player of all time, Newell William Banks." Sherman Pelphrey hobbled three-legged into the church, banking mightily on his hickory stick to keep him plumb while holding his hat to his chest to honor his old friend. Looking around, he shook his head, seeing only a few of the old hags from Van Lear way sitting back-straight scattered here and there in the pews. There were no other men to be seen from the back of God's house to the front. Sherman thought the cold sweat of the missing men's fear stank up the church.

The Knights were having trouble finding enough niggers to hang to keep them busy and it didn't seem like since the detectives had rolled into Van Lear that there were as many fornicators neither. The niggers, they guessed knew that the Knights didn't want nothing to do with the sugar maple grove, so they stayed on their hunkers for most of the daylight hours and only slicked at night. Word was this was upsetting to the newly appointed grand Cyclops, Colonel Simmons of Stone Mountain, Georgia who said that the Klu Klux Klan was a fraternity for white Christians. The niggers were upsetting the natural order of things and this is why they had to be stopped like plagues of vermin before they had the chance to decimate a good wheat crop. It was disappointing to Colonel Simmons who was said to be so upset that he had a conniption fit every time he thought about all those niggers slicking right out from under the noses of the Knights up Van Lear way. But conniption fit or not, no Knight ventured into the sugar maple grove.

Since the killing of Elmer Picklesimer the cold-eyed mustache man now rode through the junction nearly every day come rain or shine. Some were whispering that he rode up regular to the widow Betty Butter's homeplace, yonder just north up the trail leading into the mountains. The Butters had homesteaded that part of Johnson County long before Kentucky had even been divvied up into counties. Betty Butter's husband Buddy had been shot down in Paintsville one night while waiting for the #1. No one ever claimed to know why. But just like President Abraham Lincoln, Buddy Butter had been shot one time right behind his left ear. The doc who'd stuck his finger into the wound feeling around for the bullet said he'd found it lodged right behind Buddy Butter's left eye. Betty Butter had just come into her sixteenth year and was just about to deliver their second son when she was informed by the constable that her husband had been shot dead. Said it was that she just sat down on the floor, shook her head, and said "Lordy, Lordy," over and over again. That'd been about ten years or thereabouts now. Betty had done a good job raising her and Buddy's boys. Burke and Buck Butter were known down in the junction to be good boys who'd do just about anything for their momma, never giving her any cause for concern. But one day, for no reason at all, Burke and Buck, just barely having a few what could barely be called chin whiskers, up and left. Someone said they saw them walking right about dusk south towards Prestonsburg. But no matter, Betty Butter never heard from them again, later figurin' that they decided that it was time for them to be venturing on.

Buddy Butter's first set of boys had been ruffians all their lives. But, folks would say, it was because Buster and Butch had been beat up the side of the head so many times by their father that it had caused them not to be right minded. Birdie Butter, Buster and Butch's momma, had died of ricewater stool not too long after Buster was born. Buddy, having to make ends meet an all, wasn't around much, so Buster and Butch were left to fend for themselves, getting in trouble stealing just about anything that wasn't nailed down or accusing somebody of saying something they didn't say and then wanting to go fighting about it. Buster and Butch would eventually be sentenced on the same day, in different parts of the state, "to hang by the neck until dead," for murder. Buster had beat a man named Wallace Buford to death on the exact same day that Butch beat to death Buford Wallace. When Buster and Butch were hanged, Betty bowed her head and said a prayer for Buddy who'd suffered the shame of Buster and Butch being his kin by not thinking he had the right to hold his head up when he walked.

Betty Butter, even though being somewhere around twenty-six or so and having come from good breeding stock, still had her looks about her. It seemed that once the cold-eyed mustache man had come upon Betty Butter whipping her stubborn mule that he'd become downright smitten. Dismounting his steed that day, he uncurled his trigger finger, tipped up the cupped end of his derby, nodded, and said, "Ma'am." It wasn't too long afterwards that when folks began to see the well flicked black Tennessee Walker tethered up to the deep-rooted scarlet oak tree right outside of Betty Butter's bedroom window. Some of the church going women said you could set your clock by it.

Chapter 19

Happy Jack Lewis had come up from Midlothian county, Virginia somewhere around 1890. He was the oldest son of a miner who himself was the oldest son of a miner. There'd been some trouble down home way and about five years before he'd decided it was best to trode north with just about nothing but what he had on his back. It later came to be found out that the horse he'd come up on wasn't even his. Happy Jack had panhandled here and there before coming to Van Lear, having heard the mining was good. He'd been swinging a pickaxe with Flem and his crew for better near a year now and no matter how much Happy Jack tried not a one of the other miners could stand him. As a matter of fact, Frank Tuzzy, who was about as righteous as any man who'd ever walked the face of the earth, said there was something so wrong about the man that if the Lord God Himself told him to he wouldn't piss up Happy Jack's ass if his guts were on fire.

It'd seemed somehow to have gotten decided right after the cold-eyed mustached man had beat Elmer Picklesimer to death that no more union talk would be done topside. "Walls have ears," was what folks were saying. It was best to keep things underground.

That morning when Flem and his men began their roll down the shaft, Happy Jack wouldn't shut up, going on and on about this and that. But, even with all of his clattering about nothing, the miners, usually easily riled by his wearisome tall tales, sat quiet, mostly just staring ahead. Not a one even piped in with a hymn.

Happy Jack was the first one out of the hopper, disrespecting the seniority of the other miners. Once he'd even knocked Frank Tuzzy, who had rheumatism so bad he walked like a bent dog, out of the hopper climbing right over top of him. The fall had corkscrewed him up so bad when he hit the coal bed that Flem and another miner had had to pull old Tuzzy apart like a twisted biscuit. It seemed like all the talking toos that Happy Jack had gotten just went in one ear and out the other. One morning, even before first light, Flem looked down and saw him wearing just about the best looking boots that he'd ever seen. High tops going damn near up to his knees with thick welts that'd stop coal shards from stabbing into the bottom of his feet. Hell, they even had fancy fringed Kiltie flaps coming right down to the top of the steel plated toes. Flem asked Spencer Duty if he'd sold them to Happy Jack, but he said he'd never even seen a pair of boots like that before in his whole life. But he was sure going to inquire of him about where he'd got them, wondering if someone was treading in on his territory.

As soon as Happy Jack's new thick-soled boots hit the coal bed, he made for the vein they'd been working for the past week. It was being about as stubborn as a vein can be in giving up its bounty. With the swing of the tip of every pick, it was like the marbling in the rock retreated deeper and deeper, making the miners work harder and harder. As soon as Happy Jack stood over top of the vein that morning he began arching the pickaxe. And, in between the cadence of each swing, he, talking to the vein like it was living, breathing and bleeding, reeled off the same dirty ditty he'd been spewing now for a week, "*You're just like a tauntin' woman, sometimes you give it up, sometimes you make me work for it, don't matter none to me, either way, you ain't gonna stop me from gettin at it.*" After each round he would rest his pick on his shoulder, tuck his index finger into the crook of his thumb, bend over, and plunk the bits of coal that had wedged in between the Kiltie flaps just like he was some kind of fancy hoodlum knuckling down with a good taw readying to shoot for an auggie duck.

Right after Happy Jack had finished a round and was bent over with his curled up pointer tauted right up against the pad of his thumb, he felt a warm stream of water flowing in between his parted fingers dripping down onto his boot. He cocked his head to see old Frank Tuzzy standing there pissing on him. But before his words had even boiled enough to come steaming out of his mouth, he felt Flem's coal-caked boot shove his face down into the sooty settlings. The other miners encircled the now unhappy Jack Lewis dowsing him with their piss. As soon as the men's piss ran dry they began spitting on him. He knew why the miners were debasing him. What he didn't know was if he was going to make it out of the hole alive. Old Frank Tuzzy hauled off and kicked him in the face, breaking his nose. Folding up into a ball, he lay covered in coal dust that was now caked to his piss-soaked clothes. Frank Tuzzy pulled his Boker, flipped out the blade, bent down, and cut the laces of his boots. Then he put his foot between Happy Jack's legs and used his balls as a boot jack. He screamed as Frank Tuzzy twisted and tugged at his boots, grinding his foot into his privates. By the time Old Frank Tuzzy had finished debooting him, the other men, even in the dim sooty light of the mine, could see the crotch of his canvas pants starting to billow.

Flem suspected right after he had asked Spencer Duty about Happy Jack's boots what'd been going on. He went to Old Frank Tuzzy first, thinking that maybe he just disliked Happy Jack so much that his thinking wasn't the way it should be. But after figuring on it together, there simply weren't no other way the cards could fall.

It wasn't just his boots. Frank Tuzzy had heard tell a few weeks before about some of the other tent town miners catching a whiff of pot roast weaving itself through the camp like a withering snake and settling right under their hungry noses. The scent led right to his splayed open tent flap. And there he sat, spooning down a piled plate of pot roast like there was no tomorrow. Happy Jack, hardly looking up, just kept eating and eating, not even bothering to do the Christian thing of offering a bite to those with such longing in their bellies.

He strutted around the tent town like he had a pot to piss in and a window to throw it out of. He'd even tuck his thumbs up under his suspenders when he was going on and on, making like he was a somebody. The miners' women folk were the first to notice how nosey he was, wanting to know about who's doing this and who's doing that. Always being too friendly and acting like he knew you better than anyone would ever let him. When the good Rev. S.C Honeycutt came by, he always seemed to find his way up to Happy Jack's tent, after meandering around for a while looking for a stray soul to save. The good Rev. S.C Honeycutt was the only one it seemed that liked to spend time talking to the man. It did strike some folks as odd though, once they began figuring on it, that when someone other than the good Rev. S.C Honeycutt was talking with Happy Jack, everyone knew what he was saying. A man of soft tongue Happy Jack was not.

But when the good Rev. S.C Honeycutt dropped by his tent, folks would only see a hand reach out and pull the tent flap shut. For the next little bit not a sound could be heard coming from inside. After not much time having passed, the same hand that had pulled the tent flap closed flipped it back again and tied it off. Then out came the good Rev. S.C Honeycutt walkin' all bent over. Preacher'd put his hands on his hips and groan as he pushed himself upright. The devout ladies of the tent town that tended to the Sunday afternoon Bible study for the good Rev. S.C Honeycutt figured he'd been praying with Happy Jack, trying his God given best to save his sorry soul.

If it hadn't been for those Kiltie flaps no one may have even bothered to notice Happy Jack's boots. But they flipped up right at their pointy tips drawing an eye right to them. It was hard to keep ignoring something like that. Happy Jack didn't help matters none by always reaching down and rolling the tips of the Kiltie flaps between his thumb and forefinger, trying to get them to mind and lay flat. Then he'd dust them off with a slap of the back side of his fingers. The other miners cut cardboard insoles with their jack knives to cover the holes in the soles of their boots. Most of them didn't even have a pair of socks to their names. The water from the mines had leached under the cardboard insoles. It wasn't long before ringworm foot rot would set in and they'd be hobbling around, turning their ankles this way and that, trying not to step right down on a bleeding scab. Happy Jack used to do the same thing until that day when Elmer Picklesimer had seen him come into the company store and made mention of his boots. That was the first time Happy Jack had played checkers with Elmer Picklesimer too. It wasn't long after that that Happy Jack and Elmer Picklesimer would play downright near every day for what seemed like a month of Sundays, at least until the cold-eyed mustache man beat him to death. Right after the tent massacre, Happy Jack had sat for long whiles listening to Elmer Picklesimer lament about who'd known what, when. "How could they have known?" Elmer Picklesimer would rattle on the tail of a black lung breath. Happy Jack would sit uncharacteristically quiet, listening, sympathetically shaking his head, then see an opening on the checker board and say so everyone could hear, "King me!" Elmer Picklesimer would look down, king Happy Jack, and say, "Goddamnit."

Elmer Picklesimer had told him all about his life, from his time in

Deadwood to here and to there. He also told Happy Jack he'd been in Indiana County, Pennsylvania on November 1st, 1919 when the great John L. called out for the first major union strike of the mines. Four hundred thousand miners had walked off their jobs. Elmer Picklesimer said in that speech of John L. he heard more religion being preached than he'd ever heard come from any man waving a Bible. That was when the mining companies decided that men from the Baldwin-Felts detective agency were needed to quell the union unrest that they said was spreading through the mining towns like a plague. Happy Jack listened and listened. The more time he dedicated to listening and learning the ins and the outs of union organizing, the better his life got. Brand new this and brand new that, it always seemed he had something new to show off, either by folks noticing or him just outright bragging it up.

Old Frank Tuzzy thought Happy Jack should be kept an eye on. He thought Flem should be the one to do it. Flem began watching him go here and there. He wondered if Happy Jack had had some relations in Van Lear that he'd never spoke about because he took long walks up to Cumbo cemetery. As often as he made the journey, Flem figured it was maybe his momma or daddy that'd been laid to rest atop Cumbo. Flem would hide just on the other side of a briar thicket and watch Happy Jack come and go from Cumbo. He didn't even have to follow the man anymore, knowing now that just as soon as he was through playing checkers with Elmer Picklesimer, Happy Jack would leave the porch of the company store, walk right over the railroad tracks, make a right and then a left, and in just a bit be at the bottom of the switch back that led up to Cumbo mountain.

A trail that'd grown up pretty good ran up the back side of Cumbo. Getting more curious, Flem started up the trail figuring to wait to see what tombstones Happy Jack visited when he got to the top. He was surprised that the trail had been mashed down and littered along the way with piles of horse shit. Right as he approached the crest of the ridge he heard a horse whinny. Flem ducked behind bushes. There sitting astride his Tennessee Walker was the derby-topped cold-eyed mustache man. It wasn't long before Happy Jack came around a fork in the road and stood admiring the detective's tall, fancy snakeskin boots tucked into the leather-hooded stirrups.

Flem saw Happy Jack take a white canvas bag from his black-gloved hands, talking and waving his arms all the while. He couldn't make out the words going back and forth between them but Happy Jack was sure spieling on and on about something. The cold-eyed mustached man, looking high-falutin', stared down at Happy Jack. After a few minutes of talking and nodding, the standing man stuffed the canvas bag inside his coat, turned, and began making his way back down Cumbo. The cold-eyed mustached man pulled on the reigns, turning the horse toward the mashed down trail. On the way down the mountain Happy Jack ate the fried chicken legs and two pieces of corn bread that the widow Betty Butter had baked up. It was said that there was no better fried chicken in all of Johnson County.

Chapter 20

OLD FRANK TUZZY KICKED and cursed the traitor again and again. Flem finally had to pull him away before he kicked him to death. Happy Jack looked something awful, laying there on the coal bed, nose busted and bleeding, eyes swollen. A couple of his displaced teeth blinked on and off on the ground through the black sooty mist. Two of the men dragged him by his sock-covered feet and tied him to a support beam, where he'd sit until the shift was over. Old Frank Tuzzy kicked him in the face one last time when he was being pulled past his boot.

The sun was just about ready to close its eyes when the shift ended. Old Frank Tuzzy sat beside Happy Jack with the blade of his Boker tipped right up against his side. "You make a sound when we get to the top and I'll gut you like a fish." Happy Jack said nothing back nor did he say anything when the hopper rolled back into the light.

Instead of walking over to the bath house, Flem, Frank Tuzzy, and the other men huddled around the bloodied man and walked in a clump up over the hill toward the train tracks. Old Frank Tuzzy pulled out a bottle of sour mash and began swigging it high, passing it around loudly so others could see the goings-on. Flem, about as loud as he could be, told Happy Jack to drink up, putting the bottle in his hand. Old Frank Tuzzy still had the blade of the Boker up against his side. Happy Jack took the bottle, downing as much of the corn liquor just as quick as he could.

By the time the miners made it over the hill the sun had laid down for the night. About a half mile out of Van Lear, the #1's tracks curve under a rock canopy that had been left when they were blasting through the sandstone to cut a route into Prestonsburg. For the engineer of the #1, it was a blind corner.

Old Frank Tuzzy shoved Happy Jack onto the tracks. They'd all expected him to beg but he never spoke a word, he was about as drunk on his helplessness as a man could be, lost in the suspense of how he was going to die. His life hadn't been worth much from the day that his momma had been raped by a has-been confederate soldier. Hell, his momma, when she'd told him that he had no daddy, said she didn't have no reckoning of how the has-been was able to get the seed that had become Happy Jack from him to her.

Old Frank Tuzzy swung the awful pipe over and over again, never missing his head, coming just shy of killing him. Flem slipped his toe under his ankle and lifted his leg up onto one of the tracks. Then Flem raised his boot and slammed it into Happy Jack's knee, breaking it about as many places as a bone could be broken. Even though his head was leaking out what little brains Old Frank Tuzzy said he had, he still gurgled a scream when Flem snapped his knee. Old Frank Tuzzy leaned down and took his twisted foot and wedged it under one of the tracks.

One of the other miners soaked his clothes with hooch, making him smell like turpentine. Having a few drops left, the miner lifted his head by his matted hair and filled his pulpy mouth with the remaining mash. The miner looked into his eye slits and then let his head fall onto the railroad tie.

The men made their way back up the hill to a thicket of trees. They didn't have to wait long before they heard the whistle of the #1 making its weekly run to Prestonsberg.

The seesawing of the Hemlock trees in the moonlight played tricks on the engineer's eyes making him blink frantically, trying to catch sight of for sure what it was up ahead splayed across the tracks. By the time the engineer had figured it out, it was too late to pull the emergency brake and Happy Jack had exploded into a plume of red and brown tenderloin as though he had never been.

Being that he was running late as it was, the engineer, after smelling corn liquor coming off of the mess of sinew, had one of the Micks shovel up what was left of Happy Jack and toss it onto the tail end of a flatbed. They found one high top boot dressed up with what the Mick called a Kiltie flap. Seemed like the man had taken off his boots before imbibing and passing out on the tracks. "Poor bastard," the Mick uttered in a thick brogue. Happy Jack's other boot with its fancy Kiltie flap would forever sit on the rock he'd spent the last days of his life working to best.

Happy Jack Lewis was the only man anywhere near Van Lear who'd worn fancy flap boots. Word spread pretty quick it'd been him that'd been run over by the #1, the night before. "Scooped Happy Jack with a coal shovel I hear," Old Frank Tuzzy said under his cap, buying penny candy at the company store.

Smiling and nodding, waiting his turn for penny candy right behind Old Frank Tuzzy, was the cold-eyed mustache man, standing tall in his snake-skin boots, looking like he was not in agreement with his own character. Flem and Spencer Duty were sitting on the porch playing checkers in Elmer Picklesimer's old spot. When the detective came out of store, he walked over and stood staring down at the checker board right as Spencer Duty triple-jumped Flem. "You let him get the best of you, Flem," he said. Then he walked off, mounted his Tennessee Walker, lightly spurred his horse's side, and trotted up the road. Spencer Duty could barely take his eyes off the snake-skin boots disappearing in the kicked-up dust, longing to someday parade around in fancied-up boots of his own. From afar, another set of eyes was keeping watch on the tall man bobbing up and down to his horse's three-beat gait.

No one around Van Lear much cared that Happy Jack had ever been born. It wasn't likely that anyone was going to give a damn that he was dead. Anyway, the back-fence talk was saying he was a no-account drunkard. The good Rev. S.C Honeycutt, whenever he heard Happy Jack being slandered about, gave them a piece of his mind. He'd got to know Happy Jack as a good and God-fearing man that always wanted to do right by those who'd paid his way. He was going to be preaching a special sermon on the dutifulness of obedience, raising Happy Jack up as the pinnacle of such a man. A dedicated man like Happy Jack should not have died in vain. His story should be told to inspire others into standing tall for those who provide for your needs. Not a man or woman showed up for church that Sunday morning.

Chapter 21

A COUPLE OF SATURDAYS after Happy Jack had been struck down by the #1, the annual barn dance was going to take place, featuring Marion Baiotto on fiddle and Jew's harp side-by-side with his boy Bill, playing the button accordion. Calling the dance was going to be none other than Lloyd "Pappy" Shaw, probably the greatest square dance caller that'd ever lived. Some folks called him the Pride of Kentucky. He'd even penned a book, *My Square Dancing Life*. Said it was that Pappy was a relation of Nora somewhere along the line. God bless her, the church women would say for months after the dance, for writing her cousin, Mable Feazell over in Hazard, who was for sure a kin of Pappy's, asking her to ask him if he'd grace their dance with his calling. Word came back to Nora from cousin Mable not long after that Pappy would be happy to show up and give the night his all. Once word got out that he had said yes, bolts of Dotted Swiss and yards of taffeta ribbon sold off the company store shelves like hot cakes on a cold day. It wasn't long before the women of Van Lear were suffering from thimble-finger after sewing up so many fancy this and thats, preparing to pretty themselves up for the special dance. The miners were even dusting the soot off their Sunday finery, looking forward to swinging their women to the do-si-do.

Chapter 22

THE SCHOOL HALL LOOKED about as nice as anyone could ever remember seeing it. There wasn't a speck of coal dust anywhere to be seen that could fell a pair of sashayers. Flem had painted a "WELCOME PAPPY," sign and nailed it right over VAN LEAR school. That sign would hang there for a good twenty years more, letting folks know about that special night when the Pride of Kentucky graced Van Lear with the best calling that anyone could ever remember swinging their partners to.

Pappy'd come over from Hazard the night before the dance and stayed with cousin Nora and Flem, eating what he said was some of the best chicken and dumplings he'd never taste the likes of again. Cousin Nora told Pappy it was none other than his momma who'd taught her the way of rolling the dumplings just right when she was but a youngin'. Pappy thought his momma'd be right proud of cousin Nora carrying on the family's way of rollin' out dumplins'. But cousin Pappy was most honored when an apple truck, as clean as it had ever been, pulled up in front of cousin Nora and Flem's to take him to the dance. But even more surprising was the constable, attired out in a white hat and silver-buckled belt, sitting atop his blond mane mare, ready to ride in front of Spencer Duty and his apple truck, giving the Pride of Kentucky the first ever escort right through the heart of Van Lear. The road to the school hall was lined with impatient feet just yearning to dance. And, as the apple truck rolled by, those tingling feet fell in right behind. Pappy looked back smiling a big smile, shaking his head, never having seen anything quite the likes of, thinking to himself that those dancing feet had done taken over the very bodies that they were meant to serve. Spencer Duty drove with about as much

106

pride surging through his spine as he'd ever felt in his whole life as he held tight to the reins of the temperamental apple truck, careful not to run over top of the constables equally temperamental mare.

And, unbeknownst to anyone, the constable, after seeing that Pappy had his due and after having figured on it for a good while, kept on riding hard into the night, until he reached the Tennessee border, planning on giving up constabiling and taking up homesteading. Maybe even taking a wife and having a slew of youngins. Part of his figuring had been looking from atop his mare at the pile of tent town miners torn apart by the potato-digger. He'd seen it in the war but there he was young enough to have fought back and have other soldiers with him side-by-side, but that weren't going to be the case in Van Lear. If he was insisted upon by the folks of Van Lear to take up his gun against the detectives, there be no one at his side.

Between those folks swishing and swaying behind the apple truck and those waiting outside of the school hall barely able to control their dancing feet, it seemed like all of Van Lear was going to be whirling and twirling long into the night. As the apple truck crested over the hill, Pappy caught sight of all of the folks congregating in front of the schoolhouse, already squaring up, hardly able to wait to hear his sing song voice trail off the last word of each call like an auctioneer's cattle rattle barreling out a train tunnel. When Spencer Duty pulled up in front of the school hall, the folks in the crowd applauded so loud that Pappy thought it was a good thing they weren't clapping with their feet or they'd have tuckered out their soles before they even had a chance to partake in the festivities. Several of the men helped Pappy down from the apple truck and formed a circle around him as he walked into the school hall and made his way to the stage, where the best fiddlers from Van Lear and "Professor Banjo" up from Paintsville were already tuning up.

It wasn't long before Flem stepped up to settle folks down and reluctantly asked the good Rev. S.C Honeycutt to open the dance with a prayer. The good Rev. S.C Honeycutt stepped forth and said he usually didn't ask the good Lord to bless the likes of folks dancing and all but he'd asked God's help in figuring on it and felt that since the good Lord had offered up a man with as much renown as Pappy it must be something He approved of. And, on that, the good Rev. S.C Honeycutt bowed his head.

In an hour, maybe more, arms were alinkin' and petticoats were atwirlin' with each saucy twist of a hip. The good Rev. S.C Honeycutt though, out of respect, had draped his coat over Jesus' picture that hung over the stage. Never could anyone recollect having had such a grand time.

After that first hour had passed, folk's feet were needing a few minutes of well-deserved pause. Pappy had called so many square dances that he could see when the twirlin' began slowin' that folks needed to take a while to rest their twistin' hips.

The good ladies of the church had put out punch bowls filled with the best fresh-pressed apple cider anyone could remember ever having quenched their thirst. There wasn't a soul anywhere to be found in the school hall that hadn't been taken over by joviality. And then, it happened.

Chapter 23

LATER FOLKS WOULD SAY that it was the devil's breath that had blown open the school hall door. But the good Rev. S.C Honeycutt said it was "Jesus' way to welcome all to His table."

A collective gasp was heard when the cold-eyed mustache man walked through the door, arm in arm with Betty Butter. As they stood at the crest of the door, the lead detective and his date cocked their heads and looked around like they were expecting someone to announce them like they were somebodies. But the only one who showed them any Christian mind was the good Rev. S.C Honeycutt who waltzed up and shook the tall man's white gloved hand, nodding all the while to Betty Butter who was dressed in a yellow store-bought dress and shiny, slick-soled dancing shoes.

Pappy, not knowing anything about the goings-on of the past, interrupted his resting, stood up, spread his arms, thinking the couple *were* someones, and told folks to welcome the most dapper dressed couple he'd likely ever seen grace one of his callings.

And then, with what sounded like a hollow hall filled with infirmed arms, folks' hands followed Pappy's call and in unison came together once and only once, to clap a paltry clap to a silent recalling of Job 27:23 "*It claps its hands at him and scorns him from its place.*" On that, Pappy, knowing something had gone awry, called for the fiddlers and Professor Banjo to commence fiddling and picking while he softened his voice to the warble of a silver-throated thrush. In what seemed to be no time at all, folks began to turn toward Pappy like children following the Pied Piper of Hamelin away from a plague-infested rat.

Before too long, the air in the school hall was being whipped up again with all the whirling and twirling. It happened more than once that the cold-eyed mustache man and Betty Butter tried to link arms and join a circle. But the crooks of the dancing arms missed them just enough to make it look from afar like one or the other was made of smoke. *Poof, poof, poof,* round and round they went, leaving the two forever on the outside.

In a huff, the good Rev. S.C. Honeycutt threw back his splenic shoulders and strode up to Flem, now resting his dancing feet right outside the school hall doors. With a waving finger, the good Rev. S.C. Honeycutt began to blister him with God's retributing in Thessalonians of the man who wrongs his brother. Flem, having had about enough and without saying so much as a word, backhanded the good Rev. S.C. Honeycutt right across the mouth, opening up his thin lip like a blown coal vein. There wasn't much he could do except stand there and bleed. As Flem walked back into the dance, he thought to himself that he hadn't even respected the good Rev. S.C. Honeycutt enough to hit him like a man.

No one saw anymore of the reverend until the next Sunday when he preached what he said was Samuel 15:23, *Rebellion of the hand that feeds you is but the sin of witchcraft, and stubbornness to see what is right is nothing more than iniquity and idolatry.* Talk of unionizing was starting up again, he said he'd heard. Bullies were thinking they could do as they pleased without God retributing against them. The good Rev. S.C. Honeycutt said he'd even heard that folks in Van Lear were becoming more accepting of niggers and that even the Knights were getting lazy with their sworn Godly duties of enforcing the fire of the Word. "Amen," after "Amen," after "Amen," could be heard all the way down the block after each of the good Rev. S.C. Honeycutt's declarations and calls to get back to carrying out each and every man, woman and child's duty as a Christian soldier. After the service there was handshaking all around and a pot full of biscuits and sawmill gravy to fill the redevouted bellies. The good Rev. S.C. Honeycutt was sure to say, right before he offered grace over the bounty, that it had been generously paid for by Mr. LaViers himself. "A good man amongst good men," he was, the good Rev. S.C. Honeycutt offered.

It'd been months now since the steel-plated truck full of black-suited detectives had been seen anywhere around Van Lear. And the cold-eyed mustache man laid low for weeks after being humiliated at the dance. Even Betty Butter had not shown her prettied-up face anywhere near the company store to the point where folks were figuring on how she was getting by. The good Rev. S.C. Honeycutt continued to preach on the sins of organizing. "Look what had happened to Jesus," he'd say. "When the Captain of our salvation said, *Father forgive them for they know not what they did,* He wasn't talking about the cowardly thieves hanging beside Him. No, Jesus was saying that no matter how hard He had tried to persuade those twelve Jews from organizing around Him, he knew it was going to come to a bad end, but they wouldn't listen to reason and look what happened. *That's* what the Prince of Peace was saying."

When standing at the back of the church on any Sunday that the good Rev. S.C. Honeycutt was preaching, heads could be seen fervently nodding up and down.

Chapter 24

ONE AFTERNOON, RIGHT AFTER one of the good Rev. S.C. Honeycutt's fiery sermons denouncing the sins of organizing, somewhere about three or so, the armored truck rolled up in front of the company store filled with the black-coated derby-topped detectives with .30 caliber Winchesters propped up from between their legs. Not a one of them moved until the rims of their derbies in concert could be seen turning to the approaching sound of hooves announcing the coming of the cold-eyed mustached man. He strode up to the side of the truck and tipped his hat to the detectives. No one had seen the armored car for months now. No one even knew where it'd gone to or where it'd come from. If anyone asked the folks around the junction to describe the faces of the contemptible detectives there only recollection other than their killings was that they were forgettable. It'd been payday that morning and the company store had just gotten supplies from the #1 the night before. Lots of scrip was changing hands, flour, sugar, and cuttings from bolts of cotton were going out the door just as fast as they'd come in. Usually the men didn't come down with their women but on this occasion Flem had hitched up the wagon deciding to come along with Nora. Just as they were about ready to depart, Nora saw Flem eyeing a pack of Sweet Caporals that most likely had been brought up from Virginia ways. She was sure Flem was thinking that a pack of Sweet Caporals showing up in Van Lear was about as rare as shit from a rocking horse. Flem'd been rolling his own cigarettes out of cut plug since he was thirteen. He wasn't a man who desired much more than to provide for his family. Since he'd been switched he'd been about as devout as a man could be. And, to Flem's confoundedness, Nora had begun making it known that she enjoyed him turning her over.

Nora tucked a yard of cotton under her arm, walked over to Flem, reached out, took the pack of Sweet Caporals from the counter, and told the store to take the extra eighteen cents off their scrip. "You never ask nothing for yourself, Flem Lemaster," she said as she slipped the pack into Flem's one palm. Pay had been good lately. He had been pushing his men hard and production had been high. He tucked the smokes under his armpit and tore open the red, black, and blue sunburst pack, pulled out one of the fat cigarettes, tapped it against the glass counter, slipped it between his lips, pulled a stick match from his pocket, and flicked it to life with his thumbnail. Nora watched the sweet blue smoke unfurl from Flem's nose as they walked arm in arm toward the door. A breaker boy, having watched Flem open the pack, kept his keen eyes on the prized cigarette card that he had tossed to the floor when he'd opened the pack. The boy, in snatching up the card, damn near knocked over the crippled-up Mrs. Slacum, who'd come off the mountain to get her monthly bag of flour and sugar. She scolded the pleased-up boy something awful for being so unmannerly.

Right after he crested the archway of the door, Flem glanced down at his sooty boot. As his head leveled back up with his shoulders, a single .32 caliber bullet entered his brain right between his eyes. The smoldering Sweet Caporal was still clenched between his teeth when he fell to the ground. Nora, beside herself, sat beside her husband, cradling his bloody head in her lap as he lay dying, begging for someone to help. Three other miners' wives, carrying their goods, stepped around Flem, careful not to get any blood on their shoes. And, at the very moment that he passed away, and unbeknownst to anyone of this earth, Flem saw the same white-frocked itinerate that his granddaddy had held his head by the hair and made him look at as a youngin'.

The cold-eyed mustached man holstered his pistol, looked at Flem lying dead on the porch, shook his head, and said as he was riding off, "Goddamn ridge runners, they never learn." The armored truck followed right along behind, the detectives not so much as having had to point a rifle.

Chapter 25

WHEN HIS TWIN BROTHER Isaiah had been killed in the mine explosion back when, everything had changed. They'd always been together, since they'd been born somewhere about 1883 or thereabouts, give or take a year or so, in the St. Francois Mountains on the southeast Missouri side of the Ozark Plateau. Or at least that was what their momma had always said but she'd also said that she couldn't be none too sure as having eleven living children with five or so having passed on before they were barely a year or so made her lose track with who was born exactly when. But she said she figured that was pretty close should anyone with a need to know ever ask.

Being twins and all was a sight for sore eyes or so folks would say when they saw them dressed up alike not being able to say which one was who. Even their voices and mannerisms were so close to being the same that they spent many a long years fooling folks. Somewhere along right before their fifteenth birth, their momma started having a flux and fever so bad that they heard their daddy say that her insides were coming out her rear end. It wasn't long after that that they were holding her down in bed 'cause she was shaking so bad with the fever that their daddy was fearful that her bones would break. Her breathing was more like gasping and her eyes were rolled about as far back in her head as they could get. And then, with an awful sucking sound coming up from her lungs and out her rectum, that had in fact pushed out of her, bursting open from the outside in, the boys' momma passed on into the hands of the Lord Almighty. It was likely she'd died from the cholera and more likely others in the family wouldn't be far behind her. But their momma was the only one who'd come down with it. Their daddy said that he wasn't going to have time for raising up the twins much more and in fact he was thinking of moving on somewheres else himself. So the boys, now being solely on their own, signed up to fight in the Spanish-American War, which had just begun.

Both the boys proved themselves to be brave soldiers during the Battle of San Juan Hill just outside of Santiago. But aside from their bravery, and both boys in a short time having developed an affinity for explosives, was the fact of seeing how brave the colored regimen fought right alongside of the white soldiers. Even with the Spanish laying down fire faster than anyone could have imagined, the colored soldiers leveled their Springfields with deadly accuracy and, when their magazines went dry, rushed the Spaniards with their bayonets thrusting, likely killing as many of them by hand as by bullet. But it seemed to Isaiah and his brother that the bravery of those colored soldiers wasn't even beared witness to by Colonel Roosevelt, with him strutting here and there, patting his white soldiers on the back and ignoring the shoulders of Captain "Black Jack" Pershing's men. As a matter of fact, right when the battle was supposed to be done with, a Spaniard, who was equally supposed to be dead, raised up and just before the hammer dropped on his rifle, which would have sure as not killed Isaiah, a Negro threw his bayonet landing it right in the heart of the greaser. Bayonets were never meant for throwing, so the Negro who lobbed something as ill-mannered as a rifle bayonet making it stick and not hit like a club was a man not only of great strength but also a man of great skill. Forever and a day, Isaiah would be grateful to that nameless man. Even though cavorting with the coloreds by his white soldiers was not permitted by Colonel Roosevelt, that lifesaving Negro soldier would always be in their daily prayers. Isaiah would never forget looking into the greaser's eyes right as he was leveling his Mauser and then just about as quick as thought, seeing the butt end of a bayonet protruding from his chest. He looked around and saw that colored soldier, seemingly not much older than him, now looking into his eyes. Both men, who not long ago had been just boys, not having any words to say, squeezed their lips together nodding one to the other.

Isaiah's one-minute older brother came back from the War nicknamed King Fisher the Terrible. The Spaniards called him an *aparición*. King Fisher, being more of a loner of the two boys, would go off on his own, always at night, seem to appear like he had just been blown in on a puff of smoke and cut the throats of Spanish soldiers. Sometimes he'd slice a head clean off, shove the neck down on a thick stick, and prop it up in the mud, which there never seemed to be a shortage of. When the enemy would come upon the heads of one of their own, it was like they'd been turned to stone. Then, King Fisher would shoot them down like fish in a barrel. Sometimes, he'd blow them to bits. His fellow soldiers called him King Fisher after the gunfighter John King Fisher, the outlaw turned sheriff who'd died when he was just about thirty ambushed by a group of bad men. The other soldiers figured that King Fisher was so good at what he did that he was likely not to fall for such an ambush as his name sake.

Once they returned from Cuba, the boys got a job as express messengers for the Barlow and Sanderson Company, making sure the bandits couldn't take advantage of what the coach driver and the messengers saw as nothing but ne'er-do-wells. At least the first class riders who, if the stagecoach got stuck, would sit on their behinds not offering so much as a shoulder to push it out of what was usually an unseen hole of mud from a downpour the night before or a hole that'd come up in the road after a hot sun cracked it open like the crust on a hot loaf of bread. Hell, sometimes the messenger had to level his sawed off shotgun through the window to get the ne'er-do-wells up off their lazy asses and out of the coach so the second and third class passengers could roll the wheels up out of the thick muck.

There were times with some when road agents would pull a hold-up that the Jehu and the messenger wanted to go ahead and give the first class passengers on up to the bandits. But neither King Fisher nor Isaiah would relinquish their fiduciary responsibility and so rather than give over the most likely good-for-nothings to the outlaws, they'd level their coach guns at the robbers blasting them right out of their saddles. Usually, King Fisher would take the run from Kansas City to Tulsa and Isaiah would take the run back. But the drivers never knew the difference.

Isaiah and King Fisher stayed on with the Barlow and Sanderson Company until the railroads put the stagecoach lines out of business. It was on one of those days that they began their trek east thinking that opportunities for steady work would await them. A few months later in the coal fields of Pennsylvania, mining the Pittsburgh Coal Seam, they first began swinging pick axes deep inside the earth. The men were strong and unafraid of a hard day's work. But it was difficult for them to stand by and watch miners being beaten and at times even kicked to the ground and pissed on by the boss man. Every time a boss man took it upon himself to give a miner a *don't-forget-your-place* beating, there were always other boss men's eyes peering from here and there, keeping a look out for any sympathetic miner who might be foolish enough to take it upon himself to interfere with the public flogging. Afterwards, the beating boss man would shove the beaten miner into a nearby mud pit. Rumors started about a year or so after they began working for the Pennsylvania Coal Company that Isaiah had beaten one of the boss men to death with his bare knuckles after he'd sapped a breaker boy about the head so bad that when he tried to talk he just stammered, not making any damn bit of sense what-soever. Unbeknownst to any of the onlookers, it was actually King Fisher who'd killed the boss man, having had just about enough of the beatings and killings of men and boys just trying to make ends meet for their families. And so under cover of night, the brothers made their way south down toward Van Lear having talked to some of the miners who'd made their way up north. It took about two weeks or so, having to hide out from the constables, who'd by that time heard about the boss man being made an example of by Isaiah Kitchen. But once they crossed over into West Virginia there was no more cause for concern and the uptempo'd gallop of the horses' hooves beating against the dusty road became but a well-tempered resonant adagio.

As the brothers leaned back in their saddles, talk turned to their littlest of sisters, who no one got to know well at all because she drowned in a stream barely a foot deep when she was hardly two or there. They remembered their daddy taking them and her down to Lone crick, wanting to pull out a few small trout for dinner that evening. They'd not been there long, and while they were setting their poles with night crawlers, Isaiah looked up from his now squirming hook and asked where Effie May had gotten to. Their daddy threw his pole down and began fast walking the edge of the stream, when not that far out of eyesight he saw Effie May's little feet sticking out of the water. In what seemed like no time at all, from when he saw her to when he got to her and pulled Effie May out of the water, their daddy couldn't get her out of Jesus' strong arms no matter how much he pushed on her back, no matter how much creek water came flooding out of her lungs, no matter how much he cried like they'd never seen a man cry before holding her pressed against his chest, thinking maybe that somehow his big beating heart would start up her little one.

They watched their daddy that night pound together a small coffin, pick up Effie May like he was gathering up a bundle of loose sticks afraid of them coming apart, and lay her down on a stitched quilt filled with eiderdown. They buried her the next day underneath a tall Hickory that had more rings than the entire Kitchen clan put together. A wooden cross marked with her name said she was buried beneath. Not so many years later, after the wind and weather had had its way with the cross, it fell over and was buried in the thistle that had taken over the field and now run right up against her resting place. Once, when they made their way back through what was left of the homeplace, the brothers kicked away enough of the cockleburs to find the crossbar of Effie May's marker, her name long washed away.

The more they rode the more they talked, reminding each what the other had forgotten. And, what neither wanted to remember, they dreamed, tossing and turning in their painful timeless twilights.

Crossing over from West Virginia they followed the Big Sandy river until where it met up with the Levisa Fork just on the outskirts of Prestonsburg, Kentucky and then made their way back north over the ridge between Butcher Holler and Van Lear, finding just about the prettiest sugar maple grove either man had ever seen.

After a month of Sundays they'd built themselves a small tin cabin nestled underneath the sturdiest maple and began cutting wood for the upcoming winter. They'd seen plenty of deer, squirrels, and rabbits on the way over the ridge so meat most for sure wouldn't be a problem. It didn't take long before one or the other would see a colored boy and sometimes a whole family sneaking around in the woods, hiding in this or that clump of bushes. The brothers would put a canvas sack of dried meat in some of the densest brush for anyone who might be trying to be making their way up over the mountains to Ohio. Whoever said coloreds weren't still held in bondage was full of bullshit. Hell, anyone with any sense knew the southern plantations still chained the legs of their Negro workers each and every night. Usually on one end of a cotton field sat one man on horseback holding a rifle while one sat saddled up at the other. And if a picker was to manage to get away he had to be mindful of the Invisible Empire of the South who strung up any colored boy they'd catch anywhere they considered him not supposed to be. For Isaiah and his brother the plantation owners were just another kind of pharaoh and the KKK were its chariot drivers.

It was just in between the birth of our Lord and one year going and another one coming that they heard the beating on their cabin door in the early morning hours. Standing on the plank porch was an entire family of Negros; Father, mother, and two youngins. "Says that you might be friendly to helpin' out a man and his family. If you ain't then we just be on our ways." The wind was winding through the trees like an uncoiling snake blowing the falling snow every which way. Isaiah yelled for his brother to get out of bed and heat up the squirrel stew they'd made just that very day. Mr. Willis, Mrs. Ola, the girl Pearl, and the boy Willis made their way into the tiny shack and warmed themselves about as close to the fire as they dare get. Not saying so much as a word, King Fisher spooned out bowls of hot stew until he was scrapping the pot for the bits of meat and potatoes stuck to the bottom. Isaiah untied a sack of bacon they cured from a wild pig they'd shot a few weeks back and wrapped some up in a tight bundle and laid it out for them to take when they got back on their way. Mr. Willis said he'd escaped from Devils Half-Acre, the slave jail, in Richmond and made his way over to the plantation in Tennessee, where he'd stole his family because he didn't have enough money to buy them from the family who'd owned his family since his granddaddy'd been bought a many long years now before. They made their way up over this ridge and that, almost getting caught just before they crossed over into Kentucky. Other colored boys they'd run into said if they lived long enough to get to Butcher Holler and up over the ridge to the sugar maple grove, men with good hearts would help them.

The storm pushed hard against the cabin for a full two days, not letting up for even a minute. The brothers, Mr. Willis and the boy Willis, slept on the floor while Miss Ola and Pearl were offered the straw beds. After the storm quieted, they figured it was best if they be on their way. Isaiah filled a canvas bag with the boar bacon and some boiled potatoes, which would keep them eating until they made it to the Ohio river, where they'd be able to find more help. As they were walking away, Pearl turned, ran back, and wrapped her arms around the tall legs of the brothers. Mr. Willis turned and tipped his hat in thanks right as they were just losing eyesight of each other.

A week or so later, the twins were in need of more meat to get them through the rest of winter. As they crested over the top of a hill that dropped down into a steep gully, there hanging from two tall maple trees were Mr. Willis, Miss Ola, the boy Willis, and Pearl. They cut them down and dug one grave, laid them side by side and spoke words from the Good Book. Then they rolled a rock over top, marking the spot where they were buried. After a while, and like Effie May, the fact that they passed of this earth would be forever forgotten.

Other than that time of being separated, King Fisher and his one-minute younger brother had been together throughout their lives. Until of course the one-minute younger brother'd been blown up deep in the mine on that awful day.

They were raised with a strong sense of doing the right thing and as long as it was two-sided, treated those who they crossed paths with dignity and respect. But when wrongs were wrung they'd only stand by for so long. Now that the one-minute older brother was the only one left, King Fisher figured things had gone on long enough. The killing of Flem hit him hard. He'd respected the man who he saw as only wanting to do what was right, taking up the mantle, though somewhat reluctantly, after Elmer Picklesimer had been beaten to death. Other than the one other person who'd moved on since the explosion, Flem had been the only one who knew about King Fisher and his brother. Sometimes they'd meet and talk private about the goings-on. King Fisher warned him there was going to be trouble but Flem figured that if he tried to bring things about by talking rather than striking that Mr. LaViers and the mine bosses would be more apt to listening. Things had begun to change in West Virginia, it had to change here too, Flem would say. It couldn't go on like this forever, maybe now was the time. King Fisher said no it wasn't, it was still too early, talk don't bring about that kind of change, not with those kind of men. "Like a dog marks its territory with piss, those bastards mark their territory with blood," he would say. The only thing that'd make them change was fear. Not fear of a strike or organizing, but the fear of another man. "And Flem, no disrespect intended," he said, "you ain't that man." King Fisher didn't take any solace in having warned him.

It'd been a few weeks now since Flem had been shot. And just like the times before, everything had gone right back to the way it'd been. This time though, there wasn't any talk of organizing or unions going on underground. The miners reported for work, went down into the earth, dug out the coal, came back up, went home, washed up, ate supper, and did the same thing the next day, never causing any ruckuses.

Years ago, King Fisher remembered a man in Kansas City showing around what he called an automaton. The puppet master would turn the key in its back to make it bend over, pick-up a ball, stand back up, and then toss the ball. Then the mechanical man would wind down and just stand there waiting to be wound up again to do the same thing over and over again. That was how he saw the miners now. Except they were all afraid, every damn one of them. A storm had come to Van Lear and blown the life right out of every living soul. Everything was jumbled up and nothing seemed to be going toward the natural order of things.

Right after the pallbearers had lowered Flem's box in the ground, the good Rev. S.C. Honeycutt had tossed the first handful of dirt on top of the coffin, saying that we start out as dust and we end up as dust. When Nora, right at that very moment, leaned over the side of the grave and threw herself astride Flem's casket, the good Rev. S. C. Honeycutt jumped right atop Flem's final resting place, put his blessed hands on Nora's grieving head, and began sing-songing in his holiest of holy voices, Revelations 3:20, "*Beholda, I stand at the doora, and knocka: ifa any man hearsa mya voice, and opens upa the door, I willa come in to him, and willa supa with him, and hea with mea.*" Nora, beginning to come to her senses, tried to claw her way back up the side of the grave but the good Rev. S.C. Honeycutt kept pulling her back down and sing-songing the verse over and over again, screaming that Nora needed Jesus' salvation to carry her through this hard time. She'd wandered away from Jesus' love, the he said, and now it was time, here and now, right in the same holy hole where her blessed husband's body would spend its eternity, to confess her wayward ways and beg the Lord's forgiveness. Nora, trying to make sense through her grieving, didn't even know what wayward ways she'd been guilty of. The crowd had stood and watched, bowing their heads, begging for forgiveness at being in the presence of one who had lost her way, but thanking the Eternal Light for having brought them to this, her moment of salvation and return to the flock.

As their arms raised in a re-welcoming of Nora to the fold, Spencer Duty stepped out from the forgivers, jumped down into the grave, pushed the good Rev. S.C. Honeycutt aside, and lifted her out of the hole. Most folks by now had turned their heads so high to the sky that one could swear they could hear necks a crackin' and poppin' with the holy strain. As Spencer Duty was himself climbing out of the grave to attend to Nora, he stepped on the good Rev. S.C. Honeycutt's Holy hands, breaking both pointer fingers with his polished up, high-lace Sunday boots.

Chapter 26

THE DETECTIVE WHO'D MANNED the potato digger that had tore the miners apart in the cook tent that awful night didn't have any disinclinations about much of anything. He was an older fella, and had served in the Great War himself, and probably a few wars before too.

Even though he'd manned the potato digger, his preference was for a long-bladed saber, always saying that it was the spray of blood when the polished blade severed a pumped-up artery that drove him from conquest to conquest. He'd never liked the impersonalness of the potato digger.

As his thin, greying hair crawled back farther and farther away from his face, his forehead got broader and broader, making the finger-thick scar on his brow look like a freshly gorged leech. It'd been said he'd killed his only offspring with a shovel when he was just a lad and was the biggest braggart amongst the other detectives about the dago bitches he'd raped in Italy. The .45 always at his side was an 1878 Schofield he'd liberated from a Texas Ranger set to do him harm somewhere in the early '90s.

When the detectives had first rolled into Van Lear, they'd already set up camp on a ridge round the back side of Cumbo that only a few of the old timers even knew was there. On a fog-free day, the detectives could watch the goings-on undetected from a clump of trees. Before the cold-eyed mustache man began shacking up with Betty Butter, he commanded a front flap tent all to himself.

The detectives got their supplies when the #1 would stop halfway between Paintsville and Van Lear and drop off a few of this and that beside the track. The engineer had been told where to stop the train and to order the brakeman to push the metal strapped crates out the boxcar door and then be back on his way. Depending on the size of the crates, one or more of the detectives would dress like dirt farmers and take a flatbed to fetch the supplies. Saturday, every other week, the engineer would toss off a leather and canvas mail bag with news of loves staying and straying. On mail day only one of the detectives rode a draft horse down the mountain to bring back letters of what they did or didn't want to know.

On this particular Saturday, the potato digging detective mounted a draft horse that had a notch seemingly cut out of his topline just shy of his withers. He hated just about any horse except his own steed, especially a goddamned, bowed-backed useless pensioner with a hanging sow belly. It was the most uncomfortable ride in the fucking world, he would say, smashing his balls all the way up to his chin.

The potato digging detective followed the tracks, rounding a bend a couple of miles or so down from the Cumbo crossing. His sack coat was buttoned high to his thick neck and his wide-brimmed beaver-fur hat was pulled down right to the top of his bushy brows. Lying a few feet away from the tracks was the bruised and scarred mail bag. Its once polished brass rivets had long lost their luster. The potato digging detective rode up alongside the pouch and swung his leg up over the back hind hump of the swayback. Right about the time he slipped his left foot from the stirrup, the bushes to his north began to rustle. He swung around, jerked back his sack coat and started to cross draw his Schofield. Before the potato digging detective could wrap his fingers around the grip, a boot kicked him so hard it knocked him to the other side of the tracks. When he tried to roll over he only saw a thick waffled sole coming down onto his face, breaking his jaw and knocking out what was left of his front teeth. Standing above him was a big man, looking down, quiet as an invalid, no words even resting on his lips waiting to say their peace. There was nothing more to be said. There was no ceremony, there was only the muzzle blast of the Colt 1911 turning the top of the potato digging detective's head into a canoe. King Fisher stood astride the dead man, stepped over his cupped stagnant chest, and walked away.

Chapter 27

SPENCER DUTY HAD BEEN born somewhere else but raised up in Van Lear, even graduating from high school. He'd always been a good boy, helping with chores most of the time without even being asked. He'd had a sister, Effy May, who'd been born with more of a snout than a nose and dark-shadowed eyes that stared out of boney falcon sockets. There was something wrong with the size of her ears too, not to mention that folks would tuck their heads to their chests and whisper that the shape of her head never looked quite right either. No matter what, Spencer Duty's mommy and daddy knew Effy May would never be right no matter how many whippins' she got or no matter how many times she had her mouth washed out with lye soap for saying things that would best be left unsaid. By the time she was fifteen or so, she'd gotten to be a mighty big girl, eating just about anything she could put in her mouth. Spencer Duty, even as a young boy, had tried his best to keep his sister from eating chips of paint peeling off the back pole barn where his daddy'd put up hay to weather over the winter.

After many a night fretting and figuring and coming to a knowing that she would never be any better stock than she already was, Spencer Duty's mommy and daddy thought it best not to let her wander too far from home. His daddy built a shed tucked away into the back end of the pole barn where they collared Effy May and kept her chained to a fence rail not letting her out all too often. But they kept her clean and fed good until she died late into her seventeenth year, likely from dropsy. At least that's what the company doctor who'd come to look at her, not long before she died, had said. She hadn't come to know anyone and no one had come to know her, so there wasn't any grieving that needed to be done. Spencer Duty's mommy and daddy buried her far back in the woods and put a rock with a cross etched into it atop her grave. Spencer Duty always having been a strong boy and because it had to be done, dug his sister's grave.

Chapter 28

A FEW WEEKS BEFORE he'd been gunned down, Flem had been walking up Cumbo to pay homage to his momma and daddy, who lay buried atop the mountain. They'd been there a long while now, his daddy having gone on sometime before his momma, some would say so he could be holding the door open for her when she got to Heaven some years later.

Right before he crested the ridge where the eye can catch a glimpse of a rod iron fence that surrounds the plot full of Picklesimer's, Flem stopped his one foot from moving in front of the other, tipped his ear, and heard an old barn owl hoot. It wasn't just a *hoot, hoot, hoot* like he was used to, no this was a *hooooot, hooooot, hooooot,* long like, drawn out, not just *hooting* but calling, calling to him. That set off a strong sense of worriment in Flem, knowing that the *Kwakwaka'wakw* Indians said that when you hear the owl call your name, your time to die is sitting just around the next fork in the road.

Flem wasn't a man to take signs lightly. Even though he'd ignored the brush on his porch and continued having adulterous relations with Runa. When he didn't have his loins driving his good judgment, Flem had always been a man who paid attention. After he bowed his head in front of his momma and daddy's graves, Flem made his way down the backside of Cumbo and then went to look for Spencer Duty.

"You have to understand what's happened here", Flem said when he came upon Spencer Duty. "Some men want to disappear, want to live alone and not be bothered by anyone. That's what *King Fisher* wanted and was settled to doing, particularly after his brother was killed. He'd just wanted to be left alone but now it seems the Lord is calling him out. It's started and it's going to be on King Fisher's terms. There's only one other who knows that King Fisher's alive and she's not even around these parts anymore," Flem said.

Spencer Duty swore on his momma's grave, that he'd never show the other side of his face by saying anything Flem had trusted him enough not to tell. Flem nodded and said that if things went bad for him he wanted Spencer Duty to think about befriending his boys too. Spencer Duty looked up from his shoes and told him he'd do whatever need be done.

Right before Flem walked on, he went on to tell his friend about the sound of the owl and how, at that very moment, he knew he had to tell someone else about the goings-on in case the owl's call was the good Lord telling him to set his things in order. That night, Flem told Nora too and said that if the owl came for him, that she shouldn't be pining for him for too long like the other widows in the Junction.

Chapter 29

IT'D BEEN LONGER THAN it need be and the potato-digging detective hadn't returned with the mail pouch. He'd been known around the camp as eternally irascible, never giving any mind to throwing down on any man. They'd figure it out after one of us is dead, he'd say.

The cold-eyed mustached man and two other riders saddled up and headed down the mountain, following the tracks going west towards Paintsville. They heard the swayback whinny before they saw the potato digger's bloody body splayed across the tracks. His horse was hitched to a tree. The men dismounted with their fingers gripping their revolvers, their eyes keen.

The cold-eyed mustache man had been the first off his horse, taking long strides over to the body with a fresh bullet hole right between the eyes, looking like a red dot that marked a spot on the map of the digger's face, now pale as bread. He bent down and pushed his thumb into the bulbous hole. The shot had been clean, fast, right where it'd meant to go. The round had gone straight through the brain, flowering out the back of his head like a Black Jade rose bursting open in springtime. There was a boot mark that been ground into the right side of his face, as much to leave the ambushers mark as anything.

The other two riders kicked rocks and rattled out railroad spikes, while the cold-eyed mustached man went on about his business. This wasn't the work of a pissed-off miner looking to get some cowardly revenge. Who'd ever done this had looked square into the eyes of the potato digging detective before he'd blown his brains out. They slung his body over the swayback that'd been tied to a tree and led it up the back side of Cumbo out of the sight of any prying eyes.

Even though there was sagebrush rancor about reprisal, the

cold-eyed mustached man tamped it down like a smoldering pipe. Something was wrong. Not so much in the way the potato digging detective had been shot but in the brazenness of it. Not like the brazenness that he'd beat the old checker player to death or shot Flem when he had his cadre of men ready to gun down any man who threatened to be a paladin in front of his rib. No, this was a different kind of brazenness. Whoever *he* was, he knew what the cold-eyed mustached man was capable of, and yet he didn't care. *He* also knew that the detectives weren't going to go gunning down miners in the street for no cause. And, the cold-eyed mustached man knew, it'd eventually come down to the two of them.

Later that day a telegram was sent to Mr. LaViers: "*YOUR PRESENCE IS REQUIRED ******** WITH REGARD TO A MATTER OF URGENCY. ******** PLEASE WIRE YOUR ARRIVAL DATE.*" Two days later, Mr. LaViers arrived with carpet bag in hand. His solution was to mow down the sonofabitches. The cold-eyed mustached man thought better of it. Instead, an one hundred dollar reward was offered to anyone that provided information as to the murderer of the potato digging detective. Many days passed, going right past Thanksgiving and on into Christmas, and yet not a word was spoken.

Chapter 30

THE NIGHT BEFORE THE celebration of the birth of our Lord, Spencer Duty and Nora, having been spending time together since not too long after Flem had been shot, were readying presents for Flem's boys. Brand new boots that Spencer Duty had gotten as a bonus for being the best Mason Company shoe dog *not* just in Johnson County but in all of Kentucky. Thing was, Nora and Spencer Duty were just about the same age. Spencer Duty always had a hankering for Nora, thinking she was without a doubt the prettiest of the Prater girls; and, with being plagued with an abundance of shame over his scars, Spencer Duty hadn't ever been able to call up enough gumption to inquire about courting her. Then Flem had come along and he too seeing her prettiness married her right up. But given that Flem had blessed Spencer Duty spending time with his boys, he saw nothing unchristian about him and Nora spending time together too. Even the boys liked Spencer Duty and minded him just about as good they had Flem.

About eleven or so that Christmas Eve, the boys had gone onto bed and the two adults were watching the snow blow sideways across the barren cornfield. At about ten 'til midnight they pulled on heavy canvas coats, Nora wrapped a scarf around her head to protect her from the blowing snow as she and Spencer Duty walked out to the barn. There, in their stall, three cows and two pigs were down on their haunches, offering up reverence to their Lord. She quickly undid her scarf as he clasped his pocket cap over his heart, then both, right at the very same time, bowed their heads.

It was also on this night that Spencer Duty entered the world of manhood with Nora as his guide. They hadn't planned it that way, but since she'd discovered her tickler and the God like shaking that ensued when it was played with, she figured that it was something entirely holy and that if the good Lord had put something on her body that gave her such pleasure, then it couldn't be a sin, most especially if rubbing it to where she was shaking made her espouse the good Lord's name over and over, seemingly like especially right before she began shaking and then like some of the women at church who talked with the Lord in a language only they could understand, Nora, as she was trembling out of control, had sounds come up from her insides that the likes of which she'd never heard before.

Spencer Duty, only having self-abused his own private parts, each time, checking his palms afterwards for warts and even one time going to see the doc to have a few droplets of colloidal silver put on a brown spot that'd come up right in the middle of his hand a few days after he'd abused himself, explaining to the doctor that even though he tried to ward off the temptation with hard work and pure thoughts, it'd just got the best of him and he found his hand where it shouldn't be and then the worry of warts started right back up again. But now lying beside Nora, after having relieved himself in the way a man was meant to be relieved, Spencer Duty for the first time since he could remember was not having any worry of warts.

Chapter 31

In late March of that year, there was another blast. This time fourteen miners, mostly from tent town, were blown to pieces leaving parts of seared flesh and bones stuck to this and that rock face. Once the rescuers reached what they could of the cavern where the miners had been digging, it was decided that there weren't no reason to try to bring what was left of the miners back top. There wasn't enough left to bury or worry about. A charge was set and the hole was closed up for good. The good Rev. S.C. Honeycutt offered up the twenty-third Psalm at a special Sunday service dedicated to the tent town miners. Seemed like about the best anyone could up and do. Just about all of the miners that'd died that day didn't even have last names, or at least last names that anyone ever cared enough to know. Hell, most of the men didn't know who they really were or even when they'd been born for sure. So when the roster of the dead was read, it was only a list of Jebs, Nebs and a few Silas. There'd been a Red and a Crazy Legs too.

None of the other tent town miners showed up for the service and no one sitting in the pews praying for the lost miners' souls knew who they were. As far as anyone could recollect, not one parishioner could call up even a memory of any of the dead men's faces. Mr. LaViers sat in the back of the church that day, right alongside the cold-eyed mustached man, offering up their prayers for the dead. They stood right beside the good Rev. S.C. Honeycutt, shaking hands with the devout after the dead's souls had been lifted up.

Folks these days seemed just to go on about their business and mind it too. No one wanted to have much else to do with the other, especially after the cold-eyed mustached man had shot Flem right between the eyes on the porch of the company store.

Production in the mines was about as high as anyone could remember it ever being but none of the men were seeing much more scrip in their wage than before. Mr. LaViers had moved his wife and three youngins over from Ashland into a just put up white house with a wrap-around porch that sat right on the bank of the Big Sandy river, where he could walk right out his front door and fish all day long, perched on a boulder he'd had the miners roll down and place where he wanted it. As a matter of fact, things were getting so prosperous for CONSOL that they were even building the good Rev. S.C. Honeycutt a brand new church. One that would have his name, painted right up on a sign, announcing to anyone who came to worship that he was the conductor on the train to the Lord Jesus Christ Himself. And yet, for all the good that the good Rev. S.C. Honeycutt preached on the weekly day of redemption, it wasn't enough to turn up the downturned mouths that faced him from the pulpit, week after week.

Chapter 32

KING FISHER WATCHED FROM afar. There lined up, day after day, stood the miners; heads bowed and yet no lips moved to utter a prayer or a song for their safe return. Even though a miner could earn enough for a steady plate of beans, word got around about the troubles they were having in Van Lear. And to the consternation of the other miners, Mr. LaViers had to put the word out that niggers could work side-by-side with the white miners and he personally guaranteed that no harm would come to them. Getting the black gold out of the ground was all that mattered and one way or another, it'd be done. Underground none of the white miners ever spoke a word to any of the niggers. Digging orders had to be passed on from only the mouth of the crew boss. Niggers even had to find their own cranny to piss and take a shit in. Mr. LaViers had commented to the cold-eyed mustache man that it broke his very heart to have to pay wages to a bunch of wild-eyed niggers, who scratched their private parts like untamed beasts and could barely walk upright. With no reservations as all, the cold-eyed mustached man nodded in agreement.

Up top, Mr. LaViers enforcers strode right beside the miners. The knobs of their leather saps jutting out from the back pocket of their dungarees cantered to the beat of the hatchet men's hips. On this day, a redneck who'd been working his way from one side of the country to the other, picking up odd jobs here and there, stepped out of line, deciding at the last minute to go his own way. Two of the henchmen knocked the redneck to the ground and began beating him about the head with their saps. Yet, not a one of the other miners dared to make a move from the line to fend them off, keeping their long chins tucked to their collapsed chests as nameless boot after nameless boot thrashed the nameless redneck, now lying face down in the muck-filled trench. It didn't take no time before lurid crimson striations began tainting the brown Crider mud.

About the time the redneck was being beaten senseless, the cold-eyed mustached man sat with a distraught Betty Butter. She hadn't been liked much before because of her snootiness and fancy-leaning ways. Then he'd come along with promises and nice things, making her, for the first time in her life, a someone. And now, as time went on and she couldn't hide what was growing inside her womb, she'd be seen as nothing but a whore. You could only let a sleeping dog lie for so long and then as the months wore on that dog'd shake itself and wake up. Then *everyone* would know.

There was a nigger woman over Ashland way who'd take care of it, he told her. They'd fancy up and take the train over together, better sooner than later, before she started showing. No one'd be the wiser. Best though if she moved on after it was done, rather than go back to Van Lear. He'd help her get along once the nigger woman took care of what needed to be done. She wanted to know if it was going to hurt, "Not too much," the cold-eyed mustache man said straight away.

Chapter 33

THAT NIGHT SITTING AT supper, Spencer Duty told Nora he had something to ask her. It was soon, he knew, but thinking that she had feelings for him the same as he had feelings for her, Spencer Duty asked Nora to become Mrs. Spencer Duty. He said he'd raise Flem's youngins as his own. It didn't take much figuring for Nora to say she'd be proud.

There was going to be talk, he told her. Matter of fact, folks were already beginning to make insinuating sighs when Nora crossed their path at the company store or even church for that matter. One of the miners' wives had even just come up and jerked her daughter right away from Nora's moving mouth, just as she was about to give her opinion about crocheting a lace doily; the mother muttering something about not allowing her daughter to be taking up with a strumpet. There just weren't enough time that'd gone by from being brokenhearted, the daughter-jerking woman would say to another.

Nora stood with more backbone after Flem had been shot dead. There weren't much she was afraid of now, and what she was afraid of wasn't so much for her but for her youngins. Spencer Duty told her that her hair had gotten even redder since Flem had died. It looked like she'd run through hell with her hat off, he'd kid.

The newly-engaged shoe salesman had been figuring too on some-time opening a shoe store over in Paintsville. A real store, where people would come and go. He even had an idea for cutting two doors, a tall one for the mothers and a pint size door for their youngins. Paintsville was changing and he was convinced that folks' attitudes about their feet were changing too. He spent day in and day out educating people about proper foot health. He'd also talked to the home office of the Mason Shoe Company and they said he'd be able to keep selling Mason shoes even if he opened his own store. The big boss, Mr. August Mason, had even sent Spencer Duty a letter personally, congratulating him on wanting to keep bettering himself. Mr. Mason said that he had brought his boy, Bert, up to believe that a hard day's work was what lends pride to a man's life, and now Bert was running the company right alongside his daddy. Later on, when Spencer Duty opened his own shoe store, he'd be hanging that letter right beside all of his shoe-fitting awards. He even had an idea for measuring folks' feet where they wouldn't have to draw their soles on a piece of paper and hold it up to the bottom of the shoe. Spencer Duty then did something that was just unheard of, at least south of Cincinnati. He told Nora that she should be a part of his shoe selling business and the very next day after receiving the letter from Mr. Mason himself, he called up Mr. Mason directly asking for special permission to start training Nora to become an expert shoe fitter. Mr. Mason, saying it was indeed a pleasure to talk person to person to one of their top salesman, responded that it'd be highly unusual for a woman to be selling like that. He just didn't know how men would take to a woman touching their feet and all.

Then, as they were continuing to converse, he told Spencer Duty that his bookkeeper had just handed him the latest sales figures and that he, Spencer Duty himself, had achieved the top honors of being the number one salesman in the entire United States themselves. How *was* he doing it? Mr. Mason asked over and over again. *Did* he have help? Was Nora already helping him? No, Spencer Duty said, it was just him driving his apple truck hither and yon, making his sales pitch. He explained that the trick to selling was to get folks' feet inside the shoe after a proper measuring. Once they felt how good a shoe that fit their feet felt, why the sale was all but made. Heck, for example, he would say, even miners from Van Lear would go over to Paintsville on a day off and pick up some extra work doing this or that, just to make enough real money to pay three dollars fifty cents plus shipping for a pair of good fitting shoes. And folks in Lexington and Louisville, who were folks of means, hadn't ever even had a proper fitting. Add up that proper fitting with a well-made shoe and there weren't much more that needed talked about. Mr. Mason said he couldn't be more impressed and gave Spencer Duty the go ahead to start training his fiancée. He said he'd even have a special certificate made up with Spencer Duty's name embossed in gold, stating without any equivocating, that he was a certified expert in training others in shoe fitting. The number of his certificate would be '1', making him the first expert in shoe fitting that the Mason Shoe Company had ever declared. Mr. Mason also said that he was sending Nora a salesman suitcase with everything she'd need to start her shoe selling career. There was no need to send ten dollars like Spencer Duty had had to do. This was "on the house," Mr. Mason said. And then, right after Spencer Duty said his goodbye and took the phone away from his ear, he told Nora that he felt like he'd been struck by lightning, when Mr. Mason up and said, "Spencer Duty, I want you, from here on out, to call me Bert."

Chapter 34

THE CHICAGO, MILWAUKEE AND St. Paul Railroad ran northwest up through Minnesota, along the high line of North Dakota and Montana, eventually dropping down into Butte, Montana where copper mining had made it the richest city in the United States, spouting up the best schools west of the Mississippi.

It had taken Mary Mary and her youngins a month of Sundays to make their way from Hillsboro, Ohio, where she'd gotten educated as a teacher at the Hillsboro Normal College, being now duly qualified to educate others, to Butte. Mary Mary had sent off a letter saying she was looking for work as a teacher. And, having said in her correspondence that she had great familiarity with miners and their families, she convinced Mr. Robert M. Young of the Montana Board of Education that it'd be a good idea to hire her right then and there. But right before the letter had passed from her hand to the postmaster's, Mary Mary got a knowing and told her youngins that they'd for sure be moving on west. It seemed like it hadn't taken no time at all for Mary Mary to hear back to the affirmative. She and her youngins didn't have much. Every penny she'd made cleaning houses went to getting her education. But she'd manage to keep food in their bellies and shoes on their feet. As a matter of fact, figuring that she wasn't going to find any shoes any better, she had drawn an outline of her and her youngins feet and mailed the drawings off to Spencer Duty with eight dollars eighty-five cents. And, just three weeks later, a package arrived directly from the Mason Shoe Company itself with about the finest shoes that she or her youngins had ever had the pleasure to lace up. It would be a long while before they'd be needing shoes again; that was for certain. It also wasn't long after that she'd received a letter from Spencer Duty with a second letter folded up inside that she never thought she'd receive. And when she unfolded it and saw whom it was from Mary Mary felt her heart flutter.

From the moment that Mary Mary and her youngins lifted their six eager feet from the last knurled step of the coach car, to the first feel of Montana against the soles of their shoes, they knew they'd found them a home where they'd all likely be 'til they died. Even when they'd made their way up through Cincinnati and Chicago, they'd never seen such hustlin' and bustlin' as they were witnessing in Butte.

Mr. Robert M. Young had said the Board of Education was going to pay her a housing allotment because they needed qualified teachers so bad. But, unlike CONSOL, Mary Mary would get paid in real U.S. dollars and could go into any store and buy whatever she could afford. After they checked into the Butte City Hotel, run by proprietress Mrs. Flora Cushing, and settled up a bit, sponging off the dust from the trip, the mother and her children took to walking here and there. Folks nodded and tipped their hats when they walked by; seeming to be just about as friendly as could be. As they stopped at the corner of Idaho and Montana streets, figuring out which way to go, she thought that they were standing at the center of the world. She'd never heard so many different ways of pronouncing words in her life. But most especially, she and her kids had never laid eyes on Chinamen, much less heard them talking. Mary Mary had seen pictures of them in books for certain but also for certain she'd never seen one up close. "How do they see out those squinty little slits?" she whispered to one of her boys. And, unlike other folks she'd ever seen, they scurried here and there like squirrels looking for nuts. When Mary Mary had been up in Ohio getting educated, she'd seen Negroes walking the streets like it was nobody's business, but she'd never seen anywhere nears as many Negroes as she saw Chinamen in Butte. Making a left turn into an alleyway right off of Galenna Street, she and her youngins thought they'd dropped into a hole in the earth and ended up in China itself. Mary Mary would learn later that they had stepped into China Alley that ran in between Galeena and Silver Street. There wasn't barely anyone without round eyes anywhere to be seen. Right about in the middle of the alley hung a sign over and establishment that read, Pekin Noodle Parlor Specializing in Chop Suey. They even had their servings spelled out in the window, saying that you could get a plate of chop suey with this and that for forty cents. As they made their way out to Silver Street, Mary Mary, no matter how hard she tried, just couldn't get over how fast Chinamen could walk just by shuffling their feet. They all seemed to wear little black flat shoes that made a swishing sound as they scooted along.

She would be going tomorrow to meet with Mr. Leo H. King. Mr. King was the principal of Washington Junior High School. After their meeting, Mary Mary would spend the rest of the day getting her lesson plans ready for teaching.

Chapter 35

EVERYONE WAS WOKE UP when the explosion happened about two that morning. It seemed like every mine shaft must have blown at the same time, never had there been anything like it anywhere that anyone could remember, except Charles Pelphrey who, when he was shook from his bed, thought he was back in the great war, being pounded by those goddamn German howitzers. Motherfuckin' Germans, he was always saying, had beaten him senseless when they took him prisoner, so much so he'd never quite be the same. Other folks were coming out into the road now too, thinking that those they knew and those they loved had been blown to smithereens. But, when they looked up toward the mine, there was no smoke, no fire, and heard no siren calling for all to come and help. But, on the very top of Cumbo mountain, a smoke cloud billowed from a burning hell.

The detectives were still encamped right where Flem had watched the cold-eyed mustache man appeal to Happy Jack Lewis' hungry belly. As a matter of fact, if you stood on Betsy Arms' headstone, who'd been burned to death when hot embers had jumped from the family fireplace like they were alive, catching her little white dress covered with pretty pink bows ablaze, three years ago or there about, you could look right down into the center of the detective's goings-on. Walking the perimeter, all day and all night, were two detectives, passing each other at the exact same place like they were hands on a clock.

Since the sap-carrying hooligans had been brought in, anyone who took to backtalk or being headstrong and refusing to do what they were told was made an example of. The good Rev. S.C. Honeycutt likened it each and every Sunday morning to pharaoh's soldiers whipping Hebrew slaves, saying that they wouldn't have gotten those whippins' if they'd aminded their manners, not engaging in back-talk and done as they were told. Just like the plantation owners had understood that the nigger needed tended to, the mine owners now were tending to their flock in much the same way.

Mr. LaViers, after figuring on it with the cold-eyed mustached man, thought it best if the detectives just stayed put. As long as folks knew what would come if they stepped out of line, the more likely it'd be that they'd up and mind. He'd learned that from his daddy, who'd fought right alongside General Braxton Bragg, at the battle of Chickamauga. His daddy had also said that if General Lee had let General Bragg move on north like he'd wanted to than niggers would still know their rightful place. Every time Mr. LaViers told anyone who'd listen to the story about what he'd learned from his daddy, he always ended it by sucking his spit back between his teeth and making a *tis, tis, tis* sound while shaking his head in disgust.

Like Elmer Picklesimer, King Fisher had served with the Rough Riders 2nd Calvary Brigade. They hadn't known each other and, just by happenstance, fate seemed to have brought them together to talk about those days, sitting on the porch of the company store. It'd only been over a game of checkers and a jar of white mule, not too long after dismounting, that they'd come to realize they'd both rode with Colonel Roosevelt. They'd also discerned, after many jumps and one proclaiming to the other "King me!" that they shared an interest in dynamite.

The lead detective was still staying up at Betty Butter's old place, now that she'd moved on. That night, right before the explosion had roused him and everyone in Van Lear out of a deep sleep, he dreamed of the last time they had been together.

He had told Betty Butter right before they boarded the train for Ashland that it'd be best if she pack a bag and bring things that were important to her, because she'd not be coming back to Van Lear. Once the nigger woman had done what needed to be done and the bleeding had stopped enough for her to be on her way, she'd be likely heading up north.

Fifty miles or so before they reached Ashland, and right as their train was approaching the trestle over the gorge at Cabin Creek Junction, he stood and took Betty Butter's dainty hand in his, lifted her gently from the seat, and kissed her. They walked arm in arm to the back of the train and stepped out onto the platform, the cold-eyed mustached man having whispered that he wanted her to see the splendor of the gorge as the train traversed the bridge. It *was* beautiful. Looking down at the thrashing Red River swirling around this and that boulder and watching fallen trees jump like jack rabbits when they got caught in the whitewater of the frothing rapids brought tears to her eyes. He put his arm around her diminutive waist, pulled her close to him, and for a moment, she gazed deeply into his eyes. When he told her that he was sorry, she iced over in terror as she felt her feet leaving the surety of the platform and falling seemingly forever to the equal surety of her death.

Before he was jarred out of his twilight remembering of the events of that day, the cold-eyed mustache man had a vision of Betty Butter's shiny slick-soled dancing shoes, twinkling like besprinkled dew that'd caught the rays of a searing sun, tumbling end over end through a tempestuous sky.

———————

Spencer Duty had been restless all that day, Nora would have said, had somebody asked. Pacing here and there, doing this and that, telling Flem's boys to mind when they weren't doing nothing. Feeling him climb out of bed, she watched him walk over to the window just right before the explosion, like he somehow had a foretelling or something.

When Spencer Duty looked out the window he saw Charles Pelphrey running down the road, wearing a Brodie on his bald dome, and carrying his Springfield rifle, ready to kill any Bosch that were surely invading Van Lear.

The detectives, more accustomed to causing mayhem, were getting about as restless as men could get. And, in that restlessness, their blusteredupness made them stiff-necked, violating the cold-eyed mustached man's commandment of being *more* vigilant after one of their own had been murdered. The lead detective had sat right atop of the armored car one evening and said that if an one hundred dollar reward wasn't going to bring the killer to justice, then they had to be ready for just about anything. But, like the Israelites who'd ignored Moses and sinned and cavorted, the detectives were sneaking around and going down into Van Lear, carousing with floozies and drinking corn liquor. Spencer Duty had even been giving them jar after jar of just stilled white mule to take back to the other men, saying it'd make it easier going for them being stuck atop Cumbo, alone and all.

On the night of the explosion, the detectives were about as tight as a man could be and still be walking upright. Truth be told though, most though were passed out, having drunk jar after jar of the sour mash that Spencer Duty had had to go atop Turkey Knob to get. He'd even slipped up, telling one of the detectives that Rosella Pelphrey, one of the biggest bitches and finest moonshiners anywhere in Kentucky or West Virginia for that matter, had cooked up that batch herself. "It's white and it had the kick of a mule," Spencer Duty had said.

King Fisher had ringed the dynamite around the camp. Setting the charges so when he pushed the plunger on the detonator, each blasting cap would fire off at the same time, encircling the detectives in a ring of fire. There was also a charge set down into the gas tank of the armored car, which would cause a secondary explosion, spraying out sizzling shards of steel, searing into anything within fifty yards. Years later, folks would still be finding burnt shives of metal embedded in the tombstones of their loved ones.

One of the detectives was teeter-totterin' around the camp, at-temptin' his best to do his due diligence of staying on point, grab-bing on to this and that, trying to stay upright, then, thinking in his sorry state that he was seeing things through the reflection of a buckled mirror, thought he saw a bundle of dynamite strapped to a tree. Standing right there, the detective reached out and tried to take hold of the rust-colored bundle, missing his mark the first and second times, only to more or less throw himself into the tree on the third try, wrapping his arms around the trunk and shoving his face about as close as one can get to something that one was trying to make sense of. Right about the time that the detective figured out for sure that it truly was dynamite, he, along with every other detective, left this earth quicker than they'd likely come in.

None of the detectives in their moment of death never even had time to figure on what had happened. As King Fisher watched the detectives die, he thought that dying sometimes just isn't enough of an atonement for the wrongs one does in their lives. "It's almost bootless", he would say. The smoldering potato digger, which had been blown out of the armored truck, was laying on its side bleeding molten brass.

King Fisher pulled himself out of the hole he had dug for cover and walked through the carnage. There, at the far end of the camp, lay a detective. Just a few minutes before, the man had had arms and legs where now there was just thick black gristle that looked like blackened chicken skin. He was still alive, barely, his eyes batting like frantic moths flickering around a candleflame, his chest heaving, his shredded stumps trying to run like they still had legs. Sometimes, shooting someone crosses the line right where mercy meets murder. King Fisher unholstered his forty-five and shot the gimp detective in the head and walked on.

Chapter 36

MARY MARY, HAVING BEEN sleeping soundly, woke suddenly with a knowing so strong that she had to shake her head just to make sure she was where she was. There was an explosion in her knowing, the mine she thought, *here* or *there*, she was confused. Then she saw fire, fire through his eyes, not hers. She saw him moving now, like she was watching a Tom Mix picture show.

Not running away like you'd think but skirring across the top of a rippleless pond. Then, like no time had passed at all, King Fisher was somewhere else. It *was* like a picture show and now, for the first time in her life, Mary Mary thought, but only for a moment, that old lady McCarty had been right all along. Her doubtfulness left her when her knowing let Mary Mary see where King Fisher now was. It was then Mary Mary knew forever and a day that she wasn't, no matter what old lady McCarty had said, a witch.

Chapter 37

FOR THE LIFE OF him, he couldn't divine when the night became day which one of them would be alive and which one would be dead. But the cold-eyed mustached man knew without a doubt there was no one to stand behind him with rifles at their ready or a finger on the trigger of the potato digger, not now. He pulled on his pants, slipped his arms into his shirt sleeves, tucked the tails down into the waist, and snapped the suspenders over his shoulders. His .32 lay beside him on the feather bed he'd brought over from Ashland for Betty Butter, it was never out of arms reach. On this night, the lead detective didn't bother even holstering his pistol, instead tucking it into the waistband of his trousers.

And then, right when he walked under the dried out mistletoe that Betty Butter had nailed to the crossbeam of the archway of the door coming out of the bedroom just that past Christmas, he looked like a dog trying his best to figure out a riddle when he saw the black semblance of a man topped off in a tall Carlsbad hat, rocking back and forth in Betty Butter's mother's rocking chair. Resting to the left of the outlined man's right hand was a Colt 1911. Neither man made a move to kill the other, and for a moment, each unspokenly respected the other for staying alive this long having one way or another lived a life of ruthlessness.

"No reason for you to die dressed downed; get on getting dressed," King Fisher said. The cold-eyed mustached man sat down on the brocaded couch that'd been left to Betty Butter by her daddy's momma, and pulled on his snakeskin boots, smoothing his pants legs over the top of the shafts, briefly brushing a tad of coal dust from the tip of the black and yellow scales with the back of his hand. Without ever looking up, he then stomped each sole against the wooden floor to seat his heel in the boot.

They sat for a while just looking curiously at each other, not so much sizing each other up but turning their heads this way and that, like a woman might look at another's knick-knacks. Then, the silence was broken when a rock broke through the front room window and bounced across the floor stopping right in between King Fisher and the cold-eyed mustache man. And then another and another and another. They were all coming, the whole goddamn junction, even the women were coming down the road lugging pick axes swung over their shoulders. Leading the brigade, raising his dog-eared Bible, with his name embossed in gold leaf on the cover high over his head, was none other than the good Rev. S.C. Honeycutt himself calling his flock to cast out the very King of Hell now that a blessed hellfire had been brought down on the Diablos releasing the junction from its bondage.

Standing on Betty Butter's porch, the good Rev. S.C. Honeycutt thrust his upturned hands toward the crowd, preaching to the angry congregate. "You, the chosen people of Van Lear, have laid your retributing before God Almighty and I have raised up your pleadings for salvation through my prayers. And now, like Samuel had gone and done before the Lord to Agag, he who has walked before you in his serpentine boots must be hacked into pieces for his seditions." About as far as eyes could see, tips of pickaxe after pickaxe began to rise towards Heaven looking like crosses shadowed against the moon shine.

"A bullet must be seeming mighty good right about now?" King Fisher said to the cold-eyed mustache man, who nodded in agreement, looking out toward the good Rev. S.C. Honeycutt's wagging silhouette perverted by the runny windows of Betty Butter's house.

After a moment or two of figuring the lead detective's fingers began curling around the grip of his revolver. "Folks are going to be saying you're a man of dauntless stout-heartedness," he said to King Fisher.

"No matter," King Fisher replied, "I'll be gone before your last breath takes leave of your body. I've never understood men like you. Not that I'm asking, mind you. Just never understood your kind," he added. He watched as the man's fingers caressed the back strap of his pistol like he was encircling one of Betty Butter's nipples.

The horde outside of the dead woman's homeplace was rotating around like they were one body caught in the furry of a twister, trying to figure, now that they had gotten to where they were going, what to do next. Most of the windows were busted out now, rocks, some big, some small, lay here and there all over the front room. "Funny, ain't it?" King Fisher said. "You know you're gonna die, there ain't no way out in here or out there and I'm given you a chance to blow your own brains out, but you sit there hanging on to each and every livin' breath. It's different deep down inside a man when he knows death is standin' out on the porch, waitin' for him to walk right through the door." The cold-eyed mustache man moved his hand away from his pistol like he'd just buried an old friend and nodded an answer to a question that hadn't been asked.

Before his head had raised back up from his confirming nod, King Fisher squeezed the trigger of his .45 and put a bullet in the exact same place that the cold-eyed mustache man had put a bullet into Flem's brain. The lead detective fell over on the divan bloodying the brocade and in that dying moment, clawed at the weave of the tatting like a broken cricket.

The sound of the shot that killed him echoed through the pickaxed crowd like a blanket thrown over a roaring fire. And, for a moment, after the sound of the blast had blown on its way, there was nothing to be heard but quiet.

With the bayonet fixed on his empty chambered Springfield rifle, Charles Pelphrey, thinking the mob was his lost Battalion, jumped on Betty Butter's porch and threw his boney shoulder into the door, uttering words that a good Christian man shouldn't a been uttering. And there bleeding from the hole between his eyes, on Betty Butter's daddy's momma's brocaded couch, was the cold-eyed mustache man. Charles Pelphrey, having seen the goddamn Germans play possum before, twisted the Springfield's mounted bayonet into the cold-eyed mustache man's heart, making sure, beyond any doubt of doubts, that he was dead.

The good Rev. S.C. Honeycutt, after making sure that all danger had passed, walked into Betty Butter's front room and upon seeing the body declared that any man who'd delayed his righteousness should step forward and see what happens to those who resist the Lord's commandments and so began preaching over and over again from Jonah, "*Salvation is of the Lord,*" the good Rev. S.C. Honeycutt yelled at the top of his lungs, to those folks now mingling around, so to be able to say they'd seen the cold-eyed mustache man's stiffing up body.

Jedediah Veech stood there looking down at the corpse. Throughout just about every moment of his life he had blasphemed the very meaning of his name, that being one who is *Beloved of God*, with his very fornicating and drunkenness and because his momma and daddy had homesteaded some of the widest swatches of land in all of Johnson County, the good Rev. S.C. Honeycutt was determined with all of his soul, to bring Jedediah Veech above all other sinners to salvation and upon resting his holy hand on Jedediah's shoulder called for his deliverance from the abomination of his sins by reciting Leviticus, *"Behold, if the leprosy have covered all his flesh, he shall pronounce him clean that hath the plague."* And, there in the presence of all who had come for deliverance from Beelzebub who had brought his evil among them and in the very specter of the cold-eyed mustached man who'd been sent to meet his make and who lay there with eyes so cold they'd brave the pecking of a raven's beak, shouts of *"hallelujah"* after *"hallelujah"* for as far as an ear could hear so consumed Jedediah Veech that he collapsed in the splendorous forgiveness of the Lord Jesus Christ coming right through the good Rev. S.C. Honeycutt's searing palm, surging through Jedediah's body like he'd been struck by lightning. In this holy moment, the good Rev. S.C. Honeycutt stepped forth and in the very presence of death itself brought one of Van Lear's most prominent families' sons back to life.

Chapter 38

THE COAL OIL LIGHTS cast an amber pall throughout the clean white house that sat along the bank of the Big Sandy. From the trees on the other side of the river, the shadows of the LaViers could be seen dashing like scurrying mice from this room to that. Mrs. LaViers, who had a penchant for big words and linens blended from silk and cotton, and who had insisted that she needed at least three of the miners' wives to tend to her ever-evolving needs, was as confused as confused could be as to why Mr. LaViers was disconcerted. It was just another mine explosion, Mrs. LaViers had said, when Mr. LaViers had suddenly sprung up in bed, not long after having drifted into a blissful somber from engaging in relations with Mrs. LaViers. But Mr. LaViers, now in an unsootheable state of dither, knew that when a mine shaft blew the vacuum of the blast created a back draft that made a sucking sound when the methane ignited. But mostly, he knew the direction of the blast had come from atop Cumbo, not from the mine.

He began squealing like a coyote snared in a leg trap, not seeming to make a damn bit of sense, screaming out this and that order. Until Mrs. LaViers noticed a flame in the distance and then another and another. And as the husband and wife looked out their crystal-clear windows, they could see torch after torch marching up and down with the canter of each of their bearers. A lanky-looking man, who, Mrs. LaViers had been told, sold good shoes but had said she wouldn't put anything on her feet that came from "those people," could be seen forging his way across the shallow eddy that'd been spinning at that spot in the Big Sandy for just about as long as anyone could remember. Never before in his life had Spencer Duty ever seen himself doing what he was about to do.

Glory suited-up Knights followed behind him. Having tired of being ordered by Mr. LaViers to leave the niggers be, the Imperial Wizard, Dr. Hiram W. Evans, had come all the way over from Alabama to see the goings-on and to witness for himself that niggers were even coming into the company store buying up goods that hard-striving whites needed to get by. Having had been promised a free reign to keep the rightful order, the Knights were now having to kowtow to a slick-haired chinless man delivering up commandments to "do this" and "don't do that" like he was Moses just having come down from the mountain. Spencer Duty, despising everything the Night Riders stood for, promised Dr. Hiram W. Evans and every man who followed him a new pair of boots, at great cost to himself, if they'd do what they did best, burn to ash the big white house that marred the bank of the Big Sandy. Spencer Duty also pledged to Nora and the Good Lord that he would do his retributing for laying with the Knights by making a colored woman, in spite of all that he may have to endure and suffer, the first Negro to be employed waiting directly on the public in all of Kentucky. And further, Spencer Duty had proclaimed, almost like he was giving a speech, that he'd raise up Flem's youngins and any children that he and Nora may be blessed with together to keep the Lord's commandments toward *each* and *every* man.

Spencer Duty threw his torch like an Indian tossing a tomahawk. End over end it tumbled, looking like a fireball hurling through the night. The Knights, having surrounded the big white house, threw theirs in unison after they saw Spencer Duty's torch strike its mark, setting the porch ablaze.

One right after the other, the LaViers ran out a side door, Mr. LaViers first, followed by Mrs. LaViers, clinging to a ruby encrusted clutch that folks in the junction had said was never far from the grip of her spindly fingers. Then the youngins came tearing suit, their mouths moving like dumbed-up puppets above the roar of the inferno. There they stood, hovering together, trembling, at the fierceness of the fire. Spencer Duty, standing crossed arm, looked on to what he had wrought, remembered Isaiah, "*For, behold, the Lord will come with fire, and with his chariots like a whirlwind, to render his anger with fury, and his rebuke with flames of fire,*" as a whipping wind came winding through the trees catching the ascending glowing cinders in an pitiless gyre.

Dr. Hiram W. Evans strode in a broad stride reminiscent of a fine Tennessee Walker up to Mr. LaViers and Mrs. LaViers, who clung to her ruby-studded clutch and their youngins, all of whom were covered in the thick sooty remains of what was left of their fine white house. Standing toe to toe, Dr. Hiram W. Evans looked up a good six inches or so into Mr. LaViers' blackened face, whose white eye sockets made him look like a target waiting to be shot. "First time I heard about you, I knew you were a nigger in the wood pile," and on that, Imperial Wizard, Dr. Hiram W. Evans, reached up and backhanded Mr. LaViers so silly that the thick filthy slag that had coated his face cracked like a piece of hot glass that'd been thrown into a cold pond. The bewildered man looked up from the ground, and upon seeing the revolver now pointing at his head, lost all control of himself in front of his wife and his three children. Dr. Hiram W. Evans cocked the hammer and readied to pull the trigger when King Fisher seemed to turn up like a puff of smoke.

"Jesus Christ, it's him," Dr. Hiram W. Evans heard a quivering voice whisper behind his back say. And upon hearing that quivering voice, Dr. Hiram W. Evans lowered his pistol, turned around, and saw each and every Knight running off through the goosegrass like a cat with an ass full of turpentine. King Fisher walked over to Mr. LaViers, pulled him up by the hair, and told him to take his family and be on their way.

"It's over," he said. He also reached out and took the ruby clutch from Mrs. LaViers, who protested to Mr. LaViers, who promptly slapped her across the face. Imperial Wizard, Dr. Hiram W. Evans, propped up by his undaunted courage, failed to grasp why his cadre of Christian Soldiers had scampered like they'd up an seen a ghost. In his pluck, Dr. Hiram W. Evans began to spout this and that about them and those and in his pluck King Fisher reached out and grabbed the pointed purple hood from Dr. Hiram W. Evans' head and threw it onto the smoldering embers of the big white house that had once soiled the bank of the Big Sandy. Dr. Hiram W. Evans covered his snarling wea-sel-looking face with his hands, peering through the space in between each finger and screaming into his muffling palms something about having King Fisher's goddamn neck stretched. What startled King Fisher, a man not easily startled, was not the threat of his demise but how short Dr. Hiram W. Evans was without his purple-pointed hat.

As they watched the last shadows of the family shamble into the woods, King Fisher handed the ruby-studded clutch to Spencer Duty. He'd pass it along to Nora who'd already made arrangements for what'd be done with it. The two men's hands met with King Fisher nodding his respect to the man Spencer Duty had become. Once King Fisher turned and walked away, they would never lay eyes on each other again. But through a lifetime of letters between the two women who would eventually become their wives, Spencer Duty and King Fisher would keep each other up on their goings-on. "Tell Spencer Duty…" this or that King Fisher would say when he saw his forever bride writing a letter to Nora. Nora, on the other hand, would hear from over her shoulder, "Be sure and tell King Fisher now…" and so both wives would dutifully serve as scribes, until one day many years later a registered letter arrived sadly saying that one of the men had passed on. It'd been sudden, she'd say, one minute here and the next minute gone, the time between discovery and loss ever so short, he hadn't been one to do any lingering in his living and when his time came he hadn't lingered in his dying either.

Chapter 39

It wasn't long before the miners called for Mr. Bill Blizzard to come over to Van Lear from Logan County, West Virginia and serve as constable. William H. "Bill" Blizzard had been the commander of the miners' army during the Battle of Blair Mountain and stood strong against a crooked man amongst crooked men, Sheriff Don Chaffin who, like the cold-eyed mustache man, had been responsible for murdering dozens of miners and their families. But, unlike the cold-eyed mustached man, Don Chafin had escaped over to Huntington, started up the Guaranty Bank, where he swindled more folks out of their farms and land than he had killed in Logan County. But he was so fearful of someone shooting him in the back of the head that he lived in almost total seclusion in a fortress like penthouse that he had built especial right on top of the bank building. Said it was that he had died a broken man after having heart attack after heart attack, finally succumbing to an infection of some sorts that consumed his mind shortly after surgery to remove his cancerous testicles.

It must have been just about the same time that William H. "Bill" Blizzard left the train station in Logan County to come to Van Lear that CONSOL dispatched another man to take the place of Mr. LaViers, who, not long after he and his family had scurried through the black smoke of their smoldering white house, had all contracted smallpox. In a short time they were all covered in suppurating sores and, in even less time than the time before, they were all dead.

The newly appointed constable, William H. "Bill" Blizzard, met the new man from CONSOL right as he was just about to put his left foot down onto the track-bed. And in that second before the sole of his boot met the oily ballast, William H. "Bill" Blizzard slammed the butt end of his Browning 1897 12 Gauge shotgun into the chin of the CONSOL man, breaking his jaw in so many places that he never spoke another word again in his life without sounding like a warbling bird. William H. "Bill" Blizzard had hated the company men over in Logan County and he let it be known that he was going to hate them in Van Lear too.

Chapter 40

NORA HAD NEVER SEEN anything the likes of Cincinnati. Buildings so tall they disappeared in the early morning clouds and the noise with motor cars going one way or another, honking at each other to get on and folks running this way and that going here and there but never seeming to get where ever it was they were going.

Bert Mason had liked Spencer Duty's idea and had because of his business dealings knew of someone in Cincinnati who would give Nora a fair price for Mrs. LaViers' ruby clutch, *if* it should turn out that they were real rubies and not just cut glass, which a lot of those kinds of things were, he had cautioned, not wanting to get Spencer Duty's hopes up.

A.G. Schwab and Sons Jewelers sat right in the middle of the block on Sixth Street. The first clerk that Nora went up to told her that Mr. Abraham Gabriel Schwab himself was expecting her and escorted her through a marble-pillared maze and into an oak-paneled office where he introduced her to Mrs. Helen Abramowitz, secretary to Mr. Abraham Gabriel Schwab. Mrs. Helen Abramowitz waved for Nora to take a seat in the most comfortable chair she had ever sat in. Mrs. Abramowitz then pushed a button on a box with many buttons and announced to Mr. Abraham Gabriel Schwab that Nora had arrived for their appointment. In just no time at all Mr. Abraham Gabriel Schwab stepped out of his office and took Nora's hand in his saying how pleased he was to meet her.

It wasn't long before Mr. Abraham Gabriel Schwab was explaining that most rubies that folks brought in were really purple sapphires with some pink tinting the purple to make them look "red like." But a *true* ruby, Mr. Abraham Gabriel Schwab would say, was, "Red, red,

red!" And, upon asking to see what she had brought, he skeptically turned the clutch over and over again in his hands, casting light this way and that across the crown of the stones. Then Mr. Abraham Gabriel Schwab shook his head disappointedly saying that from what he could see, the stones were just cut glass. But, as a beam of light shone through his tall, clearest of clear windows, there was a twinkle that crossed a facet of one of the gems. The jeweler muttered an "ummmmm" to himself, pushed out his chair, and stepped to one of the windows with a loupe cupped to his right eye. Seeded throughout the worthless cut glass was a dozen or so Pigeon Blood Rubies. He stood shaking his head, looking at each ruby this way and that. "Beautiful," he kept saying over and over again.

Nora didn't remember much from the first of Mr. Abraham Gabriel Schwab "ummmmm's" to his last but she did remember putting the promissory note that he gave her in between the pages of her Bible, right at John 6:50-71: "*This is the bread which cometh down from heaven, that a man may eat thereof, and not die.*" Mr. Abraham Gabriel Schwab wired Mr. Bert Mason and wrote that the rubies were some of the finest his eyes had ever been blessed to envision.

When Spencer Duty cupped his hands around Nora's waist and lifted her off the platform of the train, he knew by the look in her eyes that her trip had been worthwhile. And, just about the same second that Spencer Duty helped Nora into the apple truck, Mrs. Thelma Music, proprietress of the company store, yelped out the door that he had a phone call from someone named Mason in Wisconsin.

Chapter 41

WHEN SHE LEFT MRS. FLORA Cushing's hotel that morning, Mary Mary was about as jubilant as she could ever remember being. When she had been told she would become Samuel's wife, Mary Mary was just fifteen and had barely started having her monthly reminder that she was now of begetting years. Now Mary Mary stood, waiting for the man who, from the first time they'd laid eyes on each other, knew she loved. But given the circumstances of their lives they had never confessed to themselves and certainly not to each other that they could simply be who they were when they were in each other's presence, without any pretending or showing off. It was like, Mary Mary would remember one day, that they didn't act like fawning peacocks. He had agreed. And as he would walk amongst the trees in quiet prayer, he often felt like he was committing acts of transgression when he found himself rendering prayerful sounding utterances of asking the good Lord to let him be blessed enough to find a woman *exactly* like Mary Mary.

After Samuel and his brother were killed in the mine blast, it took a lot of reconnoitering within himself not to mention reconciling with his Maker. And now, as the train pulled into the Butte train depot, he felt just about as bad a case of nerves as he had ever known. The passenger cars were coupling up against each other one after the other, telling the ready departers that their journey had come to an end. He swung his leather satchel over his shoulder and saw his trunk had been thrown out the baggage car door. Straightening his stiff back and taking a deep breath, he walked down the aisle behind the other passengers coming for their own reasons to Butte, Montana.

Mary Mary, not usually one to be in someone else's way, was clearly annoying folks who were trying to get off the train, craning her neck this way and that. Each passenger that left the aisle and stepped onto the platform at the back of the train disappointed her. He *has* to be the next one, she kept saying to herself, passenger after passenger, until there were no more. Then she turned around, believing that he had not come after all, or that he had had second thoughts and got off in Minneapolis and as she raised her head from looking down into her despair, there stood Moses 'King Fisher' Kitchen.

It seemed like time came to a standstill. They just stood there, not speaking or moving towards each other, they just stood. It looked like they weren't even breathing when, momentarily breaking the spell, Moses walked over to Mary Mary, extended the crook of his elbow, and upon feeling her slip her arm into his, walked away as though they had become one.

Chapter 42

SIX MONTHS HAD GONE by since Nora had come back from Cincinnati. The weather was just beginning to start to turn bad and all the barefoot youngins were running a lot faster to the school house. It wasn't an uncommon occurrence for some of the boys and girls to lose a toe or two over their school years trudging through the snow mostly barefoot. Some of their mommies and daddies would cut burlap from feed sacks and wrap it around their feet, tying it up with baling twine. But it didn't help much, most especially when it got wet. Sometimes the wet burlap would freeze on the walk to school making matters worse. You could always tell the boy and girls who lived closest to school because they just about all had the most toes.

On this particular day, the school principal, Mr. John Horn, had told the teachers to have all of the children down at the assembly hall at "Three o'clock on the dot," he said. He wouldn't tell them why though. As the students came rambling through the door, Mr. Horn had the boys line up in one line and the girls line up in the other, from oldest to youngest. And there, sitting in front of those youngins, were stacks and stacks of shoe boxes. Boys' shoes on one side and girls' on the other. Nora would be tending to the girls and Spencer Duty would be tending to the boys. For, thanks to the rubies that studded the clutch of which Mrs. LaViers had been relieved, each and every boy and girl, right when the weather began to turn bad, would get a specially made pair of Mason shoes, designed by Mr. Bert Mason himself and paid for from a trust set up from the sale of those rubies. The Mason Shoe Company had never made boys and girls shoes before. But thanks to Spencer Duty's suggestion and Mr. Bert Mason's God given generosity, the company had decided to

163

cobble boys' and girls' shoes for the cost of material only. They didn't make a dime of profit and Spencer Duty figured they might have even lost money which made him want to work harder to put a pair of Mason's shoes on each and every man and woman in Kentucky.

Nora wrote Mary Mary right after the fitting telling her it was quite a sight, seeing boys and girls, many of whom had never had a pair of shoes on in their entire lives, getting used to walking in them. Some of the boys and girls, Nora wrote, walked like ducks, shaking their feet out this way and that. But, she also wrote, never had she seen so many youngins so proud of anything in her whole life.

Chapter 43

SEVERAL YEARS HAD GONE by now, and Mary Mary had done so well in her teaching that she was made the principal of Washington Jr. High School. It wouldn't be long after taking over as principal before she was called to meet with Mr. Robert M. Young to tell her that if she would consider it, he would take pride in supporting her to run for president of the school board, in addition to her teaching duties "of course," when he stepped down the following year. It had come up Mr. Robert M. Young said, that some of the parents were making accusations that she had supernatural powers, but he didn't see that as an obstacle to her becoming school board president, writing it off to the rumor mongering of a bunch of busybodies calling themselves the PTA, who thought they knew something about teaching children, headed up by big mouth Mrs. Evelyn Crider. "But", Mr. Robert M. Young said, "I have it on good authority that Evelyn Crider, *Mrs.* Evelyn Crider, that is, was having untoward relations with a man other than her husband."

Moses Kitchen, after a while of figuring, decided, even though he really knew nothing about law making, to run for the Montana Legislature. It was foolish, he knew for sure, but being one who had never backed down from foolishness, he decided to talk to friends he had made and friends he respected. It was different now for Moses. He had a family, youngins that he loved as though they were of his flesh. And, maybe in some way, the most important of all, he didn't have to hide or be peering over his shoulder. It had taken a while for him to get used to both women and men tipping their hats when they walked by, most of the time with a smile on their faces. He'd also never in his life had known the likes of a Butte winter. It seemed like his bones were cold from October 'til April. And what they called summer in the northwest felt more like fall. Moses began campaigning for the legislature about mid-1931, refusing no matter what was said about him to retaliate with being despicable and underhanded. In November, 1932, Moses Kitchen, who at that time owned one tattered suit, was elected to the 1933 legislature. Folks, when asked in Silver Bow County, said that the reason they elected Moses was because he'd come and talk with them not at them. He'd even say when he didn't know something and if they would be willing to trust him, he'd find an answer to their concerns and come back and let them know what he'd found out. Not one time did he fail to return. And, as best he could, sometimes he'd come back and say that he couldn't get any straight answers from anyone. So, he'd straight up say that he failed but, if they'd vote for him anyway, he'd do his best to find out the answers when he got to the legislature. If there weren't any answers, then he'd say that too.

It wasn't long after he was elected to the legislature that Moses realized that his knowledge of the law was about as thin as March ice. In talking it over with Mary Mary, who being educated, advised him to think about applying for an apprenticeship to become a fully-barred lawyer. The law firm that represented the Butte-Silver Bow school district was Corette and Corette. In 1935, Moses Kitchen entered a three-year legal apprenticeship and in 1938 sat for the bar in the state of Montana.

It wasn't long after Moses passed the bar that Mary Mary's water broke while having a meeting with the principals in her district. Two of the principals helped her into a Model A, stretched her out in the back seat, and drove uptown to the Sisters of Charity of Leavenworth Hospital, while another ran off to get Moses, who got there right when one of the nuns came out into a group of waiting fathers to be, asking for Mr. Kitchen, saying that he was the father of a beautiful little girl. She would be known as Eleanor.

Chapter 44

DUTIES BOOTIES OPENED ITS doors in downtown Paintsville just a few months after Eleanor Kitchen was born. As a matter of fact, not long after DUTIES BOOTIES opened its doors, specializing in children's shoe fitting, Nora gave birth to Spencer Duty Jr. Spencer Duty and Nora had got married right after Mr. LaViers had been run out of town and Constable William H. "Bill" Blizzard had brought order back to the junction. As a matter of fact, it was Constable William H. "Bill" Blizzard who stood up for Spencer Duty and Nora when they said their "I do's" to each other. DUTIES BOOTIES sat right in between Hobbs' Five and Dime, owned and run by Lacy A. Hobbs herself and Martin Luther Price's barbering business. It was at Martin Luther Price's barbering business where Charles Pelphrey, who became a local somebody after having plunged the bayonet into the cold-eyed mustache's man's heart, and at the insistence of Mr. Martin Luther Price himself, opened up the first two-seater shoe shining stand in all of Kentucky, "settin' shoes to shinin' so bright," he would say, that folks "had to turn their heads when they walked by so as not to be blinded by their reflectivity." It didn't take long before his reputation grew throughout Paintsville and before any man did anything of any importance what-so-ever he'd have his shoes shined up by Charles Pelphrey himself. It got so that if a man, most especially a proprietor of sorts, a banker or even the undertaker, walked the streets of Paintsville in scuffed up shoes that folks would look down on them, commenting about so and so not takin' pride in themselves, most especially now that pride had come to Paintsville. And *always*, right before Mr. James W. Auxier, Mr. John E. Buckingham, Dr. J.H. Holbrook, Mr. A.J. Kirk, Mr.

John C.C. Mayo, Mr. J.L. Patterson, Mr. George W. Preston, Mr. H.B. Rice, Mr. H.M. Stafford, Mr. John W. Wheeler, and Dr. F. M. Williams would gather together to discuss the goings-on of the Paintsville Bank and Trust Company, they would summons Charles Pelphrey to bring his shoe shine caddy to the boardroom and set the toes of their wingtips ablaze, whipping his horse hair buffing brushes so fast this way and that across the crowns of their shoes that board president, Dr. J.H. Holbrook would boisterously declare each and every time that Charles Pelphrey's hands, even though they were gnarled and mangled from being broken time and again by the goddamn Germans, were marvels of swiftness and agility.

There were two doors right side by side going into DUTIES BOO-TIES, one for regular size folk and a pint-size door for their youngins. Inside Spencer Duty had built a merry-go-round with four horses carved by none other than *The Kentucky Whittler* himself, L. A. Edward. Boys and girls would come through the pint size door, hop on a horsey and go round and round and round while their mommas and daddies would cock their ears to listen to *Master Shoe Fitters* Spencer and Nora Duty explaining the intricacies of being fit with the proper footwear. On any given day, folks would walk by and look in the window of DUTIES BOOTIES and see a wall of youngins shoes on one wall and shoes for older folk on the other. And at the back of DUTIES BOOTIES hung a sign that said they proudly carried Mason Shoes. DUTIES BOOTIES was, they said, "*YOUR SOLE SOURCE FOR SHOES.*" The townspeople of Paintsville were learning all about *shoe cookies, pronators, Thomas heels* and later on DUTIES BOOTIES had the first ever *St. Alban's Pedoscope* for x-raying feet in the entire United States. And, DUTIES BOOTIES even had a charge account program where folks could pay for their youngins shoes on time. DUTIES BOOTIES put up a big sign that Spencer Duty had Willie Ratliff himself, the best sign painter in all of Johnson County, do up letting to let parents know the importance of foot health for their youngins: "*Every parent will want to know this important news! Now, at last, you can be certain that your children's foot health is not being jeopardized by improperly fitting shoes.*" And after their feet were looked at from every which way, the boys' and girls' mommas and daddies would get a special certificate that showed them the *scientific way* in insuring their youngins' feet would be forever healthy.

Never before had so many folks seen so many youngins walking so straight and tall. It seemed like no time had passed until Spencer Duty Jr. was walking around the store with a Visumeter, a special foot measuring instrument, developed and patented by Spencer Duty himself, hanging out his back pocket like a doctor would have a stethoscope hanging from around his neck. In years to come, Spencer Duty Jr. would take over what was now more than a half-dozen DU-TIES BOOTIES all over Kentucky, including Lexington, Louisville, and Frankfort.

One of the proudest moments in all of Spencer Duty's life happened just a few years before he passed on when he was asked to serve as a "visiting *professor* of chiropodist sciences" at the Ohio College of Chiropody in Independence, Ohio. There, men and women would come and listen to Spencer Duty talk for hours about the importance of proper foot health and he would say at the end of each and every lecture, "Remember now , you treat your feet well and they'll carry you right through to the end of your days." For the life of him though, but always making Nora as proud as could be when she heard it, Spencer Duty could never get used to being called "*Professor*." It'd been a long road from Van Lear he'd think to himself, each and every time a foot doctor to be put "*Professor*" on the front of Spencer Duty's name.

Chapter 45

AFTER THE NIGHT THAT the good Rev. S.C. Honeycutt delivered Jedediah Veech from the clutches of Satan himself, Josiah Veech, Jedediah's daddy, deeded the good Rev. S.C. Honeycutt a swath of land that cut right across Miller's Creek. It wasn't long before the good Rev. S.C. Honeycutt's congregation began contributing time and lumber to raise him a place where he could pray for their very souls. The many that he brought to salvation right in the blessed water of Miller Creek were testaments to his prayerful prowess. The good Rev. S.C. Honeycutt was particularly good at bringing girls who were just entering the throes of womanhood and sitting on the very brink of waywardness into the glory of redemption. It was on one of those very days when the good Rev. S.C. Honeycutt was chasing after Wanda Brunstetter up a steep hill that crested right atop an overlook clearing. Wanda, who, just having turned fourteen, was causing her momma Thelma Brunstetter to pull her hair out with her defiance and backtalk. Thelma said that she even caught Wanda smoking picked-up cigarette butts that her daddy, Malcolm'd, tossed away. Giving her lickings with the belt or extra chores didn't do one bit of good what-so-ever. That day the good Rev. S.C. Honeycutt saw Wanda weaving this way and that running faster than a jack rabbit, he said to himself, but he also said to himself that it was of no mind. He'd had to run youngins before and he'd always caught them. Wanda though was taking him round about this way and that to countryside he'd never traversed before. Clear it was that Wanda had run this way before, likely going up over the backside of the mountain to meet a boy over in Butcher Holler.

Wanda disappeared from the good Rev. S.C. Honeycutt's sight

when she went down into a gully but just as quick as not she came right up the other side. It was right then and there that the good Rev. S.C. Honeycutt decided that when he got close enough to grab Wanda by the hair that he'd throw her down to the ground, pull her pants down, and give her the bare butt whipping she'd been deservin', all the while prayin' up to Jesus to free her from the evil that was setting her on the road to harlotonism.

Right when the good Rev. S.C. Honeycutt set his foot atop the rim of the gully, he saw Wanda stop. Then just as precipitously Wanda turned around to face the good Rev. S.C. Honeycutt, and upon seeing Wanda's face, a verse from *Revelations* came into the forefront of the good Rev. S.C. Honeycutt's mind, *I stood upon the sand of the sea, and saw a beast rise up out of the sea, having seven heads and ten horns, and upon his horns ten crowns, and upon his heads the name of blasphemy.* Then, Wanda heard the good Rev. S.C. Honeycutt's hollow scream when he stepped down into the gully and vanished into an abandoned mine shaft that'd been there likely fifty years or more. Wanda'd been all over those hills and yes she had come across that very shaft when she and one of the Skagg boys were looking for a place where he could fuck her. Wanda'd been awful worried that she'd come to be with child if she let the Skagg boy have his way with her, but he'd pushed a hollowed out rind of a lemon inside of her to catch his seed.

When Wanda walked back atop the rim of the gully, she heard the good Rev. S.C. Honeycutt's echo faintly calling out her name saying he was broken and bleeding real bad. Blood was swirling around the big bone in his leg like turbulent water battering boulders swelling up out of the Russell Fork of the Big Sandy. With each pulse, the good Rev. S.C. Honeycutt drifted further and further back into caverns of his recollections, remembering when he was but a small boy being whipped with a switch by his momma right outside the Baptist Church at Pottinger's Creek for embarrassing her by not remembering a Bible verse when called upon by preacher. Not only did he shame her in front of God Himself but S.C. Honeycutt shamed his momma in front of the whole congregation, making them think less of her. On the back of his lids when he closed his eyes for the last time, he saw the vision of a young girl, with a lion's snout and a mane of fire with a strong man's arm holding a lightning bolt. At the very moment

171

that the last drop of blood was spilling from his body and riding right upon his very last breath, the good Rev. S. C. Honeycutt redeemed himself in the eyes of his momma by remembering word for word Revelations 9:11, "*And they had a king over them, which is the angel of the bottomless pit, whose name in the Hebrew tongue is Abaddon, but in the Greek tongue hath his name Apollyon.*"

Wanda sat right next to the open shaft with her pretty legs dangling over the side of the hole until she could hear the good Rev. S.C. Honeycutt dying no more.

Many a summers later, when a fellow would lower himself down the long shaft by a rope harness, he'd find a crumpled skeleton with its fingers still dug into the side of the shaft wall, like whoever it'd been tried to claw himself out. The legs of the skeleton were splintered up so bad that it wouldn't have mattered one iota if he'd clawed this way or that, the best thing anyone could have done for him in those days would have just been to shoot him like a lame horse.

Chapter 46
Tailpiece

SOMEWHERE AROUND TWO ON a June afternoon in 1950 the senior partners of Corette, Corette and Kitchen were reviewing a case when seventy-four year old Moses began to feel a tightening in his chest. The Corette who was older than Moses by a few years had said right before Moses grabbed his left arm that he was starting to take on a pale look and right before the older Corette said what he said, Mary Mary got a knowing so strong that she leapt up from her office chair and dashed out the door, causing confusion in those who felt her breeze blow by, ran as fast as her legs would carry her to the corner of Montana and Granite streets, turned left, and seemingly as though time had not passed, found herself in Moses' office cradling his dying head in her lap. "He needs to go up to the accident ward," executive secretary Mrs. Alta Eckstein said, nervous that not only Moses was dying but that he would die in his office and she would have to contend forever and a day with his spirit milling around. As a matter of fact, Mrs. Eckstein was now *insisting* that Moses be taken up to St. James Hospital where they could either save him or pronounce him dead. She'd never really thought much of Moses having said time and again that he wasn't an actual lawyer because he didn't go to law school like the Corettes. But it was well known that the older and considered the wisest of the Corettes never failed to go to Moses with a question about this case or that as Moses could stand up in court and quote case law after case law better than any *Juris Doctor* that the older Corette had ever heard litigate. There wasn't a judge that Moses ever stood before that didn't hold him in the highest of regard and there had even been talk of him running for District Judge.

The younger Corette grabbed Moses' shoulders while the older Corette slung his arms under Moses' legs and carried him out to Mrs. Eckstein's brand-new Studebaker Scotsman 2-door station wagon. Mary Mary hung over the back seat stroking Moses hair, while he more feebly clutched his chest with each increasingly shallow breath. The ride to the hospital from Corette, Corette and Kitchen took all of three minutes running this light and that. Corette and Corette carried the now limp Moses into the accident ward. When Nurse Lou Ann Meriwether saw the pallid-colored man being carried through the doors she called Dr. Huie Pock, who was behind the other curtain examining Gary Cooper, who'd been born right outside of Helena. Once he became a Hollywood movie legend he came back to Montana and bought himself a ten-thousand-acre ranch just north of Butte. That day he'd come into the hospital because he was pissing blood and having all kinds of shooting pains not too far up his rectum, he would tell Dr. Pock. Right after Dr. Pock finished telling Gary Cooper that he was pretty sure he had prostate cancer and Mr. Cooper in no uncertain terms pooh-poohed the notion, Dr. Pock heard Nurse Meriwether calling for him to come right away.

At the direction of Dr. Pock, Corette and Corette lifted Moses onto an examination table. Dr. Pock opened up Moses' shirt and began listening for a heartbeat. He moved the bell of his stethoscope over different spots on Moses' chest making no utterances that might reveal his dismay at hearing only the faintest of irregular beats. When Dr. Pock's long thin fingers lifted the lid of one of Moses' eyes, it looked like someone had glued it in place and his pupil was so big that if a man *was* alive he would have squinted at all the light burning its way in when the curtain had been lifted. When Mary Mary saw his staring eye, she remembered a verse from Psalm 141, *"But mine eyes are unto thee, O GOD the Lord: in thee is my trust; leave not my soul destitute"* and so she softly said it aloud. In those brief moments that Dr. Huie Pock had begun examining Moses Kitchen, his breathing had stopped.

A coldness came over Mary Mary. Colder than after the mine explosion and Samuel's death, colder with all the years of being without heat and going hungry, colder than having gone without shoes and undergarments, and colder than all of her knowings ever combined. But never could she remember ever having a knowing where tragedy in one way or another wasn't its minder and to this very moment, never had she ever known such coldness.

She watched Dr. Pock frantically give Moses an injection of mercupurin and then cut an incision into his chest and insert a Southey tube, to drain off any fluid that may have been building up around his heart, trying to get it to start up again. But Mary Mary didn't need her knowing to tell her that Moses had moved on. After listening for a heartbeat one last time, Dr. Pock, in his thick Chinese accent, respectfully bowed his head, and told her he was sorry, but there was nothing more he could do. Moses would be staying dead.

Since that day now, so so many years ago, that Moses Kitchen extended his elbow and Mary Mary had slipped her arm into his, had she ever opened a door for herself or ever eaten a meal that Moses didn't insist that he share his with her. Especially if Mary Mary had taken a particular liking to *his* food, Moses would feign his immediate fullness and not wanting good food to go to waste importune her to finish what he claimed he could not. Once he had begun practicing law he enjoyed saying "importune" just about every chance he got. Although she tried her best to conjure up a for sure knowing that they would share eternity together, it had taken them so long to find each other, it would only be on her deathbed that her last knowing would finally come to her, now she just had to believe that Moses had gone ahead of her to hold open the door to the other side when her time came to join him. Up the hill a bit toward the backside of Mount Moriah Cemetery sits Moses' gravestone. Chiseled into the marble reads his name, the best guess of his birth date, and the for sure day he passed on. Below the chiseled "MOSES KITCHEN" reads the only poem Mary Mary ever knew him to write:

> *Two lovers walking, talking*
> *looking to the horizon*
> *Raise their hands like*
> *brims of an old hat*
> *to shield their*
> *eyes from the late afternoon sun*
> *as though they are one...*

It just about broke Spencer Duty's and Nora's hearts when the registered letter came from Mary Mary telling them of Moses' passing.

About a year or so later, the shoe sellers at just about the same time began to have problems swallowing. And, in not too long after that, shortly after Spencer Duty had finished talking to the 1951 incoming class of chiropodists, Dr. Lester E. Siemon, the dean of the college came up to him and said that Spencer Duty's neck looked swollen and puffy. He thought it'd be a good idea for him to have himself checked out. Spencer Duty said that Nora's neck was looking just about the same as his but they figured since they were getting up in age and all that it wasn't nothing to be worried about. Dr. Siemon said he disagreed and called Dr. John H. Hines who'd graduated at top of his class from Wake Forest Medical School and had become a specialist on thyroid cancers, having researched the Nippers who'd survived the Hiroshima blast. Dr. Siemon thought Dr. Hines was just the man to take a look at the husband and wife.

When Dr. Hines laid his eyes on Spencer Duty and Nora he figured that what he'd find wasn't going to turn out to be what anybody would want to hear.

One right after the other, they had X-rays from this way and that, and when Dr. Hines saw how big and twisted their thyroids were, he called back to Dr. Siemon and said their necks looked just like those slant-eyed devils he'd examined who'd been doused with heavy doses of radiation after we'd dropped the bomb on them. Dr. Hines said he was sure that each and every Jap he'd looked at back when he was a Captain in the Army Medical Corp. was dead now, and pictures he'd seen of the babies that the Jap women had had showed some of the worse birth defects any doctor anywhere had ever seen. A lot of papers were being written on what the radiation had done to their thyroids, Dr. Hines said. The biggest problems doctors saw was how the thyroid absorbed radiation like a dry piece of toast sopped up hot soup. "Had Spencer Duty and Nora been in Japan any time after the war?" Dr. Hines asked. "No," Dr. Siemon said, but they had been using the *St. Alban's Pedoscope* for just about longer than anybody, so likely they'd gotten their fair share of radioactivity. Dr. Hines said he had just read an article by the great English doctor Leon Lewis who he himself, after having raised so much Cain, had the Pedoscope banned from ever being used again in Europe because shoe salesmen were dropping like flies from the most awful cancers.

Dr. Hines decided it would be prudent to do a few more X-rays and found a baseball size tumor starting to press right up against Spencer Duty's vena cava and tumors just about everywhere in Nora's lungs. She'd been coughing blood now for a while and told Dr. Hines she'd thought it'd been from a bad tooth she'd been meaning to have Dr. Clayton back home to take a look at. Dr. Hines said there wasn't much he could do as the cancers had spread just too far for anything to help and they sure couldn't try and treat them with any more radiation. "Just go on back home and take care of what you need to take care of, but do it quick," Dr. Hines said, "Because there won't be much time left for either one of you."

It'd wasn't long after Spencer Duty and Nora got back to Paintsville that they began getting sicker and sicker, ending up in the Shadyville Rest Home run by proprietress Della Dixon, whose grandchildren Spencer Duty and Nora had fitted in their first high tops and kept their feet healthy and straight all the way through the eighth grade.

Dr. Conrad Baker Rice, folks called him "Dr. Con," would come every day on his way home and give Spencer Duty and Nora enough morphine to get them through the night and then come back again the next morning on his way to his office. Dr. Con's children's feet had also been taken good care of by Spencer Duty and Nora so he said it was the least he could do. Problem was Spencer Duty's pain was getting so bad from the tumor getting so big that Dr. Con had on two separate occasions to take him into surgery and cut some of the nerves in his spine just to keep Spencer Duty from dying from the pain alone.

In what was just about the exact same moment and just about the exact same time, Spencer Duty and Nora knew their passing on time was just about there. Evanescent beings from the other side were swarming, gnat like, calling out to Spencer Duty and Nora who both were reaching out to touch the little angels' hands. It was a sign as sure as not.

The colored woman, Sarafina, named after the divine messenger that forever and eternally protected the throne of God and whose momma had revealed to her early on in her life that she a was a Urshu, had been running back and forth between Spencer Duty and Nora's sick rooms, taking care of them just about round the clock now. And given that as an Urshu, she not only had the gift of being able to see when folks were being called for their Messianic banquet, Sarafina was also charged with leading those who'd seen the good Lord looking in their window to the middle of the swinging bridge where she would pass them on to the Archangel Gabriel, whose waiting hands would escort their souls into blessed eternity. And in that, Sarafina pushed Spencer Duty's bed that screeched along the floor to the point where one of the other colored help said that that alone was enough to wake up the dead, into Nora's room where she moved it right alongside. Then Sarafina took Spencer Duty and Nora's limp hands, intertwined their fingers like they were walking together to a picture show, and then cupped their hands in hers. Then Sarafina waited.

It wasn't long before Sarafina began rocking back and forth, feeling the sway of the swinging bridge. All of the other colored help had gathered to watch, having heard but never seen an Urshu delivering up souls. Sarafina was gyrating now, round and round like a spinning top on a table. And the colored woman, Hildreth, who'd been the first to see what Sarafina was, right when Sarafina let go of Spencer Duty and Nora's hands, saw that their chests, right at the exact same time, had stopped moving up and down. Hildreth, who'd ran and got a rag dipped in cool water, said that Sarafina's poor hands looked like she'd done reached into a fire pit and grabbed a smoldering log, Sarafina said never mind, they'd always ended up being burnt when the Archangel Gabriel took the hands of those being passed on from one side to the other. Sarafina then bowed her head, turned, and walked away. Hildreth said she watched her just seem to disappear into thin air. It would be a few years on before Sarafina was again called back by Gabriel.

Spencer Duty and Nora's bodily viewing and funeral brought folks from as far away as Louisville on one side and Prestonsberg on the other. But, surprising to all, came a man from as far away as Wisconsin that Spencer Duty had met when he was just coming up in the shoe business. The man respectfully requested of the beloved Pastor C. Hoge Hockensmith Jr., who'd come to serve the folks of Van Lear and Paintsville in the name of the Lord, after the good Rev. S.C. Honeycutt had one day just up and disappeared, that he be permitted to say a few words. And, the beloved Pastor C. Hoge Hockensmith Jr., who knew only of the man from his many talks with Spencer Duty and Nora, was happy to oblige him his request.

When the beloved Pastor C. Hoge Hockensmith Jr. called for Mr. Bert Mason, the President of Mason Shoes Incorporated, to say a few words, attendees were in awe. Bert said that in all of his days he had never met a man like Spencer Duty, a man with a burning desire to better himself. And not just to better himself so he could turn his nose up to those less fortunate, but to better himself so he could do the right thing. When Spencer Duty had come to him about using the ruby-crusted clutch to buy shoes for youngsters, many of which Bert learned didn't even have full sets of toes, it'd never come up in the conversation that Spencer Duty or Nora ever wanted one red cent for themselves. As a matter of fact, the couple *insisted* that Mr. Abraham Gabriel Schwab be the one to handle all of the money going to pay for the shoes for the youngsters. And, because of Mr. Abraham Gabriel Schwab's investing the money the way he did, not only would shoes continue to be given out to those boys and girls in need but that there was so much money in the shoe fund that Spencer Duty and Nora, a few months before they'd passed on, and in talking with Mr. Abraham Gabriel Schwab, had decided that an education fund be set up to pay for high school graduates who wanted to go onto learn a trade. From here on it would be known as the Spencer and Nora Duty Endowment.

At the end of his sermon, the beloved Pastor C. Hoge Hockensmith Jr. called the pallbearers to come forward. Spencer Duty, Jr. was at the right front side, with Flem's eldest son on the left. The rest of Flem's boys took their place alongside the casket. Then Bert, feeling honored at being asked to serve as a pallbearer, took a spot behind Spencer Duty, Jr. Then to everyone's surprise, the beloved Pastor C. Hoge Hockensmith Jr. helped Charles Pelphrey stand up and walk him to the side of the coffin. Charles Pelphrey, even though his gnarled fingers were now long infirmed and had passed his shoe shine business onto his only begotten son, James, had insisted that he himself polish up not only each and every pair of pallbearer's shoes but also the pair of Mason Executive Imperial Oxfords that Spencer Duty had wanted to be wearing when he walked hand-in-hand with Nora as they stood face-to-face before their Lord and Savior.

Charles Pelphrey said that no man had ever given him the opportunity that Spencer Duty had, and he didn't have much left havin' the sugar, liver spots, bad blood, weak bones, and now the cancer, and if he were to drop dead serving as a pallbearer for the great man, then he would die in the good Lord's graces. The other pallbearers were sure to place Charles Pelphrey in the middle of the coffin where he wouldn't have to bear any weight. Once they'd loaded up Spencer Duty they'd come back in and get Nora.

When Edwin "Pinky" Jones, funeral director at Jones-Preston Funeral Home, opened the door for the pallbearers he saw that his hearse had been moved and in its place sat Spencer Duty's apple truck. He'd kept it all those years. Sometimes he'd go out to the barn where he had it parked in a stall, start it up, and feel the engine spit and sputter, shaking him this way and that, and then he'd get tears in his eyes which he'd quickly wipe away with his sleeve. He'd once told Spencer Duty, Jr. that when they passed on he and Nora wanted to be taken up to Cumbo on the back of the apple truck. Spencer Duty, Jr. said he'd see to it if he had to push the apple truck up top Cumbo himself.

The pallbearers had sat Spencer Duty's casket on one side and Nora's on the other. Their boy primed the carburetor by holding down the foot accelerator and then turned the key. The apple truck fired up with its usual shaking and trembling and then, and like never before in its life, the vehicle began to purr. Flem Jr., sitting right beside Spencer Duty Jr., said he figured that the old girl had decided that Spencer Duty and Nora's last ride should be a smooth one.

Once they got to the top of Cumbo and got his parents buried, Spencer Duty Jr. and Flem Jr. got back in the apple truck and cranked the engine until there was no juice left to crank. They got out of the apple truck one last time, pushed it in between two tall oaks to let it go to rust. Now there sits nothing more than a pile of crimson-colored steel that year after year collapses more and more into itself. And for those that make their way up Cumbo to pay their respects to loved ones and gather blackberries that grow along the road, who know nothing about what was once the apple truck, almost always say snotty things about someone needing to get rid of that mess or shake their heads in awfulness like they'd just found a plate of moldy food under their bed.

It'd last been since the day of Moses' passing that Mary Mary had had a knowing. It wasn't until she was breathing in her last breath that she *knew* that her knowings were still with her. Mary Mary, having just celebrated her last Feast of Tabernacles, had for about as long now as she could remember looked out at the world through a thick opaque film that started clouding her eyes. So bad it was that Mary Mary had never laid clear eyes on her grandchildren, only having seen her children's children as ghost like beings that gave off the illusion of floating from here to there. And had moved on with their own lives from here to there.

Eleanor had come from back east to tend to her mother's imminent passing, having become a law-school-graduated lawyer herself. As a matter of fact, a Harvard law school graduated lawyer, who'd taken up the causes of the underprivileged.

Where most mothers read their children this and that fairy tale, feeling proud when they'd impress him and her with their prowess of memory, Mary Mary instead had told Eleanor nightly tales of growing up poor, mining explosions, and stories of a man, who Mary Mary later told Eleanor personified evil, that'd come to Van Lear acting like he'd up and bought himself a cotton plantation filled with his own personal slaves. Like most plantation owners, he hadn't been one to get his hands dirty, and had his henchmen do his whippings and most of the murdering. But finally, Mary Mary said, right about the time that Eleanor got too big to be told fairy tales, that it was her daddy and one other man who'd been this ignoble man's undoing.

It was also right about that time that Eleanor began wearing a black beret cocked just to the left, barely obscuring her eye, making her raise her brow just like she'd seen Simone de Beauvoir doing in a picture book while looking inquisitively at Jean Paul Sartre. Later Eleanor developed a liking for bright red lip stick and cigarettes. She also developed an early penchant for cursing, "goddamn" being favored.

On Mary Mary's last day, Eleanor arrived at the Butte airport, having been routed from here to there, through this snow storm and that.

Mary Mary lay in the bed that she and Moses shared for 'not long enough,' she would have said if she could still have talked. Up until the past few months she'd still got around by herself, having paths forged around her and Moses' house so as not to fall, not leaving home of course unless she had someone's arm to escort her here or there. And then, seemingly, just one morning, Mary Mary began to fail. It wasn't long before her hair began falling out, and then the weight started coming off her just about as fast as her hair was taking leave of her head. Mary Mary climbed into bed for the last time and told her caretaker, a black woman named Willamina, to summon Eleanor.

A frail, liver-spotted hand reached out to Eleanor as she crested the archway of the bedroom door. It was so old and light that it seemed to hover above the quilt. Mary Mary's hand grasped for air. Eleanor long ago had been told what to do when this day came. She walked over to the night stand that had been on her mother's side of the bed forever and a day. Pulling open the drawer, Eleanor saw a piece of wood that had been wrapped in deer hide with the ends covered in the fur of a hare. From one end were strung blue and purple glass beads. Eleanor took what Moses had called an Apache staff of eternity and tenderly slipped it into Mary Mary's waiting palm. The staff, Moses had said, would allow them, no matter what form they may take in the afterlife, to always recognize each other. Then, upon opening her eyes to take one last blurry look at this world, Mary Mary curled her fingers one by one around the end of the staff. Many winters before Mary Mary had crossed over from the other side into this world, shrouded in a caul. Now she would leave this world to cross over into the other, enveloped by the only knowing that she'd ever truly sought. Right at the moment that her lids began to close Mary Mary felt Moses' hand take the other end of the staff.

Part Two

ELEANOR KITCHEN

Chapter 47

AFTER I MOVED TO Paintsville, the first thing I did was look up Spencer Duty, Jr. We discovered that between us we had hundreds of letters and photographs that, no matter what Nora or Mary Mary had told us, couldn't compare to what was revealed in their correspondence. Some of the older folks around Van Lear still remember getting their first pair of shoes because of Spencer and Nora Duty. It may not seem like much to someone who has had shoes all their lives, but to someone who didn't have ten toes and whose soles of their feet bled day in and day out and were only warm six months out of the year, getting shoes made a lasting memory.

After the Baldwin-Felts detectives, the cold-eyed mustached man, (who no one ever found out his name but the folks I talked to said that name stuck about as good as any other), and Mr. LaViers had all been killed, run out of town, or died, there was talk back then that the *ghost of the sugar maple grove* had come back from the dead to put things right. Even to this day, folks shy away from the sugar maple grove and especially what is left of the old dilapidated tin shack that rots away in a hovel. "Honey," they say, "…let sleeping dogs lie."

Chapter 48

It wasn't long after she arrived in Van Lear that Eleanor began causing a ruckus. Moses, having been responsible for sending the cold-eyed mustache man and the cadre of Baldwin-Felts detectives to hell, and now his blood had come to Van Lear with a puffed up sense of right and wrong, seeming to lots of folks of wanting to pick up where her daddy'd left off so many years ago. "Bitch," was the word most used among themselves, and anyone else within ear shot, to describe Eleanor. Things were different now than they had been in her daddy's day. There weren't no more detectives to contend with and the beatings by the foremans were, if they were going to happen at all, done where folks would only see the aftermath rather than the foremath. But what was and would forever be the same was the mines. Except more of them, having sprung up like rabbit litters. Everywhere you looked there was a tipple, some big operations like the 151, which was still producing after all this time and smaller ones where men would for the most part just dig a hole into the side of a hill, shovel out the coal, and move on, leaving goddamn pock marks all over the mountain faces.

Eleanor had brought with her a law degree and a suitcase full of money that she'd come into possession of when her momma had passed on. Having not to worry about making ends meet, Eleanor didn't have to be beholden to anyone. She also had a penchant for reading that communist, Nelson Algren, about those, who no matter what they did, just kept getting beat into the dirt. Her beret pulled down over just one eye, that she'd gotten used to wearing after spending upwards of a year in Paris, and smoking right out in public, made her look not just goddam queer, but also like a whore too. Most especially when she painted her lips red, which the miners' wives would say made her look like a floozy. It was said by some that she was even more of a harlotan because sometimes she'd been seen by some of the church women unabashedly drinking *Kentucky Bourbon*. The other lawyers in town though would say unbeknownst to their wives or preacher that under her finery they thought Eleanor likely had a fine female form hiding naked as a nut in its husk.

Eleanor herself, even though she'd been raised up believing in God the Almighty, had, once she'd been converted to a bohemian way of thinking by associating with red devils herself and all, rejected her God-fearing upbringing as "nonsense." So, forever and a day, Moses would pray for her redemption, asking the good Lord to give her plenty of leeway for forgiveness, promising if He could see His way fit to do so, that Eleanor would end up being one of the good Lord's better representatives of what He'd put man on this earth to be. The last two thoughts that Moses Kitchen had right before he took his last breath was professing his eternal love for Mary Mary, figuring that she'd likely hear him talking to himself as he'd never been able to keep anything from her anyway, and prayerfully asking to speak with God directly upon getting to Heaven about forgiving Eleanor for veering from His flock. But truth be told, Moses had come to figure by watching Eleanor that being one of the faithful didn't just mean going to church on Sunday and asking for forgiveness for Monday through Saturday's sins. No, Moses figured now that being faithful was more about being a decent human being. One who didn't profess empty beliefs but lived their faithfulness by offering up their prayers in the way they treated others and spoke up against wrong doers.

Eleanor had taken a room in Paintsville at Wanda C. Music's boarding house. From there she could walk to her office right in the middle of Jefferson Avenue. Mostly Eleanor took on cases of women suffering terrible at the hands of their husbands. She almost always lost too.

Mason and Mandy Ratliff showed up at Eleanor's door, shortly after three o'clock on a Friday afternoon, right after Eleanor had got back from court, having had tried to argue for Belinda Ratliff, who'd been caught by her husband Sammy Ratliff reading *God's Little Acre*, and that and that fact alone, Sammy Ratliff's lawyer, Johnny Pelphrey said, proved that Belinda Ratliff was unfit to continue to carry on caring for Sammy Ratliff and his six God-given boys. "Why," Johnny

Pelphrey had said in court, "Sammy Ratliff had found that book, which had been brought before the courts in as nefarious a city as New York, by the Society for the Supervision of Vice, and put up for banning." "And now, like vermin crawling off a filthy ship from somewheres overseas, it had been brought into the God-fearing house of Sammy Ratliff, who everyone knew was about a devout a man as ever had been, and now his house of repute had been turned into a house of ill-repute and because of this Sammy Ratliff was asking for a divorce from one said Belinda Ratliff, and further," Johnny Pelphrey said, "Sammy Ratliff wants back his name from Belinda Ratliff, who having soiled the Ratliff name, should go back to being Belinda Blevins, whose family hadn't ever amounted to anything anyways. And he, having given her his name had offered her respectability, which she had deliberately soiled."

Eleanor raised this and that objection, even resorting to threatening the court, but in the end, Judge Herbert Van Hoose said that everything Johnny Pelphrey had said was true and ordered that Mr. Sammy Ratliff would in fact be granted a divorce and that no shame should be cast upon him or his children because of said facts, and that Belinda Ratliff would relinquish not only all rights to ever seeing her boys again, having known full well the consequences of violating the hoi polloi of not only the Sammy Ratliff family but of the whole of Johnson County, Kentucky. It'd probably be best, Judge Herbert Van Hoose said, if Belinda Ratliff hereby now known again as Belinda Blevins just packed up and went back to where she'd come from, having assumed that one of her kind wouldn't have ever come from Paintsville.

Eleanor stormed out of the courtroom, slamming the swinging gate that separated the spectators from the opposing parties so hard that it tore part of it right off its nails. She hadn't calmed down by the time she got back to her office to meet Mason and Mandy Spradlin.

They were there, Mason said, because he wanted to take his law-fully-wedded wife Mandy to court. "For whatever for?" Eleanor said, thinking to herself that Mason didn't quite seem in his right mind. Then, after sucking into his black lungs what little breath he could, Mason went on to reiterate in his iterating that he had known suffering all his life. Fellow miners who'd been blown up down in the hole and some who's just been in a blast and left for dead with the mine company deciding from atop that they were dead at the bottom. He'd even known suffering like he thought no other when on a snowy December night in 1945, when he and Mandy's only boy Peto had been killed while serving as chauffeur to none other than General Georgie S. Patton. But when the Chaplin and the Captain from the War Office had showed up at Mason and Mandy's door brushing the snow off their shoulder boards, one of the first things they had said was that neither Mason nor Mandy was never, as to be sworn to God and under penalty of law, to say to anyone other than themselves that Peto had been killed while driving the great general himself. It'd be said officially that he'd been killed serving his country while driving a truck delivering medical supplies to a field hospital tending to soldiers who were still too critical to move anywhere else and that, because of his gallantry of driving over shelled-out roads and having lost control of his truck, and even though it was after the war had ended, Peto would be awarded the Medal of Gallantry.

Peto's body arrived back from Germany a month or so later, the coffin welded shut with only a small little window cut right up at his head. When Mason Cupped his hands against the thick smoky glass he saw Peto, looking shined up like he was made out of wax, with the brown bill of his visor cap pulled down so far over his forehead that Mason couldn't even see his eyelids. Right after that Mason collapsed onto the floor having to be picked up by his daddy, Zollie. The day that Peto had got on the bus to take him to the enlistment station over in Lexington, Mason promised him that his 1939 Studebaker could stay put right under the overhang at the north end of the house. And there it sat rusting away over these many years, this part and that falling off here and there. Likely someday, the axels would give way and it'd fall right to the ground.

After Peto was lowered into his forever resting place and the last shovel full of dirt covered his grave, he was never spoken of again.

Mason said, in his complaining that day to Eleanor, that he wanted what was "rightfully" his, namely Mandy's virtue, just like it'd always been all these years, with Mandy *never* one time refusing to hamper him in taking care of his needs. Yet now, with all his wheezing, Mason couldn't even go to the toilet by himself, with sometimes Mandy finding him passed out, slumped over the hole from straining up his bowels. Mandy even went so far as to think that he was forgetting how to even make himself go. Just like he'd gone on to forgetting how to make himself a man. Mason now though pointed the finger at Mandy for what he couldn't no longer do and was *insisting* that Eleanor have Judge Herbert Van Hoose *order* Mandy to make him "…reconnoiter with his manhood." Mason sat rocking to and fro, waving his hands and contorting his mouth, making more and more less sense as he went on and on, looking like a tree limb whose bark had been whittled away to a dried-up stick. Eleanor wondered sitting in Mason's presence how blue a man had to turn before being declared dead.

Mandy, not wanting to speak up and say the most personal of personal things to Eleanor, and in fact had never even said the most personal of personal things to Mason, at least until recently when she'd had to go see Dr. Hammond Vaughn, who'd gone to medical school in Georgia, complaining of itching in her private area, and then and only then did she learn the name of her most private part, the "vagina" Dr. Vaughn had said, but Mandy not hearing as well as before, thought Dr. Vaughn had said her most private of private parts was called "Virginia." She figured because her most private of private parts was down below, as she would say, and Virginia was south that was why a woman's most private part was called Virginia.

Hell, Mandy did say though that Mason couldn't do much of *anything* now, not even being able to take Abraham Lincoln Salyer, his nephew who'd been once removed by divorce, down to the dump to shoot rats scurrying here and there looking for food, without getting winded just raising the rifle to his shoulder. Thing was, Mandy said pitifully, and like Eleanor knew, Mason wasn't the only one suffering and behaving like they'd up and lost their minds. The West Van Lear Rest Home was filled with men of little use and who'd soon enough be widow makers themselves because of the way their black lungs forbid the air from making it up to their brains.

After the meeting with Mason and Mandy, Eleanor sat feeling useless. She'd always had a fire in her belly but each and every day Eleanor felt her embers being dampened down, knowing the reason folks retained her was because she mostly didn't charge them for losing their cases. She didn't have no kin that she knew of anywhere in Kentucky, much less Johnson County and hell, Eleanor would say, when somebody did bother to listen to her, after her step-brothers had been killed in an avalanche in the Crazy Mountains, and then after her daddy had passed on and then her momma up and died, hell again she would say, there was no one. Even in law school she'd not made any long-lasting friends, most especially not at Harvard not having come from a *good* family, as she rarely was left to forget.

It was a just week later when Mandy showed up at Eleanor's office by herself. Mason had took too a coughing fit, not being able to get enough air the day after they'd met. He was dead before Mandy and their other boy Bud could get him over to the Golden Rule Hospital there in Paintsville.

Chapter 49

THAT NIGHT THERE WAS going to be a meeting, listening to folks coming to talk about the lung sickness, the black lung that eventually'd get all the miners. They'd come to let the miners and their families know it weren't really the mines that were causing the black lung. And as a matter of fact, they would say when they went here and there, putting on their dog and pony show, "…has *anyone* here ever *seen* a black lung?"

"There's what we tell them, and then gentlemen, there's what we don't tell them," spoke Mr. Cecil Preston, the president of the local UMW. "Each and every one of these goddamn families wouldn't even be here if it weren't for the mines. It feeds them, clothes them, builds them goddamn schools, churches, and they just want more and more. If it don't stop, the goddamn government'll step in and bring a shit bucket down on the whole kit and caboodle."

A half dozen heads nodded in agreement with Mr. Cecil Preston, and most especially Dr. William H. Brady, who'd been brought in from as far away as Kansas City, Kansas to provide an expert opinion that *silicosis* was caused by silica and not by coal dust and further that there was "no such thing as the black lung." Dr. Brady, being a pathologist, had done just about more autopsies than anyone and he'd say he'd *never* seen a black lung, "not even inside a Negro," he'd always add with a knowing laugh.

Over the years, coal mining had become more mechanized and now, not only were the trains better that took the miners down into the holes, but so were the pneumatic drills which had pretty much eliminated, at least in the deep mines, pick and shovel mining. Problem was that the drills spewed out more coal dust than the picks ever did. So what had been a problem with black lung before the drills had gotten a hell of a lot worse after they came to be used. But the drills also meant that production had gone up and when production went up so did the miners pay and contributions to the pension fund. The UMW had fought for miners' rights since John L. had forged the way. But, John L. also himself *insisted* that silicosis was *not* caused by the coal dust but by silica and forbade *any* UMW representative from ever uttering "black lung." Ordering instead that it wasn't coal dust that was the culprit and that the miners should get down in those holes and use those new drills with the confidence that the colossal pitch-black plumes being kicked up wasn't doing their lungs one iota of harm. And hence, Dr. William H. Brady had been retained to go on a talkin' tour to tell coal miners from West Virginia to Kentucky to Pennsylvania about there "not even being a medical condition known as black lung." He'd even written scientific papers on it and had x-rays to prove what he was saying, "Look at those lungs," he'd say pointing to the x-ray, "their white, there just ain't no better proof." Invariably at the end of each part of his community meeting a wheezing miner would stand up and challenge him. Dr. William H. Brady, being undeterred, would look the miner square in the eyes and say, "Sir, I can only present to you what medical science reveals the facts to be. And, only you sir, can present your feelings about whatever the condition is you suffer from. But again, Sir, I will tell you and every man here that medical science does not support your *feelings*." Littered throughout the school gymnasiums where the meetings mostly took place, was a dozen or so men who were traveling right alongside Dr. William H. Brady, who'd applaud at just about everything he'd say. And when Dr. William H. Brady showed the proving-his-point x-rays, the littered men's peppered, whispered tones, could be heard saying things like, "Well, will you look at that…" "Amazin, ain't it…" "Doc sure knows his stuff…" Setting off a round of contagious comments that drowned out the raspy miners struggling to get air to say something back.

Eleanor, at the beckoning of Mandy, sat in the back of the meeting place, shaking her head at the *goddamn* lies being espoused. And the wheezing miners who'd actually made it to the meeting weren't the ones in the worse shape. Those men could barely make it from their chairs to the outhouse to take a leak, complaining as best they could, that each breath was like taking in a lung full of broken glass. Some didn't even bother, instead keeping a chamber pot right beside them or just giving up and floating in puddles of piss. It just didn't seem right, that each lifegiving breath should feel like a man was being suffocated from the inside-out.

Waiting for Dr. William H. Brady was none other than Patsy Arms herself, the self-proclaimed Queen of Van Lear. She'd been crowned the queen of her eighth-grade class and decided that since there was no doubt that she was the prettiest and most popular girl in all of Van Lear that she was well due the title and "anointedment." Pasty had made sure she became close to President Cecil Preston when he'd been brought in as the head of the UMW in those parts. And, upon hearing that Dr. William H. Brady was going to be passing through, Patsy insisted that she have an opportunity to be seen taking a meal with him at the Pig Stand Café, who anyone, who knew anything about roasting pig came from miles on end to eat at, with the meal being so good it'd get talked about for weeks on end. Cecil Preston offered up this and that excuse to no availing, but, in the end, Patsy got her way. And now she sat right up front, blinking her long, store-bought eyelashes at Dr. William H. Brady, making him forget where he was in his talk when he'd looked down at her, knowing he'd not only be eating some of the best roast pig a man could ever hope for but also likely be smooching with the Queen of Van Lear.

Patsy, over these past few months, had even offered Mr. Cecil Preston to take her with him when he was getting signatures on signaways from breathless miners before they died. She had a way of sweettalking men, she'd tell Mr. Cecil Preston, each and every time they left a dying miner with their names or their 'X' signed to the piece of paper that released the UMW and the mine from "*any and all responsibility, and that no family members shall now or in the future make a claim in the signatories name,*" for a miner's ills whatever they may be. Mr. Cecil Preston thought Patsy Arms could be pretty hard to take at times, but it was like watching a preacher saving a blind man at a burlesque house, the way she worked her miracles with the dying miners. Hell, she'd even say "God Bless," to the poor sonsabitches right as she was folding up the signaway and handing it to Mr. Cecil Preston. And, Mr. Cecil Preston always showed his appreciation by helping her out with this or that expense directly from the miners' fund.

Eleanor hated Patsy Arms. It didn't matter to Eleanor one bit that that woman was a trollop. It was her eagerness to prey on her own people. Eleanor had noticed when she saw Patsy Arms this time around swinging her legs in front of Dr. William H. Brady that her make-up was getting thicker. She wondered how long she was going to be able to cake on enough rouge before she began to look like an old has-been stripper who still 'took it all off' at the Mayfair Opera House over in Louisville.

Patsy Arms had never known who her daddy was. Her momma had told her that he'd been a Knight Rider, who held it in his heart of hearts to protect each and every white man, woman, and child from coloreds who had the audacity to try and settle down like they were white. It'd not be long 'til they took over like vermin. And, Patsy Arms' momma would whisper into her ear, that they didn't bathe neither. But her momma would never say who her daddy was, only that he'd been killed right before she was born by the nigger lover that lived in a shack up in the sugar maple grove. "Shot your daddy right off his horse," she'd say. "The nigger lover got what was coming to him though, died in the big mine explosion, and good riddance." And, she'd add, "I saw that nigger lover lowered into the ground with every other miner who'd been taken that awful day. The preacher back then buried him right alongside the other men, good men, knowing full well about his sympathetics. But, then not that long after he'd been buried, that nigger lover came back from the dead, killing folks right and left. He was the devil incarnate hisself."

Patsy Arms always listened to her momma when she talked of her daddy. Even though she never said, and Patsy Arms never asked out of respectin' her momma and not wanting to make her feel terrible, that her daddy and her momma were never married under the cross-beam of Jesus Christ. Even though Patsy Arms was the Queen of Van Lear, she knew she'd forever and always be a packsaddle's daughter.

Chapter 50

SPENCER DUTY JR. HAD taken over his daddy's shoe store right after he graduated from the University of Kentucky. Not long after that, taking what he'd learned in school, he figured out a way to begin expanding DUTIES BOOTIES throughout the whole state. He'd grown up with a strong sense of right and wrong and watched his daddy and momma endure the Knights' burning crosses in their front yard and threatening to kill them for hiring Gladys Applewhite, the colored woman who'd had the "audaciousness to touch the feet of the purest white, God – fearing folks," the Knights would scream and yell while waving pick-axe handles above their white pointy hoods.

When he was a youngin' he'd asked his daddy if the Knights heads were pointy too underneath their hoods. Moses used to say to Eleanor that a brave man would look you square in the eyes before he killed you. The Knights he said were gutless cowards, hiding under a mask under the cross of redemption.

The fact was though that Mrs. Applewhite was not only the best clerk Spencer Duty had ever hired, she had also spent more than twenty years working with Spencer Duty and Nora and was also beloved by her customers. She'd even on an occasion saved the mayor's granddaughter from certain death one summer afternoon.

It'd been about four o'clock or so and the Skagg brothers were known to drive their jalopies like a bat out of hell swerving this way and that right down the middle of the road. They didn't give it any mind that they might run over somebody. That afternoon little Naomi Bonham, who they used to call "Nay Bug" because she was fearful of ladybugs, was walking hand in hand with her mamaw, when around the corner the Skagg boys came roaring, the rear end of their car that'd been put together with this and that parts fishtailing like a bucking horse just let out of the chute. Just when Nay Bug and her mamaw were right in front of DUTIES BOOTIES, Mrs. Applewhite happened to glance out the window. There she saw the Skagg brothers, whose daddy was known throughout the hills to be some kind of a Wizard in the Knights, barreling down on Nay Bug and her mamaw. Mrs. Applewhite had been bent down tending to a Mary Beth Pringle's hammer toes, when she jumped up, tore toward the door, throwing it open so hard it broke the glass as it slammed into the display window, raining down sharp shards everywhere. Right before the Skaggs ran over little Nay Bug and her mamaw, Mrs. Applewhite spread out her arms hooking them around their waists and shoving them out of the cars veering path. And in doing so, the clerk fell face first with her legs sticking straight out behind her. The Skagg boys ran right over top of Mrs. Applewhite's stocking covered legs, breaking them in about as many places as a leg had to break.

Johnny Pelphrey defended the Skagg brothers too in court, with again Judge Herbert Van Hoose presiding, seated right below one of the true Stars and Bars, that'd flown over Fort Sumter in Charleston Harbor, in 1861. His Honor held that flag in such deep and abiding respect that he'd had it hung especial right behind his bench.

The defense council said that if the colored woman hadn't run in front of the Skagg brothers' car she wouldn't have gotten run over and that was one of the problems with the Negro not knowing how to be in a civilized society without the guidance and help from white folks. But, in this instance, even the mayor testified against the Skagg brothers. The jury came back with a unanimous guilty verdict. After the verdict was read Judge Herbert Van Hoose spoke up and said he'd known the Skagg brothers all their lives and their daddy was like a brother to him. He knew the brothers to be good boys who'd never do nothin' to hurt no one so he couldn't let good boys go to prison and agreed with Johnny Pelphrey that Mrs. Applewhite shouldn't have jumped in front of their car no matter what and in her decision to do so had made the decision to forfeit any liability should she get from being injured. "It ain't no different than when a man goes hunting a bear. You go out knowing full well that if you don't get the bear first, then the bear will get you. And in the case of *Applewhite verses Skagg* the bear got Mrs. Applewhite. Therefore I am rendering the verdict of the jury null and void and redeclaring the Skagg brothers innocent of all charges." Then Judge Herbert Van Hoose, looking right at the clerk, leaned down to his bailiff, shaking his head like he'd just witnessed something awful, and said in not a hushed tone, "No matter what you dress 'um up in they just never look quite right, do they?" The bailiff looking over at Mrs. Applewhite nodded his head in solidarity with Judge Herbert Van Hoose.

Until the day she passed on she walked with something awful of a limp, needing side-by-side canes just to get from here to there. After being hospitalized for up more than six months convalescing, she came back to shoe fitting for DUTIES BOOTIES and never missed another day's work. Spencer Duty and Nora visited her in the hospital often and every Friday Nora took Mrs. Applewhite her regular pay just as if she'd been working day in and day out. A few months after she was back tending to folk's feet, the Skagg brothers, having gotten liquored up, pulled up right beside the #1, throwing up dirt and gravel like they'd drove right into a dust devil. Up ahead was the railroad crossing just outside of Paintsville. They had the notion of playing chicken with the train, sped up at the last minute, cut in front of the train, yelping and hollering like two damn fools. Likely because of being liquored up, whoever the Skagg brother was who was driving didn't accelerate enough and right as the car turned onto the tracks the #1 slammed into it so hard that it exploded into a fireball, burning up whatever was left of them. The undertaker said there weren't nothing to bury, unless they just put the crumpled-up mess of melted metal in the ground. And that was just what they did. A simple white cross marks the spot on the Skagg homestead where the Skagg brothers were laid to rest. At the colored church Mrs. Applewhite asked that they be remembered in prayer on that Sunday morning.

Eleanor had lost each and every case she'd ever had appearing in front of Judge Herbert Van Hoose. "It weren't a woman's place to be in the courtroom unless she was supporting her husband or was a defendant herself," he would say, just about every chance he got. And he hated Eleanor, especially how she tried to up an act like she was as good as a man. Judge Herbert Van Hoose figured that her daddy had done her a disservice by letting her think that way, instead of taking the strap to her when she was a youngin' and whippin' some of that vinegar out of her. "Hell," Judge Herbert Van Hoose would say to Johnny Pelphrey. "Just because niggers walk upright it don't mean they ain't monkeys tryin' to imitate white folks." When Judge Herbert Van Hoose talked about the moral decay of society, he often cited Mrs. Samuel Gompers, whose husband, Samuel Gompers, was a self-made man. Having been the President of the American Cigar Company and the Georgist Labor Union Leader, fathering upwards of twelve children. Mrs. Gompers *knew* the dangers of women's thinking going past the walls of the home that her husband had worked liked a dog to give her. She'd proclaim, "A home, no matter how small, is plenty large enough to occupy a wife's mind and time." Women working outside the home is "unnatural," she'd say, chiding women for taking jobs from men who needed them. Mrs. Gompers along with the help of her husband, was instrumental in starting up The Women's Bureau, which asserted that wives who held outside jobs were destroying the integrity of their families and set out to prove that women possessed qualities best suited for the "sanctity and security" of keeping a home for her husband and children. Judge Herbert Van Hoose said he admired Mrs. Gompers just as much as he admired his own mother, who'd certainly done right by him.

Chapter 51

ELEANOR HAD READ INTO the early morning hours at Wanda C. Music's boarding house, having fallen asleep propped up. The smell of Miss Music's buttermilk biscuits wafted up the stairs and snuck under the door to her room, causing the young lawyer to twitch, knock the book from her lap onto the floor, and look down realizing that she'd fallen asleep in her good clothes.

Mr. Conrad Twinkledink thought that she looked like something the dogs had dragged in, nodding over to Mr. Roger Tinkenfeld, sitting at the breakfast table shrouded in his blanket-lined ducking-coat smoking his own rolled cigarette. Mr. Twinkledink and Mr. Tinkenfeld were in Paintsville proclaiming the goodness of graham crackers made by the Christian Baking Company. Pointing out to grocers where it was written right on every box of graham crackers, that "*Before each batch is baked, every mixer and blender bends down on their knees in holy reverence and asks the good Lord to bless the fruits of their labor, just like the Israelites had asked for each clump of straw and mud to make a good brick, these bakers are dedicated to making you a graham cracker they'd be proud to serve up to the Almighty Himself.*"

Mr. Twinkledink and Mr. Tinkenfeld figured Eleanor had been up half the night drinking hard liquor, which they'd heard she regularly imbibed. Bowing their heads, they silently prayed for her deliverance as she pulled out a chair and put her hind end to wood.

Mr. Tinkenfeld was an overfed man, some might say he was well-up-holstered, others would say he looked like a baby elephant. Reverent and at times even bowing his head, as he hawked the consecrated graham crackers, constantly putting one after the other into his mouth, declaring that eating the unleavened crackers was like having "Jesus in my belly."

Mr. Twinkledink would always echo Mr. Tinkenfeld, nibbling graham crackers right alongside.

Mr. Twinkledink and Mr. Tinkenfeld always told jokes to lasso folks into hearing about the goodness of their graham crackers, but never ones that were off color, unless of course they themselves had run across a good joke about coloreds.

Mr. Tinkenfeld liked to say, "The Bible says niggers are cursed," quoting Moses as he stood cradling the Ten Commandments against his chest, "'For behold, the Lord shall curse the land with much heat, and the barrenness thereof shall go forth forever; and there was a blackness that came upon all the children of Canaan, that they were despised among all people.'" And Mr. Twinkledink would nod *fervently* in agreement, bowing his head saying, "Amen."

On this very morning Mr. Tinkenfeld was just beginning to tell the "tail" of a colored woman he'd heard just the other day down in Huntington from one of his graham cracker "devoters." And right at the very moment that Eleanor sat down, he was reaching for one of Mrs. Wanda C. Music's biscuits that seemed to linger just barely above their plate, Mr. Tinkenfeld just starting to laugh his fool head off at his own joke, grabbed his throat, and started to choke. He'd just gotten "Nigger" to come out from the back of his gullet when he began gagging on a hunk of smoked pork chop that he'd been chewing on while talking up the divineness of his graham crackers, while Mr. Twinkledink jovially nodded his head in anticipation like a Vaudeville straight man, getting everyone at the breakfast table sitting on the edge of their seats readying to hear the summit of the best "nigger tail he'd ever heard." And upon the uttering of those final words, Mr. Tinkenfeld grabbed his bulky neck and flew face first into his bowl of Wanda C. Music's thick brown sausage gravy.

Mr. Roger Tinkenfeld's fat, jowled cheek fit about as perfectly into that big bowl of sausage gravy as just about anybody could imagine, and, Mr. Tinkenfeld also looked just about as dead as anybody could imagine, with his eyes glassed up like cat eye marbles and his tongue allol off to the side of the pretty porcelain bowl. Eleanor jumped up and began slapping him right between his shoulder blades. But because of the rolls of fat across his back, the vibrations of her slaps likely never caused enough tremors to even make their way to the gob of meat blocking up his throat. There, having just come from the kitchen, stood Wanda C. Music holding a plate of right-out-of-the-oven biscuits, tearfully praying for her roomer to come back to them and finish his story. But Mr. Tinkenfeld was never to return.

Mr. Twinkledink however, after relating the demise of Mr. Tinkenfeld to their customers, came back to the Christian Baking Company with the largest number of orders ever received. He even got the salesman of the year award which came with a fifty-dollar bonus. A special prayer and deliverance service was held right around the graham cracker dough mixer for the dead man.

A while later Pinky Jones arrived in his hearse to pick up the rightful remains of Mr. Tinkenfeld. Pinky had got his nickname from having been one of those lads whose daddy had taken him snappin' turtle hunting right about the time he was making his turn towards manhood. Having been in the business of "preparin' folks for bur-yin'," as he liked to say, Pinky looked at Mr. Tinkenfeld's substantial body and knew he'd need to do some figuring to get him out to the hearse. Wanda C. Music said that someone should notify his kin that he'd passed onward. But Mr. Twinkledink spoke up and said that, being a man of such portliness, his dead associate had never been able to find himself a suitable wife and his momma and daddy, three sisters, and four brothers had been long gone, all having come down with the enteric fever and dying one right after the other, while by some miracle he had been spared by the graciousness of the Good Lord, which was what drove Mr. Tinkenfeld to spread the word of the *Holy* crackers.

Pinky stood for a bit and came to fully figure that there was only one way to get the corpse from Wanda C. Music's rooming house. He made a phone call to his assistant, Mr. Elijah Waterbury, and then, seeing himself with the authority of a captain on a ship ordered the living to depart and not come back until late in the afternoon. When Mr. Waterbury arrived he brought with him two carpenters' handsaws, whereby Pinky and Elijah set forth to dismember Mr. Tinkenfeld at the joints, trying not to make too much of a mess, just like one would take apart a rooster for Sunday supper.

Once they got all the parts of Mr. Tinkenfeld back to the funeral home, Pinky and Elijah allotted themselves the task of putting him back together with bailing wire, figuring that would hold him together long enough to get him atop Cumbo and into the ground.

Chapter 52

SHE'D LEFT HER OFFICE about four in the afternoon or so having just met with three already-croaking miners, barely over thirty. Their wives and youngins were in tow, helping to prop up their daddies while they tried to make a case for being disabled so as to apply for benefits to keep from starving and having to depend on the church for food, clothing, and getting close now to shelter too. They just kept coming to her and Eleanor just kept saying the same goddamn thing, there wasn't nothing she could do. The mines weren't going to give them a plugged nickel and they'd have to find what they needed somewhere beside the coal yards, maybe even considering moving up to Dayton or Detroit to get work. Day in and day out she had to turn away families from begging her to help them. But the other lawyers in town wouldn't even take the time to sit down with them.

Truth be told she didn't have much more left in her, not to mention the fact that she was about as lonely as one can get, as not many folks wanted to be seen with her. Like reading a book waiting for the plot to start, Eleanor waited for the direction of her life to become clear.

Even taking supper at Wanda C. Music's rooming house, roomers would nod their heads while courteously ladling out a helping of chicken and dumplings, but once her plate was full, and she'd drawn it back away from the spooning hand, the eyes that had briefly caught Eleanor's to make sure they didn't drip a drop of soup would cast right back down to their own plates and begin eating. After dabbing their mouths with the 'WCM' hand stitched monogramed napkins, the other roomers would espouse the deliciousness of that which was being served up hot, with satisfied heads nodding in every direction but Eleanor's.

It was either because they knew in their hearts of hearts that she was a harlot or that the lawyer had tried to cause a ruckus between the life-giving coal and the miners who were breaking their backs to put food on their families' dinner tables. No one forced one goddamn man to start digging coal, there were plenty of jobs to be had doing this or that, the espousing miners would retort when anyone said anything above a whisper.

It was right about the time that CONSOL discovered it was best to do any beatings that needed to be done, out of eye and earshot, and to let the broken bones and bruises speak for themselves, they also came to figure that full bellies brought about more loyalty than empty ones. Once Eleanor had finished her supper, she retired again back to her room.

Chapter 53

WHEN ELEANOR HAD ARRIVED in Paintsville the first thing she did was look up Spencer Duty, Jr. Having taken over DUTIES BOOTIES from his daddy and momma, he'd branched out all over Kentucky and traveled seemingly hither to yon, visiting each and every store as much as he could, making sure that the managers were living up to the standards that his parents had set right from the beginning. He too was called a nigger lover, hiring colored women to work right beside white women, even when he could have hired a white woman, who needed the money to help support her family, and further, more even though when having been given permission by her husband to suffer the humiliation of having his women work in the first place!

Upon meeting Spencer Duty Jr. for the first time, and looking at this picture and reading that letter between their mommas, Eleanor felt about as close a kinship as one could feel having not come from the same blood. The young lawyer also, if truth be told, had fallen in love with Spencer Duty, Jr. He was handsome, unlike his daddy, who, folks would say, was nothing to look at because of the awful acid etched scars burrowed into the flesh of his face. The same folks would even say they didn't know what Nora had ever seen in him. But his son had dark wavy hair and was as good lookin' as any Hollywood leading man. Eleanor had never up and told Spencer Duty Jr. about her truest feelings for him but anytime anyone saw them together folks would talk and whisper that she, being the whiskey-drinkin' strumpet she was, had likely ruined him for ever being able to marry a good Christian girl. Of course, Spencer Duty Jr. being a nigger lover and all also made matters worse for the mommas and daddies when he was known to go courting. Especially those who he didn't know were back-door affiliated with the White Knights. Once, he'd gone to pick up Ella May Ratliff, whose family had come to Van Lear to dig coal back in 1909. When Spencer Duty Jr. had gone to pick her up to go to the community dance, her daddy threw a bucket of cow piss in his face and told him that if he ever set foot on his land or came around Ella May again, then he'd kill him and feed him to the pigs. Certain though that Mr. Ratliff had no compunction about his boy Elmer taking money from the Spencer and Nora Duty Endowment to go onto trade school to learn welding. It was said that Mr. Ratliff told Elmer that he was as proud as a daddy could be of a boy and his last living act being to pass on his white cowl with its red tassel in hopes as he stepped in front of St. Peter that Elmer would pass it onto his boy and so on.

The young couple went on picnics regularly and talked of their mommas and daddies. Spencer Duty Jr. told Eleanor that there wasn't much of anything that his daddy wouldn't have done for Moses, saying that on the night that Spencer Duty had led the raid against Mr. LaViers house he'd become a man, unwilling from that point on to ignore injustice whenever he'd encounter it.

Chapter 54

IT WAS ON AN EARLY evening in late June, with a wind swirling maple leaves and the clouds growing dark and tall, when Bobby Maynard, who'd up and been born with a harelip that cut just about up to his left nostril, showin' a couple a chisel-pointed teeth that hung onto his gums for dear life, and who barely muttered a word, other than a grunt sayin' he wanted this or that, and Randy Gabbard, who'd only been known as "Boy" all his life, had just been fishing up at Greasy Crick. The crick had come by its name when a trapper'd, who'd been lockin' back the jaws of a leg trap after cutting the throat of a mostly dead beaver, saw a bear sittin' up on a ridge. The animal was readying to come down and refresh himself with some cool water. The trapper set the sight of his Hawken .50 on the bear, thinkin' to his self what a pelt would bring, not to mention the meat. And, in his usual fashion, the trapper ceased the bear from living for a second longer than the time it took the lead to leave the barrel of his Hawken, until it bore a hole right through its head, causing him to tumble down the cliff into the water below. Problem was, once the bear fell into the crick, the trapper couldn't get him up to the bank, havin' to leave him there to swell up somethin' awful, leakin' this and that, makin' the water so slick with the animal's innards remnants that from that very day forward, it became known as Greasy Crick.

Boy, carrying a stinger of smallmouths, had to relieve himself behind a mulberry bush, when, just as he was holding himself, about to relax and let his water flow, he looked down and saw what he first thought was more mulberry juice caking up the dirt than he'd ever seen in his life. Then from under some long-hanging branches of a thorny Cockspur Hawthorn dusting the ground, Boy saw the splotchy purple fingertips of a Negro's hand. He began running about as fast as a boy could run throwing the stinger of small mouths at Bobby who caught it right before a couple of the fish who were still gasping gave up and died. Dodging this and those branches hanging down and catching up in his feet, Boy got to Lincoln Miller's service station with barely a breath to spare, where Linc, as he was known about Paintsville, was just finishing up washing the windows of widow Willard, whose husband, Peck, had been found dead in the bed of Helen Rice, who had an unsavory reputation in and about Paintsville and it was said that Peck hadn't been the *first* husband who'd died in her bed. Said it was she did things to the men who she'd beguiled into occupying her bed that no God-fearing wife'd *ever* do with their men. Folks just figured that the poor men's tempted hearts just couldn't take the unchaste Helen Rice's debasing ways. It was said that hung above the widow Willard's forsaken bed was needlepointed a verse from Proverbs 7: 21-24,

> *With her enticing speech she caused him to yield,*
> *With her flattering lips she seduced him.*
> *Immediately he went after her, as an ox goes to the slaughter, or as a*
> *fool to the correction of the stocks,*
> *Till an arrow struck his liver. As a bird hastens to the snare, He did*
> *not know it would cost his life.*

Boy went screaming up to Linc saying that he'd found a dead nigger up by Greasy Crick. "Linc, *I say, I say,* Linc *I say, I say*" which was what Boy always added into what he was about to say. "I say, I say, there's a dead nigger up there in the briar patch right this way of Greasy Crick, I say, I say Linc."

"Don't you be bullshitin' me Boy. You do an I'll slap the shit outta you, then your momma 'l go an beat your ass too," Linc said.

"I say, Linc, I wundt' bullshit no one, no how, 'bout no dead nigger, I say, Linc."

Linc got on the phone and called the police station. Deputy Duffy Deeter answered and said constable Thaddeus Yates was he figured sittin' at Nellie's right about now havin' his well-deserved lunch, and why didn't Linc call him up there? Well, Linc went ahead and called Nellie's asking if the constable was there when Ethyl, Nellie's straw-haired bastard daughter, who'd just gotten her womanly blood and had a big gap sitting right between her two yellow front teeth, answered the phone. "Yes sir, he's a sittin' ri-chunder by the window lookin' out and I'm just a gettin' ready to cut his blackburry pie. Whose should I say is callin' for him?"

Linc told Ethyl to shut the hell up and go get Thaddeus on the phone.

The constable came to the phone explaining that he was just getting ready to eat his pie and disturbing him had better be goddamn important. Linc went on to say that Boy had come runnin' up to him when he was washin' Widow Willard's windows and said there was a dead nigger up in the briar patch right along Greasy Crick. "You called me 'cause of a dead nigger, you disturb my lunch after I've been patrolling all goddamn morning in this goddamn heat and all these goddamn flies and you interrupt me feedin' my hunger 'cause of a dead nigger."

Linc, not one to take any guff, said he'd keep Boy there and for Thaddeus to come on over to the station when he'd finished his pie and he'd have Boy take him on up to the dead nigger. Thaddeus slammed the phone down and waved to Ethyl to go ahead and bring him his dessert. Ethyl'd made sure that she scooped the seedy syrup oozing from around the extra big piece she'd cut. Having spent time with Thaddeus in his patrol car, she knew how much he liked to search for those blackberry berries from between his teeth with his tongue when he was on patrol right after lunch.

Thaddeus picked up Boy and Linc, Linc telling his brother-in-law Dewey Blevins to mind the station while he was gone and issued him a warning that every goddamn penny'd better be accountable for when he got back. Dewey, liking to dip his hand in the till at just about every opportunity he got, nodded his head understanding that Linc had had just about enough of his dishonest ways, brother-in-law or not. Thaddeus also issued a warning to Boy that there'd better be a dead nigger right where he'd said or he'd drown the little bastard in Greasy Crick. Boy said, "I say, I say that dead nigger ain't goin nowheres, you'll see, I say."

There sittin' by the side of the road was Bobby Maynard, still holding the now still stringer, whistling to no one, waiting for Boy and whoever he'd be a' bringin' with him. Thaddeus got out of the patrol car telling Bobby first thing that if they was lying he was going to beat them within an inch of their lives. Bobby, looking up from their later dinner layin' there dryin' in the dust, muttered for sure they weren't fibbin', pointing his thumb back over his shoulder to indicate the location of the dead nigger. Boy jumped out of the car with Linc following, telling Thaddeus he'd show him. Traipsing through the brush with his two companions close behind, Boy took them right to the spot where the colored girl's hand poked out from under the thick colorful wet maple leaves covering the forest floor. Thaddeus looked down and said, "Well I'll be goddamn right you were Boy, that sure looks like a dead nigger to me." He bent over and pulled back the limbs and leaves that had been placed atop the child's body. "Goddamn," Thaddeus said.

"That's the Hick's girl, Hattie," Linc spoke up and said.

"Goddamn you're right."

"I say, I say she ain't got no clothes on," Boy said.

"Get on outta here Boy, go on get the hell outta here," Thaddeus ordered.

"She sure enough didn't get here on her own," Linc was saying as Thaddeus nodded his head up and down. She was beat up pretty good too.

"Her momma and daddy's the ones that come over from Germany, they're the only niggers I ever knew who spoke Kraut," Linc said. "First time they came into the station and was asking for gas for their jalopy, I recognized that accent from when I was in the war. But a couple of niggers in the great state of Kentucky, with a German accent, I thought I'd heard it all. Come to find out they'd been a part of the Human Zoos, the Krauts called them, they had some Kraut name for it, *Volk Tiergarten* something or other. Damn people started complaining like they do, but the Krauts gave those niggers a place to live and a couple of squares a day and all they had to do was to be niggers and let folks walk by and look at them scratchin' their asses. Here tell Aberdeen and Sarah Hicks, Sarah was the name she gave herself when folks here couldn't say 'Saartjie', left their keepers high and dry, owing them for food and the likes, hid away on a freighter and came over to the U. S. of A., the old man worked up in Pennsylvania in the mines there and when those ran dry they came on down here."

Thaddeus had heard it all before, like Linc, though he hadn't ever heard a nigger with a German accent. And now the Hicks' pickaninny had been murdered.

Chapter 55

AFTER PINKY AND ELIJAH had finished cutting up Mr. Tinkenfeld and the commotion at Wanda C. Music's boarding house had died down, Eleanor made her way back down the stairs and walked on over to her office, nodding to Lacy A. Hobbs herself, who owned Hobbs' Five and Dime right there on Main Street.

"No finer a woman has ever walked the face of the earth," folks would say right out loud, whenever they passed her by. Why she'd even been known to take money right out of the cash register to make up for folks who couldn't afford to buy their youngins school clothes, if they came up short while paying for their goods. She charged them interest of course for her generosity. She was the mother of her boy Boyd, named after his daddy, who'd stepped on a land mine in Italy during The War of International Jewry. Said it was that Boyd the first had come upon a Nazi *Spähtrupp*, just he himself, suddenly fighting the Krauts to save his battalion, spraying bullets from his machine gun, not realizing that he'd entered a Devils Garden, when he stepped right down on a glass mine. Right before he suffered his mortal wounds he said he heard the glass breaking under his boot the very second before the mine blew off both his legs and his manhood. Somehow or other he didn't bleed to death right then and there, draggin' himself to the 15th Evac Hospital in Riardo, with not much left below his waist. The doctors trimmed off this and that, tucking this where that should go and that where this should go, giving him penicillin, trying to stop gangrene and blood poisoning from consumin' his body. But there just wasn't enough left of Boyd the first to fight with and he passed away a week to the day that half of himself had disappeared in a crimson mist. Lacy A. Hobbs never forgave the Jews for starting that war in the first place and sending Boyd the first to be with Jesus rather than his earthly family, leaving her to raise up her boy Boyd and the girl Gayle. Like a black cloud hanging over her head, bad fortune again struck

Lacy A. Hobbs when her boy Boyd and the girl Gayle were rough-housing behind the homestead, Lacy A. Hobbs spending the better part of her days hollering at them, trying her best to get them to mind, specially her boy Boyd, when on that day the boy Boyd came running inside yelling his fool head off that the girl Gayle'd fell down the well shaft. Lacy A. Hobbs went a tearing outside, leaning over the well shaft as far as she could, looking down into the blackness, seeing nothing, trying her darndest to pull up the bucket, but no matter how hard she pulled the rope just seemed to stretch out the more. Lacy A. Hobbs told boy Boyd to run over the holler to get Mr. Yarborough, who'd sometimes come to visit Lacy A. Hobbs when the boy Boyd and the girl Gayle had gone onto bed. Lacy A. Hobbs kept screaming into the well, telling the girl Gayle help was a comin' but all she heard was the ringing of her own voice. In what seemed like forever to Lacy A. Hobbs and what seemed like in a flash to her boy Boyd, Mr. Yarborough came hurrying along through the woods. Mr. Yarborough was wheezing hard but kept inside him enough breath behind to crank up the bucket pulley with all his might. When the bucket broke water, there was the girl Gayle, tangled up dead as could be in the ropes, with most of her head stuck in the bucket. Mr. Yarborough untangled the girl and broke apart the sides of the bucket so he could unwedge her head, wondering to himself how it could've got barred in like that, it just didn't make no sense to him. It looked like she'd been shot out of a canon and her little head'd been a direct hit into the cask. Mr. Yarborough squatted down, holding the girl Gayle dripping in his arms, trying his best to comfort Lacy A. Hobbs, who'd was about as beside herself as one could be. Boy Boyd didn't seem too bothered one way or the other.

Chapter 56

BOY HAD DONE MADE it back to town, having run all the way, leaving Bobby trailing behind carrying the stinger full of smallmouths, kicking stones off the dusty path along the side of the road.

Boy upon getting into Paintsville ran into the barbershop and started stammering, "I say, I say that Kraut nigger girl, Hattie Hicks, I say she's dead, found her up yonder by Greasy Crick, buck naked, dead as dead can be."

Getting trimmed up, Shug Bayes sat under the barber's bib, his spindly arms hanging out from underneath, lined with carmine veins that looked like spleenful snakes arcing this way and that under his sylphic hide. Unbeknownst to anyone else, when old Bayes moved his head this way or that, he could hear his neck bones scrapping together, which every time caused him to squinny up his eyes making it look like he had some kind of tick, and because of that old Bayes tried as he might not to get going on something that would make him get riled up and start throwing his head around, but when he got to talking about niggers he just couldn't control himself.

"Niggers, just like my daddy told me and I'm tellin' you, it all went straight to hell when we were made to stop hangin' um. Now, every goddamn time something goes haywire, a nigger's got their fingers in it somehow."

Just like old Bayes, the half dozen or so others sitting waiting for their trims were getting just as riled up and tossing their heads around in his resolve. Boy, standing there, getting caught up in the nodding himself, just kept stammering, "I say, I say, I say…"

Thaddeus and Linc pushed back the mulberry stems, grabbed young Hattie's ankles, and dragged her out from under the brush.

When they got her freed up, they could see there was a piece of hemp rope tied so tight around her neck that her head was purple and her eyes were buggin'. Her knickers were pulled down and hanging off one of her ankles. It sure looked like she had bite marks just about all over her trunk. Linc tucked the toe of his work boot under the small of her back and rolled her over. From the way she was all twisted up it looked like someone had stomped on her spine.

Underneath the dead child was a pack of Nigger Boy Licorice Cigarettes. Lacy A. Hobbs' boy Boyd had been chewing on Nigger Boys just about as long as anyone could remember, his teeth always black as black could be. Some folks'd say that when he opened his mouth it was so black with licorice all you'd see was the dark of night. He always had a ready supply being able to walk right into Hobbs' Five and Dime anytime he so well pleased and fill the pockets of his dungarees.

Right out of the corner of his eye Thaddeus saw Linc take the same boot toe that he'd turned over young Hattie with and kick the Nigger Boys back up under the brush. "No need to cause a stir when one ain't needed," Linc said, shaking his head back and forth. "These niggers run around like wild animals getting into this and that, goddamn."

"This is a bad one," Thaddeus said. "Depraved, I'd say."

The two men picked up young Hattie by her feet and hands and carried her back to the police car. Thaddeus lowered his end to the ground while he opened up the trunk, then he and Linc picked her back up and heaved her in. Her body came down hard on the jack, making a sound like something inside her back that was already busted got busted up some more.

Chapter 57

THE CONSTABLE PULLED UP behind Jones and Preston Funeral Home and parked right up alongside the hearse. Linc went on in and told Pinky what had gone on and that they had the young Hicks girl in the trunk. Thaddeus had opened the trunk and was looking down at how swollen and bruised her private parts were when Pinky and Linc came on out. Pinky leaned into the trunk and moved the child's head around and squeezed on the back of her neck.

"Even with the rigor her neck has been broken six ways from Sunday," he said. "She's a little thing, no doubt about that, but whoever did this was a strong boy the way her vertebras are separated from each other. Hell, just feel back here, her ligaments are ripped hither to yon."

Thaddeus reached into the trunk and felt around the back of young Hattie's neck. "It don't seem like there's much holding her head on 'cept the rigor." Linc watched Pinky nodding up and down. "Go on bring her on in," Pinky said.

Thaddeus threw a canvas over top of young Hattie when he and Linc carried her inside. Pinky, pointing, said, "I've been busier than a cat covering shit on a marble floor today. Just lay her on the other table."

The two men obeyed. There, laying right beside young Hattie on the other table, was all the parts of Mr. Tinkenfeld, who Pinky had just begun wiring back together. Pinky looked over at Thaddeus and Linc saying, "Go on now get outta here and let me do my job. I'll tell you how she died after I do the post. I suspect you're going to talk to her family and all? Seems pretty obvious she was choked to death but you just never know 'til you get in there and take a look."

Chapter 58

THADDEUS DROPPED LINC BACK by his station and headed on out to the Hicks' place at the end of town, right before you head upwards to Turkey Knob. The dirt road leading back to Hicks' homeplace was holey, maybe too much, Thaddeus thought. When he pulled up, Sarah was out front pulling the last drop of milk out of their cow while Aberdeen was prying the top off the milk can.

"Whatchu want sheriff, we ain't done nothin'," Aberdeen spoke up and said.

Thaddeus looking long in the face, said, "Mr. and Mrs. Hicks, I'm afraid I've got some bad news for you, some real bad news." Aberdeen and Sarah stood there lookin' at Thaddeus who just stood there too, not sure of how to say what he had to say. In all the time he'd been sheriffin' he'd never once had to tell a family their youngin' had been murdered, Negro or not. Killed by this or that way, an accident as such, but never murdered and most especially like young Hattie'd been. "I guess everyone starts this way when the news is this bad, and I don't know of any way to say it so it'd be any easier but your youngin's dead, she's been murdered."

"What you sayin' sheriff?" Aberdeen asked, his throat beginning to choke up. Then without hearing what had happened, Sarah fell to the ground wailing, slamming her fists into the dirt, "Lord have mercy, Lord have mercy," Sarah kept saying over and over again. Aberdeen now leaning over, tears caking in the dust that coated his jowls, having just come in from plowing the back field. "What done happened sheriff?" Aberdeen asked.

"We're just not sure of it all yet, but we think she was strangled," Thaddeus managed to get out.

Sarah seemed to take one last wail, looked up at her husband and the sheriff and then passed on out from the worst heartache she'd ever known.

Aberdeen picked her up and carried her into the homeplace, laying her down on the straw-filled mattress that he had made for them right after he'd helped Frank Brumley, who'd gotten too old just hisself to do the cuttin', get his hay in. "Brum," as he'd been called since he was a boy in those parts, let Aberdeen harvest enough straw for the mattress after he'd stripped off his barley. It'd been the first time he or Sarah'd ever slept on anything other than a hard floor or the dirt on the ground.

Aberdeen was beside himself, trying to make sense of what Thaddeus had said. "Killed? That don't make no sense," he kept saying and shaking his head. "Where's she at?" Aberdeen asked.

"She's at Pinky's, he figurin' on what happened to her so we can get to investigating."

Sarah was beginning to come around now, with her husband sitting beside the bed holding her hand. Thaddeus asked the parents when was the last time they'd laid eyes on their girl.

"She'd gone off to school early, said she was helping Mr. Horn, her teacher, cut out some pretties from a book to hang up in their classroom," Sarah was able to say. Aberdeen added, "We wus just wondering right before you come around what wus takin' her so long comin' on home. She's a good girl, never had one day of trouble from her, she's a good girl."

Thaddeus drove on away, thinking to himself about how to proceed about something he didn't know nothing about. First off he thought about calling in the state police out of Frankfurt, but that could go stirrin' up a hornet's nest that likely didn't need stirred up. Then he thought it best if he caught the one to blame, get them arrested, tried, and executed.

When Thaddeus got back to the station, Linc was waiting for him, wanting to know how it'd gone out at the Hicks. "About as bad as you'd expect it to go," he told him.

"You gotta get to the bottom of this quick like, Thaddeus, words starting to get on around, Boy's already gone spouting off over at the barbershop. Folks ain't gonna be taken kindly to this, even if it was a nigger. Gonna get their bowels in an uproar. You're gonna be looked at real close like, how you handle this, Thaddeus."

Chapter 59

EDWIN ROSSKAM'S FAMILY HAD migrated down from Chicago, back right after the war. His daddy, Beauf, as a boy had suffered under the cruel whip of the plantation Overseer, Boon Polk, of the Estate of Francois Gaurenne, havin' had eighty-three slaves in their day. Even upwards of 1895 they'd still had slaves, and that if they'd get caught tryin' to sneak away goin' through the Devil's Swamp, and even though it was their God-given right, they'd be taken back to the plantation sufferin' the consequences, sometimes even castrating the real troublemakers to take the rascality out of them.

Hetty Lemee, Edwin's wife, now known for more than forty years as Hetty Rosskam, was the offspring of Emile and Delphine Lemee and had been put with the Rosskam family when she was just around two or three after Emile and Delphine had been found runnin' away again from the plantation. They'd been whipped so many times before that Master Gaurenne thought it best, them being unrepentant and incorrigible and all, that they go ahead and be hanged. Master had been about as frustrated as one could be, each and every time whippins and the like didn't do no good. It had been gettin' to the point where the other slaves were beginnin' to lose their respect for their Overseer. Master Gaurenne even took to his diary, writin' that, "The slaves Emile and Delphine Lemee have been lacerated with whips, paddles, and red pepper, and salt rubbed into their mangled flesh, and hot brine, and turpentine poured in their gashes, and being stubborn as they are they left me no course of action but to go ahead and hang them."

Right after the hangin' Master ordered their offspring, Hetty, be brought up by the Rosskams like she was one of their own. Edwin

Rosskam, being the older of the two, took to Hetty, and she took right to him, and they never let go of each other, even after they were finally able to leave the plantation, becoming a lawful husband and wife, and settlin' up just a ways from Hager Hill, east a bit from Paintsville, where other coloreds had put down. Some of the strappin' Negroes even got work in the mines, not so much down in the hole, but up top, where they could be better kept an eye on by the boss man. Edwin and Hetty only were blessed with one offspring. Hetty, who'd almost bled to death bringin' Robert Lewis into the world, figured it'd be best if she did a dousing with a concoction that'd come down to her from her momma that'd come down from her momma. It was being a brew of cocklebur roots mixed with bluestone right after her and Edwin'd had relations.

When Robert Lewis came backwards out of Hetty, he came out slow, and he'd been that way ever since. He'd also come out about as blue as a colored baby could get. And when Edwin saw how dispirited Robert Lewis was not only in his color but also in his vitality, he didn't even bother wipin' him clean, instead puttin' him right away in a pot of water sittin' atop the cook stove and covering it with a sackcloth to warm him up. After a few minutes or so, the blue in the newborn's lips began to drain away, and he began paddlin' his arms around in the pot like'd he was swimmin' inside his momma again. But, no matter, he'd always be one to move slow and think even slower. Good thing was that he was a strong boy, able to toss hay bale after hay bale right atop a tall stack of hay bales all day long, with nary breakin' a sweat. When just about any member of the congregation of the Colored Baptist Church spoke of Robert Lewis they always spoke of him in the highest of regard, and they'd almost add that even though he was slow at catching onto things, he was a hard worker and a good boy. Some of the folks around Paintsville said he had just about the best constitution of any imbecile, especially for a colored boy, they'd ever come upon. Only thing anyone ever got upset with Robert Lewis about was his stealin' of onions. Come late August, folks'd see him out in their fields, sittin' there with brown onion paper blowin' on about his big black head, and him eating those onions like they was the biggest and most delicious apple that any man had ever partaken of. Then, upwards when winter set in, the grocer'd have to run him out of the store, just about every other day, chasing him with a broom to keep him away from the onion bin. And, for some reason or other that Hetty could never figure out, her son also liked to eat butter. Not just on his bread, mind you, but as big a handful of butter as he could scoop out of the churn right after she'd finished whipping up the fermented cream Edwin had just brought over from one of the white neighbor's farm. Edwin went over once or twice a week and helped old lady Beauchamp, whose husband, Wade, died early on, likely from being henpecked by the old hag, who now had to rely on just about every man, colored or white, to help her to tend to the farm. There wasn't no one man who could stand to be in her very presence for more than a couple of days a week.

There wasn't much other than work for Robert Lewis to do but sometimes he'd go down to the railroad tracks outside of town to look for ball bearings that'd been thrown from the wheel casings of the #1 as it passed outta Paintsville on its way to Van Lear. Days there weren't many bearings and others when he'd come home with three or four. Robert Lewis had him a mound of them stacked up out back that Hetty always said looked like what she figured the Tower of Babel must have looked like. Edwin and Hetty had been taught comin' up to read pretty good and Hetty, especially when Robert Lewis was but a boy, had read the Bible to him just about every night. And even though Robert Lewis couldn't himself read, he remembered the stories that his mother devotedly read to him. In her remembering, Hetty couldn't ever recall Robert Lewis having backtalked her.

He was just about as good a boy as the Good Lord had ever blessed a momma and daddy, slow or not.

Chapter 60

THE BOY BOYD RAN the only other filling station in Paintsville, beside Linc's. Folks had been coming to Linc's for about as long as anyone could remember. Linc could tell just from resting his ear against a screwdriver pressed up against a sputtering engine what was making the sputter. The boy Boyd never was able to learn the ins and outs of engines and so he only fixed things that weren't really broken. When a customer pulled up to get gas, the boy Boyd'd be standing there filling them up when he'd see things that he said was wrong that needed to be fixed right away. "Just wouldn't be safe otherwise," he'd say, always insistin' that he take the time to serve his customer even though he had other things to do. He was a crackerjack at seeing how low folks' tires were gettin' on air, especially when he was filling up their tanks. Sometimes when he was pumping gas, tires would just up and go flat, right out of nowhere. "Bad rubber," he'd say. Folks figured it was just good fortune that they were sittin' gettin' filled up when they lost their air. "Good thing you're right here takin' care of me…" was what he heard most. Jacking the car up right then and there, pullin' off the flat, rollin' it into the station, and fixin' it lickety split always added to the day's till.

It got to be so commonplace that the boy Boyd had to be careful the number of flats he racked up in a day. When he'd been a boy he got chased just about every day making his way to school by the same damn hound. For some reason or other the dog just hated the very sight of him. The boy Boyd, having gotten fed up with being bit up, figured out a way to shove a spike through the front part of his boot. One morning when the sun was just starting to melt the dew off the grass, the hound came tearing after him. He turned around, faced off with the mongrel, and caught him right under the chin with the spike, driving it clean up through his jaw and out the top of his snout, with the poor dog crying and trying his best to free himself off the nail. The boy Boyd, laughin' his fool head off, taunting, "Gotcha now, you sonofabitch," shoved his heel on the ground, grabbed the dog by the nape of its neck, and pulled it up off the spike, cocking his foot back to kick the hound again. The dog managed to get away and take off like a bat out of hell, with the spike just grazing his ass, never to bother him again.

When he opened up his filling station, with the help of his momma's money, one of the first things he did was to push a spike through the front of his boot, where he could just about flatten any tire with one swift kick. No one was ever the wiser.

Chapter 61

IT WAS JUST A day or so after young Hattie Hicks'd been found dead that Thaddeus began investigating. He'd had to wait until Pinky'd done and said for sure how the colored girl'd been killed. "Her neck was broken in about a dozen different places," Pinky had said. "The vertebra there that connects right down on top the spine," he said, pointing to the back of his neck with his fingers, "'d just been ripped right away. And the rest of the bones in her neck were just torn apart. Don't know why somebody'd go to the trouble of puttin' a rope around her neck after they'd done and killed her. There ain't no doubt that she was well on her way to Heaven when he did. Must not have been too awful long after she died though, you saw the ligature marks. He'd taken' the rope, wrapped it around her neck, and pulled it tight enough to cut through down through the skin and cause the blood that'd been pooling from her neck being mangled to start seepin' through the trough he made by pulling up on the ligature. But, like I said, she was dead before he'd did that.

"And, well, I've seen many a dead bodies," he continued, "but whoever he was that did what they did to her privates was more like an untamed animal than a human being. It was bad enough what he'd done to her neck, but he tore her insides apart. Hell, she'd a died from blood loss alone, even if he'd hadn't a broke her neck. I can tell you this Thaddeus, you're lookin' for a strong man to be sure, filled with fury and ferment."

Chapter 62

SITTING RIGHT AT THE top of a cut off road atop Hager Hill was Lacy A. Hobb's big house. Matter of fact, it was the biggest house east of Lewisville. Lacy'd done right fine for herself, her Five and Dime being the only Five and Dime within forty near miles or so, sold just about everything a housewife could want, and not only that but the house-wife'd always be met with the friendliest of smiles and helpfulness.

Just about the only time you saw a man frequent Hobbs' Five and Dime was to insist that they stop selling useless this and thats to their wives. "We work hard for every red cent we make and here you are browbeatin' our women into spendin' it as fast as we make it. It just ain't right," they'd say. But, "The worst of it was when there weren't no money to be had and the tight-waisted help with too much red lipstick on, actin' like a livin', breathin', walkin' billboard'd reach under the checkout counter and pull out a wooden box, and just write down the name and the amount of what was being bought and the housewife'd just go on about her day." Then come the end of every month Lacy A. Hobbs'd go back to the backroom and figure interest into the amount *that had been incurred unto her for delaying payment of a rightful debt*, she'd write on each and every bill, the men would complain about. Lacy A. Hobbs said in jest at church one Sunday that she had so many folks obligated to her that she never had to sell another thing as long as she lived. She'd send her boy Boyd out knockin' on doors, if at least the interest on the housewife's indebt-edness weren't paid right the day she said it would be. Housewives would be scramblin' all month to add pennies to the tobacco tins they kept hid behind the bread box just to be able to keep up so Lacy A. Hobbs' boy Boyd didn't make good on his threat to go to their husbands, wantin' to collect what was "rightfully and dutifully" owed to Hobbs' Five and Dime.

When Thaddeus got to the top of Hager Hill that day, he saw the boy Boyd, leanin' against a fence post, drinkin' a nice cold lemonade, and chewin' on Nigger Boys.

"Mornin' Boyd," Thaddeus said, nodding his head.

"What is it you wantin' Constable?" The boy Boyd said, feelin' himself filled with highfalutin rancor.

"Your momma here?" Thaddeus asked.

"You ain't got no cause to be askin' anything about my momma, where she's at or where she's not, Constable."

"I think we should have a discussion Boyd about what you know about Miss Hattie, and I figure Miss Lacy'd want to be here when we have our discussion."

Boyd sat himself upright, rigid as a nail, furrowin' up his eyebrows and said, "What makes you think we're gonna have a discussion about anything, Constable?"

Thaddeus had been figurin' on him actin' just about how he acted, but he had to do his job.

Chapter 63

Death was on his doorstep, he figured. For the most part he felt like a hollow tree. There was no way to tell if he'd kept up with the lies he'd told over his now many long years of service, or those who he'd had a vendetta against, who he'd made pay in one way or the other.

He hadn't had a bloodless shat for months now, which made him even more irritable than a man who'd been thrown butt naked into a patch of stinging nettles. Never far from being plagued by fond memories of when his bowels were working as a man's bowels should, Rudolph Sword brought perdition to each and every man he prosecuted for *any* and *all* crimes that came before him as the Johnson County Attorney, having been elected on the justice enforcing slogan,

*'HE WILL LOOSE THE FAITHFUL LIGHTENING
OF THE TERRIBLE SWIFT SWORD'*

<u>ELECT</u>

RUDOLPH *SWORD* FOR COUNTY ATTORNEY

When he heard about the nigger girl who'd been violated and murdered, Sword figured it'd likely be his last time to send what had to be another nigger who'd done it to his own kind to die in *Old Sparky*. Sword had spent his professional life bringing swift *Lex Talionis* to God fearing folks who'd been wronged one way or another by niggers. He'd made it known long ago that them even being within ten feet of a white man or *especially* a white woman would be met with iron-fisted justice if he or any man in his office was called upon to bring forth charges of an infraction. Sword had been singled out from the bench, over and over, again and again, by Judge Herbert

Van Hoose for dedication and exemplariness to his office. The other two counselors who worked for him, either by respect or fear, often offered a verse from *Psalm 96*: "Declare his glory among the heathen…" when offering up his name about this or that. It was a rare occurrence, when Sword was sittin' under the barber's bib, that he didn't get asked about July 13th, 1928, when seven men were electrocuted, one right after the other, in the space of an hour and fifty-seven minutes.

"Y'all can't want to up and hear 'bout that again," knowing good and well that the men sittin' waitin' for a trim, some havin' heard Sword tell the story what seemed to be a hundred times or more, would start scooting to the edge of their chair, the barber would stop snippin' and some would swear that the ever sleepin' hound dog who was as much a part of the barber shop as the barber would wake up, when Sword slipped his hand up under the barber's bib and pulled out the browned-brittled article from the *Madera Tribune*, that Sword always seemed to have in his pocket, each and every time he came in.

Sword always clenched his lip to one side before he read from the snipping to show his reverence to the decree of a just court. "It was justice at its very best men, justice like I've never seen meted out before, I was just startin' out, mind you, made me want to be a voice for the law, just like Jesus *is* the voice of his Daddy in meting out the law put forth in the Book of all Books, I knew that I had been led to witness the rightful demise of those idolaters of sin personified. You know, boys, I went back and studied what they'd done and how they were brought to justice." And then Sword would take to reading the snippet, always finishing up by adding on his own, "Out of the seven was three niggers, that's *almost* half, Willie Moore, beat the brains out of Anna Eslick with a beer bottle, Clarence McQueen shot another nigger in the back with a shotgun, and James Howard stabbed someone named Lucy Buchner. She was a nigger too.

"When I got to the Castle on the Cumberland, that's what they call the state prison there at Eddyville, it was like I'd been lost and then up and found. The warden, now he was just about the nicest fellow I'd ever met, John B. Chilton was his name, like I said, as good a Christian man you'd ever want to meet, died while he was serving up justice. We became friends, me I was just a young lawyer, wet behind my ears, disgusted by what I was seeing day in and day out and more than half of each and every case I had to prosecute was a nigger, always killin' each other. I told the warden how much I got tired of facing off with some two-bit defense attorney, 'representing *their* rights,' like they had any rights, hell they didn't give one hoot about any niggers' rights any more than I did. But, what Warden Chilton, who'd also sat on the bench before wardening, said to me that right then and there made me the man I am today, he put his arm around my shoulder and like a father teachin' his youngin' how to make it upright in the world said, 'Rudy, each time a nigger comes before you, it don't matter if he's guilty or innocent, your job is to make sure they get the most merciless sentence the court can muster out. And you can't concern yourself with whether or not somethin' comes up indicatin' that truth be told they aren't guilty of that *specific* crime, because it don't matter. Each boy that comes before the court is the good Lord bringing forth an opportunity for justice. And by virtue of when you laid your right hand on the Good Book and swore you'd be that purveyor by overseeing and superintending the coloreds, you were behested with the magisterial responsibility of rightfully subjugating the Negro. When you have the opportunity to put them where they belong, you exercise that responsibility, just as I did with each and every opportunity I had when I was judiciating. They're gonna rape a white woman or kill a white man one day or another, you're just administratin' a comin' redressen sooner rather than later.

"Those words men," Sword said, "those words were what set me free. And, you know, darndest thing, Warden Chilton died exactly one day lacking the one-year anniversary of his proudest moment of presiding over those one right after another executions. They found him deceased in his quarters at the prison just the night before."

Chapter 64

Rudolph Sword never stopped yelling the whole afternoon at Thaddeus, telling him he'd have the effrontedness to be talking to Lacy A. Hobbs' boy Boyd about anything so much as even relating to that dead nigger girl.

Lacy A. Hobbs herself had shown up at Rudolph Sword's office that morning, bright and early, even before opening up Hobbs' Five and Dime, consumed with such discomposure that folks walking along on the sidewalk could hear her letting Rudolph Sword have a piece of her mind. Thaddeus had always had it in for her son, even when he was a youngin', he'd been ridin' him, never having taken a liking to him, thinking the worse. Even insinuating to the Chief Constable before him, that truth be told, the boy Boyd had had something to do with the tragic demise of the girl Gayle. But the constable before him, Emile Savage, took Lacy A. Hobbs up in his arms one night, sittin' down by the bank of the Big Sandy, and told her what his new constable was inquiring about her child. Constable Savage told her right then and there as he was commencing to kiss her mouth that not she nor the boy Boyd should never *ever* answer any questions from anyone about that day. He should say he couldn't remember nothing about the goings-on that day. The Chief Constable had spoken to Mr. Yarborough, who said it seemed fishy to him too, the girl Gayle's head being pushed down in the water bucket that way and all. It wasn't long after that when Mr. Yarborough likely fell backwards while stacking hay bales right onto his pitchfork which he'd appeared to have been negligently left lying on the ground. Lacy A. Hobbs herself found him. Then she rang up Constable Savage, weepily telling him that Mr. Yarborough had the five tines of his pitch fork stickin' right out the front of his chest, the fork'd even popped off the buttons of his overalls, she said. And that was exactly the way Constable Savage found Mr. Yarborough when he arrived, the tines protrudin' out his chest and his drawers havin' fallen down around his ankles from his dungaree buttons being torn right off their stitch. After comfortin' Lacy A. Hobbs in her state of distressedness after having witnessed such a spectacle, Constable Savage declared Mr. Yarborough's death accidental.

It wasn't long after Constable Savage left Mr. Yarborough's that a school bus was rounding a bend on Route 23 when it slammed right into the back of a slow-moving wrecker. The bus driver tried as he might to keep the bus on all fours, but it reared up like an ill-tempered stallion and went skiddin' down an embankment, rollin' upside down and landin' in the torrent of the Levisa Fork. The wrecker driver waded into the swirlin' waters and took hold of twenty-two of the forty-eight youngins that were able to make it out through the busses busted out windshield. They were cut to pieces with shards of glass stickin' in them just about everywhere. Right as he was grabbin' hold of the last little girl the Levisa seemed to get just about as angry as anyone had ever seen it. A swell rose up out of that damn river the likes of which had never been seen before and threw that bus downstream even further than any man could ever hope to reach, drowning the other twenty-six youngins and the bus driver, who'd probably, truth been told, was already dead.

When Constable Savage got to the accident there were two rows of thirteen dead wet children layin' right along the side of the road. Just about every reverend from just about every church was there prayin' for Jesus to take hold of the youngins' hands and lead them personally through the doors of Heaven, makin' their journey easier than their deaths had been.

It'd just been a couple of days before the Levisa took the lives of the youngins that the father of Pentecostalism himself, William Marrion Branham, came through Prestonsburg and offered to save the souls of the lost and wretched, the most vile of the most vile who'd been born of the Serpent Seed and were now rottin' in the Floyd County jail. The good William Marrion Branham said of his own anointment by John the Baptist himself, "As John the Baptist was sent to forerun the first coming of Jesus Christ, so *your*" (William

Marrion Branham liked to emphasize that part) "message will fore-run His second coming." The Rev. William Marrion Branham met more than a dozen prisoners right where the school bus went down the embankment and led them one by one into the great waters, dipped even the biggest of them back, relyin' on the Good Lord to give him strength while beggin' Jesus to save their damned souls. To a man, *to a man*, every soul, *every soul...* was saved. By the time the last head of the last prisoner was immersed into the water the Levisa Fork looked like it was boilin'. William Marrion Branham said he'd never witnessed such salvation before in his entire life. But, for days on end, folks who lived near the Fork said the Levisa looked like it was damned up, not able to go downstream and certainly not able to go upstream.

Right after the last child was pulled out of the Levisa that day, it quieted down. Quietin' to the point where it seemed like time had drifted off to sleep. Mable Dietz, who taught Housekeeping at the schoolhouse where the boys and girls had been headin' to, lived just up the road and heard all the commotion. Standin' there right beside Constable Savage lookin' down at the twenty-six bodies of the boys and girls she taught day in and day out, she just kept shakin' her head back and forth, finally looking up at the Constable, and said, "When we heard back in the holler about those convicts comin' this was to be saved, we all came down and tried to tell the Sheriff he needed to stop what he was goin' to let happen, not knowin' what he was dealin' with and all. Every one of those men who went into the water made the Levisa madder and madder, we tried to tell the Sheriff Jesus weren't savin' those men from *nothin'* no matter what that preacher was sayin'. It was each one of those sinners' pelts of evilness that was being washed off into the Levisa, one right after the other, just fillin' up the Fork with all that balefulness. It ain't no wonder what that poor river up and did."

It also wasn't very long after that that Constable Savage said his goodbyes one mornin' to his wife of twenty-seven years now, liquored himself up, drove about half-way up the road leading to Turkey Knob Cemetery, pulled out the PO8 he'd taken off a dead Kraut, and allowed the rounded tip of the cold blue barrel to warm against his pale temple while squeezing the trigger so slowly that it seemed like he was trying to scare himself to death, right before the firing pin let loose killing him dead. The confoundedness of what he'd done still was alive and well and discussed at the barbershop whenever there weren't more pressing news. He was buried right beside little Jr. McKenzie, who only lived long enough to breath but a few breaths outside of his momma's womb.

Chapter 65

LIKE EVERYONE ELSE ALL over Paintsville, Eleanor heard about the dead colored girl, folks saying this and that, and Boy going around to whoever'd listen tellin' how he'd found Hattie Hicks all covered up in thorny briar patch stalks, "I say, I say," he'd say, "that nigger girl was just lyin' there, dead as dead could be... I say, couldn't see much under the briar patch, not much, but she was fer sure dead. I say, ain't no doubt 'bout that, dead fer sure."

It wasn't long before Spencer Duty, Jr. came knocking at Eleanor's door, saying he'd heard over at the barber shop that Thaddeus had talked to Lacy A. Hobbs' boy Boyd about Hattie Hicks and that Rudolph Sword had raked Thaddeus over the coals for only talking to the boy Boyd, he didn't even close his office door, like it'd a mattered, Spencer Duty, Jr. said. Eleanor sat and listened, thinking that for once it wasn't something she'd have to have a concern about.

Chapter 66

THADDEUS HAD BEEN TOLD in no uncertain terms that the boy Boyd had had nothing to do with the nigger girl's death. Rudolph Sword said also in no uncertain terms that he was tired of reading about niggers thinking they were deserving of the same rights as the white man. Dropping one of his chins to his chest, he shook his thick neck this way and that, saying that he was "severely discomposed" by the Supreme Court's ruling on desegregation and that he had fully supported the good Governor of Arkansas, Orval Faubus, when he stopped those nine colored boys from marching right on into a white high school. But that Goddamn Eisenhower had the audaciousness to order the U.S. Army to intervene and walk those niggers in just like they were as deserving of the same rights as whites. And now, some nigger girl is killed, and Thaddeus goes off half-cocked asking questions of Lacy A. Hobbs' boy Boyd. Before walking hangdogged out of Rudolph Sword's office, Thaddeus had been told he'd better be out finding the nigger who gone off and killed one of his own.

Thaddeus didn't have nothing against the colored around Paintsville. They went their way and he went his. When a Negro was causing problems, it was mostly because they drank too much making their runs back from the stills down in Harlan County. For the most part though they minded their own business.

And Thaddeus had never in his life seen anything like what'd been done to Hattie Hicks, Negro or white.

Chapter 67

IT WAS LATE THAT night when he could be sure that no one else would be pryin' eyed up where Hattie'd been killed that Thaddeus went prowling. Once he winded this way and that he came upon where Boy had found Hattie Hicks. He bent down and shined his Hunter spotlight around until he found the crumpled pack of Nigger Boys. Linc hadn't just kicked it aside with his foot, he'd ground it down into an undergrowth of stingin' wood nettles. Holding the flattened pack in his palm, Thaddeus pointed his spot, reading the Nigger Boy slogan: *Licorice cigarettes of all the sweets so full of joy the best of all is Nigger Boy.* Slipping it into his dungarees, the constable made his way back to his patrol car and drove back into Paintsville.

Chapter 68

Linc found the boy Boyd in the back of his garage nuzzlin' up to Reba McCracken, who'd developed earlier than any fourteen year old had a right to do, causing many a men to act foolish around her scaggy ways, struttin' around like a damn fool she did.

One thing the boy Boyd said for sure was that there was a nigger he knew who was good for taking care of girls who'd gone and gotten themselves knocked-up. When the time came, he'd for sure have to hold Reba McCracken down good while the nigger Effy Boone spread her legs and poured lye soap and turpentine up her cogie. Grandpa Hobbs, who'd come over from Scotland, used to take him aside and tell him all about the pleasures "milking the cogie," and then laugh up a storm as the boy Boyd just stood there lookin' at him, not knowin' this or that in those days about "cogie" anything. The boy Boyd figured Reba McCracken couldn't get any more knocked-up than she was right then when goddamn Linc came pushing his way through the back door interruptin' him, causing his manhood to go and peter out.

"Lincoln Miller," he shouted, "what's you goddamn up an doin' here interruptin' me and Reba McCracken?"

"We are needin' to have us a conversation," Linc said to the boy Boyd.

"Go on get outta here, old man, before I go and take a hammer to you." Just about the time that the boy Boyd was starting to cinch up the pigtailed hemp holding up his drawers, Linc smacked him silly across the back of the head, telling him to get his ass right on outside. "I found yer Nigger Boys up there where they found the dead colored girl," Linc said.

"No mind, I ain't been near there and I sure ain't been near no colored girl," the boy Boyd said back.

"I tried to kick them aside but Thaddeus, I'm for certain, saw me, so I don't know what he's goin' to be up to."

"He's done and been around, up and insinuatin' this and that. I hear Thaddeus was put right in his thinking and told in no uncertain way to find who'd done what'd been done to that nigger girl and leave *me* be and..."

Linc interrupted the boy Boyd, saying, "I've known your momma for just about all my life and you're goin' to have to take care of this, you hear? No matter what you might think, Thaddeus, he's like a dog that can't stop huntin', he ain't goin' to go arrestin' someone that he don't believe is guilty, so you need to take care of this."

Linc looked into the boy Boyd's eyes, thinking there was nothing there to behold, just an endless well of indelible ink.

The boy Boyd, sure not to be out done and not appreciating much being told what to do, went on about his day, but figuring long and hard, until, when his mind was made up, that he had convinced himself that killing Thaddeus was his own good idea. And how Thaddeus should die for the awfulness that he was accusing the boy Boyd of was just as important as him being gotten rid of in the first place.

Chapter 69

Spencer Duty, Jr.'d been raised up right in the church. He could just about quote the Good Book forward and backwards. But, as he became more of a man, he figured that putting food in someone's belly was a sneaky way of tricking the Devil, more so than just offering up this Bible verse or that especially when folks were goin' hungry. Thanksgiving was, for most of the miners around Paintsville and Van Lear, nothing to be thankful for. So it began every year that DUTIES BOOTIES put on a "*Come-as-you-are Thanksgiving Celebration*" with enough turkey and all the fixins that guaranteed nobody'd leave hungry. Folks didn't take pridefully to handouts so if someone wanted to bring something to offer up then so be it, but if there weren't nothing to bring then come they could and partake of one of the best belly-busting meals in all of Johnson County. Spencer Duty, Jr. even got Eleanor cooking and serving up folks.

The boy Boyd loathed Spencer Duty, Jr., thinking him queer, being a man who'd go about touching feet and all. But even more, he hated Eleanor, actin' with no shamefacedness and blaspheming the word of the Lord by smoking, being seen without her sobriety in mind, partaking in Crab Orchard Whiskey, and wearing rouge and like a Jezebel whore painting her lips ruby red. Like the nigger girl Hattie, who he had regularly watched bathing in the river, and whose cheeks he saw dimple when she washed her private parts, the boy Boyd imagined that Eleanor did unspeakable, unclean things to herself when she was unseen. It took the Lord, holding the boy Boyd's head fast, so as not to be able to turn away from the sinfulness when he saw Eleanor strutting the streets, that Jesus would up and burn the boy Boyd's mind with the words of *Revelation*, "*And upon her forehead was a name written, Mystery, Babylon The Great, The Mother Of Harlots And Abominations Of The Earth."*

Unbeknownst to most of the folks around Paintsville, the boy Boyd's uncle by marriage was none other than Rev. George Went Hensley, who taught his nephew just about everything there was to know about snake handlin' and cleansin' oneself of the Evil One. He'd also taught the boy Boyd the importance of delivering yourself up to God almighty when you have committed a sinful deed. The boy Boyd remembered when he was just a youngin' and walkin' down the road, listenin' to Rev. George tell him that somewhere about 1922, when he was doing his best to make ends meet, delivering up folks to the Lord, that he was sentenced to a chain gang for running liquor. But the Rev. George said to the boy Boyd, right before he smacked him across the back of the head to make sure he had his attention, "Sometimes you gotta do what you gotta do and then once you've done it, you gotta throw yourself at the feet of the Lord and beg forgiveness for your doins'." And the boy Boyd took that to heart. Each and every time he up and committed a sin worth beggin' forgiveness for he'd ask Jesus to see his side of why he'd done what he'd done what he did.

The boy Boyd's momma, Lacy A. Hobbs, had been the sister to Rev. George's third wife, who'd up and passed on right after havin' surgery on her goiter. Lacy A. Hobbs remembered rightly pleadin' up and down with Sister Inez to let Rev. George lift her up in Jesus' name and drape a snake around that swelled-up gland while havin' the good Reverend's members of the Church of God with Signs Following pray for her deliverance from the orb of trespasses that was now occupying what was left of her neck. But she steadfastly refused, instead believing that a doctor could cure her of what the Lord Jesus had not, she would say, irratin' the Rev. George. And in that the Rev. George had never learned to read or write and Sister Inez had to read up Bible verses during healing services, the Rev. George always was distrusting of her devoutedness, making sure she read the Word just as it was supposed to be read.

The good Rev. George took a likin' to the boy Boyd shortly after the girl Gayle had up and fell down the well, likely, he thought, havin' being swallowed up by Satan, who Rev. George was convinced lived deep in the darkness, himself makin' *sure* to bless each pale of water that he was ever known to drink once a well bucket broke light. The

Rev. George would account to just about anyone who'd listen, and lots of folks listened regular, that the boy Boyd had the greatest gift for snake handlin' than anyone he'd known other than himself.

The boy Boyd took it mighty hard when in July, 1955, as he was just a ways into manhood, that the Rev. George while preaching a service for folks who were *just* comin' to the Lord and whose faith was being challenged day in and day out by Beelzebub was listening to his newly wifed Sister Sally reading up Luke 10:19, *"Behold, I give unto you the power to tread on serpents and scorpions and over the power of the enemy and nothing by any means shall hurt you."* Member folks were yellin' *"Praise Jesus,"* fillin' up with the Holy Spirit, when Rev. George reached down inside the lard can and grabbed the vile rattler by its neck and jerked him up above his head. Swingin' that soulless reptile this way and that, wrappin' it around his shoulders and kissin' it right on the mouth, while that serpent's tail was rattlin' fearful of Jesus' love that was fillin' up the deserted blacksmith shop where the service was being held. And right as Rev. George uncurled that rattler from around his neck and began lowering it back down into the lard can, he felt it. There was unsettledness in one of the members, his faithfulness was being infirmed by the very presence of a demon. Then, right as Rev. George started to drop the head of the serpent into the can, it struck twice and bit him on the wrist. Rev. George screamed out in agony, his wrist turnin' black as a colored man. All the way up his arm the blackness continued like a slithering plague, and Rev. George screamed through his pain, *"And the LORD sent fiery serpents among the people, and they bit the people; and much people of Israel died."* Sister Sally bent over Rev. George offerin' him confortin'. Right before he lost his consciousness the Rev. George pointed out at the member who just wasn't fortified enough in his faith to keep the Evil one at bay, and in the last words that he would speak on this earth, the Rev. George said, "I forgive you." In that precious moment, the member, on his knees, askin' for forgiveness, tears streamin' down his face knowin' what he'd done, was delivered. Rev. George died the next mornin'. None of his thirteen children by two of his four wives knew he'd even passed on until he'd been well laid to rest at the Mount Olive Cemetery. The boy Boyd wept for the daddy he'd never had when the Rev. George passed on, kissin' Satan's messenger full on the lips, just up an darin' him to strike.

Chapter 70

LINC THREW HIS ARM up at Thaddeus driving by his station heading up early to Turkey Knob, likely looking for moonshiners, Linc figured. Old lady Kreg was sittin' at the pump draped in patience while he checked her oil and water. The old bat had been widowed longer ago than anyone could remember, with most folks wondering if she'd drove poor Mr. Kreg to shoot himself in the head with her ever insistin' and complainin' about this and that, never seemin' to let up. Everyone knew that she'd never at first offer up criticism and seem to be thankful of whoever was doin' what for her, but then when she got to lookin' or thinkin' nothing was ever done right enough.

When Linc finished checkin' her oil he brought around the dip stick and said she was down a quart and he'd better go ahead and add some seeing that she didn't want to end up blowin' a rod. He went into the garage and found an empty oil can, pushed the oil spout down into the already punched hole in the top of the can and came carrying it out, balancing it careful to make it look like it was full and ready to slosh out the top. Linc tipped the spout into the waiting oil hole, lookin' over the engine like he was watching the oil pour right down into the crank case. Mrs. Kreg looked appreciatingly through the crack right there at the bottom of the popped hood and the firewall. In a few minutes Linc took a greasy orange rag from his back pocket, wrapped it around the spout, and lifted it from the hole, making sure to act like he was sure to catch any drippings. Then he pulled up the dip stick again, came around to the car window, and showed Mrs. Kreg that her oil was *now* "Right where it should be. That'll be one dollar for the gas and forty cents for the oil," Linc said. Mrs. Kreg fished out the money from her change purse, nodded her thanks, and drove on her way. Linc sat the empty can on the oil saturated work bench, put the money in the till, and then picked up the phone and made a call. There was an understanding at the other end of the line.

Chapter 71

IT WAS JUST A bit after Thaddeus and Linc had thrown their hands up to each other that Thaddeus turned up toward Turkey Knob, rounding the fork that goes up beyond Turkey Knob Cemetery, where most of the dead and buried go so far back that the plots have sunken and swallowed up the grave markers, leaving it to anybody's guess who's laid where.

There sittin' alongside the road was the boy Boyd, his and his momma's homeplace being just up behind the cemetery if you come in from the backway anyways. Thaddeus saw the boy Boyd's truck being shaded by a hedge apple tree, with so many of the gnarly green orbs smushed up underneath the truck's tires that he figured there were many a good girls who'd gone bad parked up under that tree.

Thaddeus pulled up beside the boy Boyd, stopping his patrol car just shy of the truck's door, and looking out from the passenger window said, "What you doing sittin' out here all alone?" The boy Boyd looked up from his lap, nodded back to Thaddeus, and with that final look and not so much as uttering a word, flung two rattlers through Thaddeus' open car window. Last night he'd pulled them out from under a wood pile. Both sets of fangs struck the constable's neck and face, his hands flying every which way trying his best to pull them off. Screaming in an agony like he'd never known before, Thaddeus' throat began to swell up to where what little breath that was coming into his lungs was from gasping. And then, in the last vision he'd ever know, he saw one of the rattlers arch back its thick triangular head and strike him in the eye, tearing out most of his eyeball with its fangs. His head felt like it was being burned up from the inside out, and in but a few more seconds, with the venom going straight from his eye to his brain, Thaddeus began convulsing and then mercifully died. The boy Boyd looking on, prayed for Jesus to save Thaddeus' soul, and walk him Himself into eternity.

The constable sat all slumped over in his patrol car, the one eye that was still left in his head frozen open looking like it'd been staring straight into hell. The boy Boyd got out of his truck, reached through the police car window, grabbed Satan's Serpents, and wrapped them around his neck, listening to the rattler's rattles, taking the head of one and letting its forked tongue flick his lips.

The boy Boyd walked back to his truck, put the snakes back in the lard can, and drove away, heading over to have a piece of pie at Nellie's Diner just far enough away from where Thaddeus sat stiffinin up.

It was late in the afternoon when Spencer Duty, Jr. just happened to be coming down from the top of Turkey Knob when he saw the patrol car nestled up under a hedge of apple trees off the side of the road. He'd known Thaddeus since they'd been youngins but being a few years older than Spencer Duty, Jr.

Thaddeus was one of the boys who'd benefited from getting his first pair of shoes from Spencer Duty's daddy. He'd always said how appreciative he was, once he figured out how not to walk like a duck. After Thaddeus' daddy'd been crushed between two coupling coal cars, Thaddeus took to coming around DUTIES BOOTIES wanting to talk to Spencer Duty just about every chance he could get. Spencer Duty, Jr., having been raised around feet, came to know the constable pretty good with them taking a liking to each other, and after a while getting just about as close as brothers get.

Spencer Duty, Jr. pulled up alongside the patrol car. His head was slumped over the steering wheel and was all swelled up about as big as a melon, with most of his right eye not even in its socket. Spencer Duty, Jr. couldn't believe what his eyes were saying to him, seeing Thaddeus like this and he couldn't even be sure what'd done this to him. He got back in his truck, feeling about as shaken as a man could feel, and drove as fast as he could, right to the police station, saying how he'd just found Thaddeus. Then he went to Eleanor's, telling her about what he'd seen. Eleanor only knew Thaddeus from him testifying in court, but she also knew he seemed to be a man of integrity where the truth was involved. "He was all slumped over the steering wheel, his head all black. I've never seen nothing like it before," Spencer Duty, Jr. said to Eleanor. Nor was it like anything

Eleanor had ever heard of before. But it didn't seem like it was what might be called a natural death either. "His eye was gone, just a big black hole was left in his head. The rest of his face looked like it'd just been torn apart by something."

Chapter 72

WHEN RUDOLPH SWORD HEARD what'd happened he went out to where Spencer Duty, Jr. had found Thaddeus. There he was looking just like the young shoe salesman said he did, face all swollen up and all. "What likely did this?" Rudolph Sword asked Pinky Jones, who'd been called to figure out what'd gone on. "Any notion what happened here?" Rudolph Sword said in his demanding voice. Beginning to pull Thaddeus out of the patrol car, moving his head this way and that, Pinky looked for Thaddeus' missing eye. "Well, I don't quite know how, but lookin' at his wounds, he was killed by rattlers, and more than one, from the way it looks. And, figuring in my experience, I just can't see this being no accident. Rattlers keep to themselves, one rattler ain't goin' be setting up a nest with another one."

Pinky had Thaddeus loaded up in his hearse. Rudolph Sword announced that he was going to take personal control of the case, getting to the bottom of and making sure who'd ever done this would get the chair.

Chapter 73

ONCE THE CORONER HAD Thaddeus on the table, cleaned him up, and got ready to embalm him, he had a better chance to get a look at what'd happened to him. The wounds were deep and there must have been a dozen bites or so, which was unusual for rattlers, being that when they strike they leave it at that. But the constable had been struck and struck, he was figuring, like they'd come at him, not crawled up from under the seat or the likes, which was the only thing he could reconnoiter. Plus, Pinky took note, he hadn't recalled seeing any signs of snake shit anywhere in the patrol car. If they'd been living there, they'd a shit somewhere abouts.

Thaddeus may have been able to survive one or two strikes, but not so many, and most assuredly not the one that tore the eyeball out of his head. When the viper'd struck his eye, Pinky reckoned, the venom had gone right back into his brain, which was still swollen so bad that when he pushed down on the eye that was left in his head, it squeezed some of Thaddeus' gray matter right through the hole behind where his other eyeball still shoulda been sittin'.

"Damnedest thing I ever saw..." Pinky said out loud to himself.

Chapter 74

ROBERT LEWIS, JUST THAT morning, had happen to have been helping out up top Turkey Knob. Here tell, he'd get paid upwards of fifty cents a day for helping to load up moonshine into the back of cars whose back seats had been cut out so as to pack in more hooch. He was such a strong boy, and not knowing much about much of anything, there weren't much he could say if ever inquired about what he'd been doing here or there about this or that. He'd been meandering his way back down the road when he saw the goin'-ons right as Rudolph Sword was shaking his head in awfulness and watching Pinky pulling Thaddeus out of the patrol car.

Robert Lewis just stood there, looking about as dimwitted as a man can look, Rudolph Sword thought. He could never understand why, when you can tell right when they come out of their mommas, that they were just goin' to be good for nothins, folks just didn't put them in a bag, take them down to the Levisa, and throw them in. It'd be saving folks a lotta trouble later on.

Right when Thaddeus' lifeless boots hit the dirt, Robert Lewis took a bite out of an onion that he'd just tore the skin off of with his teeth, turned, and then went along on his way. As Thaddeus' dragging heels made their first skid marks on the dusty road being lugged toward Pinky's hearse, Rudolph Sword saw the pack of Nigger Boy's fall from Thaddeus' pants pocket. Pinky, not paying attention to any more than not dropping Thaddeus, didn't see Rudolph Sword bend over, pick up the pack, crumple it up, and stare at the back of Robert Lewis as he walked away down the road.

Rudolph Sword thought it'd be best to let things die down for a couple of days, giving him more time to figure on how to go about catching the culprit who'd brought shame to Johnson County, and, when he did catch him, bring fame to himself. Instead of heading on back to his office, he drove up over top of Turkey Knob to do some conversing with the boy Boyd.

Chapter 75

ELEANOR HAD JUST LOCKED her door and pulled the shade down in her office when Spencer Duty, Jr. began tapping on the window. She peaked around the curtain and smiled when she saw him. He told her that last night someone had thrown a rock and smashed a window at DUTIES BOOTIES, and wrote something about '*niggers...*' on the sidewalk in chalk, that'd mostly washed away from the early morning rain.

Suggesting that they get dinner at Nellie's, Eleanor said she was tired of being whispered about just loud enough so she could hear by the other roomers at Wanda C. Music's boarding house, Miss Music's buttermilk biscuits withstanding.

Driving out towards Nellie's, on past the Turkey Knob turn off, they could see that the scuff marks of Thaddeus' dragged heels still hadn't all blown away.

Walking in, all eyes turned toward Eleanor and Spencer Duty, Jr. They slid into one of the yellow upholstered booths toward the back and ordered pork tenderloin hot shots, Spencer Duty, Jr., askin' for extra gravy.

Everyone in the diner seemed to be talking about Thaddeus' death. The people in the booth right behind Eleanor and Spencer Duty Jr. was figuring that being that he died at the mouths of Satan's Serpents that he'd likely not been a good man at all, like folks had all along said, and was instead filled with transgressions and trespasses. One husband, saying to his wife, said he was likely on his way up to Turkey Knob to engage in illicitness when Jesus'd had enough and just stepped back, lettin' the Devil have his due.

Sittin' right beside the lawyer and shoe salesman was Brack Auxier,

Pinky's helper down at Jones and Preston Funeral Home, who now, after being with Pinky so long, upwards of thirty years or thereabouts, did most of the draining and embalming. Pinky did the figuring about what'd killed whoever was layin' dead on the table, then 'Aux"d, as he liked to brag, "Plug um in, drain um out, and fill um back up."

He was remembering for the other folks sitting around when Louisa Ferguson, just barely twenty-one, had been shot four times by Billy Coffey right when joviality had just taken hold of those folks who were enjoying themselves something awful during the Skaggs pie festival, held that year at the Wheeler Schoolhouse. Said it was that Billy Coffey became about as affronted as a man can be when Louisa Ferguson jerked her arm away right as he was about to snag it during a twirl and whirl during the squares and pairs dance, causing him to slip and fall which made three more pairs of dancers go down right along with him. Billy, tryin' his best to get his humiliation off top of him, couldn't no matter how hard he tried get to his feet, and then all the hotfooted stompers began their goddamn sniggering. Bending down and bashful like, Louisa reached her hand out to Billy, then, right as Billy reached back, Louisa pulled her hand away again. Billy, lookin' to recuperate his self-respect, reached under his coat, pulled out a pistol, and shot her twice through the head and twice in the chest.

Using the dead as dead can be Louisa to right himself, Billy got to his feet and took off running about as fast as any man has ever run in his life. No one, with any knowing of Billy Coffey ever in the whole of their lives, said they saw him again.

And even though the constable at the time said he sought out to arrest Billy for what he'd done, standing above lifeless Louisa and hearing how she'd treated poor Billy, he shook his head from side to side figuring just to himself she'd deserved what she'd got. After noddin' that he'd come to an understanding about what'd gone on, the constable left the schoolhouse, looked this way and that, and not seeing Billy figured he was long gone. Wouldn't do much good, other than waste time, to go lookin' for him. The constable figured he'd up and arrest Billy if he ever showed his face around those parts again.

Ethyl came jugging the hot shots in the crotch of her freckled arms and sat down one each in front of Eleanor and Spencer Duty, Jr., almost dropping the bowl of extra gravy precariously balanced on the edge of one of the plates, catching it right at the last minute by pinching the brim of the bowl with her thumb and forefinger, licking off the gravy she'd gotten all the way up to her first knuckle, apologizing all over the place for the mess she'd just about made.

Ethyl's cracked lips rode up so high over her yellow bucked teeth that her thick, rhubarb-colored gums made her look like she was always ready to raise up and whinny. Spencer Duty, Jr., said it was no cause for apologizing and thanked her, pushing the bowl of extra gravy aside with his fork. Eleanor said he could have some of her gravy knowing how much he liked it.

Just about any time snakes came up the boy Boyd's name came up along with them, being known for snake handling and all more than for his filling stationing, but seemingly for some reason, Eleanor nor Spencer Duty, Jr. heard not a word from any of the other tables mentioning the boy Boyd. All the overheard talk was about Thaddeus maybe having gotten what he deserved indeed if rattlers had gotten the best of him. Rattlers weren't an uncommon sight around those parts, slitherin' from under this or that. The back of a shovel usually took care of the threatening snake be it a copperhead, cottonmouth, or rattler. If that didn't take care of it a shotgun did.

Much of the back and forth between Eleanor and Spencer Duty, Jr. was about their mommas and daddies with the young shoe salesman always talking about how Moses hated the Knights more than any man he'd ever heard tell. Eleanor always shook her head in agreement, remembering how Mary Mary was the one who'd always told her of Moses' doing this and that, and when she asked her daddy about what her momma had said, he'd mostly just nod and say that her mother told a better story than he ever could, but to always remember how *no* man was never better than any other. She also saw how Moses never failed to take up the cause of those struggling to just get by, whether he was legislating or lawyering. Eleanor also told her companion how she was growing weary of handling the same kind of case day in and day out and then no matter what she did or how she did it, the court, mostly Judge Herbert Van Hoose, would slap her down every chance he got, believing about women as he did.

Chapter 76

A FEW DAYS AFTER Rudolph Sword had his talk with the boy Boyd, Robert Lewis' father Edwin Rosskam was pushin' the hand plow he'd made from hewing two bent pieces of hickory, a warped tractor rim he'd pounded back to more or less round, and then hammerin' through some nails about every few inches or so. And when he'd figured out how to fit on the head of a broke hoe he had himself a pretty good workin' plow.

It couldn't no how be denied how hot it was that day and Edwin was sweatin' outta just about every pore, wippin' his forehead with his wrist which was likely more wet than his brow. As he stopped right next to the woodshed he heard what sounded like cold teeth chattering in a piss pot. Edwin jerked the spade he always had rope-tied to his plow, given if he hit a soft spot in the earth he could pry his blade out without making his sweat no worse, and looked behind him before taking a step back. There, just to his right, were two rattlers, coiled close to each other with their rattles shakin' this way and that. Edwin spun the shovel around in his hands, lifted it above his head, and slammed the back of the blade onto the heads of the snakes, killing one right off. The other one just didn't want to die, taking three or four more swings before it stopped its threatenin'. Breathin' hard, Edwin stood lookin' down on the head flattened dead rattlers, confused how there'd be two snakes all curled up together, ready to strike. He'd seen plenty of rattlers, killed plenty too, but he ain't never seen two curled up like they was one. He'd had his pants legs rolled up to his knees, so if they'd a hit there wouldn't have been nothin' for them to strike but the bare flesh of his legs. He'd a been a goner, that'd be for sure. Then Edwin's confusion turned to curiosity when he heard a siren coming up the holler road.

The dust was swirling like a dirt devil when Deputy Duffy Deeter skidded the patrol car to a stop, sticking swirled up grit and grim all over Edwin's thick sugary sweat. When the deputy leapt from the patrol car he already had his revolver at the ready. Rudolph Sword flung the door open on the other side, brandishing a double-barrel shotgun. Edwin's bones were now rattling about as much as the vipers he'd just beat to death. "Whats you want up here?" Edwin asked. It was Rudolph Sword who began demanding to know where Robert Lewis was, saying they had a warrant for his arrest. Not even fully sure what that meant, Edwin, just trying to figure on what they'd be wanting with Robert Lewis, said, "Whats you…" when Rudolph Sword swung the butt of the side by side into Edwin's jaw, breaking it so bad that his teeth'd never fit together quite right again. With Edwin still laying on the ground, Deputy Duffy Deeter and Rudolph Sword marched upwards towards the shack, ready to shoot that simple-minded nigger should he come runnin' up on em. When they got to the shack, Deputy Duffy Deeter kicked open the door, tearing it right off its rope hinges. Siting by the cook stove was Robert Lewis, an onion in one hand that he'd likely stolen from some white farmer, and some just churned up butter in the other, just going up into his mouth.

His mother Hetty was hunkered over a wash board scrubbin' up and down on the stains in the rag she used for when she got her womanly blood.

"On your feet, nigger," Rudolph Sword commanded, levelin' the shotgun right about where Robert Lewis' eyes would meet each barrel. Hetty began screamin' nonsense, bein' taken right back to when she heard tell of her granny sayin' how the Master'd when they'd get to punishin' their slaves'd cut off part of their ears or be whippin' em to death, right just as Edwin fell through the door opening, still bleedin' from his mouth with his one good tooth on that side hangin' by its nerve.

Deputy Duffy Deeter came up behind Robert Lewis, lifted his revolver high up over his head, and began pistol whipping him, driving his head down onto the table Edwin had built out of the barn siding that the old lady down the road had said he could have "…just enough of" when he helped her tear down what was left of her outhouse after a big storm.

"If you ain't stupid before nigger, you're gonna be stupid after I'm a done with ya," Deputy Duffy Deeter kept sayin' with each blow to Robert Lewis' now pulpy head. Rudolph Sword had swung his shotgun over at the terrified parents who were as beside themselves as could be, still tryin' to figure why the lawman was beatin' their boy. Hetty kept screamin' that she'd make sure he would never steal another onion again if they'd just leave, "He never meant to do no harm, it's *just* an onion," Hetty kept sayin'. Right before the deputy swung the last blow atop his son's head, Edwin tried to get himself up off the floor by grabbin' what was left of the leather strap where the door'd been. Rudolph Sword knew how strong niggers were said to be so he just about blew off Edwin's right knee, spinning him around what seemed like a half a dozen times. Edwin, grabbing at his knee, screamed in a pain like he'd never known before in his life. Deputy Duffy Deeter hooked his arms under Robert Lewis' shoulders and began dragging him out the door. Hetty, screamin', "Why you takin' my baby for stealin' onions?" Rudolph Sword bent down, grabbed her by her nappy hair, looked into her brown eyes, and hollered, "This ain't about no goddamn *onion*. He's being arrested for killing and raping that nigger girl Hattie Hicks. And I'm personally going to throw the switch on that sideshow freak sonofabitch."

Hetty stared up into Rudolph Sword's eyes not blinking, not screamin', not movin'. He threw her back onto the floor like she was about as disgusting of a thing as he'd ever touched. Deputy Duffy Deeter was just lifting Robert Lewis up into the patrol car, his arms now handcuffed behind his back. When he closed the door he looked back and saw Rudolph Sword wipin' his hand on his pants from where he'd been holding Hetty's hair. Every time he had to touch a nigger, he heard his daddy sayin' how if you touch one too many times, it could be catching. He always remembered that. When he got to the patrol car, Deputy Duffy Deeter was just climbing in behind the wheel. He looked at Rudolph Sword, being right then about as proud as a lawful deputy can be about doin' what he'd done, and said, "Twis the midnight ride of Paul Revere, through the woods and over the fence, I've got a can if you've got ten cents." Rudolph Sword had no idea what Deputy Duffy Deeter was talking about and just ordered him to get Robert Lewis back to the jail before he came back to life.

When they pulled up in front of the police station, the *Paintsville*

Herald photographer was already there, and began taking pictures right as soon as the deputy grabbed Robert Lewis by his feet and dragged him out of the police car onto the pavement. Two other deputies were right there helping to pick him up, take him on into the station, and throw him into a cell. They figured they'd leave him handcuffed for when he began to come back to what little senses he had. And, later on that day, for the first time ever in their history, the *Paintsville Herald* ran a special edition. A headline blazed across the front page,

RUDOLPH'S SWIFT SWORD BRINGS KILLER TO JUSTICE.

Chapter 77

RANDY GABBARD'S MOMMA, DRUSA, had him when she was just about to be able to say she was fourteen. She'd just met an older drifter who'd promised her this and that, delivering up a good nothing of his assurances. But he did manage to get her knocked up, then going off and drifting somewhere else never to be heard from or seen again, probably knocking up someone else along the way. Drusa had a bad lisp from bein' a harelip and always seemed to whistle when she talk-ed, especially hissin' her R's. Folks'd say that they had trouble seeing directly into her eyes because her cheeks were so porky they looked like a squirrel that'd been gathering up nuts for the winter. Her thick snouty nose had pores just about as big as most other folks' nostrils.

Her daddy had named her youngin' Randy when he was born, saying she had no say in too much of anything after the shame she'd brought on a good Christian family and all. Not to mention havin' to bring her up his self after her momma had died of consumption. But she couldn't say 'Randy' without it sounding like she was just about ready to sneeze each and every time she said his name, it was just easier to say 'Boy.'

It'd been pretty much a hand to mouth life so far for Drusa and Boy. Her daddy died after being gut shot by a revenuer while running shine. Took him a few days of writhing up and writhing down in pretty bad pain, even for a hard man. The last thing he said to Drusa was that God was going to retribute her being the tramp she was and bringing that snotty little bastard into the world. Then, as she looked down at the disgust in his eyes for her, Drusa's daddy stiffed out like a dying chicken, twisting up his hammertoed feet like there were joints where there weren't, futilely gasping for just one more breath, likely to grab for Drusa and drag her down to hell with him.

Boy was a about as dumb as a boy could get. Where Robert Lewis'd been born that way, Boy didn't have the gumption to do much of anything, especially any learning. And, truth be told, Robert Lewis was about as helpful and right-minded in his wrong-minded mind as a man could be, even with his being slow and all he'd always made Edwin and Hatty proud, *except* for his stealin' of onions. Boy though would lie about whatever he could lie about to get whatever he could get. So when the boy Boyd called on Drusa and told her that her days of eatin' scraps and livin' in a shack could be done and gone if Boy could get it straight in his head what he'd seen that day when he found that dead nigger girl. Drusa said she'd be working on Boy about being sure about what he'd seen and who'd he'd seen runin' down from the other end of Greasy Crick. The boy Boyd said he'd be mightily obligin' upon Drusa's assurances that Boy would be able to say, "I say, I say…" to a jury of the good men and women of Paintsville who'd insure that Robert Lewis'd get what was deserving to him. Believing in lawabiddedness, the boy Boyd said he was just wanting to make sure that justice was served.

Chapter 78

IT WAS LATER THAT day, once Edwin and Hetty got a way into town, that Eleanor heard the bell above her door dingle and saw two deeply beleaguered folks walk in, look around, trying their best to figure on what had just happened. Hetty had wrapped what was left of Edwin's knee in rags and he was using a 2x4 with a cross piece hammered across the top for a crutch, dragging his leg across the floor. The left side of his face looked like sausage that been ground with too much fat and his tooth was still strung up by its nerve, with a piece of a burlap feed bag rolled up and shoved into the split gum. When Eleanor walked out of her office she couldn't believe the sight she was seeing. Hetty was helping Edwin as much as she could given' her own beat down self. Eleanor reached out and helped Edwin into a chair asking, "What in the goddamn hell happened to you?" Then Eleanor said she'd be right back and ran out the door to DOOTIES BOOTIES telling Spencer Duty, Jr. she needed his help. When they got back, Spencer Duty, Jr. looked at Edwin's leg. There was buck shot peppered just about everywhere and his knee cap was beetling out from its ligament looking like a piece of cracked clay. Eleanor and Spencer Duty, Jr. wanted to take them on over to the hospital but they insisted with as much life as they had left in them that they had to say what had happened and that they needed Eleanor's help. Problem was, Hetty up and said first off, they didn't have nothing. Only their land and they'd give it and their milk cow on over to Eleanor if she'd be willin' to help their son.

Eleanor knew who Robert Lewis was, seeing him sometimes right out her rooming house window, which ran right beside Webb's grocery store. He'd be refiling through the wood-slated produce crates, throwing the withered lettuce aside, a rotten tomato here and there until he found himself a tossed onion that looked good enough to skin and eat. But until this day Eleanor had never heard of him ever causing anyone a lick of trouble. Spencer Duty, Jr. would call on him to help unload a shipment of shoes off the truck during their weekly delivery. He'd always been not only reliable but as honest as anyone he'd ever had do any work for him. Later on when Eleanor talked to Spencer Duty, Jr. about Robert Lewis, he told her that one day he'd seen him walking by right when the delivery truck pulled up. The delivery man had been running COD orders all over town that day and had left his money bag laying on his seat. Spencer Duty, Jr. had happened to see him walking down the street when he called for him to help unload the truck. Well after the truck was unloaded, the driver hopped back in his cab and drove on away. But the money bag with hundreds of dollars in it had somehow fallen out the door. Robert Lewis was carrying the last of the boxes inside to the back room of DUTIES BOOTIES when he eyed it. He came into the stock room, found Spencer Duty, Jr., and handed him the bag, saying, "Mr. Duty, Jr., the shoe man dropped this and drove his truck right over top of it, softenin' up the dollars like mashed taters." There was more money in the bag than Edwin and Hetty had probably ever even seen much less had ever earned and Robert Lewis handed it right over to Spencer Duty, Jr., without giving it a second thought.

In more of an unreflective urge than a well thought out thought, Eleanor said she would help, refusing to take Edwin and Hetty's land or milk cow. Spencer Duty, Jr. went to the back alley and brought around his car to the front of Eleanor's office and took Edwin and Hetty on up to the Paintsville Hospital where Nurse Fannie Blankenship called Dr. Louie C. Hall, as soon as she saw Spencer Duty, Jr., and Hetty coming through the door with Edwin slung between them.

Dr. Louie C. Hall said right away, without taking much time to look over Edwin, that he'd be limping rather than striding for the rest of his life, and that he'd do what he could to put him back together the best he could. Dr. Louie C. Hall'd been back from Korea not for too long now and had to sew this to that of men who'd been blown this way and that by those goddamn Zipperheads, he figured he'd likely do about the same thing to Edwin. Hetty needed some stitches and tending to but her beating hadn't taken nearly the toll on her as Edwin's had on him.

Chapter 79

ELEANOR, AFTER SHE HEARD back from Spencer Duty, Jr., went over to the jail and said she was representing Robert Lewis and demanded to see him. Rudolph Sword and Deputy Duffy Deeter were talking with Brower Stubblefield, who'd won this and that award for upstanding reporting from the *Paintsville Herald*, about how they busted the case wide open with good policing under the guidance all the way by Rudolph Sword himself, who kept belaboring how he'd taken over the case, offering up his expertise in bringing criminals to justice and seeing they got what they deserved for the crimes they'd done.

Rudolph Sword grabbed the young lawyer by the arm and escorted her into Deputy Duffy Deeter's office. "See here Miss. Kitchen, if you are taking this case, just to inform you, it will be the end of you. This boy killed that nigger girl, committed sexual intrusion, and then up and killed Thaddeus when he was getting close to figuring it all out." Eleanor stood with her mouth agape at how ludicrous he sounded. Robert Lewis, she figured, barely had the sense to come out of the rain much less figuring on how to not only cover up the killing of young Hattie Hicks but how to plan and carry out the killing of Thaddeus. When she said this to Rudolph Sword, he looked square into her eyes and said, "Miss Kitchen, I only have to say he did it, I only have to tell folks what they already know, while *you*, Miss Kitchen, have to prove he didn't do it and to convince folks that they don't know what they know." Deputy Duffy Deeter had gone on and dismissed reporter Stubblefield and was leaning up against the door frame, thinking how harlotonian Eleanor looked with her ruby lips and beret cocked down over her left eye.

As Rudolph Sword turned to walk out of the room, he said, "By the way, Miss Kitchen, we also have an eyewitness."

Chapter 80

DEPUTY DUFFY DEETER LED Eleanor back to Robert Lewis' cell. He was laying on a cot, his face caked with dry blood and his eyes glazed over. A look on his face made Eleanor think what little mind he had was in a state of thoroughgoing shambles. She walked over to him and sat beside him on the cot. Clearly he needed to see a doctor from the pistol whipping Deputy Duffy Deeter had inflicted. "Robert Lewis, I'm Eleanor Kitchen, I'm going to be helping you." He looked up at her and through slurred words began apologizing for stealing onions, saying how his momma had always told him to mind his business, but he'd never do it again, he'd never eat another onion, can he go home now? he asked. Eleanor told him no, he wouldn't be going home for a while.

When she came out of the cell, Rudolph Sword informed her that Judge Herbert Van Hoose had ordered that the "Nigger be brought before the court, first thing tomorrow to say whether he was pleading himself to be not guilty or just going to up and admit what he'd done and do the right thing before our God, so when they strap him in the electric chair, Jesus, when He's passin' judgement'd, look more favorably on him than the court had.

"Remember, Miss Kitchen, He reminds His hearers that "... *Judgment is without mercy to one who has shown no mercy.* You don't do what that boy did and not expect retributin' in both this life and the afterlife. I expect after we're done fryin' him, he'll burn in hell for eternity."

As Eleanor walked out the door she knew that Robert Lewis was a man who was already dead, he just didn't know it yet. When she got back to her office Spencer Duty, Jr. was waiting for her. Eleanor was despondent, knowing she had just agreed to, no matter what she did, shepherd a man all the way to the electric chair. There *would be* no goddamn *innocent until proven guilty*, there *would be* no goddamn *fair trial*, there *would be* no goddamn *equal justice for all*. She would be nothing more than an observer who, like a doctor with bad news, didn't say to the patient, "You've got six months to live." No, they just lied and let the patient believe everything was going to be okay. Robert Lewis was being held for a rape and two coldblooded murders and he thought he was sitting in jail for stealing onions.

Chapter 81

Boy was telling the men sitting around over at the barbershop that he "saw it all, I say, I say, saw that nigger runnin' away from Greasy Crick, I say" *and...* that he and his "momma ain't goin' to be goin' hungry no more" and "we'll be a stayin' in a homeplace with a roof that don't leak no more when it rains cats and dogs." Boy said both of those things together, one right after the other, Carl the barber told Spencer Duty, Jr. when he came in to get his little daughter by marriage her first pair of high top walkers havin' married Vergie Honaker not long after her husband'd been beat to death after the Knights had given him fair warning after fair warning for his adulterations. Carl the Barber stepped up right and married the widda, raisin' her child as his very own—he himself being widowed just a few months before, after being married for forty years to the most, "God fearin' woman that'd likely ever walked the face of this earth," he would say, every time her name was mentioned.

Eleanor was confused, what did that have to do with anything about Boy being *the* witness, as Rudolph Sword had threatened more than said? Bobby Maynard had been with Boy when they found Hattie Hicks but she knew he could only grunt and point. Eleanor sat, trying to conjure up how Robert Lewis could ever have figured out how to kill the Hicks girl, cover up what he did, and then kill Thaddeus on top of that to keep him from finding out what he'd done, *let alone with snakes*. Not only didn't he have that kind of ability to reason out how to do what, when and where, but it would require being conniving and Robert Lewis was *not* conniving. Hell, he didn't even try and hide when he was stealing onions, he'd just sit out in the middle of a field, pick um, peel um and eat um. It wouldn't even dawn on him to try and hide what he was doing.

Chapter 82

THE BOY BOYD RAISED the thick-bodied timber rattler over his head, declaring to those in his furtive congregation of followers that the fear of death should be no barrier to their faith in the Lord Jesus Christ, to protect them from the serpent's fangs or in drinking the strychnine he was boiling up with a blow torch. Miss J, as she was known in the congregation, as each member only went by an initial, and if they saw each other outside of the sacred service it was forbidden to speak of the goings-on or suffer the consequences of violatin' the boy Boyd's direct transmissions from God himself, and draining away the power of the Lord's shield, makin' every member and their family powerless to Beelzebub, Miss J, who some would whisper was Lacy A. Hobbs herself but none would ever say for certain, was sittin' against the wall, toing and froing, clenched in Jesus' furor when across her lips came the gift of tongues, "*Shurumo te mote Cimbale. Ilunu teme tele telunu. Onstomo te ongorolo. Sinkete ontomo. Isa bulu, bulu, bulu. Ecemete compo tete. Olu mete compo. Lete me lu. Sine mete compote. Este mute, pute. Ompe rete keta. Onseling erne ombo lu mu. Outeme mo, mo, mo. Ebedebede tinketo. Imbe, Imbe, Imbe,*" and, through Miss J's pencil, the Great Spirit wrote on the wall.

The boy Boyd unrolled his tongue from his mouth meeting the two tines of the fork of the rattler's in that space where death either lives or dies. And, in that he screamed, "*When the Holy Ghost descended upon the apostles, there appeared unto them cloven tongues of fire, and it sat upon each of them…*" And from the congregating came, "Praise Jesus, Praise Jesus," over and over, again and again. And then Miss J fell to the floor and was consumed by the Holy Ghost, as the members encircled her, laying their hands on her body hoping to be burned by the fire of the Lord. And finally Miss J began calming, her limbs now limp, her lips blessedly worn thin from God twistin' around in her mouth and explodin' in words not meant for understandin' but for bein' consumed by their power.

The boy Boyd encircled the serpent around his neck and began prayin' for the heathen nigger who'd killed the little colored girl and done things to her that were so unspeakable that it proved that he was so consumed by the Devil Himself that the only thing left was to rid this world of his earthliness.

A bowing of heads, a raising of hands, a swayin' of bodies in unison as the boy Boyd called Mr. M forth to drink of the boiled poison. And in that moment of the testing of his faith under the shroud of Jesus Mr. M was taken over by the collywobbles and stormed toward the barn door. His wife Miss. P suffered overwhelming mortification at Mr. M's bringin' more shame to their family than ever thought possible. And in that moment of torment Miss. P ran in the opposite direction toward the boy Boyd, took the tin cup of blistering strychnine, and began pouring it down her throat. Miss. P immediately began screaming and threw herself onto the floor convulsing, froth oozing from her mouth like a rabid dog, her eyes rollin' back in her head while tryin' her best to get a full breath of air through her constricting throat and into her rupturing lungs. Mr. M, hearing Miss. P screamin' through her gurglin', came runnin' back through the door and took her in his arms one last time before her body twisted up in a way a body weren't meant to twist, and then mercifully dying.

After a few minutes of holding Miss. P, Mr. M lowered her to the dusty floor feeling his arms burning from the poisoned foamy spittle still flowing from the dead woman's burned swollen mouth. The boy Boyd, realizing that her faith had not been strong enough to ward off the effects of the strychnine, ordered each and every member of his following to cast aside the woman in her failin' of faith and so ordered Mr. M and his cowardiceness to take up Miss. P's body and get on out of that Holy place, *never* speakin' of what had happened that day, now or in any other time.

Mr. M saw it as a curse that'd follow his family for generations to come. And, further speaking, to make sure that the slow-eyed nigger got what was assuredly coming to him, the boy Boyd told each member of his congregation to seek out the good, tried, and true Rudolph Sword and volunteer themselves up for jury duty. Miss. J, now properly propped against the wall and having witnessed the goings-on, screamed, "Hallelujah."

Chapter 83

RUDOLPH SWORD AND THE boy Boyd were pushing back the hanging branches of a deep-veined willow that'd likely been witness to coloreds being strung up for this or that should have known betters in the hackberry that'd stood side by side now for a hundred or more years or so. Deputy Duffy Deeter, Rudolph Sword was tellin' the boy Boyd, had just last night gotten Robert Lewis to confess that he'd up and killed the Hicks girl and Thaddeus. The nigger'd even told how he'd done it, spyin' on the Hicks girl being back there by Greasy Crick, being unclothed an all. He just couldn't take it no more, lost what little mind he had, and that was it.

Thaddeus'd done figured it all out, Robert Lewis had said to have said to Deputy Duffy Deeter, and on that Rudolph Sword reached into his pocket and handed the boy Boyd the crumpled up pack of Nigger Boy's, not saying so much of a word, which the Boy Boyd then tossed into the smoke pit, causing an arc of yellow and red to burst upward toward the Heavens and then just as quickly vanish.

Rudolph Sword didn't go on and say how Robert Lewis had said how he knew Thaddeus'd figured it all out, but... that could be figured out itself when they had his murder trial. But again, his confession'd been written down "word for word," so as to be able to be sure the jury knew exactly what he'd said of his own free will.

Deputy Duffy Deeter, being the hound dog that he was, had gone back to Edwin and Hetty's and gathered up those two rattlers that Edwin had killed with his shovel, never explaining how he knew they were there in the first place. Rudolph Sword said he'd be introducing those as evidence against Robert Lewis who right about now was at the Paintsville Hospital getting the fingers of both hands taped up having all been broken when he started resisting during his interrogation. His nose needed to be fixed too after he'd broke it when he slipped and fell face first onto the concrete floor. But, Rudolph Sword said, it weren't really necessary to do much fixin' up of a man that was going to be "*barbequed*," adducing, right at that very moment, his most *favorite* story "Want to See an Execution?" that had appeared in the true crime magazine *Front Page Detective* where that rascal reporter, Allen Rankin, had wrote about for the first time ever, "barbecuing" four sonsabitches, who like Robert Lewis were rapists and murderers, deserving of being "fried to a crisp," Rudolph Sword would add from there on out whenever he'd go on and on recounting the *Front Page Detective* story to anybody whose ear he could bend into listening.

Chapter 84

ROBERT LEWIS, HIS BROKEN fingers wrapped and still having dried blood around his mouth and nose, having not been cleaned up by the nurses at the Paintsville Hospital, the nurses not wanting to touch him anymore than they had to, plus anyone who'd do what he did wasn't deserving of being fixed up much less healed up, and so he sat rocking back and forth on the bed that the deputies had somehow fastened down to the floor with horseshoe nails, figuring if they didn't, Robert Lewis, being just barely up from an animal and all, 'd try an kill them with the legs he'd end up breaking off the bedframe.

But the inmate had barely said a word, mostly asking if he could go on home and promising over and over again that he'd never steel another onion. Deputy Duffy Deeter would sometimes go back and taunt him, telling him how he was going to die for killing the little nigger girl and then up and killin' poor Thaddeus too, one of their own, Deputy Duffy Deeter would add. Robert Lewis would sometimes begin crying, saying he'd never done nothin' to nobody. Then Deputy Duffy Deeter would remind him how he'd confessed to what he done and how now he was going to die for not just breaking the most important of the Ten Commandments, but he'd broke it so bad that God Himself was gonna personally be sendin' him straight down to burn in hell. Robert Lewis didn't know how to be as scared as he was, never having faced the prospect of meeting God Himself not to mention having God being so mad at him. He also didn't remember what he'd said, not having had any sleep and nothing to eat as Deputy Duffy Deeter and a couple of other deputies'd been beating him with their fists and stomping him the back of the head when they'd knock him onto the floor. One of the deputies, much later in his life, and a few weeks before he died from the voluminous lungs, would say how he proud he was of the night when they'd gotten that colored boy to confess.

It was about as painful a sight as one could imagine watching, when the deputy was remembering, once a strong enforcer of the law now not even being able to walk to take a piss, laughing on as best he could through his awful wheezing and then hocking up a bolus of red stippled yellow phlegm, as he told his three grandboys one last time how he'd beat the nigger up the side of the head with his leather sap, held him down on the cell floor while Deputy Duffy Deeter, who he'd then say was about the best lawman as there ever was, ground his boot onto Robert Lewis' fingers, crushing them one by one until he finally confessed for what he'd done.

"Hell," the deputy said. "That boy's nose got broke three ways from Sunday. Every time the Duff would crack one of his fingers, and you could hear um breakin' right at the joints, that nigger'd scream, raise his head as best he could and then the Duff'd slam his face right back down onto the cement floor. The sonofabitch didn't even have enough sense to turn his head, hell he done went and broke his *own* goddam nose, just goes to show you how stupid he was."

It wasn't long after that, when the deputy was sitting on the toilet, that he succumbed to his heart up and dying on him. His poor wife, Mildred, smellin' something burnin' from under the door and not hearing his never endin' croakin', went on in and found him sitting on the pot, his body leaned against the hissin' radiator that'd been building up steam to keep the toilet from freezing up, the bathroom being built just off the back of the house and all. The deputy's belly, which had gotten so big from enjoying Mildred's chicken and dumplings all those years, had flopped over against the heat pipes just about settin' him ablaze. Seeing the scorch marks when she pulled him onto the floor off the toilet, Mildred believed that the Devil, for some reason unbeknownst to her, had marked her husband for perdition, and after being together for more than forty-seven years, she wouldn't go near his body from that very second until they lowered him into the ground three days later. Never telling another living soul, but especially their God-fearing children, about her suspicions. In the end it was the children who were stymied when their mother and devoted wife of their father chose to be buried up over a hill, far away from her husband.

Chapter 85

ELEANOR HAD MET WITH Edwin and Hetty, the parents of her client, trying as best she could to find out if their son had acted unusual around the time that Hattie Hicks had been murdered or when Thaddeus had been killed by the vipers. They told her that they were about as hampered in their figurin' as anyone could be about their son's being accused of doing anything like they were saying he did. He had never been a bad boy, always helpin' out whenever he could, even with him being real slow and all. Edwin spoke up and said how strong Robert Lewis was, being able to swing a hay bale right up over his head. What about the snakes? Eleanor asked. Where'd they come from? Edwin sat and for a moment figured, but couldn't for sure say, only that they'd just slithered out from under the wood shed, though he'd never ever seen two rattlers being coiled up side by side like that.

Like Eleanor knew, rattlers weren't uncommon around those parts, showing up here and there but this was like nature'd turned itself inside out. And there was *nothing*, *nothing* that made any sense about Robert Lewis killing Thaddeus. If, Eleanor thought, he had killed the Hicks girl, he'd a been watching her at Greasy Crick, and like Rudolph Sword was accusing, being retarded, he just couldn't help himself and attacked her not meaning to kill her, then things just went bad, she started screaming, Robert Lewis panicked, started choking her to get her to stop, and not having all of his wits about him, and being as strong as he was, squeezed her neck so hard it not only cut off her air but also broke it. But. Thaddeus. The snakes. Clearly, Robert Lewis was not guilty!

Chapter 86

EACH TIME SHE TALKED with Robert Lewis, it was always the same, he thought he was in jail for stealing onions, and he'd never do it again, and he wanted to go home. He'd be a good boy, he'd say. He also said he knew nothing about the Hicks girls, hell he didn't even know her by name, only that he remembered sometimes, he would say, seeing her walking here or there. But Hattie, like most other folks, didn't pay much attention to him when she'd see him, some folks would say he was like a stray dog that was always around here and there so much that nobody took any notice of him.

How could the police have gotten this *so* wrong? The only thing that Rudolph Sword would say for sure was that they had an eye witness and she knew it was Boy from the talk going on over at the barber shop.

Eleanor asked Spencer Duty, Jr. to come with her up to Drusa Gabbard's to see if she could talk with Boy herself. Drusa had built her a shack along the bank of the Big Sandy, right where Rabbit Hash and Monkey's Eye Hollers marry up against each other. Monkey's Eye was known for being just about the best place for winter goose hunting in all of those parts, and even with her thick snout nose throwing off her sighting, Drusa had figured how to flatten her right nostril against the stock of her shotgun, take aim at a good fat goose, and get supper for a week or so, for her and Boy. When winter wasn't upon them, Drusa would make a big pot of muskrat stew or catch a fish or two.

It took a bit to get back up into the junction of the hollers. Eleanor and Spencer Duty, Jr. found Drusa bent over a fire pit, dryin' goose breasts shot that mornin'. Just right about when Eleanor called out to her, Drusa picked up her shotgun and squeezed the trigger, and in those hair's breadth moments, Spencer Duty, Jr. spun himself around in front of Eleanor and took a full load of birdshot in his backside. He would later would say that it felt like his pants were on fire from the burning pellets that had lodge in the cheeks of his bottom.

Eleanor screamed at Drusa, trying to make clear they meant her no harm, they just wanted to talk to Boy, and just about the time that Drusa was cocking the other hammer, the boy Boyd came out from behind the shack wondering what the goddamn hell all the commotion was about. Upon seeing Eleanor and Spencer Duty, Jr., who was scootin' around on the ground, trying to cool his behind, he told them to get on outta there before he took the shotgun and loaded it up with shot that'd blow the shoe saleman's ass clean off next time.

For the life of her, Eleanor couldn't figure on why the boy Boyd was up there with Drusa, much less why he'd be threatening them.

She'd seen the Boy Boyd here and there, but had no remembrance of ever so much hearing his voice, which she thought sounded squeaky, like it just wasn't greased enough to smooth up the words as they came up out of his throat. Spencer Duty, Jr. picked himself up, walking half bent, his hands on his knees to keep upright. Drusa was now walkin' towards Eleanor with her shotgun resting on one of the cliffs of her hips. "Go on now, get on outta her, go on," Drusa said.

"Please, we just want to talk with your boy Boy," Eleanor pleaded. The boy Boyd came up beside Drusa and said they'd better be on their way before their trouble got worse than it was. There wasn't going to be anything that'd be done here today, Spencer Duty, Jr. said, as Eleanor lifted his arm over her shoulder, limping him on down the hill. As they crested around a bend right before their feet made level land, it came to Eleanor that Spencer Duty, Jr. had put himself between her and Drusa's shotgun. He could just as likely have been shot to death than not, but he didn't hesitate in making himself Drusa's target.

Chapter 87

WHEN THE BOY BOYD had heard Drusa's shotgun he'd told Boy to crawl under the straw bed and stay put. There wasn't much to haul down the mountain being they didn't have much to begin with. Drusa had just killed a goose fattened up for winter so she was *insistin'* on dryin' it before making their way down anyways. Boy's prize possession was his leather pouch he'd stitched up for his slingshot that he'd used to kill nightjars sittin' quiet on branches, restin' up during the day. Boy'd see them there, eyes closed, their long wings catchin' a bit of an upturn as a breeze'd swirl through the branches of the chestnut oaks.

He'd get him a bead on a nightjar with his right eye perched in the crotch of the V of his slingshot, then Boy'd stretch the rubber back as far as his arms would let him, feelin' the most perfectly rounded rock he coulda ever a found pushin' back from the leather pocket against his fingertips, "steady now Boy," he'd say to himself, and then let the sling snap, and before the rubber'd even lost all its tension the nightjar's neck would break as that most perfectly rounded rock collided with the delicate scruff shrouded by soft downy furled feathers, fallin' off the thin branch onto a bed of sun-warmed Autumn colored leaves. Boy'd then go lookin' for another nightjar and then another and then another after that and sometimes even another. Then he'd go on over to Carl the barber carryin' a box filled with nightjars, showin' off his prowess with a slingshot. Homer Hare, havin' about as little sense as a man can have, always seemed to be sweeping up hair for Carl, who day in and day would say that the only thing "Homer Hare is in fact good for *is* sweepin' up hair." And every time Boy'd bring in a box of limp-necked nightjars, Homer'd get stuttern' so bad that his mouth made his arms stutter right along with it, which in fact made him unable to do what Carl'd always say was the only thing he was good for in the first place. Even with some of the most prominent men of Johnson County regularly occupying a chair waitin' or not for a 'trim me up,' discussin' the these and thats of the this and those, they could never fully figure why Homer Hare got so worked up by a box of dead birds, leaving it as one of those mysteries that every town has to reckon with.

It was that very night that Drusa and Boy'd been moved by the boy Boyd into a real homeplace, just up over the ridge tucked away under the canopy of a dense pine forest. Their new dwellin' place, small though it was, would be dry being protected by the towering trees, had a cook stove that when she was fixin' up this or that'd keep them warm and would be the first ever roof over her head, even being when she was a youngin' where she wouldn't have to crouch in a corner so's not to get wet on a stormy night or flecked with pounding snow finding its way through the same holes mice'd use gettin' in an then eatin' what little food they had scrounged up for a supper. The boy Boyd'd done and kept his word so far, promising Drusa to forever after take care of her if Boy'd do the right thing and say he'd done seen Robert Lewis runnin' away from where Hattie Hicks'd been done unmentionable things to. When the boy Boyd sat Boy down on a lightning-struck stump right before he began keeping his word, he asked Boy what he'd say when Mr. Rudolph Sword asked him what he'd seen the day when he found the little colored girl.

"I say, I say, I'll say like momma said I should say, that that nigger sittin' right yonder over there," the boy Boyd telling him it'd be important to point towards Robert Lewis, who'd be sittin' at a table, likely handcuffed to a chair, likely being the only nigger in the courtroom who'd be handcuffed, Boy'd have no trouble figuring out who he was. Then he went on, "I say, I say, I'll keep sayin' he took off like a cat with a fire up his ass, when he'd seen that I'd seen him squattin' down over that dead colored girl, I say.

"I say, I say, I figured he'd done been takin' him a crap but sure enuf right cheer was that dead nigger girl, an she was sure enuf dead as dead could be, bein' swelled up and all like a pawpaw that'd been layin' on the ground too long with no one comin' along and eatin' it, I say.

"I say, I say, too she was missing her knickers, I'll say." And, in the end, the boy Boyd was pleased that Boy was in fact being a good boy, saying just what he'd been told to say. As a matter of fact, since Boy was the star witness, Rudolph Sword would be helping him along too, making sure that when Eleanor questioned him that he'd have answers about what to say, but mostly if he just kept repeating that he saw Robert Lewis over top of the dead girl, that would be for sure enough for the jury.

Chapter 88

SPENCER DUTY, JR.'S BEHIND looked like it'd come down with a case of the chicken pox. Each pellet was setting his butt ablaze. Being as humiliated as any man had ever been, he up and refused to go on over to the hospital to drop his drawers to have *each* and *every* buckshot plucked *from* his butt as he knew had to be done.

He had laid in the back seat on his belly all the way back from the brow of Rabbit Hash and Monkey's Eye Hollers. Eleanor pulled up in the alley behind her office so they could go in the back way, making him flinch with each limp not being so conspicuous. "I have to do this and you know it," she implored him. "It's either I do it or they have to do it at the hospital, that's likely old shot that Drusa has cut out of the squirrels she's killed, it's not going to take long for those to get infected!"

Eleanor went over to the Big Sandy Drug Store and bought a bottle of hydrogen peroxide while Spencer Duty, Jr. cleared off her desk. When she came back she made sure all of the blinds were closed tight and all but her desk light was on. He had never been unclothed in front of a woman. Even in college he had been shy, and now a woman, whom he was privately in love with, but had dared not say, was going to be unceremoniously digging buckshot out of his naked hind end.

It so happened that Eleanor just yesterday had bought herself a new La Cross manicure set at Hobbs' Five and Dime, which she had put into her center desk drawer. "Take your pants down and stretch out across the desk," she said. Spencer Duty, Jr. dutifully turned away from her, lowered his pants and boxer shorts, and stretched out on the desk.

Eleanor remembered being a young girl in Butte, when a dog

had hobbled into her yard with his hind end peppered with .410 birdshot. Moses had said it'd do her good, never knowing what life might present to you, to help him get the pellets out of the dog's butt. Her daddy'd held the canine, wrapping a piece of cloth around its snout, while Eleanor pulled back the fur and grabbed each ball from the hound's behind with a pair of her momma's tweezers. Fortunately, she thought Spencer Duty, Jr. didn't have fur on his butt. "Grip the sides of the desk," she directed. He grabbed the side of the desk and locked his jaw. Eleanor counted thirteen welts, most of the pellets were for the most part sitting right atop the boils beginning to fester up; some were more deeply embedded. Doing the worse first, Eleanor took the cuticle tool and pressed it against the side of the welt, pushing down and pulling back at the same time, opening the tiny crater, exposing the shot. Spencer Duty, Jr. felt tears well up in his eyes when Eleanor set the tip of the tweezers against the top of the ball and then, as gently as she could press underneath the shot with the cuticle tool, lifting the ball in between the tines of the tweezers. When the rim of the pus-filled bursa let go of the lead, he felt the air rush from his lungs and his hands release against the sides of the desk. Each pellet was silenced as Eleanor dropped them one-by-one onto the smoked butts of her last day's cigarettes. After the thirteenth pellet was extracted, Eleanor doused each empty pustule with peroxide, feeling comforted as it foamed out any infection that may have started to set up.

"I feel so humiliated," Spencer Duty, Jr. softly said.

Leaning down, she brushed his sweat-matted hair, looked into his eyes, and said tenderly, "You saved my life. If you hadn't jumped in front of me I'd be using my guts for garters. You didn't even hesitate."

Chapter 89

ROBERT LEWIS PACED. BACK and forth to nowhere, day in and day out, waiting for he didn't know or understand what. Eleanor went to see him most every day, trying to help him understand why he was in jail and what the police were saying that he had done. But it was like some foreigner came to you every day and tried to make you understand what they were saying even though you didn't speak a lone word of their language.

When Eleanor would talk about the police saying that Robert Lewis had killed Hattie Hicks, he would just stare at her with no more recognition of what she was saying than not. She could get nowhere.

Rudolph Sword was giving interviews every week to Brower Stubblefield, keeping him up on the investigation, saying without any doubt that they "had their man" and folks had no reason to be concerned for their safety. Mostly that would be the headlines in the *Paintsville Herald* in one form or another every week. Brower Stubblefield even took pictures of Rudolph Sword with his suit coat pulled back over the ivory gripped butt of his Detective Special, and even though he wasn't a sworn detective, he always carried his revolver in a tipped forward quick draw holster, wanting everyone to know that it was *he* who was protecting them from dangerous criminal elements that may want to do them harm, he especially wanted them to know at voting time. He also said Robert Lewis'd get what was coming to him. He'd see to it!

There was no physical evidence, nothing that the accused man had *ever* done would indicate that he'd have been capable of something like this *and* he was retarded. But Rudolph Sword was going to say that because he *was* retarded and was known to be seen here and there stealin' onions *and* was further known to wander about, that a man like this was capable of anything and with him being witnessed and all leaving the scene of the crime that he was *surely* guilty, not to mention *that* fact, "ladies and gentlemen, yes ladies and gentlemen, not to mention *that* fact." Apologizing to the court about his language before he'd say it, Rudolph Sword'd say, "… it don't matter for a *tinker's dam* ladies and gentlemen that there weren't any witnesses to Robert Lewis Rosskam killing constable Thaddeus Yates. It *don't* matter one bit, but what *does* matter is that," and on that, Rudolph Sword would hold forth the two dead rattlers that Deputy Duffy Deeter had had the good sense to collect, and present them to the jury as evidence of the accused man's "heathenistic ways." As she envisaged Rudolph Sword's chicanery, Eleanor imagined the jury nodding their heads in agreement while right side by side wanting to take her client out and hang him right then and there.

Eleanor couldn't figure why the boy Boyd'd be helping out Drusa and her boy Boy, not to mention them taking a pot shot at her and Spencer Duty, Jr. The boy Boyd was known abouts as a despicable character, not doing nothin' for no one unless there was something in it for him. And now she was hearing that he wasn't tending too much to his filling station, folks sayin' they'd be pullin' in and finding a 'CLOSED' sign hangin' on the door.

Spencer Duty, Jr. had for the longest time heard about the boy Boyd being a preacher of a snake-handling church and that Lacy A. Hobbs herself too had been reared up in the church. But whenever it was mentioned amongst folks standing around just about everybody'd get real quiet with someone always changing the subject onto something else, understanding that the boy Boyd wasn't someone whose ire one wanted to stir. Not that long ago, as a matter of fact just a couple of days ago now, Spencer Duty, Jr.'d heard about Millard Burton, who ran the ticket office over at the bus station. His wife Polly, having been showing no signs of being ill, just up and died, Millard had said, but Pinky Jones had been heard sayin' that her mouth and throat were so burned up it looked like she'd been drinking lye. Millard had decided that it be better if they had a closed casket, just sayin' Polly'd hadn't wanted anyone to be starin' at her when her time came to move on. But Pinky'd said that when he asked Millard about her mouth he'd been told just to mind his own damn business, Pinky said he'd told

Millard that he was a full-fledged graduate of the Cincinnati College of Embalming and that he'd seen just about every kind of way
someone can die and that further he'd *swear* that Polly'd drank lye
or some other kind of poison that'd burned her mouth up. Millard,
getting about as irate as a man can get and still keep his wits about
him, had gone on to say said that the reason Polly had died was because her faith in the Lord Jesus Christ had been feeble and that she
had to bear the sufferin' of the spurnin' of her devotedness to Jesus
Christ and because of her failin' faith she had brought shame on her
family ever after. So, "… Go on now and close her on up," Millard
ordered, and Pinky gently lifted Polly's stiff neck, removed the satin
pillow from under her head, lay her back down, lowered the lid, and
twisted the Crane and Breed Ever-Seal bronze casket key locking
Polly up in a box of forever darkness.

Chapter 90

THERE WASN'T MUCH TIME for Eleanor to prepare for trial. Judge Herbert Van Hoose had said, over the young lawyer's many objections, that the evidence was clear in this case and it was nonsense to go on delaying what he expected the inevitable to be. It was just eating up the court's time and he had other things he wanted to do being that he was getting up in years and all, "Do you understand Miss Kitchen?" he would say. "You are *still* a 'Misses' ain't that right?" Judge Herbert Van Hoose would *say* while acting like he was asking. "I don't understand, Miss Kitchen," he would then further pontificate, "women are up and taking the places of men in law schools, taking that place takes away a man's ability to provide for his family and... women are even gettin' admitted more and more into medical schools. Can you imagine being looked after by a woman who calls herself a doctor?" Eleanor would look up at the Bench with such incredulity that it felt like she was being gut punched over and over again.

Rudolph Sword told the boy Boyd that he thought the trial would last a week or so, with him taking up most of the time and that Judge Herbert Van Hoose would likely overrule just about any objection that Eleanor may bring up, but that he wanted to make sure that there was no room for appeal, so he was going to bring on this and that witness who'd testify about Robert Lewis' moral turpitude, sneakin' around stealin' their onions not to mention callin' Oliver Webb to testify about his stealin' out of *his* trash behind *his* hard-earned grocery store, he'll be sure and say in *no* uncertain terms how much of a pest he was, and bein' that Robert Lewis was about as black as the ace of spades he'd sometimes disappear into the shadows if it was around sundown when he was doin' his stealin' upsettin' Mr. Webb or one of his clerks. Rudolph Sword said he expected Eleanor to stand up and object, saying over and over again, "…He was taking onions out of the *trash,* this doesn't make him a thief and certainly *not* a murderer!" Judge Herbert Van Hoose would most certainly have to censure Eleanor on those occasions for her agitating ways *clearly* attempting to cause discomposure to the members of the jury.

The boy Boyd reassured Rudolph Sword that Boy'd be sayin' what need to be said to make sure that nigger'd be found guilty. Rudolph Sword was pleased to say that members of the boy Boyd's church had volunteered the time away from their farms or mining to ensure that a *fair* and *just* verdict would be rendered, once the irrefutable evidence of the nigger's culpability had been presented.

Shortly after Rudolph Sword had departed the boy Boyd's Drusa made her way down the hill carryin' a pot of squirrel stew. She had no memories of *ever* in her life havin' had to do so little to have been able to get so much. The boy Boyd took the pot of what he said was "slop" and poured it into the hog pen, causing the pigs to go rootin', looking for whatever they could find of the cooked-up rodents. "You don't have to eat that shit no more!" The boy Boyd screamed, flipping along his cigarette into the pin, causing the bright-orange glow to die with a silent sizzle in the thick pig muck. Drusa looked about as hangdogged as she'd ever felt in her whole life. It'd taken a month of Sundays to get those squirrels, dry um out and then pick the buckshot out of each one, she was just tryin' to show how much appreciating she felt for what the boy Boyd'd done for her and Boy. The boy Boyd said he'd be bringin' her and Boy supper up just about every night and if he didn't bring it on up he'd be sure and leave it sittin' on the cook stove and she could just help herself. Then the boy Boyd said there was one more thing that he expected in return for his abundance of generosity as he grabbed Drusa by the arm, led her into his homeplace, and shoved her down on his feather bed.

Chapter 91

SPENCER DUTY, JR. ONE afternoon listened to Kay Yocum who was sittin' with her sister Helen Yocum, who, both sisters having been born Spradlins married the Yocum twins on the same day and had their youngins exactly one hour apart. Helen was gettin' her youngin' Kenny his first pair of low tops, while Kay had gotten her youngin' Butch his just an hour or so before. Kenny and Butch weren't very likable boys, Spencer Duty, Jr. thought, the way they'd run up to their mommas and bite them just about anywhere their teeth could get a hold of, sometimes even slapping them too. The Yocum girls'd said they'd just come from Hobbs' Five and Dime where they'd heard Lacy whisperin' to Rudolph Sword about the Church of God with Signs Following and even though she said she shouldn't'd been sayin', Lacy said that once the Rev. George Went Hensley'd taught the boy Boyd everything he knew about rattlers and copperheads, that the boy Boyd'd realized his true callin' and *everything* he did was in the service of the Lord, even when he went out collectin' for her or pumpin' folks' gas, "...Jesus is always with him, they're right there side by side, together," she said, and that the boy Boyd was one of those whose faith in the Lord Jesus Christ was so strong that the serpent, who was Satan's emissary on earth, couldn't strike its strike in the face of the power of God almighty that coursed right down from Heaven right through the boy Boyd. *But*, Lacy A. Hobb cautioned, there were those who professed to be *of* the faithful but whose faith was doubtful and the serpent seeing the weakness in their faith'd arch back and sink its fangs into whatever hunk of flesh it could get um' into, causing Satan's demons to infect the hesitant with its venom. Those were the convicted, Lacy A. Hobb's said, "...like runnin' away from the law, the law always gets you, just like Jesus catches up with you and says are you gonna give up or not *and* if you don't throw yourself on His mercy, well then…"

The Yocum girls sat shakin' their heads back and forth, sayin' that havin' been raised up Baptist and all, they just didn't understand havin' snakes and poison too, in the House of the Lord, no matter if it was a church that'd been raised up by the devout from the earth, along the banks of the Levisa Fork or even in a barn for that matter. "Jesus'd been born in a barn, don't forget," Helen reminded Kay.

Each time Spencer Duty, Jr. tried to twist the low-top shoe onto Kenny's foot, Kenny'd twist his foot the other way and then try and kick Spencer Duty, Jr. with his other foot. Kenny likely figured he was the first one who'd ever been a bad boy while gettin' shoes, but his figuring was wrong. Spencer Duty, Jr. was squatting on his knees while fitting up Kenny because his behind was still stinging. While Kenny's momma was lookin' at her sister, Spencer Duty, Jr. gripped Kenny's ankle just above the Achilles Tendon and gave it a good hard pinch, which caused poor Kenny to startle in pain, making him to snap right back in his seat and forget his orneriness long enough for the patient shoe salesman to slip the shoe right on his cantankerous foot. After they left Spencer Duty, Jr., not at all sure why Lacy A. Hobb's'd be talking to Rudolph Sword about the boy Boyd's snake handling, went on over to see Eleanor to let her know what he'd just heard.

Chapter 92

THE TWO SAT AND figured. Eleanor had borrowed a chalk board on wooden casters from Hattie's teacher Mr. Horn, who'd gotten tired of the politicking while having been the school principal. Now though, getting to know his students he was beside himself with despair, as one of his smartest and nicest students having not only died, which in the mountains this or that accident happens but *not* dying like'd happened to Hattie. Eleanor drew out what she knew about the case and figured out loud while Spencer Duty, Jr. asked questions.

Up until Thaddeus' murder there was no explanation for Hattie Hicks' murder *except* Robert Lewis and that was *only* because of Boy saying he'd seen Robert Lewis running away from where he'd found her body. But then Thaddeus was murdered by snakes and the lines that Eleanor was drawing on the chalk board started going this way and that, until they all circled back around and began to meet up at one place.

If Thaddeus'd been beaten to death or choked it may have point-ed back to Robert Lewis being as big and strong as he was, but to have been murdered by snakes, "*murdered by snakes*," Eleanor said again, and then for Boy to be braggin' at Carl the barber's that he and Drusa'd never be going hungry or storm-wet again and then for Eleanor and Spencer Duty, Jr. to be shot at by Drusa with the boy Boyd coming from around back and then trying to make sense of him being there in the first place but *then* getting threatening himself and… just a short while ago, Spencer Duty, Jr., overhearing Helen and Kay Yocum talking about Lacy A. Hobbs talking about the boy Boyd's snake handlin', brought Eleanor to the conclusion that it could only be the boy Boyd who was the killer of Hattie Hicks and

Thaddeus. The problem was there was not one shred of proof. She knew if she called the boy Boyd to the witness stand and began to accuse him that Rudolph Sword would object and that Judge Herbert Van Hoose would immediately sustain his objections, telling her to sit down. The trial was scheduled to begin on Monday.

Chapter 93

THE SUNDAY GO-TO MEETING service at the boy Boyd's church was going to be something special on this day, held in a barn up atop Hager Hill, the Sunday before the Monday of the beginnings of the murder trial. None other than Mrs. Cecil Denkins herself, who'd been widowed from none other than Mr. Cecil Denkins himself, who'd been arrested back in 1947 and thrown in the workhouse for more than six-months for bringin' sinners to salvation through his conquering of snakes at the Dolley Pond Church Of God With Signs Following. Mrs. Cecil Denkins had been playing her guitar and witnessing to a dying cousin right over in Harlan County and was invited by none other than Lacy A. Hobbs herself to offer up a evenin' of redemption for those offering up themselves to serve as witnesses to the deliverance of the soul of the heathen Negro Robert Lewis Rosskam for, being retarded or not, defying the second most important tenant of the Ten Commandments, '*Thou Shalt Not Kill…*' second only to '*You shall have no other gods before Me…*' which Jesus had personally struck down many a for. Eleven of the jurors were the devout followers of the boy Boyd and *his* signs following. And it was said that two of those members had had family members, a daddy and a momma who'd up and defied the teachings of the boy Boyd and had suffered up the consequences by being stricken in the middle of the night by serpents slitherin' out from under their porches, havin' found a hole in the floorboards and strickin' them all about the neck and face while they were likely having dreams of lust and fornication.

There weren't many benches for folks to sit on as there was going to be so much dancing and praising of the Lord that worshipers just couldn't stay seated for very long without being caught up in the spirit of Jesus which, when the boy Boyd pulled a rattler or two out of a coffee can, was going to be like the spirit of the Lord unfurled like blue smoke and began encircling each and every member of those so congregating.

And then Mrs. Cecil Denkins stepped up holdin' her guitar in one hand and an old thick timber rattler in the other, just *daring* that viper to strike her lips as they met tongue to tongue, and then the likes of which *no one* had ever witnessed, Mrs. Cecil Denkins told the boy Boyd to take that rattler and wrap it around her face like a bunting protecting her against the cold, then Mrs. Cecil Denkins rolled her head back while the boy Boyd patted that snake around her face like he was patting putty round a drafty window. That rattler laid so still as you'd a thought it was dead, but truth be told it was Satan His very self so scared of the spirit of Jesus risin' up from Mrs. Cecil Denkins that it dared not move.

The congregating threw themselves backwards into each other like they was hit with a twisters wind, and began speaking in the tongues. Even the tail of that rattler lay quiet as it hung between the bosoms of Mrs. Cecil Denkins. And sittin' right beside of Mrs. Cecil Denkins, which she used to further draw the Lord Jesus into her like a lighten' rod, was the fingertip of Mr. Cecil Denkins which had fallen off when his faith *one* day had faltered that *one* time and the serpent felt his faltering and struck him on the finger causing the tip to fall off just a couple of days before he succumbed to the Devil's malevolent venom. Now, everywhere she went, Mrs. Cecil Denkins carried that dried-up hunk of flesh, sayin' that she'd always have a piece of Mr. Cecil Denkins with her, and as a reminder for *her* faith *never* to falter; no matter where you are, you can never be tellin', she would say, where the evil one lurked.

When the congregating's undulating stopped and the boy Boyd had curled the snakes back into the coffee can he began preaching about the importance of making sure the nigger got what was deserving of him, having done what he'd done and that to have done what he'd done he'd a have to have been consumed by Satan and for one to have been that taken over by Satan, he'd had no faith to begin with no how. Jesus had *told* the boy Boyd directly that Robert Lewis *had* to be held accountable for his sins. Then the boy Boyd added that to have killed Thaddeus the way he had could only mean that the Devil was getting his way through havin' completely taken over the colored boy and not strickin' him because he wanted Robert Lewis to do his bidding and for that there was *nothing* left to save. The boy Boyd said in his closing that him being retarded and all was just the evil one tryin' to get the devout to up and feel sorry for Robert Lewis, and through that sympathy making him not get what was coming to him. He needed to burn in hell fire on earth.

Folks were noddin' so fast in agreement that eyes peering in from the outside couldn't a kept up. It'd a been nothin' but a blur of heads of frenzied hair goin' this way and that. When the service subsided the congregating went home so full of the Holy Spirit that they could barely sleep a wink all night with their insides still gyrating.

Part Three

THE TRIAL

Chapter 94

ELEANOR HAD MET WITH Robert Lewis that morning right before the trial began. He was to keep completely quiet, she had told him. He wasn't to say anything or make any sounds. Edwin and Hetty had scraped enough money together by Edwin doing chores for folks with finally having to sell their milk cow to buy Robert Lewis a new pair of dungarees and a shirt presentable for him to wear in court. Spencer Duty, Jr. fitted him with the first pair of shoes he'd ever had that hadn't been worn by someone else and didn't have a hole somewhere in their soles. Eleanor had no witnesses except his mother and father who'd say that Robert Lewis had never given them any problems and even though he was slow he was a good boy who'd do just about anything for anybody. But no other members of the colored community would testify for fear of the Knights burning them out or them ending up being beaten just about to death and hung. At nine in the morning the bailiff called the court to order.

"The state of Kentucky, in the county of Johnson, hereby declares these proceedings to begin. The Honorable Judge Herbert Van Hoose preceding." And on that Judge Herbert Van Hoose made his way from his chambers to the bench, fluffing his robe so it pillowed down and descended like a falling feather as he took his well-worn seat. The bailiff continued, "Now comes the District Attorney, Mr. Rudolph Sword, and the Attorney of record for the defendant, Miss Eleanor Kitchen, each of them in their own proper person. They are announced and hereby ready to proceed.

"The State of Kentucky and the Johnson County Circuit Court Vs. Robert Lewis Rosskam in the charge of two counts of murder in the first degree."

Eleanor and Rudolph Sword were already seated when Deputy Duffy Deeter began to lead Robert Lewis into the courtroom. His hands were handcuffed behind him while the ankle manacles made him scoot more than walk. When he came through the door just to the right of the bench he looked this way and that as dozens and dozens of eyes came to watch the spectacle of the Negro who'd been accused of committing the biggest murders the town had seen maybe ever. Robert Lewis' frozen stare was being pushed out of his head by more fright than Eleanor had ever seen in any man. As he turned his head this way and that he caught sight of Hetty with her head on Edwin's chest, and he began screaming, "Momma, Daddy!" and tried to run toward them, when one leg got caught by the chain of the other leg, and he went falling face first onto the floor when Deputy Duffy Deeter shoved his knee into his back right above his handcuffed wrists, preventing him from doing who knew what *to* who knew what, he would say later to Brower Stubblefield, who'd be there every day to *exclusively* talk with Rudolph Sword and give folks a blow-by-blow accounting of what'd taken place that day in the name of justice. Robert Lewis lay crying in a hovel as Deputy Duffy Deeter began dragging him by his cuffed wrists to the defense table. Two more deputies helped Deputy Duffy Deeter lift him into a chair beside Eleanor. "Okay, you sit here like a good boy, you start actin' up and I'll give you a whippin' ritch here, you understand boy?" Deputy Duffy Deeter whispered into Robert Lewis' ear. Eleanor looked with disdain at the deputy and said her client understood, he wouldn't cause any problems, she said. Eleanor touched Robert Lewis on the arm and said everything would be all right, he just needed to sit quiet. Edwin and Hetty sat right behind the defense table. Hetty began to reach out to touch Robert Lewis when Edwin jerked her hand back just as Deputy Duffy Deeter's lead sap just missed her hand. "Keep your hands off the prisoner," he ordered. As Eleanor watched the spectacle, she saw the rage in Edwin's eyes, imagining that he wanted to break Deputy Duffy Deeter in two. Judge Herbert Van Hoose sat with his hands cupped in his palms waiting for things to calm down. Then he pronounced the court in session.

Rudolph Sword took to the well and began to address the jury, "Ladies and gentlemen of the jury, we are here today to present evidence that will, *beyond any reasonable doubt,* show that the defendant

Robert Lewis Rosskam, unable to control himself and being a sub-stantially-sized Negro, murdered and raped, I am sorry to have to use that word in mixed presence, one of his own kind, the young colored girl known as Hattie Hicks, only being of this earth eleven years, and then upon being discovered as the killer by Constable Thaddeus Yates, Robert Lewis Rosskam perpetrated a heinous murder upon him. We will prove the facts of this case with an eye witness. A young man who is known as a good boy throughout Paintsville and is known as a boy who doesn't back talk and who has long helped his momma make ends meet. We will also show physical evidence that relates directly to the crime that was found in the possession of the defendant directly relating to the murder of Constable Yates. It is also important that it be understood that the gravity of the crime has caused folks to live in a state of great disconsternation and has disrupted many social events for fear of whoever had done these heinous crimes would strike more members of the community at large. It was only through the good police work by Deputy Duffy Deeter and me that this lecherous animal was brought to justice." Rudolph Sword, after each breathy break in his words, began getting out-and-out stentorianly resolute. When he'd been in law school he was told that because he had a booming voice that he should use it to his advantage. "Go to the dictionary and look up 'stentorian,'" one of his teachers had said. And on that Rudolph Sword went right on over to the library and found the heaviest dictionary he could find and looked it right up. What he remembered most from the defini-tion written right there was 'loud and powerful.' When he spoke of the crimes committed by Robert Lewis, the words came out of his tumid mouth riding on the turbulence of his stentorian. Rudolph Sword tossed the pile of papers he'd had in his hand onto the desk, scrapped the legs of his chair across the wooden floor, and took his seat at the prosecution table.

Eleanor touched Robert Lewis' shoulder and told him she had to talk to all those twelve people sitting in the chairs to her right, but he would be able to see her, and for him to sit quiet.

"Ladies and gentlemen of the jury, clearly I am here representing the accused, Mr. Robert Lewis Rosskam. And ladies and gentlemen I have never seen a more miscarriage of justice. There is not one shred of evidence that ties Mr. Rosskam to the tragic murders of

Hattie Hicks or Constable Yates, nothing! And further, ladies and gentlemen, the defense will show upon cross examination that the case that the prosecution is alleging against Mr. Rosskam is as empty as a dry well. Thank you."

Judge Herbert Van Hoose: "Call your first witness, Mr. Sword."

Rudolph Sword: "The state calls Deputy Duffy Deeter."

Deputy Duffy Deeter was sworn and Rudolph Sword began his direct examination.

Rudolph Sword: "Deputy, would you please give the jury a background of the case."

Deputy Duffy Deeter then related just about what everybody in town already knew from the nonstop talk that'd gone on since Hattie Hick's had been found dead. Everything he said was straight forward up to where he began to suspect Robert Lewis of being the murderer. And when asked how he came to the conclusion of his guilt, Deputy Duffy Deeter said he'd been contacted by Boy's momma Drusa who'd said Boy'd told her that he'd seen Robert Lewis running from where he'd found the little colored girls body and she thought it her duty to report what her boy'd told her. Boy'd be testifying later on, he believed, Deputy Duffy Deeter said.

It was the first time that Eleanor had heard that Drusa had contacted the police. Mostly, as much as he could, Rudolph Sword hadn't said much about what he had or didn't have on Robert Lewis other than an "eye witness."

Rudolph Sword: "Did you interview the boy Randy Gabbard, known as Boy?"

Deputy Duffy Deeter then went on to say that he had indeed interviewed Boy and that he said that when he found the colored girl, he heard rustling in the bushes and looked up from seeing the dead girl and saw the defendant (pointing to Robert Lewis) running like a bat outa hell, throwing his arms this way and that, Boy had said, Deputy Duffy Deeter said. It was him, there weren't no doubt, Boy'd said. And he done the right thing by his momma and come forward to tell what he'd seen.

Rudolph Sword: "Would you Deputy relate how you came to be in possession of the second piece of evidence in this case, namely the two rattlers that *were* the murder weapon of Constable Yates."

"Yes sir, after we arrested the suspect I went back out to the

Rosskam place and found two dead rattlers tossed right next to the woodshed. I picked them up as evidence and brought them on in. They had about the biggest heads I'd ever seen on rattlers—damn near as big as a cats head."

Rudolph Sword walked over to the prosecution table and picked up two stiff dead rattlers and held them up to the jury, "Are these the rattlers Deputy?"

"Yes sir, those had to be the snakes that got Thaddeus. They'd had to have been that big to have done what they did to him, it sure weren't no regular rattler, that much I can tell you for sure." Deputy Duffy Deeter continued, "So figuring that the defendant, the colored boy over there," he said, again pointing to Robert Lewis, "had killed the Hicks girl just a few days before, I figured that the defendant somehow knew that Thaddeus was onto him, so he waited for Thaddeus. Everyone knew he pulled off right there where his body was found, just about every day to eat his boloney sandwich under the shade tree. So I figured that that Negro waited there for him and right as he was relaxin' came out of the bushes and threw those snakes through his window. He must have stayed close by to collect the rattlers after they did what they was supposed to do, because they weren't nowhere to be found."

Rudolph Sword: "Would you describe the events when you and I went to arrest the defendant?"

"Well, when we knocked it sounded like there was a ruckus inside and we figured that the defendant might be trying to escape, so we forced the door open and the defendant attacked us like some wild animal, coming on at us like a bull. And, as y'all can see, he's a *big* colored boy so I had to get pretty rough with him. But finally after subduing him we dragged him on out to the patrol car and brought him on back to the station."

Rudolph Sword: "What about the defendant's daddy, what did he do, Deputy?"

"Right as soon as we went through the door the defendant's daddy came at you, making you havin' to use the butt of your shotgun to get him under control, while I was scufflin' with the defendant."

Rudolph Sword: "And, Deputy, what did you do with the defendant when we got him back to the police station and into a cell?"

"Well, we, me, and another deputy, sat him down and started

questioning him about what he'd done, and it went on pretty late, for a not too smart colored boy, he was a hard one to break. And, we had to take him on over to the hospital to get patched up from his resistin'."

Rudolph Sword: "And what did the defendant say, did he finally confess?"

"Yes sir he did!" Deputy Duffy Deeter said.

"And would you please read the confession to the jury?"

On that, Eleanor stood up and *strenuously* objected, "*Your honor,* the defense, after multiple requests, still has not been supplied with a copy of the so-called confession!"

Judge Herbert Van Hoose looked down from the bench and re-torted in an exasperated tone, "*Well,* Miss Kitchen, you're getting to hear it *now* aren't you, so what exactly are you objecting to?"

Eleanor looked up at the bench and said under her breath, "Jesus Christ."

Then Deputy Deeter read the confession, "*I was walkin' in the woods out by Greasy Creek when I saw Hattie Hicks sittin' along the creek danglin' her feet in the water and I snuck up behind her and hit her in the head with a big rock 'til I was sure she was dead then I raped her. Then I'd seen that constable following me and I figured he'd done figured out what I'd done to Hattie Hicks so I collected up two rattlers and threw them into his police car when he was eatin' his lunch under that shade tree, where he always did.*"

Eleanor listened to Deputy Duffy Deeter read the confession like she was watching a silent movie with the wrong subtitles and then looked over at Robert Lewis, who was sitting there owl-eyed, turning his head from side to side, back and forth, not even understanding why in the hell he was even there. Deputy Duffy Deeter *swore* he took Robert Lewis' words down just as he'd said them. However, the words that were recited as *his* confession were no more Robert Lewis' than were the coerced words of the three black sharecroppers who were beaten and tortured into confessing for murdering a white farmer just a little more than twenty some odd years ago. Goddamn, Robert Lewis could barely string three words together that made any sense and now Deputy Duffy Deeter wanted the jury to believe that he had been able to be that fluent in a confession that was clearly obtained after being beaten and kicked all night, Jesus Christ!

Judge Herbert Van Hoose again looked down from the bench, "Are you satisfied *now* that you've heard the defendant's confession, Miss Kitchen?"

Then Rudolph Sword, turned and said, "Your witness…"

Eleanor stood up, "Deputy Deeter, when exactly did my client confess, before you beat him senseless or afterwards?"

Rudolph Sword immediately stood up, "Your Honor the defense is clearly trying to inflame and prejudice the jury and impugn the witness."

Judge Herbert Van Hoose: "Miss. Kitchen, you start those contemptable antics in my courtroom and you'll be sharing a cell with your client."

Eleanor, still enraged, reframed her question, "Then Deputy, let's go through this, at what point during your interrogation of my client did he dictate the alleged confession that you just read?"

Deputy Duffy Deeter, "I already said so when Mr. Sword was questioning me, can't you just look at that so I don't have to go repeatin' myself?"

Eleanor said, "Deputy, just answer the question."

"He's a big ol' colored boy and once we got control of him he just started pacing around his cell, jabberin' about what he'd done, then I asked him to say what he'd done so I could write it all down and that's when he said what I said he said."

"Deputy, my client *is* retarded, he has never been to school a day in his life, and doesn't even know what the word *rape* even means!"

Deputy Duffy Deeter, "Well he may not know the word as you say, but he sure as *hell* knew what it meant when he did it to that little colored girl before he'd up and killed her."

Eleanor then asked Judge Herbert Van Hoose to direct the jury to ignore the comments and direct the witness to only answer the question which he was asked and not offer commentary.

Judge Herbert Van Hoose said, "Miss Kitchen, if you're interruptin' and popping off is an indication of how you are going to conduct yourself throughout the rest of this trial, then I'll remove you from your representing. A half century ago or thereabouts, Miss Kitchen, the *Kentucky Supreme Court* up and said in *Gholson v. Commonwealth* that '*common justice demands*' that an attorney *must* be appointed when a person charged with a felony is too poor to hire his own counsel, so you keep this objecting up and trying to tell the court what the court should be doing I'll appoint Johnny Pelphrey to offer his representation to your client. And then Mr. Pelphrey can file a lean over your defendant's family's land for the court imposing such an inconvenience and encumberances that goes with such an imposition, do I make myself clear Miss Kitchen?"

Eleanor Kitchen, "*Your honor*, I am *only* doing my job by *challenging* the *clearly* misrepresentative assertions that the witness and the prosecution is presenting as *evidence* in this case."

Judge Herbert Van Hoose, "Miss Kitchen, this court at times just doesn't understand the necessity of even having a trial when the facts in a case are *so* clear and defense lawyers like you waste the courts time."

"Jesus Christ, Your Honor, what are you saying!" Eleanor retorted. "You're attacking the very foundation of your position of impartiality not to mention the very foundation of the Constitution of the United States."

Judge Herbert Van Hoose, "When I need *you* to interpret the court's foundation, I will ask for your opinion, for now though Miss Kitchen, mind your manners *and* your mouth."

Eleanor, not wanting to be dismissed from the case, acquiesced, turned, said she had no more questions, and sat down.

Rudolph Sword then called Pinky Jones.

"Mr. Jones, will you please for the court describe the condition of the deceased Negro girl Hattie Hicks and Constable Thaddeus Yates?"

In the back of the courtroom sat Aberdeen and Sarah Hicks. Sarah was leaning her body against Aberdeen's with her head buried in his chest. Sitting behind them was Spencer Duty, Jr. who, as he looked on, thought that the dead girl's parents looked like department store dummies, quick frozen from the moment Thaddeus had gone to their homeplace to tell them their little girl was not only dead but had been murdered and raped. Other than them and Robert Lewis' mommy and daddy there weren't no other Negros in the courtroom.

Pinky Jones: "Well, Thaddeus had brought the Hicks girl from where he'd found her over to the funeral home. Linc, eh Lincoln Miller, was with him, 'cause Boy, who'd done found her, ran on over to Linc's, told him, and he called Thaddeus to say that Boy'd done told him that he'd up and found a dead colored girl. And then Thaddeus and Linc had brought her on around for me to do the figuring on how she'd died.

Rudolph Sword: "And what were your conclusions?"

Pinky Jones: "Well, her neck had been broken for sure, really torn all apart inside, like when you've just rung the neck of a Banty hen, them being small birds and all, her head was just barely attached to her body, you could feel the ligaments stretched out like she'd been hung. Who'd ever'd done it was strong and I figured mad too, to have done that much damage, she was just a little thing."

Rudolph Sword: "And what else did you conclude?"

Pinky Jones: "Well she had been sexually violated, her private area had been, I would say, brutalized, and like her neck very damaged, and that is all I have to say on that matter."

Rudolph Sword: "Thank you, Mr. Jones, I think the court and the jury understand your reluctance and respect for the family. What did you determine was the cause of death of Constable Yates?"

Pinky Jones: "Well, I'd never seen anything quite like it. He'd certainly been killed by snake bites, there wasn't much figuring needed on that matter. His head was swollen up about three times normal and there were strike marks about a dozen or so different places or so. All the places where he'd been bit were necrotic, eh, that means the skin around the wounds were black and hardened up from the snake venom. Usually a rattler will just strike once then be on their way but for some reason or other these kept going on after him."

"Do you have an explanation for that?"

"No, I sure do not."

The district attorney walked over, picked up the vipers, and stretched them out as best he could being as stiff as they were. "Are these the rattlers that killed Constable Yates."

Pinky Jones: "Well I can't say for certain but they are big enough that'd be for sure."

And on that Rudolph Sword said he had no more questions and waved his hand at Eleanor.

Eleanor: "So, Mr. Jones, then as I understand your testimony you cannot say if the snakes presented to the jury by Mr. Sword are in fact the same snakes that were responsible for the death of Constable Yates, is that correct?"

Pinky Jones: "No, I cannot say for certain 'cause I wasn't there when the snakes killed him. But them being the size they are and all, I took those dead rattlers, pried their mouths open, and measured their bite against some of the wounds on Constable Yates, and they matched right up, those teeth fittin' right into the holes they'd made in his neck."

Eleanor had not been expecting that response and hadn't been told that Pinky Jones had been given the snakes for any kind of comparison.

Rudolph Sword: "Thank you, Mr. Jones, for enlightening the jury about your findings about what this animal, sitting right over there, ladies and gentlemen, did to the little colored girl and one of our finest officers of the law."

There was nowhere for Eleanor to go, no questions to ask, nothing to challenge, for no matter what she said or did, Judge Herbert Van Hoose would overrule her objections or allow the witness not to answer the question. As Eleanor looked on at the jury she saw that several of the jurors were looking towards the back of the courtroom. She turned her head and saw that they were not only looking at the boy Boyd but they seemed to be mouthing something back and forth, then looking over at Robert Lewis. Then the jurors looked at each other and nodded. Regardless of the consequences, the only recourse she had would be to call the boy Boyd as a witness and then accuse him on the stand, but she had not a shred of proof that he had been involved in any way other than a hunch, and that he had taken in Drusa and Boy. But perhaps if she tied the events together it may give the jury enough pause to have at least one or two holdouts and fail to get a conviction.

The court adjourned for the day with Judge Herbert Van Hoose saying that he liked to get things going early, huntin' season was about on us, and he wanted to get this over the sooner the better so he didn't have to waste his time on what shouldn't be wasted time on.

After that day in the courtroom, Aberdeen and Sara never showed their faces again at the trial. It was only later that Edwin told Eleanor that they'd stopped by one night as they were makin' their way out of Paintsville, sayin' that they'd decided to move on. They'd gotten back Hattie's body from the funeral home and buried on their homeplace, but there just weren't nothin' there for them no more and so it was time to be a movin' on. But Aberdeen said that he "knowed" that Robert Lewis wasn't the one who'd killed Hattie. He added: "It don't matter none now."

Chapter 95

THE ONE JUROR WHO wasn't a follower of the boy Boyd's church was Chafin. He was about seventy-five or thereabouts and had no last name, or maybe he had no first name, didn't matter though as he only knew himself as Chafin. He'd been put on this earth a while now after the Negro'd been set free, and had for the most part, when he was but barely able to walk, been taken, or so he believes, by his momma to a traveling show that'd come through somewhere in Mississippi and up and left. Supposed was that he'd been taken in by a leftover pistolero named Ebenezer 'Hody' Hurd, who went from town to town with the traveling show shooting the numbers out of playing cards whilest looking backwards through a mirror. He even taught the boy when he got to walkin' to push the cards down into the knife cut slits he'd made a long time back in a found log of hard Birch that he'd used forever and a day. It took the lad many a years to realize that that hunk of wood was *the* one and only hunk of wood and the only marks on it had been made by Hody's carrying knife. After thousands of .45s coming right at it, Hody had never missed, not even one time. Hody'd given Chafin his name, having been the name of the man who'd taken him in, when he was just about the same age as the boy. He'd also gave him, round about ten or so, his first chew of bacci and now, after many a spit-soaked plug had been hocked over Chafin's lips, a thick black lump that turned blacker with each passing day had raised up on the tip of his tongue, making each word that passed out his mouth come to voice with a sizzlin' *thhhh*.

Chafin had tagged along with the traveling show until one afternoon, right as Hody was lifting the mirror with his left arm, readying his pistol with his right, his left arm shot forward with a lurching pain, his jaw grew so stiff he thought he'd been struck by the lock-jaw and then he, in front of a hundred or show folks, fell over dead. Chafin ran over to him and rolled him over, yelling at him to wake up, but that was not to be. Still not being quite of age, and with that particular traveling show not traveling as much, Chafin happened upon someone who said he should make his way on up to Michigan and join up with the Johnny J. Jones Exposition. Which he did and ended up over the years doing just about everything you can do with a traveling show, except tending to the lions and tigers. He'd even been privileged to meet up with Henry Ford and Thomas Edison, Chafin saying he was the one who gave Henry Ford the idea for a new kind of pull-up brake for his cars. Somewhere in the '40s the Johnny J. Jones Exposition made its way through Paintsville, and Chafin, while running one of the spots for the tiger show, was asked to consider taking over as the projectionist for the SIPP Theater, the first talkie theater in all of Kentucky. Figuring he was getting on in years and he'd have a room that'd be warm on cold nights right in the theater, and his bunk wouldn't be all the time rocking back and forth on steel rails or bouncing up and down on wagon wheels, Chafin gave over the running of the show spot to a midget, bunked his paltry belongings in the room right off the projection booth, and set about figurin' on how the projectors did what they did. In two or three days he had it down pretty darn good. He'd had a few run-ins with the boy Boyd now over the years, Chafin thinking him to be a lout who, as he would say, "…weren't the kind of man even to waste a fist on."

Chafin, looking out into the courtroom, saw the boy Boyd sittin' in the back with his arms spread out across the oak bench seat, takin' up enough room for two or three folks, he thought. The boy Boyd'd mistakenly gone on over to the SIPP tryin' to strong arm Chafin during a matinee, sayin' he'd owed his momma upwards of ten dollars, when Chafin' had never in his entire life ever owed nobody. Lacy A. Hobbs herself had sent the boy Boyd to do her mistaken collectin'. He'd climbed the steps right off to the right of the concession stand, reaching under the glass, and grabbing hisself a candy bar. "On the house," he said, before he made his way up to the booth, and then burstin' through the door, just as Chafin was steppin' on the change-over peddle, pushing his face just about through the port hole lookin' out onto the movie goers. The boy Boyd'd gotten by with his hooligan shenanigans mostly by pickin' on helpless women or men built of slight stature, but not havin' known Chafin before he'd had no way of knowin' that he used to help out with the big cats and elephants and if that don't make a man about as strong as a man can get then he'd say, "nothin' would." Chafin reached back, grabbed the boy Boyd by his most private of private parts, and lifted him off the ground, squeezing so hard as he levitated him in the air that the boy Boyd thought his balls were going to explode. Not even knowing who the boy Boyd was, havin' never known him before, Chafin figured he was being burgled. When Chafin let the boy Boyd's feet touch the battleship grey cement floor, his eyes were rolled back about as far as they could go without falling off the edge of their sockets down into his skull. Whatever nerve he'd had was puddled up on the floor right along with where he'd pissed hisself from bein' in so much pain. Chafin dragged him toward the booth door, kicked it open with his foot, and pushed him down the steps. The boy Boyd thought he'd never stopped turning end over end before he came to rest right at the feet of Sally Mae Westover workin' behind the concession stand, whose momma *did in fact* owe Lacy A. Hobbs ten dollars or there-abouts. How the boy Boyd or Lacy A. Hobbs herself'd *ever* confused Chafin for Sally Mae Westover, who was about as stupid as stupid could be, and no matter how many times the boy Boyd yelled and screamed about what'd been done to him, would the reason for the confusion be figured out rightly. It took a several Sundays in a row that the boy Boyd had to miss his preachin' for his privates to get their regular color back and for the swellin' to seep on down into his legs so he weren't waddlin' this way and that like a duck.

Chapter 96

THAT NIGHT ELEANOR SAT with Spencer Duty, Jr. and lamented. "Robert Lewis is going to be found guilty and there's not a goddamn thing I can do." Spencer Duty, Jr. said he saw the boy Boyd sitting in the back of the courtroom smirking and seemed to be nodding back and forth to just about everyone on the jury. The only one who he didn't seem to be nodding too was the projectionist from over at the SIPP. Eleanor said that she believed that the boy Boyd was guilty of both murders and that Thaddeus was on his way to confront him when the boy Boyd got to him first. But the real sway was Lacy A. Hobbs, seeming that nobody she gave credit to who was ever able to pay it off with the way she charged them so much interest. Folks'd get outta work and desperate then come asking for credit and she'd say,

"Honey, out of the goodness of my heart," she'd be obligin' but that she, in order to be fair to herself and all'd, have to charge them more interest and folks needin' this or that'd then have to agree.

The Church of God with Signs Following was something that Eleanor didn't understand, what little she'd heard about it. And especially the snake handling sounded like a looney bin nothing that she, even being a nonbeliever, could imagine. At one point Eleanor said, "I'm going to find out where the boy Boyd holds his church service and attend one of the meetings."

It was the first time that the young shoe salesman had ever been abrupt with her. "No! That's not something that you should be doing. These are dangerous people, there's been rumors going back to when I was a boy and that's not something you should be doing. Look what happened to Thaddeus," he continued, "and likely others that we don't know anything about. Folks disappear from around these parts and are never heard from again. I don't want that to happen to you." He swallowed. "And I guess the truth is that it's likely that you'll lose this case."

Eleanor changed the subject and told him that Robert Lewis had said he'd been out walking looking for onions when he'd seen a policeman pulling another policeman out of a police car. He "wudn't be moving" Robert Lewis'd said. "Like when Daddy'd has to lift his arms up real high and hit a cow in the head with a board, they's a movin' then they's a ain't."

Chapter 97

RUDOLPH SWORD PREPARED TO call Drusa to the stand, likely only because she was Boy's momma. When she was called the bailiff presented the Bible and said, "Do you swear to tell the whole truth and nothin' but the truth so help you God."

Drusa looked right into the eyes of the bailiff and said, hissin' through her hair lip, "I ain't sworin' at God, so if I gotta swor up at God then I ain't sayin' nothin' that I ain't doin' so I may as well go right on back to sittin'."

Judge Herbert Van Hoose looked down from the bench and interrupted, "Bailiff I don't think we have to ask Drusa to swear at God so she can go ahead and be seated."

Rudolph Sword then began asking the witness on the stand this question and that. *Did your boy that folks around here know as Boy say anything to you after he'd found the dead colored girl?* Drusa pushed herself up in her seat and looked right back at the boy Boyd who was noddin' his head that she should say what he said she should be sayin'.

Drusa: "That he did, he said he found that little dead nigger girl and up an seen that nigger sittin' right over there" (pointing to Robert Lewis) "runnin' like a jack rabbit through the bushes up there around Greasy Crick. Boy done said that he didn't think a nigger could be movin' so fast, them bein' lazy and all." Rudolph Sword then said he had no further questions.

Eleanor stood up, turned around, and pointed to the boy Boyd, "Drusa, why do you keep looking back at the boy Boyd?"

"He's a nice man who done a nice thing helpin' me an Boy out the way he's done," Drusa said.

Eleanor: "What has he offered you, Drusa?"

"He's a God fearin' man who brought us down from Rabbit Hash and Monkey's Eye to be livin' in a homeplace where the roof don't leak and you ain't got to be cozyin' up in one of the corners so's not to catch the draft comin' between the cracks."

Eleanor: "Why would he do that, Drusa, did you know the boy Boyd, are you related to him, I don't understand why he'd up and do this for a stranger."

"Like I done said, he's God fearin'."

"Drusa, isn't it true that the boy Boyd has told you everything to say here today and that you doing what you are told is why you now have a dry roof over you and Boy's head?"

"No, ma'am, that ain't true, I can't tell what's in a man's heart, only what he does and that tells me what's in his heart, so the boy Boyd showed me what's in his heart when he come up to my and Boy's shack and made the Christian offerin'."

Rudolph Sword: "You honor, can we stop this berating of the witness?"

Judge Herbert Van Hoose: "Miss Kitchen, you ain't even said that much and I'm already worn empty with your talkin' and tryin' to see how far you can push this court. If you got a question to ask, Miss Kitchen, ask it, if you ain't and you've only got one of your opinions then keep it to yourself."

Eleanor: "Jesus Christ!"

And on that Judge Herbert Van Hoose stood up and shoved his chair back, causing the Stars and Bars to quake with the jar to the wall, "I've had it with you, Miss. Kitchen! I may give you some latitude in my courtroom for your disrespectin' ways, but you *ain't* goin' be disrespectin' our Lord and Savior Jesus Christ."

From the courtroom, cries of "Amen" were shouted. And then the boy Boyd dropped to his knees and began asking the Lord Jesus Christ "to forgive the heathen in our presence, who'd viled His name, who'd shown her contempt for His teachins' and who'd debasted His demand for *justice* by offerin' up lies in the face crushin' testimony that that nigger, sittin' ritch yonder, in ways as debasin' as debasin' can be, up and killed that colored girl and then up and killed Constable Thaddeus, Lord Jesus Christ, forgive those of us bein' exposed day in and day out to this heathenness."

Just about all of the jury was on their knees, rocking back and forth, McKenzie Wark, who everyone knew as 'Mac,' was ballin' her eyes out now fearful for her salvation bein' in the presence of such debauchery and there sittin' just down the bench from the boy Boyd was none other than Lacy A. Hobbs herself who'd been so moved that she began speakin' in the tongues. And when the jury heard Lacy A. Hobbs herself bein' used by the Lord to up and announce His very presence they reared back off their knees, threw their hands into the air, and felt the *assuredty* of their salvation restored. The only one still sittin' was Chafin. Watching the spectacle, Eleanor was at that moment ready to make a motion for a mistrial when she looked up at the bench and heard Judge Herbert Van Hoose scream, "Hallelujah!" On that, the young lawyer felt her words become hot in her mouth from the fire fueled by her hatred and then turn to dust on her tongue as her breath disappeared. She shook her head in disbelief of what had just happened and sat down. Brower Stubblefield was writing as fast as he could about the goings-on, never himself having seen the likes of.

Chapter 98

AFTER THE JURY WAS prayed out, the bailiff stood and said, "The court calls forth Randy Gabbard, also known around these parts as Boy." Up from the back Boy came hobblin' up the aisle, hobblin' because when he was more of a youngin' than he was now he'd been playin' a game of mumbly peg and threwed his pocket knife clean threw two of his toes, losing one of his big toes, never goin' to the hospital bein' so far up in the holler and all, Drusa had to sit on top of him while she'd done cut off the hangin' tendrils of what was left and then take the end of a burnin' stick an sear right where most of his toe'd come off his foot. Boy took himself a second or two to frolic with the swingin' gate at the bar separating those talkin' from those watchin'. Rudolph Sword clasped his fingers around Boy's shoulder squeezing to a hard pinch causing him to flinch. The bailiff then directed him on up to the witness chair, whispering to go on and sit on down and mind his goddamn manners.

"Boy..." Rudolph Sword began to say, when Boy himself spoke up and said, "I say, I say, if yer wantin' me to say I saw that nigger sittin' over there runnin' away up yonder there by Greasy Creek, well I done seen him, I say, I say that's fer sure."

Rudolph Sword: "Boy, can you tell the jury what you were doing up at Greasy Creek and who you were with?"

Boy: "I say, I say we wus..."

Rudolph Sword: "Who were you with, Boy?"

Boy: "Bobby Maynard, he's a hairlip like my momma, cept my momma has two hairlips but he don't know how to talk very good and when he tries an say somethin' he spits in yer face."

Rudolph Sword: "Boy, you said you saw the defendant running away from the dead girl?"

"That nigger he's a runnin, I say, I say, he's a runnin' like a jack rabbit who'd just been up and shot but ain't dead just yet. I ain't never seen a nigger runnin' so fast."

Rudolph Sword: "And then when did you discover the dead colored girl?"

Boy: "I say, I say, I up and felt the urge an said to Bobby Maynard I wus gonna piss an wus pushin' back those cockspurs when I done seen that nigger girl layin' there dead."

Rudolph Sword: "And then what did you do?"

"I kicked her with my foot, I say, I say, and when she didn't do nothin' I done figured she was gonna up and stay dead, I got on with pissin' an I say, I say, I said to Bobby Maynard to up and stay there and I up and runned on over to Linc and said I say, I say I found a dead nigger."

"And what did Mr. Sinclair do?"

"I say, I say, he said if I wus lying he'd beat my ass an I said, I say, I say I wudn't lyin' to no one about no dead nigger an he up and called officer Thaddeus and we went on back up to Greasy Creek, I say, I say and I showed um right there where that nigger girl was dead, she didn't have no clothes on neither, I'd ain't never seen a dead nigger girl with no clothes on, I say, I say."

Rudolph Sword: "And when did you see the defendant running away?"

And on this Boy forgot what he'd been told to say.

Boy: "Ummmm, I say, I say, it was before I went on down to get Linc. I say, I say, he wus a runnin' like a jack rabbit who'd just been up and shot but ain't dead just yet."

Eleanor noted how Boy repeated the same thing word for word. Then Rudolph Sword said he was finished with his direct questioning of Boy.

Eleanor: "Boy, I'd like to ask you some questions."

"I say, I say, you're that bitch who'd come on up to Rabbit Hash and Monkey's Eye tryin' to cause trouble for momma an she had to get her shotgun to get you to be on your way, ain't you, I say, I say."

Eleanor: Boy, I just want to ask you a couple of questions, then you'll be done. Has anyone told you what to say here today?"

"I say I say, there ain't no one who'd told me what to say, ain't no one, most fer sure the boy Boyd."

On that Chafin looked back at the boy Boyd, who was sitting

about as straight up as a man could sit, with no look of worry etched out anywhere on his face." Then Rudolph Sword leapt to his feet and objected to Eleanor questioning Boy's forthrightness. "You honor, how many times does the prosecution have to object to Miss Kitchen's antics? She clearly has no defense and so the only thing she seems to think she can do beside plead her client as guilty as he is is too impugn the good name of these good folks who are coming forward to see that justice prevails."

Judge Herbert Van Hoose: "Miss Kitchen, the court has heard nothing from this young man that would lead it to believe that he is being untruthful, I don't know how much longer this court can allow you to behave the way you're behaving without finding you in contempt. Watch yourself, Miss Kitchen!"

"Boy, at the risk of being found in contempt, when you described my client, who you're refer to as 'that nigger' running away from where you found Hattie Hicks, would you tell the court again what you saw."

And on that, Boy said, "I say, I say, he's a runnin' like a jack rabbit who'd just been up and shot but ain't dead just yet."

And then Eleanor said, "But Boy, if you haven't been told what to say, how is it that when you described my client running away from the crime scene that you now, on three separate occasions, have described it using the *exact* same words each time, *exactly*. I can ask the court reporter to read Boy's statement back if Mr. Sword would like?"

Then Boy, clearly pissed off, said, "They'd done said you'd be tryin' to get me to look like I was sayin' what I wudn't. I say, I say, I don't say what I don't say, I say, I say the boy Boyd's done been feedin' us real good, he's a good man doin' what he's done, I say, I say."

Then Rudolph Sword stood up and told Boy to shut up. Eleanor looked over at the jury and most especially at Chafin and then said she had no more questions.

During the entire trial Robert Lewis had sat, mostly rocking to and fro in his seat, looking back at his momma and daddy, and at the end of each day, he stood up, started to walk back toward Edwin and Hetty, and then was grabbed by the arm and taken back to his cell. Eleanor always brought him an onion which she laid on the table and he picked up and put in his pocket, he hadn't had any butter forever and day though. He never so much as uttered a sound other than an occasional sigh, then reached under himself, scratched his butt, and then went on back to being the way he'd been. Edwin and Hetty and most particularly Hetty never stopped praying that Jesus would touch the hearts of the folks on the jury and guide them in His love to see the wrong that'd been done. Hetty even promised that if He could see his way to helpin' her son that she'd never stop praising His name and bringing as many souls to His altar as anyone who'd ever praised His name had done. Hetty said in her prayers that she'd been workin' her fingers to the bone most every day that she'd been alive and she'd be workin' harder for Him than she'd *ever* done worked. Robert Lewis was a good boy, she'd say in her prayers, he ain't never done no body no harm no way and his only sin was stealin' hisself an onion or two and he'd done promised that he never be doin' that again neither.

Edwin mostly held Hetty's hand and tried with all his might to hold back the tears that kept weepin' out of their sockets and go rolling down his cheeks. He also tried as he might to keep his head out of the line of sight of Lacy A. Hobbs and the boy Boyd who'd keep lookin' on over their way seemin' to unfurl a malevolent curse with their eyes.

Miss Eleanor hadn't bullshitted them, saying that just about everything in just about every way was stacked against their son. The worse part was that Rudolph Sword had a witness who'd just taken the stand and under oath had said that he saw Robert Lewis running away from where Hatty'd been murdered. There was no way of proving otherwise, even if he had been somewhere else, and even if someone saw him somewhere else, they sure weren't going to come forward and say so.

Eleanor knew Boy was lying, but the jury hung on *every* word and she saw that the jury believed him. Plus, even though everyone'd known Thaddeus, Rudolph Sword was mostly focusing his prosecuting of Robert Lewis on the murder of Hattie Hicks, figuring that the murder of a young girl, Negro or not, would inflame the jury more. Not to mention, just looking at Robert Lewis it would take a mighty long stretch to see how he could have not only killed Thaddeus but planned it all out too. But unless someone got on the witness stand and confessed to the murders, this jury was going to convict the boy who liked to eat onions.

Other than Edwin and Hetty, there wasn't one other Negro who'd come to the trial. The other coloreds were fearful that if they showed up there'd be retributing against them. And they knew that truth be told there were some folks, no matter what, that the law was goin' to protect, and that they'd likely never get their due. Figurin' that was what was happening, those folks just stayed away.

Then a few days before the trial was about to come to an end, and just right before the bailiff called the proceedings to order, the door to the courtroom opened, and a rickety old Negro woman came hobblin' into the courtroom. She had the gall to make her way past three white women and sit herself down right beside the boy Boyd and Lacy A. Hobbs herself. Seeing the old woman walk through the door'd brought an audible gasp from the folks on the jury and frowns and whispers for her impudence from the folks watchin' her disrespectful display that was sayin' she was as good as any of the whites who were there beholdin' the scales of justice tippin' toward convictin' the nigger of his wrong doin'.

When Hetty looked up from Edwin's shoulder and saw the old colored woman in the courtroom, tears began to roll down her cheeks. Edwin offered up, "Praise be to God."

Likely faster than when the boy Boyd'd run to fetch Mr. Yarborough, when the girl Gayle'd done fell down the well shaft, he took Lacy A. Hobbs' herself's hand and just about dragged her over top of the other folks who hadn't the mind to be moving away from the crippled up nigger who'd done gone an made such a ruckus by daring to show her face amongst the good Christians whose salvation had been assured by the boy Boyd and Lacy A. Hobb's rightful Holiness. But many of the folks were pinned down by their confusion, having heard stories about the old colored woman most of their lives, and thinking that likely she'd been dead and buried long, long ago, and that the stories were nothin' more than lore passed down by their mommies and daddies about how she'd just turn up here and there, not so much coming too but havin' been sent from.

Chapter 99

The night that the old nigger woman had violated the courtroom etiquette with her presence the boy Boyd called forth a special prayer service. Linc had offered up his barn so folks could congregate without the presence of the nosey.

Every member of the jury, except for Chafin, was there plus about twenty others or so seekin' deliverance from their sins and an open door to the promised bountifulness of Heaven. Betty Cain's husband, Peck, had brought Betty so the boy Boyd could cure her of the cancer that had taken over her private parts. Lacy A. Hobbs herself'd told Peck when he'd been delivering bolts of fabric to Hobbs' Five and Dime and lamenting on his wife's bad fortune that the boy Boyd could heal poor Betty from her suffering, but her heart *had* to be fully open to Jesus' love and if it wasn't then even with Lacy A. Hobbs herself speakin' in the tongues and the boy Boyd receivin' the healing power of the Lord Jesus Christ through his fingertips, well there weren't nothin' that could be done and the Infernal one would drag Betty right then and right there down to Hell.

"If," Lacy A. Hobbs herself'd said, Peck's wife "didn't care about her eternal soul" then Jesus' wouldn't either, but if she did, then the boy Boyd'd would for sure cure her of her cancer. Peck and Betty had been devout Nazarenes all their lives and had been baptized when they were youngins and long before they'd even knew each other had dedicated their lives to upholding the Word of the Lord and now with Betty's sufferin' and all and Peck barely able to make ends meet with buyin' medicine and all they were feelin' abandoned especially when the doctor said there just wasn't nothing that could be done, the cancer wasn't just in her private parts anymore but was just about everywhere in her body and the only thing they could hope for was a miracle and the doctor further said he couldn't provide that.

It weren't long after Peck carried Betty's cancer-battered body through the barn door that the boy Boyd uncurled a thick timber rattler from a coffee can, kissed it, and then wrapped it around his neck as he began preaching the Word of the Lord. Meanwhile Lacy A. Hobbs sat on the hay bale pulpit, clearly beginning to feel the spirit of Jesus pulsing through her as she began uttering utterances that only she and the Lord God Almighty understood their meaning. And even though he wasn't speaking in the tongues, the boy Boyd began to quake in the presence of Jesus who'd come to make sure that the members of the jurors' souls were scrubbed clean of sin before they began deliberating the fate of the murdering nigger. It never failed that Lacy A. Hobbs herself was able to receive the Word of God right just about the time when the boy Boyd retrieved a snake from the coffee can and then began preaching. "In the name of Jeeesuus, Hallelujah," the boy Boyd screamed, and the snakes' rattles began their own quaking, and the congregating began falling to their knees, offering up their very souls unfearful of the Dark one's presence wrapped around the boy Boyd's neck. And further there was Peck holdin' Betty in his arms, barely nothin' to her as the cancer that'd ravaged her body'd drained her like a tornado that'd spun dry a lake. The boy Boyd laid his hands upon Betty's pale forehead and called upon Jesus, who was causing Lacy A. Hobbs herself to shake so much that the boy Boyd thought himself that she might break apart like an egg, then realizin' that it was Jesus whose love had enveloped her that was keepin' his momma from flyin' apart at the seams. The burn of Jesus' love comin' through the boy Boyd's hands scorched Betty's head and she too began to feel the Lord runnin' through her like electricity surgin' through an old house that'd been left dark all too long, its rooms lighten' up with a brightness that not been seen since the lamps'd went dim. Peck feelin' Betty comin' back alive began screamin' "Hallelujah, Hallelujah, Hallelujah," at the top of his lungs. The congregating were rocking back and forth praising Jesus and Lacy A. Hobb's herself had collapsed as she usually did after being consumed by the Holy Spirit. The boy Boyd whipped the rattler off his neck and began scoldin' Satan who lived within, admonishin' that he was powerless in the presence of the Lord Jesus Christ, then the boy Boyd spun the snake around his wrist and curled him back into the coffee can. Betty was sittin' up now of her own accord and Peck was cryin' his eyes out with her healin'. The boy Boyd'd done right by him, he said, and he was goin' to do right by the boy Boyd offerin' up a hundred acres of his best pasture land that bordered the Daniel Boone National Forest for healin' his Betty. And although Betty was weak as could be she walked on out of the healin' barn on her own two feet while the believers sang songs of praise seeing the power not only of Jesus' love but of the boy Boyd.

It was the very next day that the boy Boyd'd gone on over to Peck's and secured the papers to what was now rightfully his land. And it was just a few days after that that Betty suddenly took a turn for the worse and up an died. Lacy A. Hobbs had given fair warnin' to Peck that neither he nor Betty could *ever* let their love for Jesus wain even for a second or He'd likely get perturbed for what He'd done for them, bringin' Betty back from the dead an all and just go ahead take Betty and then figure on what to do with her soul from there. Sure enough that'd been what had happened.

Chapter 100

"Those goddamn sonsabitches," Eleanor said to Spencer Duty, Jr.

"Can this go to appeal?" he asked.

"The judge can block the appeal by writing that he is confident that an appeal would be a waste of time as all trial procedures were met and there were no procedural errors. He can get by with it, no doubt. The laws read good but how they are enforced is a different matter, especially with a retarded Negro. Have you ever heard of a Negro who was charged with two counts of murder *not* being convicted?"

Spencer Duty, Jr., nodded in agreement. He then did something he had never done, he reached out and pulled Eleanor close and held her against his chest as she began weeping. She had never seen herself as weak or someone easily defeated but now she was faced with an insurmountable odd, not only with the court proceedings, but once they were over, her ability to practice law in Paintsville would be over. She had come here to help folks who had little or no representation, and then she ran up against Judge Herbert Van Hoose, whose malice, bigotry, and racism were beyond measure.

Eleanor remembered the first case that she'd had in front of Judge Herbert Van Hoose. Opal Butcher'd been living with her newly-wedded husband, Lonnie B. "Lon" Butcher, up around Mash Fork when she, being just having turned round abouts fourteen or so, and Lon being upwards of forty or so, had refused to perform her expected duties as a wife, including but not limited to cookin', cleanin', and havin' relations when Lon, being a man of mighty need felt the beck-on call. Opal, being a strong-headed girl'd, put up a fuss when Lon made his needs known by hangin' his pants on the bedpost that night. Instead of doin' what was right by her husband, she'd just tossed his dungarees onto the floor, and turned on over, lettin' it be known that she wanted no part of what was dutifully hers to dutifully do. Lon up and tried his best to let it be known what Opal was expected of. He'd done offered up a good home, land that was his, and nobody could up an take away, a job on the railroad, and more than one hundred fifty dollars saved up and kept on top of a shelf in the kitchen in a flour can. Opal's mommy and daddy'd said she weren't likely to ever find a man who'd be offerin' so much an said it be a good thing for her to go on, marry Lon, and being of birthin' age, give him as many youngins as he thought he could provide for. But Opal was a stubborn girl, throwin' fits, screamin' and yellin' about this and that. Until one day, poor Lon couldn't take it anymore, and gave Opal the beatin' that she'd been askin' for, for not long after she'd up and said "I do." He'd also taken her for what was rightfully his. Then Opal up an ran near thirteen miles, all the way from Mash Fork to Paintsville, declaring that she wanted to have him arrested for what he'd done to her. Deputy Duffy Deeter'd done the investigatin', and when Lon had figured out where his young, unhappy wife had gone, he came lookin' for her. Well, after figurin' with Lon, Deputy Duffy Deeter couldn't see how any laws had been broken excepting that Opal had clear and simple broken her marriage contract, which led Deputy Duffy Deeter to recommend that Johnny Pelphrey represent Lon in suing Opal for breach of contract for what was rightfully his to use, when and as he pleased. It hadn't been but just a few days that Eleanor'd come to Paintsville when Opal showed up at her office wanting her to represent her in defending herself, saying that she wasn't about to be owned by any man. Eleanor figured that Opal was for some reason lying until she saw the written complaint that Johnny Pelphrey'd put together and served on Opal. It clearly stated that what was Opal's was Lon's, him having provided more for her than she'd ever had, and certainly more than she'd ever have had Lon not come along. Eleanor figured and assured Opal that no judge in his right mind would find for Lon. It was just a few days after Opal was served that she was ordered into court. Judge Herbert Van Hoose liked to get these "*nuisance* cases" as he called them over "lickety-split" he would say. Johnny Pelphrey stood up and read the complaint. Then Eleanor called for immediate dismissal as the charges were ridiculous. Then Judge Herbert Van Hoose spoke up and first and foremost told Eleanor to sit down and stop her demanding for what she wasn't going to get. And then Judge Herbert Van Hoose said, "After reading the complaint and figuring on this for a while longer, *you* little girl sound like you've been up and causing problems from the time you up and said your 'I do's' well with you going ahead with your 'I doing' an with your momma and daddy's blessing you just ain't got much to say about anything. This man, far be it from me to figure on why, said he'd take care of you, and for all that he's givin' you and for all that you ain't got and never will have without him, I in fact declare that whatever is yours is in fact *his*, be it your cookin' pots, your Sunday church dress, or those parts of a woman's person which we men know are there but don't see, but in fact are there by a God-given right to use to procreate and bring forth onto this earth those which will carry on after we have, by God's grace, been taken up to Heaven."

Judge Herbert Van Hoose decision was contrary to all reason. The decision was borne out of such ignorance and stiltedness that Eleanor sat in its presence in a state of disbelief. It was certainly not the last time that she would be consumed by a state of bedlam with Judge Herbert Van Hoose's decisions.

Chapter 101

WHEN SHE WAS IN law school Eleanor had heard Mary Jane Ward give a lecture on being locked away in the Rockland Insane Asylum, coming face to face with not only incompetency but also cruelty and indescribable insanity for years. As Eleanor sat in her room at Wanda C. Music's rooming house, she remembered Mary Jane Ward talking about how at times her world seemed make-believe. "This couldn't be happening to me." All the clichés seemed real, "This is just a nightmare and I will soon wake up." But Mary Jane Ward's struggle with the nightmare went on for years. And indeed Eleanor's struggles with bigotry in every form imaginable had gone on for years, and now, the fate of a man's life was hers and hers alone.

Mary Mary had told Eleanor of times when Moses had come upon the Knights up in the sugar maple grove looking to do him harm. Little good it would have done to go to the constable with your troubles, best to take it upon yourself to solve the problem. "Funny," Mary Mary would say, "Moses having taken up lawyering and all.

"But," Mary Mary would also say, "there's a lot of mountain here around Butte, and it wouldn't have been the best of notions for any man to have crossed Moses outside of what lawyering could settle."

That morning, right before breakfast, Spencer Duty, Jr. showed up at the rooming house telling Wanda C. Music he needed to see Eleanor right away. It turned out that right after the film exchange had picked up the shipping cans for last week's movie at the SIPP and dropping off that coming week's attraction that Chafin had been cleaning up the projection booth, throwing out the burnt ends of used carbon rods he'd toss in a metal can with a flip-top lid that sat right below the lamp houses, when he heard a pounding at the door that led off out into the alley, right where the film exchange had just done their pick and swap. Thinkin' that they'd likely forgot something, he opened the door. There stood two white-cowled Knights holding pick axe handles. In that moment before Chafin could have likely done much of anything, one of the Knights brought an axe handle down across the top of his head, causing him to drop to the ground, where they proceeded to kick him just about everywhere a man can be kicked. He was known to be a nigger lover, they were saying, said he'd lived with freaks and niggers with those travelin' shows and he wasn't going to be standin' in the way of that colored boy getting what was just deservin' of him to get. And if he did they'd come back and finish what they started. Then like the Knights were known to do, they ran off into the dark.

When Eleanor got to court that day she called for a mistrial, saying that whoever had beaten Chafin had engaged in jury tampering and that a fair trial for Robert Lewis could not be gotten. Judge Herbert Van Hoose though figured otherwise, saying that it was Wednesday and that'd give Chafin five days to recover from whatever'd happened to him, citing that no one knew for sure what had happened and that for all the judge knew Chafin, who'd been known to be a drinker and not a Christian man of sorts, had been full as a tick and fallen down the steps coming out of the SIPP and was makin' up excuses for his own profane ways.

Right after Judge Herbert Van Hoose slapped his gavel against the bench, declaring the day done, Eleanor told Robert Lewis she would come by and see him later on, she also said she'd bring him an onion slathered in butter. As Deputy Duffy Deeter led Robert Lewis out of the courtroom Eleanor heard him say, "Move on along nigger. Don't go pullin' none of that shufflin' shit y'all do." Then Deputy Duffy Deeter, seeing that Eleanor had inadvertently stepped in his way and not appreciating anyone disrespecting the authority that the badge on his chest anointed him with, reached out and shoved her knocking her right over top the defense table and onto the floor, spoutin' off that she'd been tryin' to "Interfere with the prisoner." And on that, Robert Lewis, not liking what he'd seen, and who just about no one'd ever seen get angry over just about nothin', even when he'd been suffering beating after beating, being forced to say this and that, jerked himself free from Deputy Duffy Deeter grip, turned around, and screamed some kind of sound that folks left in the courtroom would later say sounded like the Devil Himself screaming up from Hell. Robert Lewis grabbed Deputy Duffy Deeter's thick neck with his cuffed wrists and lifted him a good three feet off the ground, causing him to immediately begin gasping for air while his face was turning blue and his eyes were startin' to pop out of his head. Robert Lewis shook Deputy Duffy Deeter so hard that his partial plate came flying out of his mouth, snapping in two when it hit the floor.

Rudolph Sword puffed himself up and commanded the other deputies in the courtroom to "…get control of that sonofabitching nigger," even though they were already trying their best to pull the accused's hands from around the deputy's throat. One of the deputies pulled out his billy club and began striking Robert Lewis across the small of the back trying his best not to hit Deputy Duffy Deeter who was now long past being able to be regardful. Then another deputy pulled his revolver and began beating Robert Lewis across the top of the head, finally causing him to let go of Deputy Duffy Deeter, who dropped limp as a rope onto the floor. The deputies dragged Robert Lewis into a room off the main courtroom and began pistol whipping him as senseless as a man can be whipped.

Spencer Duty, Jr. had jumped over top of the bar and pulled Eleanor, whose head was bleeding from having been knocked down by Deputy Duffy Deeter, back through the swinging gate doors.

Rudolph Sword, once Robert Lewis had been dragged away, ran over to Deputy Duffy Deeter and began slapping him in the face to try and bring him around while Judge Herbert Van Hoose, who'd up and pulled a .45 from under his robe and was standin' at his bench waving it back and forth, thinkin' that another colored may be comin' into the courtroom and get violent at any moment, was screaming for order to be restored. The boy Boyd had stepped foot into the jury box, bent down on his knees, and began praying for Deputy Duffy Deeter to show signs of life. And in that blessed moment and right as Rudolph Sword was about to deliver another conscious restoring slap to his face, Deputy Duffy Deeter begin spitting and sputtering as his lungs refilled with life giving air. Again the courtroom was filled with "Halleluiah" after "Halleluiah."

Spencer Duty, Jr. was wiping the blood from Eleanor's forehead when the boy Boyd, having delivered up another miracle for all to see, leaned down and said to him, "You'll be gettin' your due too." The sounds of Robert Lewis' screams went quiet just about as fast as they'd started once the deputies'd started beating him. Eleanor figured and in many ways hoped that he was unconscious.

Chapter 102

ONCE THINGS HAD SETTLED down, Spencer Duty, Jr. took Eleanor back to Wanda C. Music's boarding house. After she recovered a bit Eleanor would go on over to the jail and see how close to death Robert Lewis was. But just about no matter what, after what had happened, the deputies would never take him to the hospital. As he was leaving Eleanor, Spencer Duty, Jr. said he had something to take care of.

Chapter 103

He drove out of Paintsville past the "*Caution Falling Rocks*," signs that were more plentiful themselves than fallin' rocks and rounded the bend from Turkey Knob that went up to the boy Boyd's. He'd seen Drusa and Boy walkin' around Paintsville just a while ago, so he figured that the boy Boyd'd likely be at his homeplace and likely too that Lacy A. Hobbs'd be at her store proper.

Spencer Duty, Jr. parked his truck, got out, and heard a commotion behind the barn. When he rounded the corner he heard a hound still more of a pup than a dog crying out in pain with the boy Boyd beating it with a roll of thick bailing wire. The dog was bleeding from its side. Just as the boy Boyd was about to deliver another blow to the cowering dog, Spencer Duty, Jr. grabbed his arm and threw him back onto a split rail fence. "You goddamn son-of-a-bitch," roiled the boy Boyd. Spencer Duty, Jr. made not an utterance as the boy Boyd got to his feet and began strutting threateningly toward him, lifting the wire readying to strike. Spencer Duty, Jr. certainly wasn't a big man but his daddy'd said that a man should always know how to handle himself and so he began boxing when he was just a youngin' and became a Golden Glove at sixteen.

Just as the boy Boyd was about to strike him, he felt his jaw dislocate and the cartilage in his nose shatter as he now could only mutter his threats, seeing how his jaw just flopped around like it was lookin' for a way to run away from his face. The boy Boyd dropped the wire and tried to block the next half-dozen or so blows from Spencer Duty, Jr.'s fists, but was just no match for his speed or relentlessness.

The boy Boyd couldn't get out a coherent sounding word as Spencer Duty, Jr. continued to beat him senseless. Then, left laying in a bloody hovel, the beaten man managed to crawl into the tin pig pen to get away from Spencer Duty, Jr.

During the whole time he was beating him, he hadn't said one single word to the boy Boyd, but the hound was howling with what sounded like his last dying breaths. Spencer Duty, Jr. walked over to the dog, took the chain from around its neck, and carried him to his truck. He laid the dog on the seat beside him and drove to Travis O. Bramblett who'd been a horse doctor for going on fifty years or more now and who no one had ever seen without a cigarette hangin' from his lip. Folks'd say they figured he had a dip in his lip where he rested his smoke. When old Doc Bramblett took a look at the dog he shook his head back and forth at havin' seen too many beaten to the point of having to be put out of their misery, which was what he said it'd be best to do to the pup, saying he'd take a lot of tendin' to his wounds to make him worth it enough for someone to put that kind of time in. It took not more than a second or so for Spencer Duty, Jr. to come to the conclusion that being practical, versus the dog having some good years ahead of him after having suffered so much at the hands of the boy Boyd, was worth it. Fixin' him up'd cost upwards of a fifty dollars or more, Doc Bramblett said. "No matter," Spencer Duty, Jr. said back.

Henry lived upwards of close to twenty years, Spencer Duty, Jr. rarely being seen anywhere without him. He was also known to come out from behind the curtain at DUTIES BOOTIES and greet the youngins right as they came through the door. Folks that knew Henry said that likely he was the best dog that'd ever walked the face of the earth. Spencer Duty, Jr. told Eleanor that Henry knew every pair of shoes that he had. And that each night, right before bed time, Henry would go looking for each and every pair, bring them to him one at a time and wait for Spencer Duty, Jr. to look down and say, "Henry, I was just wondering what I did with that shoe, and well, what can I say, you're always helping me. If it wasn't for you why I'd be walking around bare foot. What a boy," and then Spencer Duty, Jr. would reach in his pocket and give Henry a biscuit. Much later on, Spencer Duty, Jr. said God likely had a special place for four-leggers like Henry, maybe even more so than most two-leggers.

Chapter 104

DRUSA AND BOY FOUND the boy Boyd layin' in bloodied-up pig slop. "I say, I say he's covered in pig shit momma, I say, I say," Boy said. And even though Drusa proclaimed her devotion to the boy Boyd for what he'd done for her and Boy, she also figured he'd been deservin' of whatever whoever'd done this to him. Drusa also gloated for him gettin' what he'd got for doin' to her what he'd do whenever he so desired to please himself. The boy Boyd couldn't talk with his jaw hangin' lose the way it was, so Drusa dragged him outta the hog pen and with Boy takin' hold of his feet lifted him into the back of his truck and drove him on over to the Paintsville Hospital, where the doctor had three orderlies hold him down while he twisted his jawbone this way and that back into its sockets, but, he said it'd probably forever hang a bit loose, making him "mumble" a bit when he'd up and try to say anything, especially when he was goin' on and on preachin' the Word of the Lord. The doctor also said the x-rays of his face showed his cheekbones were fractured, especially the left one, "…looks like a broken China cup that'd been put back together with the pieces not fittin' up the way they should," being all cracked this way and that. The boy Boyd's nose didn't sit straight on his face anymore neither.

Drusa and Boy took the boy Boyd on back to his homeplace and began tendin' him on back to health. Doc'd said it'd take a few days for the swellin' to go down in his face and for the bruisin' to go away but he'd be back to lookin' more or less like he did before in no time at all, except for his twisted nose.

Later that night the boy Boyd did some reflectin' on how to go about getting' back at Spencer Duty, Jr. for what he'd done. He hadn't figured ever on Spencer Duty, Jr. bein' the kind who'd do what he'd did and then bein' so fast that he didn't have no chance of even bein' able to get a lick in, so likely if he up and did anything at all, he figured that the Knights'd have to hit him about the head with an axe handle and then hold him so he could give him the whippin' he deserved for doin' what he'd up an done. But that weren't even for sure.

Truth be told, Spencer Duty, Jr. scared the boy Boyd, and he was figuring that unless he went on and just killed him that he wouldn't let a sleepin' dog lie and may finish what he'd started. Spencer Duty, Jr.'d be on his toes now too, figurin' that the boy Boyd'd try something, he hadn't done what he'd done without figurin' on that too, so likely he'd also be figurin' on keepin' clear of an opportunity for any timber rattlers comin' his way or openin' the door in the dark.

After a couple of days the boy Boyd was up and walkin' around so wrathful that he could barely see straight at havin' been done to him what'd been done, when Drusa showed up, brushed aside the swarm of flies gathered up on the screen door, and walked into the boy Boyd's homeplace, bringin' him a fresh pot of muskrat stew. And even though he'd *tried* to beat it into Drusa's dumb head that he didn't want her bringin' that slop around, she up and did her persistin' always pushin' up against his insistin'.

When she came through the door the boy Boyd smelled that shit and came ridin' on his iratedness from the other room, grabbed her by the hair, and slapped her across the face, causin' chunks of hot muskrat meat to go flyin' just about everywhere cut up muskrat could go. And then, havin' had it with her disobeyin' and unappreciatin' ways, the boy Boyd grabbed Drusa around her thick neck, feelin' the might of his rage convulsin' through his hands, and began screamin' with a voice like a man ought not to have comin' from inside him, shakin' her back and forth until her eyes swelled up out of her head and her neck went limp. When the boy Boyd came back from his vexin' spell, he uncurled his achin' hands from around Drusa's collapsed throat and let her fall to the floor.

He grabbed her by the hair and dragged her out the front door to his homeplace, bustin' up her backbone real bad as he pulled her down the scaly oak steps that he'd never bother to hewn properly. Once she'd bounced off the last step, the boy Boyd rolled her over and over again with his foot to the back of his truck, gettin' her face covered in dust that caked to the foam and blood oozin' from her gapin' mouth and nose holes. The boy Boyd leaned down and struggled to lift Drusa up into the truck bed, dropping her with a decidable plop onto the scissor jack that was layin' on its side from bein' not put away proper from when he'd had a flat. Right after that he got him a shovel from the shed, threw it in the back of the bed on top of the body, and then threw a tarp over top of her.

The boy Boyd tossed a hand up to Deputy Duffy Deeter who passed him on the road out of town. It took a while to get to the junction of Rabbit Hash and Monkey's Eye Holler and then took even more of his time to dig a hole deep enough to cover up the corpse so the bears that time of year wouldn't be diggin' her up. He pulled Drusa by her feet from the back of the truck, let her fall onto the ground, and then dragged her by her matted hair to the hole he'd just worked hard at diggin'. He'd figured long ago that draggin' a body that wouldn't ever be walkin' again on its own was about as easy as could be if they had a good head of hair to get a good drip on. It weren't so easy if the body didn't have no hair though, the boy Boyd remembered with a snigger, as he pulled Drusa through the brush.

He pushed her into the hole where she'd be up and spendin' eternity, likely scouring the hereafter for Jesus, who the boy Boyd figured had givin' up on her heathen ways long ago, then he covered her up with the pile of dirt he'd dug from the grave, smacked it down good with his shovel, smoked a cigarette, and then made his way back to Paintsville, figurin' he'd be stoppin' at Nellie's Diner for a likely pork tenderloin hot shot, with a double helpin' of mash potatoes and gravy, havin' worked himself up a hefty appetite.

When he pulled up in the front of Nellie's sure enough there was his momma's shiny new car, havin' had Linc take her all the way over to Louisville to buy it just a few days or so ago. He brushed whatever might be left of Drusa off himself and went on inside smilin' at his momma as he sat down in the booth across from her.

Lacy A. Hobbs herself said to her boy Boyd that she'd been figurin' on him needin' to take up more collections 'cause her havin' just spent a load of her hard-earned money on the new car and all, that she said she equally figured was needed to not let folks forget her rightful place that was due and demandin' of their respect. The boy Boyd nodded in agreement sayin' he was gettin' called upon for more preachin' and that his name was bein' known now here and wide, especially his healin' powers, but that he'd make sure that his collectin' picked up for his momma.

Lacy A. Hobbs herself was appreciatin' as always of the rightful dutifulness of the boy Boyd.

Chapter 105

THAT MONDAY MORNING FOLKS were wondering if Chafin was going to be in any condition to come on back to court and partake of his juryin' duty, seeing how he'd been broken up and all, but sure enough, there was Chafin, who refusin' to allow any of the other jurors to touch him, used a crutch to prop himself up while he stepped into the jury box, his head covered in a thick bandage along with a patch over his right eye. After he sat himself down, he glared out at the boy Boyd who was sittin' in the back of the courtroom tendin' to his own painful wincins from movin' this way or that.

Robert Lewis was brought into the courtroom, his ankles in manacles and his wrists handcuffed tight behind his back, by Deputy Duffy Deeter, who was still wheezin' with his breathin'. His eyes were just about swollen shut and his jaw was sittin' cockeyed on the opposite side of his now flattened out nose. Robert Lewis couldn't even put one foot in front of the other, havin' to shuffle his way to the defense table instead. When court was called to session Eleanor immediately stood up and demanded a mistrial, to which Judge Herbert Van Hoose told her to sit herself down and not to start causin' a commotion right off even before court even up and began. Then Rudolph Sword stood up and said after what'd happened with the accused showin' the jury how dangerous he was that the prosecution rested. But, he did add that with Robert Lewis' demonstration of his violent nature that it was obvious how he'd lost his mind and killed Hattie Hicks and that he was pullin' the wool over folks' eyes, and that he was smart like a fox, and had figured out how to kill Thaddeus too in the most heinous of heinous way. A cunning and murderous colored boy, this one was, he said.

After Rudolph Sword finished his goings-on, Eleanor stood and called for Drusa to come back to the stand, figuring that she'd try a different tact of trying to expose her relationship with the boy Boyd and how she may know more than she'd been willing to say. But even though the witnesses were to supposed to have made themselves available, Drusa was nowhere to be found. Boy was sittin' in the back right beside Lacy A. Hobbs herself and when Drusa's name was called started askin' where his momma was, sayin' that she'd ain't been nowhere to be seen and that weren't like her. The boy Boyd stood up and asked the judge for permission to speak, which was granted, sayin' that Drusa'd said right after Eleanor'd tried to get her to say things that weren't true that she'd had enough and that she was takin' off and for him and Lacy A. Hobbs herself to take up the rearin' of Boy. And on that, Boy began his screamin' sayin' that his momma'd never leave him, "I say, I say, she'd never up an do that, momma'd never do that!" he said. Then Boy said, "What'd you do to my momma… I say, I say?" Judge Herbert Van Hoose said he'd now heard enough and for the boy Boyd to get Boy out of the courtroom and added that he was makin' more of a commotion than the defense. The boy Boyd took Boy up by the scruff of his collar and practically dragged him out of the courtroom kickin' and screamin'. Once the boy Boyd got Boy down the steps of the courthouse, he slapped him silly, sayin' him he'd better straighten up and shut his goddamn mouth if he knew what was good for him. Boy hauled off and kicked the boy Boyd right in his private parts, makin' his hands let go of their grip and find their way down to comfortin' his crotch parts. Boy was actin' like he'd up and lost his mind, kickin' and swingin' and scratchin' like the boy Boyd'd never seen before in a youngin'. He later told Lacy A. Hobbs herself that it was like tryin' to hold onto an always angry long-tail weasel carryin' a kickin' chicken. When the boy Boyd's hands let go of Boy, he took off runnin' through this way and that, knowin' Paintsville just about as good as anyone'd ever known it, and in no time at all Boy'd twisted himself up into a side alley coal chute. He'd stay there 'til darkness fell down to the ground so he could sneak on out and make his way back up to Rabbit Hash and Monkey's Eye Holler to look for his momma.

Chapter 106

WITH DRUSA NOT BEING anywhere to be found, Eleanor called Deputy Duffy Deeter back to the stand. Rudolph Sword immediately objected, sayin' that Deputy Duffy Deeter'd already said everything he had to say and that the defense was just wastin' the court's time, when everyone knew that Robert Lewis was guilty as any man who'd ever been brought before "…this court and this nonsense needs to stop and things need to be moved on along, these good people serving as jurors have jobs to go to and mouths to feed and they can't keep havin' to deal with the defenses claptrap!" Eleanor said again, "I call Deputy Duffy Deeter to the stand, Your Honor." And on that, Judge Herbert Van Hoose annoyingly waved for Rudolph Sword to sit down and then motioned for Deputy Duffy Deeter to come back on up to the witness stand, all without ever so much as sayin' a word. After he was sworn Eleanor began her questioning:

Eleanor: "Deputy, Exactly *how* did you go about investigating Constable Thaddeus Yates' homicide?"

Deputy Duffy Deeter: "We did figurin' by deducin' that given that the defendant'd killed the Hicks girl and that Thaddeus was closin' in on him that he musta been the one'd gone and killed him, and after what that boy'd did to me when I was just tryin' to do my job, right here in this court of law, he's about as dangerous of a nigger that I've ever come across."

"But, Deputy, I asked you *specifically* how you investigated Constable Thaddeus Yates' death, so again, to repeat myself," Eleanor said, "what did you discover that directly tied my client, Mr. Robert Lewis Rosskam, to the death of Constable Thaddeus Yates?"

Deputy Duffy Deeter looked over at the jury and told them they found the snakes that Robert Lewis' daddy'd killed just before they showed up to arrest Robert Lewis for the murder of the Hicks girl, and that those snakes being where they were and all was about as "closed and shut case" as he'd ever seen in his "many years of law enforcin'."

"So," Eleanor said, "if finding dead snakes is your only *evidence*, in an area where rattlers can be found hiding under just about every rock, then to me that says that not only were you quick to jump to conclusions but that you're lazy."

And on that, Deputy Duffy Deeter leapt to his feet, pointed his finger at Eleanor, and shouted, "That colored boy sittin' right on over there strangled that little nigger girl and it ain't of no mind to me if all them niggers kill each other, but if he did what he did to his own kind then what'd you think he'd do to one who ain't his kind?"

Eleanor looked over and just about every juror was noddin' in agreement with Deputy Duffy Deeter. She then said, "Your honor, *please* instruct the witness to *only* answer the questions to keep what are nothing more than his opinions to himself!"

Judge Herbert Van Hoose directed Deputy Duffy Deeter to "Just respond to Miss Kitchen's questions being that they make any sense or not." And on that Deputy Duffy Deeter calmed himself and sat back down, waiting for the next senseless question.

Eleanor then asked again, "So again, *other than the dead snakes*, you have *absolutely nothing* that directly ties my client to the death of Constable Thaddeus Yates."

"No," Deputy Duffy Deeter replied.

"No more questions, Your Honor," Eleanor said.

Robert Lewis sat, handcuffed and tied to the chair, still knowin' that his only sin had been stealin' onions. When the lights had gone down in his cell each night, he prayed in his own way for Jesus to forgive him for havin' done such a bad thing and that he'd never do it again, if he could go home, he'd be good.

The truth was there were no more witnesses to call and nowhere else to go. It was time for the defense to rest.

Chapter 107

Upon resting, Judge Herbert Van Hoose asked Rudolph Sword if in fact he had any further witnesses to call in the "…prosecution of the Negro Robert Lewis Rosskam," who'd he said'd been accused of committing just about the most two heinous crimes ever committed in those parts and the jury was burdened now with making the final determination as to whether or not he was going to get his due or not. "It's a right-sizable responsibility and one that y'all 'il be charged with right after we get on with the closing arguments."

Eleanor stood and began to deliver her closing. "Ladies and gentlemen of the jury, I can't imagine that anyone of you has ever seen anything like has gone on in this courtroom. Here you have a man, a man of limitations, a man who suffers from mental retardation, and a man who in fact is guilty. But he is *not guilty* of what he has been charged with for the only act of violence that anyone has ever been witness to Robert Lewis Rosskam committing occurred right here in this courtroom, right after Deputy Duffy Deeter pushed me over the defense table knocking me to the floor. My client thought he was defending me and then yes, ladies and gentlemen, everyone here witnessed what he did. But outside of that the only crime that my client is guilty of is in fact stealing onions and food scraps. That also, ladies and gentlemen, is what he believes because he has no memory of committing the crimes he is being accused of because he can't remember what he *didn't* do! Again, ladies and gentlemen, Deputy Duffy Deeter just admitted under oath that other than two dead snakes there is *nothing*, *nothing* whatsoever, other than a cockamamie notion that he and the prosecution seem so fond of touting, that my client could even be capable of conniving. When the prosecution's witness Boy testified using the exact same words when he was asked about what he saw, *word* for *word* for *word*. Throughout all of Boy's goings-on when he was testifying, he repeated that he had seen my client running away from the body of Hattie Hicks exactly the same way when he was questioned by the prosecution and by me. *Exactly*, not one word was different, not one, ladies and gentlemen. And I ask you, who amongst you talks like that? No, ladies and gentlemen, what you heard was a young man who was coached and told what to say, by *someone* who brought him and his mother off a mountain, gave them a dry roof over their head, and plenty of food to fill their hungry bellies. And further, I think *we all* know *who* that person is.

"Even when Drusa testified, and when she said that when her boy Boy told her that my client was 'runnin' like a jack rabbit,' even Drusa was repeating Boy's words *exactly*. Clearly, ladies and gentlemen, *Drusa and Boy were lying*. Boy saw nothing, because there was nothing to see, because my client was *nowhere near* Greasy Creek. It is an undisputed fact that Boy discovered the body, it is an undisputed fact that he reported the death to Linc and they accompanied Constable Thaddeus Yates to the girl's body. But it is *not* undisputed that my client is the perpetrator of these horrific crimes. In fact, ladies and gentlemen, Drusa seems to have disappeared so the defense can't even recall her to the stand to confront her on these discrepancies. It is unimaginable, ladies and gentlemen, how you can reach any other conclusion in your deliberations than to find my client Mr. Robert Lewis Rosskam *not guilty!*"

Then Rudolph Sword stood up and began to deliver his closing statement. "Folks, I have stood before jurors in Johnson County for about as long as I can remember. I grew up in these parts and I've known many of you for most of my life. I've never lied to you before and I'm sure not about to start now. Now sittin' right yonder is a man who is accused of murdering a young girl of his own persuasion and then engaging in debauchery of such ferocity that the good Pinky Jones couldn't even bring himself to describe in detail what the defendant had done to his own kind. Then, as we all know, he went out and got himself a couple of vipers and threw them through the window of Constable Thaddeus Yates' patrol car. Now, Miss Kitchen would have you believe that her client is so retarded that he couldn't figure out how to go about doing all this killing. And, ladies and gentlemen, as I said to you before, don't let this Negro pull the wool over your eyes. Then the defense wants you to believe that two of the prosecution's witnesses were, as she said, 'coached' into saying something that they were told to say for a place to stay and food to eat. And that Boy when he testified to seeing this Negro running away from the Hicks girl that he'd just killed, had said it, I guess to 'perfectly' or the same way more than once. Well folks I would say that the reason he said it the same way is because there is no other way to say it if that's what you'd seen. Miss. Kitchen says there's no proof of this and no proof of that, but here she is making allegations against who we all know is the boy Boyd, who's been bringing folks to Jesus now for longer than I can remember, and whose momma, Lacy A. Hobbs herself, has been helpin' folks out around these parts for about as long as I have been protectin' folks from murderous criminals like the defendant. I suspect that some of you have been brought to salvation by the boy Boyd and are indebted to his momma for carin' about folks who are tryin' to make ends meet. Miss. Kitchen stood before you and debased the boy Boyd's good name, trying to somehow implicate him, again with absolutely *no* proof, in the murders that her client, beyond any shadow of a doubt, committed. The thing is folks, y'all saw that boy, havin' to be chained up, turn into the animal he is, just about killing Deputy Duffy Deeter right here in this courtroom! If this is how ferocious he gets with folks who are watching him you can imagine how ferocious he gets when there ain't no one watchin' what he doin'. Well good folks of the jury, Miss. Kitchen may not be able to imagine how you can find this man guilty but I can assure you that I can imagine how you can and that is because that is where the evidence takes you. If that Negro were a dog and doing what he'd done, there ain't no question that you'd put him out of his misery. But in this case he don't seem to be in no misery at all, it's us, the good people of Paintsville, who are in misery being in fear of their lives. If this boy were ever to stalk us again, there ain't no tellin' where he turn up and what he'd do. I ask you good people of the jury, find this man, Robert Lewis Rosskam, guilty of the murders and debauchery he wrought upon us."

Judge Herbert Van Hoose then slapped his gavel to its block and said all the pleading was in fact done and now the good folks of the jury had their decision to make. "It's up to y'all to decide if this boy is guilty or not, so go on and get to decidin'. Deputy Duffy Deeter will take you on into the back room and you can begin your deliberatin' there. He'll also be standin' right outside if y'all need anything. Hopefully this won't take too long." And on that Deputy Duffer Deeter led the jurors to the back room when they began their debatin'.

Chapter 108

"HE'S ABOUT AS GUILTY a colored boy as I've ever seen," said Luda Mae Bower whose twin sister was born just a few minutes after Luda Mae. Lula Mae, who was known not to talk so much and who'd suffered from the mully grubs most all her life, nodded her head in agreement, which folks who'd known the twins all their lives'd knew that whatever Luda Mae said Lula Mae agreed with. It was right after their momma and daddy'd died within the same week of each other that the twins'd been left to fend for themselves. Their parents had been sick goin' on six months or so back then after havin' gone out squirrel huntin' which was about what their daddy'd rather be doin' than just about anything else while he was in this world or any other world for that matter. Their daddy'd shot a half-dozen or so squirrels that day and carried them back to their homeplace where their momma'd done skinned them and cooked them up in a stew pot with dumplins. Once they'd done cooked up she'd crack the skull open with her teeth and scoop out the brains with a spoon. Momma and Daddy though'd never share that delicacy with Luda and Lula sayin' that they'd done the work shooting them and cookin' them and if they went to that much work they was goin' to be eatin' them too. So Luda and Lula ate up the rest of the squirrels and dumplins, fillin' up for a couple of days or so with the fixins.

Squirrel brains are just about the size of walnuts but when they was stirred into a bowl of dumplins cooked up all day with squirrel meat, well... there just weren't any better or more tender eatin' anywhere on God's green earth. It weren't long after the last time that their momma and daddy'd cooked up squirrel brains that they both began actin' just about as odd as anyone who'd ever acted odd.

Their momma had been about as sweet of a woman who'd God'd ever given breath to and their daddy, well he could get pretty riled up pretty quick if the notion took him over for some reason or other. And then, seemingly like one day, all of a sudden, Luda and Lula's momma lost her mind and began screamin' and chasin' them around their homeplace with a butcher knife, while their daddy it seemed no matter what had lost all of his gumption to get riled up about anything. Seemingly it took about all he had to just take one breath after the other. It wasn't long after that their momma and daddy got a bad case of the palsy and shook so much they thought they was gonna break apart like a dried-up tree unable to bend with the wind. That went on for a few months when they both just about the same day or so went onto sleep and never woke back up. A while later their hearts just up and stopped. Luda and Lula buried them out back just a week apart, havin' to dig their graves themselves. The twins suffered a lot for a long while after that. But, one thing for sure, never would they ever again touch another bite of squirrel figurin' it somehow had something to do with their momma and daddy up and dyin' on them.

The other jurors nodded in agreement with Luda's assertin' and Lula's agreein' about the despicableness of Robert Lewis. Junior, who nobody knew as anything but Junior, said his daddy'd of already strung up the nigger and "…it just don't seem right that good folks have to go through these shenanigans just to give that sonofabitch what he's deservin' of." The only person in that room who wasn't noddin' in the affirmative was Chafin.

An hour or so after the debatin' had begun the door opened and Deputy Duffy Deeter let the boy Boyd into the room. "I ain't here to say nothin' other than to say that Jesus is lookin' to each and every one of y'all to do the right thing. Bow your heads, my brothers and sisters," the boy Boyd said. "Lord Jesus, give the men and women of this jury the strength to make the right decision so that when they come before you on their day of judgment, you may look in your book of judgment and see that they had not fallen under the spell of Satan and cowered in trepidation. Ye recall the words of Leviticus, *Whoever takes a human life shall surely be put to death*. In Jesus name we always pray, Amen." And so said eleven "Amens." Chafin though sat with his head unbowed. An 'amen' was not heard coming from his lips by the other members of the jury. The boy Boyd told those so appreciative of his coming by that their salvation was assured, providing of course they do the right thing. Deputy Duffy Deeter opened the door and the boy Boyd then went on his way.

Aunt Birdie, who folks'd always nod to when she limped by, was only able to take a few steps at a time, havin' to stop, get her breath, while lighting a cigarette she'd take from the pocket of her apron. Every mornin' she'd always roll up a half-dozen or so, wrap them in a piece of tissue paper, and put them in her apron pocket. That way if she was out and about she'd have her greatest pleasure always at hand. More often than not when she stopped to catch her breath, someone feelin' themselves lookin' like her one day'd light her cigarette for her seein' her fumbling while tetterin'. Her daddy'd always said that Abraham Lincoln'd been a "miserable sonofabitchen traitor," and "the day John Wilkes Booth pulled that Deringer out of his vest pocket and did what God had called him to do was the greatest day of my life." And Aunt Birdie'd always felt the same way, seein' all her life what coloreds had done to the South once they'd gotten rights they shouldn't of had in the first place. "Folks should know their place," she'd say to just about anyone who'd listen, and given how long she'd been livin', folks were prone to listenin' to what she was sayin', and the boy Boyd'd always paid her her due, that was for sure. Aunt Birdie'd gotten an entire mountain top right up on Hager Hill and given that all of her next of kin had passed on, and that she was a beloved member of the boy Boyd's church, and that she was also the most devout believer in the boy Boyd's healing power and corralling Satan each and every time he reached in and pulled one of those rattlers out of the coffee can, well to Aunt Birdie the boy Boyd became "...*the Messiah who crushes the serpent's head at Calvary.*" Like all said and all believed given God had granted Aunt Birdie a long life to use her tongue to spread what she knew and had been taught what was right and now after havin' spent time listenin' to the evidence presented by the righteous Rudolph Sword about the accused nigger, Aunt Birdie pronounced him "as guilty as livin' sin itself."

Born over in Tyewhoppety, Okey Saylor had his say, sayin', "Y'all saw what that boy did to Deputy Duffy Deeter, and I fer one sure don't want that boy bein' back anywhere around these parts where he can do what he'd done to that little nigger girl and Thaddeus, who'd

I known for most of my life, matter-of-fact it was Thaddeus who'd helped my daddy, Hobart, when he'd been up and shot by 'Big Frank' Blair, ritch up there at the left fork of Little Paint Crick, and it was Thaddeus who'd said my daddy, Hobart'd, didn't have no choice but to shoot Big Frank right between the eyes with his shotgun, takin' most of his head off I heard tell, Thaddeus'd come up on my daddy, Hobart, layin' there bleedin' from that hole put in him by Big Frank, and he dragged him on into his patrol car and drove him bleedin' to the hospital. Hear tell Thaddeus even helped the doctor plug up the bullet hole with his finger so he could find the bullet that was secretin' itself up somewhere around his liver, or thereabouts. Why if it weren't for Thaddeus I wouldn't even be sittin' here with y'all in judgment of that colored boy, I mean if he wants to kill his own kind, I'm of the mind that it don't matter just one bit to me, except for the Christian side of me feelin' sorry for that little nigger girl's momma and daddy, there ain't nothin' like loosin' a youngin' I hear tell, but when he done what he did to a man like Thaddeus, well, *that* he needs to die hisself for '*an eye for an eye*' the good book says. Y'all know when ya hang a man his eyes'll pop clean outta of his head, I'm a guessin' that that's how Jesus knew what he was talkin' about havin' seen his share of hangins'."

As Chafin looked around the table he saw eleven heads noddin' up and down, just about as fast as they could in their agreein'.

"Not to mention *that* woman, sittin' there disrespectin' Judge Herbert Van Hoose lookin' the way she does, speakin' out of turn, interruptin'. Most certainly Lacy A. Hobbs'd *never* debase herself lookin' like that," said by Ellaree Miller, wife of Linc, and whose momma'd said she'd remembered hearin' stories that Eleanor's momma'd been carryin' on in a no good way with a man named Moses Kitchen who'd himself done killed some of the Knights way back yonder ago who'd been doin' nothin' more at the time than their Godley-appointed duty to be lookin' out for folks when the coloreds'd come slickin' up from the South, over the mountain top from Butcher Holler hidin' out in the sugar maple grove. "Her momma hear tell was a witch too," Ellaree Miller whispered of Eleanor. Linc, she constantly reminded folks, held his head up about as high as a man can when he was chosen to be the Knights Grand Titan of the Johnson County Province. And since he'd taken over the province he'd run the Knights with the same capability that he'd run his fillin' station, makin' sure that the coloreds knew their place, *if* they knew'd what was good for them. Chafin, lookin' up now, knew it was Linc or at least two of his henchmen who'd beat him just about to death.

Sittin' just to the west of Chafin was the Queen of Van Lear, holdin' her head proud at havin' become the wife of Dr. William H. Brady and now havin' had the opportunity to see just about all of Kentucky and West Virginia, managin' Dr. Brady's travelin' schedule, goin' here and there and just about everywhere else to talk up against the black lungs, from a medical perspective of course, he would always add. And always from the audience, Patsy Arms, who folks outside of Van Lear didn't know had been anointed Queen, would stand up and say, "In all my years of knowin' I ain't never known a better or more honest man than Dr. Brady. Y'all can believe what he says as the God's truth." Patsy Arms was known to come into the SIPP demandin' that she be recognized for who she was and given free admission to the motion picture show.

Eddie Holcomb, who'd worked as an usher, bein' just about the best usher the SIPP'd ever had, knowin' just how to shine his flashlight so as not to disturb other movie watchers while directin' folks to a seat that wasn't taken up by someone else. Eddie'd always say each and every time to Patsy Arms when she came in demandin' that her "rightful" place in the linage of Van Lear royalty be recognized, that he didn't know who she was havin' not seen an announcement in the *Paintsville Herald* of her annointin'. But that she'd have to pay the sixty-five cents to get into the movie, but that he'd sure be watchin' for when her crownin' was announced and then he'd be just as sure to make sure her royal highness was recognized and he'd be even more sure that she wouldn't have to pay a penny to see the movie and to boot he'd see to it that she got free popcorn. Patsy tried every which way to get Eddie Holcomb fired from his usherin' job, but Chafin'd said that "no phony queen of this or that is going to gyp folks by swindlin' her way to a free ticket.

"You just keep on doin' what your doin'," Chafin would say to Eddie, whenever Patsy Arms'd complain, saying he was being "... impudent" to her. Chafin hated the Queen of Van Lear.

Patsy Arms said she agreed with everyone who'd said their mind but that "bein' married to a doctor and all," she thought they should know that Kentucky had a special medical experimentation unit at the state prison there in Eddyville, where's if someone is convicted of a crime where they're goin' die in the electric chair, then they can go ahead and use those prisoners however they think fit, "they're gonna be killed anyway, they've done about as bad a things as good folks can imagine someone of the likes of them doin', so why not give their life some meaning?" The queen of Van Lear further explained that "in all likelihood that colored boy, like a lot of colored boys, had already got himself infected with syphilis but even if he don't, the experimentin' doctors are infectin' boys like him with syphilis. They're takin' the syphilis germ right from other prisoners who'd already got it and givin' it to someone who don't and then watchin' in an experimental way of course to see what happens. Dr. William H. Brady, my husband and all, says it works out best when the prison takes a good long while before strappin' a prisoner in the electric chair so the doctors can see how bad the syphilis gets.

"So that Negro could be worth somethin' in death even if he ain't worth a piss pot in life."

Most of the other jurors thought the mercifulness of prisoners being used to further medicine brought meanin' into those prisoners otherwise meaningless lives, and felt their appreciation for Patsy Arms tellin' them as such.

"I don't know how many times I've had to chase that boy out of my onion field, more times than I've got fingers and toes, I reckon," said Drema Othel-Winburne, and she knew more about fingers and toes than anyone else havin' been born with a couple of extra of both. It was likely because of her supplemental digits that her momma and daddy'd put her on the Othel-Winburne's porch in the middle of the night and in the middle of a howlin' wind blowin' snow this way and that. Dorsel Othel-Winburne'd just about fell over the basket pushed up against his and Ruby Jo Othel-Winburne's door to their home-place. That little baby was sure enough about as cold as cold could be and not movin' barely at all, when Ruby Jo brushed away the snow and lifted who was to become Drema Othel-Winburne out of the basket. Dorsal and Ruby Jo'd never been blessed with any youngins of their own, figurin' that the good Lord just hadn't seen fit to bless them that way and then on that night they refigured that the good Lord in his plannin' had destined their homeplace to be where the good Lord laid that child at their feet further destining them to rear up that little one knowin' of His ways. And that's just what they did, with Drema Othel-Winburne not havin' gone beyond much of the fifth grade or so right there at the Asa Creek schoolhouse. But, that bein' understood, Ruby Jo, each and every night from the time that youngin' was able to hold her head up by herself, read the good book to her, over and over, again and again, until Drema Othel-Winburne could quote the Bible line for line and would in just about any conversation call forth a verse or two as proof to what she was sayin'. In their conversin' about Robert Lewis' guilt Drema Othel-Winburne just kept repeatin' over and over again, "*Who so sheddeth man's blood, by man shall his blood be shed: for in the image of God made he man.*" Not another word did she speak and every now and then in between their sayin' this and that, the other folks on the jury would under their breaths say, "Praise Jesus..." in response to what they heard as Drema Othel-Winburne's devout prayfulness.

They'd always said they'd wanted a boy youngin' but they settled on a Petey May Stumbo instead of a Pete Stumbo when what was supposed to be a he come out born of the wrong ilk. Petey Stumbo even when she was just learnin' to talk'd been about as ornery as a youngin' can be, smartin' off to her momma and daddy in that wheezy high-pitch voice, with her little knobby hands goin' this way and that, walkin' with a waddle and tryin' like the dickins to make herself look taller than she'd ever in her life be. Folks'd always said that her daddy had Tommyknocker blood in him, especially with Petey just barely comin' up to her momma's waist when she was less than more growin' into womanhood and never sproutin' upwards beyond that. Said it was that her daddy, Abraham Lincoln Stumbo, had thought it best once she'd come out backwards and all to take her on down to the river and let it have its way with her, but her momma, Sadie Stumbo, said she was havin' none of that and would raise her up herself if she had to. Abraham Lincoln Stumbo then said that he now was havin' none of that and so they decided one way or another to go ahead and keep Petey on dry land. It'd been hard for her havin' to all the time be lookin' up to see who was always lookin' down at her and now that she was on the older side she'd developed a crooked neck that cocked to one side and rarely moved to the other. But her outspokenness was what folks seemed to take away when they looked down and began conversin' with her. Some folks, most especially those gettin' on in years, still thought of her as havin' Tommyknocker blood flowin' in her veins, and so they'd try as they might to shy away from her, which was sometimes hard because they wouldn't see her comin', and then she'd be tuggin' at their pants leg or dress hem before they knew it, wantin' to be conversin' about this or that, when what they wanted was to get on away from her, fearful that if she up and spilled any of her Tommyknocker blood that it'd bring bad luck upon them and theirs.

Junior'd lifted Petey from as far out as he could push his arms, mind you, onto an upside down milk crate that Aunt Birdie'd put up on a chair. "I don't know who'd be guilty if he ain't guilty and if he ain't guilty then I don't know who'd be," Petey hissed, wavin' her short, meaty arms this way and that. Aunt Birdie said that Petey had about as good a thought as anybody'd had and that she was in full agreement, "If *he* ain't guilty, then who'd be guilty? 'Cause," Aunt Birdie continued, "their ain't no one else that Rudolph Sword or Deputy Duffy Deeter'd be thinkin' about for the murder of that little colored girl and poor Thaddeus, y'all know Thaddeus was a good Christian man, not just arrestin' criminals but he'd be helpin' folks just about whenever he could, y'all remember when that flood in '57 came on us and Thaddeus, he'd be out there trudgin' through water almost up to his neck helpin' to save folks from drownin', he was about as good a man as'd ever been, and that boy up and did what he did to save his own hide and I say *damn his hide* to that." Petey was so riled up in her agreein' with what Aunt Birdie'd just said that she couldn't even get one word to pass through her hissin' lips, and with what looked like to Dr. Lucky Archer, M.D., Petey was startin' to have some kind of fit from falling sickness. Suddenly Petey broke through her hissin' and screamed out, "I'm tellin' y'all the wind blows through that nigger's head like it blows through a rail fence," and then again but this time makin' no sense at all Petey stuttered, "*Amen brother Ben, shot a rooster and killed a hen.*" There was no mistaken at all that she was agreein' with Aunt Birdie as her crooked head nodded up and down over one shoulder as the wheezin' and shakin' got worse and she threw herself off the milk crate and onto the floor.

Dr. Lucky Archer'd been just about known for his bein' a man of good reason as he was for his doctorin'. He'd been around for so long takin' care of folks and bringin' this and that youngin' into the world and seein' those that he'd slapped on their bare behinds leave this world. Folks on the jury'd decided that Dr. Lucky Archer'd be the one who'd speak up to Judge Herbert Van Hoose when the time came to say whether or not Robert Lewis had been found guilty (which for sure he was goin' to be). Folks knew also that Dr. Lucky Archer was a God-fearin' man havin' been baptized just about before he could walk and *never* strayed from the path of righteousness. Bein' sure that when he stood before Jesus and Jesus looked down at the page in His book that said the sinful things that one had done and then whether or not Jesus'd be grantin' forgiveness, that Dr. Lucky Archer's page in the book of books would be empty. It was in agreement with his wife Laureta Rita Rose that they'd only have relations to bring their progeny into this world and that they'd take no pleasure in what they had to do to do it. It so happened that on both times that they'd engaged in relations that it bore them two good sons, bein' just about the finest young men that any momma and daddy could've ever hoped for. But their lives were to be short, havin' come just a year apart, havin' lost the year older one right as the great war was comin' to an end and havin' lost the next older one to the Spanish Flu in 1918. But bein' the fine boys they were Dr. Lucky Archer and Laureta Rita Archer were sure that they were about as close to Jesus as any mortal man'd ever been, havin' been raised up to fear the Lord and whenever they did anything growin' up that went against the Ten Commandments they were met with all the everlasting torment that Dr. Lucky Archer and Laureta Rita Archer could muster out. And, as each boy moved on into manhood, they thanked their momma and daddy for their up bringin' ensuring them a special place in Heaven.

Dr. Lucky Archer early on'd been a strong believer in keepin' the races separated, mostly because when he'd spent much of his doctorin' lifetime studying eugenics he'd come to realize that miscegenation adulterated the purer genes of those of the white race. It was one of his proudest days of proud days when he made application for membership in the Anglo-Saxon Clubs of America, being one of the first folks from Kentucky to join the prestigious club. It wasn't long after he'd sent along his hard-earned ten dollars that he received a letter in the mail sayin' that he'd been accepted into membership. After that

Dr. Lucky Archer figured that one of the most important things he could do among other important things would be to educate folks about the *Virginia Racial Integrity Act.*

He'd even gone to the Kentucky legislature to educate them on the scientific principles of Dr. Lewis Terman, who showed "…beyond any shadow of a doubt that the Negro needed to be tended too and not just allowed to roam around willy-nilly" he liked to say. In 1951 Dr. Lucky Archer did further educating saying that "…*Army mental tests have shown that not more than fifteen percent of American Negros equal or exceed in intelligence the average of our white population and the intelligence of the average Negro is vastly inferior to that of the average white ma*n," in his quoting of Dr. Terman. It was right then that the legislature invoked a fine of up to a thousand dollars or five years in prison for those folks who'd go up against nature and engage in miscegenation. Dr. Lucky Archer, was just about as well thought of as any man could be, so folks on the jury were lookin' to him for his knowin' guidance.

"To the question that is put before us, ladies and gentlemen," Dr. Lucky Archer always preferred takin' a more formal tone, "…Is this Negro guilty …beyond any shadow of a doubt, and him bein' a descendant of Africa, has in the words of the great scientist Karl Pearson, and I don't expect folks to know who he was, havin' gone onto the Lord many years ago now, and I had the pleasure of meeting him once when I was a much younger man, but that is neither here or there, but, Dr. Pearson said *directly* to me, *There is for the best ascertainable characters a continuous relationship from the European skull through prehistoric European, prehistoric Egyptian, Congo-Gaboon Negros to Zulus and Kaffirs,* and I think we can see that right here with this Negro.

"And, if I may go on for just one more minute, again, y'all wouldn't be likely to know this, but I was on the National Committee for Mental Hygiene when it conducted its survey regarding race and feeblemindedness. In 1934 I helped write the law that showed the *undisputable* need for sterilization of the racially inadequate idiot. I taught Georgie T. Skinner, the main writer of a law. He and I put forth, on how a *completely harmless* operation to sterilize these imbeciles could be the best thing that'd ever happened to them. And, given his persuasiveness, he was able to convince those in the state house on how this was a truly humane, scientific endeavor. The feebleminded have no sense of reason and are prone to acts of unpredictable violence. In a civilized society we *have* to protect ourselves from folks of this ilk, you know truth be told, they can barely walk upright, and with those long arms hangin' by their sides, we know right where they came from.

"And as I sit here before you, I say that this colored boy is about the surest proof of the need for what I have worked for all my life. Being feebleminded, epileptic, insane or diseased, are defects that can't never be overcome, and when you put that together with being *Negroed*, well, my good friends, neighbors, and some of you that I've even brought into this world, that'd be the reason why we're all sittin' together in this room."

"The undertaking department of the Mountain Furniture Company prepared his body for burial," Beedie Cantrell piped up. It didn't seem particularly to make no sense until she added, "That nigger Sut Mushroe killed my daddy with his own gun, mind you, lyin' through his teeth, sayin' that my momma was in love with him and that my daddy'd better be on his way and leave them alone, if he knewed what was good for him. Sayin' as much that my momma was a whore, a no good. Heard tell that when that nigger saw my daddy reachin' in his pants, gettin' ready to pull his pistol, he hauled off and hit my daddy so hard with that big fist of his that he staggered like he'd been on an all-night bender, then he grabbed my daddy's pistol and shot him right between the eyes. Said it was that momma just lost her mind after that, that's right about when they put my poor momma in the lunatic asylum, but they hung that nigger for doin' what he'd done to my daddy, and Judge Herbert Van Hoose'd been the judge then just like he's bein' the judge now, and as fer as I'm concerned then that nigger's as guilty as sin itself."

Dr. Lucky Archer turned to Chafin, who'd not said so much as a word, askin' him of his opinion on the colored boy's guilt or innocence. Chafin looked this way and that around the room and then spoke up, "Did any one of y'all see that each and every day that they brought this man into the courtroom that his shoes were untied?"

Dr. Lucky Archer asked Chafin in a scoffing tone, "What on God's green earth does that have to do with the price of tea in China?"

Chafin looked right at each person and asked the question again, and again there was no response, except from the good Dr. Lucky Archer, who demanded that Chafin, if he had something to say, to get on with it but it wasn't his place to be askin' questions. Then Chafin said, "The man can't tie his shoes. I've seen him all over Paintsville, and his shoes ain't never tied, he can't tie his shoes, and Rudolph Sword and that goddamn crooked Deputy Duffy Deeter wants us all to believe that Robert Lewis killed that little girl and Thaddeus.

"If a man can't figure how to tie his shoes then he can't figure his way to do what they say he's done. He ain't guilty."

And on that Ellaree Miller looked down the table declarin', "If my memory serves me, it weren't that long ago that you got a talkin' to. It seems to me that'd been enough for you."

"Any man, and I mean any man, who has to hide underneath a sheet and ambush a man, is gutless sonofabitch," Chafin replied.

Dr. Lucky Archer said that it was important for them all to vote and then let Judge Herbert Van Hoose know where things stood and what the verdict was going to be. And on that the jury decided it was time they took a vote, "…say yea or nay?"

Chapter 109

ELEANOR AND SPENCER DUTY, Jr. had figured that Robert Lewis
would be found guilty and even though she would file an appeal it
would do no good as Judge Herbert Van Hoose'd known each and
every member of the appeals court and not one time in all of his time
serving as a judge had he been overruled or sanctioned. They sat in the
backroom of DOOTIES BOOTIES saying that they had imagined
things would be different now than in their momma and daddies'
days. Spencer Duty, Jr. had heard many stories about Moses and his
disgust with Negroes being hung for just being Negroes. Eleanor
said that her momma had said that Moses'd seen hangings when he
was a boy in Missouri, Negroes taken out of their huts at night and
strung up, whole families, sometimes the real youngins'd be taken
in by some white families and reared up to be servants. The beatings
and whippings right out in the street left a mark on him and when
he saw injustice like that he couldn't help himself. "Momma said the
Knights were deathly afraid of him. He'd walk down the road, and
the Knights would never go near him. They thought the sugar maple
grove was haunted and if they went near there they'd never come
out. Moses and his twin brother would leave out food for the folks
who'd come up over the mountain from Butcher Holler and leave
warm clothing for them too. Momma said that one night a whole
family came to Moses and his brother's door and they brought them
in, fed them, clothed them, and got them warm before they were able
to make their way. Later Moses found the whole family strung up."

Spencer Duty, Jr. said he'd heard stories like that from his momma
and his daddy too. And his daddy'd always said that he became a man
the night he and Moses burned down the house of the man who'd

been responsible for bringing in the detectives and killing so many folks over in Van Lear. "My daddy said that he'd always thought he made a deal with the Devil getting the Knights to help burn that house down, but when Moses reached over and tore the hood off of Dr. Hiram W. Evans, the imperial wizard himself, and told him to skedaddle, he said he thought his salvation had somehow been restored." He was grateful to Moses for that maybe most of all.

Eleanor said growing up in Butte she saw the Chinese families left over from the railroad days being treated about as badly as the Negro was down around those parts. "Moses used to say that he'd heard tell that there were a lot of slanted-eye folks buried in the mountains, but that just about anyone other than a white man was considered 'throw-outs.'

"After all," Eleanor said, "Butte was also where Dashiell Hammett helped string up Frank Little, for his union organizing against the Anaconda Mining Company. Six masked men broke into Nora Byrne's Steel Block boardinghouse, not that far down the road from I was raised, and took Frank Little out in the middle of the night, beat him with a rifle butt, and then took him to the Milwaukee Bridge at the edge of town and hung him from a railroad trestle. That was long before Moses and Mary Mary settled there but folks still talk about it to this day. They never did figure out who killed him but Dashiell Hammett had been a Pinkerton Detective before he started writing books and just like the Baldwin-Felts Detectives were back when Moses and your daddy were living, the Pinkertons would send in their detectives to break up unionizing activities, beat and kill organizers all over this country.

"It's going to take a long time before things change, Spencer, likely longer than either one of us will be alive to see."

Then a knock came at the door. The jury had reached a verdict.

Chapter 110

"THE COURT IS NOW back in session, the Honorable Judge Herbert Van Hoose is presidin'."

Edwin and Hetty sat right behind Robert Lewis and Eleanor. Lacy A. Hobbs herself perched behind Rudolph Sword and kept pokin' him in the back whispering this and that to him while he kept tryin' to shush her up. Sittin' right beside her was Brower Stubblefield waitin' with his pencil to not only write down the verdict but to get an exclusive interview with Rudolph Sword about how his swift sword had once again brought about justice. The boy Boyd planted himself all the way in the back of the courtroom. Right after the boy Boyd sat down Linc came in and sat down right beside him. Upon Linc sittin' himself down the boy Boyd reached into his pocket and pulled out a pack of Nigger Boys, tore at the perforation around the front, reached inside, and before his fingers found the licorice, he pulled out a small piece of paper readin' how Nigger Boys 'give endless joy.'

Fingerin' around inside the box he brought out a long twisted strand of the sticky black root, slipped it into his mouth, thinkin' to himself that each bite sure enough delivered the 'endless joy' they said it did.

It was the first time Linc had seen the boy Boyd with his Nigger Boys since he'd kicked the crumbled-up pack away from the dead Hicks girl, figurin' then that Thaddeus' hadn't caught on to what he'd done when he'd done it.

It seemed like the whole town of Paintsville was now crowdin' through the door, pushin' each other this way and that to see the Negro get what was deservin' of him. Why even Gwendolyn Puckett showed up with still the look of being consumed by the grief of

357

havin' buried her girl Louella who'd died just last week after eatin' fish and drinkin' a tall glass of milk chilled down just a short while after havin' come from the cow. Mr. Puckett, Louella's granddaddy, scolded Gwendolyn right after Louella took her last little breath tellin' her how many times he'd said not to let any of her youngins drink milk after eatin' fish or eat fish after drinkin' milk, but bein' as contrary as she was, Gwendolyn paid no mind and now, her daddy said, "See what your headstrongness done brought down on yourself."

Then a path began to open and in walked the tumbled-down old colored woman who looked for sure older than she'd looked just a few short days ago. When she sat at the edge of the aisle folks just about sat on top of one another to get away from her. Imojean Childress was heard whisperin' that the Negro woman lived down in Packard, there in Whitley County, and how she got on over Paintsville-way Imojean just couldn't figure. But folks knew that Packard'd become a ghost town right after those miners'd been cut down by Kentucky National Guardsmen's machine-gun bullets somewhere around 1922 or thereabouts. Things were never the same there after that and the few folks that were left behind because of circumstance always felt those miners unsettled spirits, angry about bein' enslaved when they were flesh and blood, and now that they'd gone to dust they were fated to wanderin' what was left of Packard. Sometimes one of the poor souls'd try to make his escape from eternal enslavement and strive to ply his way through the dense Cumberland forest that covered the Cumberland Mountains, only to encounter a frigid downdraft that blew the very marrow of his spirit back down the steep inclines and thickets right into the depths of valley below. Said it was that the old broken-down nigger woman, Sarafina, was the only one who could calm the spirits of the miners, and when she was called here or there for this or that the phantoms'd become unruly. It was also said it was that Patricia Neal's daddy, who was the town doctor, would even call on Sarafina himself to help calm the spirits that were causin' the non-spirited to become riled up. About 1935 or thereabouts Patricia Neal's doctorin' daddy couldn't take it no more and moved on to Knoxville. Now the only one livin' in Packard that had flesh still clingin' to their bones was Sarafina. Most of the buildings'd long ago collapsed but at the end of what'd been the main street through town was a small shack and years back when one or two government people'd seen it they couldn't figure how an old colored woman, who could barely walk, could keep up a place or fend for herself being out so far a yonder. But Sarafina'd been said to have said when asked that the wayward souls adrift in the gorge of death that was known as Packard'd seen what she'd been called to do over these many years and now they understood that their fate wasn't another kind of enslavement but instead servin' one who had important work to do when a callin' came straight from the Almighty Himself. And today, Sarafina had been called.

Sitting next to Eleanor, Robert Lewis simply looked this way and that, his left eye still mostly swollen shut from the beating he'd been given. Spencer Duty, Jr. sat beside Edwin and Hetty. There was a pall of dread that now consumed Eleanor at the verdict.

Judge Herbert Van Hoose waved his hand for the jury to be brought in and seated, "All right, let's get on with it, has the jury reached a verdict?" he said.

Spencer Duty, Jr. felt his fingernails cutting into his palms as he clinched his fist, Eleanor spontaneously took in a deep breath wondering how long she had been sitting without breathing, and Edwin and Hetty looked up to Heaven having not stopped praying since the day Rudolph Sword and Deputy Duffy Deeter's came for their son.

Then Dr. Lucky Archer stood up and responded to Judge Herbert Van Hoose, "Your Honor, we as a jury have reached a *complete* impasse. Eleven of us are in one hundred percent agreement as to the guilt of that Negro sitting right over there, but there is one amongst us who, no matter what kind of reasoning or looking at the incontestable and irrefutable evidence that the good Rudolph Sword presented, will not vote with the rest of the jury to find a verdict of guilty., so no, Your Honor, we have not and cannot reach a verdict."

In that moment, Eleanor was mired in disbelief. It was impossible to conceive of the jury coming back with any verdict other than guilty but now, at least until a decision was made about whether Rudolph Sword would retry the case or not, Robert Lewis would go free. And later that night, when she would meet with Edwin and Hetty, Eleanor was going to tell them to pack up only what essentials they needed, take him, and leave in the middle hours of the morning when few eyes would be awake, likely going by way of West Virginia and then crossing up over to Ohio once they got to Wheeling or thereabouts.

Eleanor and Spencer Duty, Jr. would make sure they had enough money to get them on their way and to set up housekeeping when they got where they were going to settle.

Judge Herbert Van Hoose looking peeved, thanked Dr. Lucky Archer and the rest of the jury, and then said they could stay or go, but he was going to say his peace.

Eleanor stood up and *demanded* that Robert Lewis' shackles be removed immediately, and on that Judge Herbert Van Hoose waved his hand for her to sit back down. Edwin and Hetty began sobbing in relief. Rudolph Sword immediately declared his intention to retry Robert Lewis for the heinousness of his crimes against the good people of Paintsville, saying he would once again be seeking the death penalty. That was when Judge Herbert Van Hoose smacked his gavel against its well-worn block and called for order.

"I've been sittin' right here now for more than fifty some odd years," Judge Herbert Van Hoose said, "and I've presided over many a cases that have come before this court, some folks' guilt weren't so sure and others, like this one, where the accused was so guilty that a trial weren't really even needed. And how a jury in its right mind could render a verdict other than guilty, well I just can't figure on it. But the good state of Kentucky—y'all know that I am the longest serving judiciary in this great state's history; there ain't no one who's *ever* served at the bench longer—this great state has appointed upon me the power to uphold and enforce the law, whenever and however *I* see fit. And given that this duly-appointed jury can't come to its senses and deliver up the verdict that is deservin', then it is up to me, the honorable Judge Herbert Van Hoose, of the 24th District, to declare that the jury's indecision leaves this court with no other choice than to make an independent judicial rendering, based upon the presentation of the evidence and given that this court has presided in an unbiased manner over these proceedings, it is now the verdict of this court that the defendant, Robert Lewis Rosskam, is indeed hereby found guilty of two counts of murder in the first degree and shall be transferred immediately to death row at the state penitentiary at Eddyville until his execution can be dutifully carried out."

Eleanor was no longer mired in disbelief but was enraged as Deputy Duffy Deeter took hold of Robert Lewis and pushed him back to the holding cell while Edwin and Hetty were tryin' their best to make sense of what had just happened. Judge Herbert Van Hoose then ordered the courtroom to be cleared.

The boy Boyd went on back to his homeplace while folks stepped aside for Lacy A. Hobbs herself to get on by. Eleanor and Spencer Duty, Jr. were shunned by everyone except Edwin and Hetty who said to Eleanor that she'd done her best.

The jury went out the side door to the courthouse, all going their separate ways until later on when eleven of them would meet at the old train depot for a special saving service with the boy Boyd. Chafin went back to the SIPP to begin splicing the coming attractions trailers into the film that'd likely be sitting there from the film exchange. It'd just be another week or so though that he'd decided it was time to be movin' on. No one seemed to take notice when Sarafina left.

Chapter 111

THE BOY BOYD MADE his way on up to Rabbit Hash and Monkey's Eye Holler, comin' up back around where he'd put Drusa. Even though he'd buried her nice and deep, there was a mound of dirt rounded over top her grave showin' where she'd been laid.

Lookin' down from the ridge, the boy Boyd saw Boy sittin' rockin' back and forth beside his momma's grave. It hadn't taken too much figurin' to figure that he'd come back up to Rabbit Hash and Monkey's Eye Holler when he'd run off the way he did. It also didn't take too much figurin' to figure that Boy'd find Drusa wasn't ever comin' back out of the holler. Boy'd likely figure on how his momma got where she was and'd be comin' lookin' for the boy Boyd once he'd figured on how to go about getting' his retributin' either now or as he grew up into himself.

There weren't any need for wastin' time and not gettin' done what need be done, so the boy Boyd cocked his '94, sighted in Boy's head, havin' to figure on when to pull the trigger as to the cadence of Boy's grievin' head rockin' this way and that. Then once the boy Boyd had his figurin' figured, he squeezed the trigger. But the boy Boyd's figurin''d been off just enough that the bullet passed right behind Boy's head, burying itself deep into the old oak tree that sat right above Drusa's grave. "Goddamit," the boy Boyd said to himself, not botherin' now to not make a sound, as Boy jumped up and took off runnin' this way and that, knowin' the hills that ran around the holler better than anyone alive, now that his momma weren't around no more. The boy Boyd took off chasin' Boy as best he could, but Boy bein' about as spry as any a boy could be had the boy Boyd runnin' this way and that until he collapsed, consumed by his exhaustion.

362

The breathin'-hard boy Boyd laid in the leaves still lyin' wet under the canopy of the trees, when he heard a rustlin' that weren't of his doin'. Standin' above him was a red-faced Boy with two barrels of a shotgun pointin' at the boy Boyd's head. The boy Boyd throughout all his remainin' days'd never figured where Boy'd got the shotgun, but have it he did. Figurin' that he had only one prospect of keepin' his head still sittin' on his shoulders, the boy Boyd rolled fast to one side, raised his rifle, and shot Boy right in the chest. As Boy tumbled backward, he pulled the trigger on the shotgun. Somehow or other the boy Boyd figured that Jesus must have been lookin' out for him that day as the buckshot only took off the top half of his left ear, dis-figurin' him for sure. Clappin' his hand over his bleeding ear, the boy Boyd used his rifle to raise himself off the ground and walk on over to Boy, who was, the boy Boyd could barely believe, still breathin', pleadin' with his eyes, mouthin' this and that. But with all his air leakin' out the gapin' hole in his chest there weren't enough to make its way up to his mouth, so likely the last words that Boy was tryin' to say, were "I say I say," which were never to be said. The boy Boyd raised his rifle and put a bullet between Boy's eyes, makin' his head slam against the ground and then bounce back up smackin' right into the barrel of boy Boyd's Winchester.

With all the blood and the bear being still awake, the boy Boyd figured it weren't necessary to go about diggin' a grave, most especially after all he'd already been through, so he picked up Boy's shotgun and walked on out of the holler. Stoppin' by Lacy A. Hobbs' herself's homeplace for some comfortin', she packed the straggles of his ear in gauze, demandin' that he hold it there for an hour or so until the bleedin' stopped. Then she called Dr. Lucky Archer, who was good enough to come by and give the boy Boyd a shot of penicillin, sayin' that he'd sure enough be mighty sore for a while and to also be sure not to sleep on his left side. Dr. Lucky Archer was also kind enough not to ask how the boy Boyd'd gotten half his ear blown off, figurin' to himself that he'd dropped his gun and it went off accidentally, givin' the boy Boyd some grandfatherly advice that he should be more careful.

Chapter 112

CHAFIN NOT HAVIN' MANY this or that's'd been figurin' on bein' back on the road, hoboin' here and there. He'd been missin' his days with the Mighty Monarch of the Tented World himself, Johnny J. Jones, and not bein' one who liked to feel much grass growin' under his feet, figured it was time to be on his way. But before he did he had to set something right.

Linc was finishing up for the day, havin' just refitted the rope that kept riding up out of the groove of the pulley that raised and lowered the garage door. When the bottom of the wooden door met the concrete of the floor the loose windows at first'd rattle and then settle on right down. Linc turned around to go on back and put his tools up for the night when out from the toilet stepped a man with a white sheet over his head, the only thing showin' were his eyes through the slits that'd been cut, so he could look out. Right after Linc said, "What the goddamn hell is this." For a second, he saw an arm raise above his head with its hand holding a three-pound sledge. Then he felt his head split open and warm blood begin pouring down his face as he fell to the ground. Chafin reached up and pulled the sheet from over his head and leaned down, face to face with Linc, and told him, "I'll show you man to man who I am, I ain't gutless like you and the rest of your kind, but figured I'd show you what it feels like to have done to you what you cowardly bastards did to me." Linc, about as dazed as a man could be, rolled his head to one side with his tongue lolling out. He was able to make out the bloody-blurred image of Chafin taking his pocketknife from his trousers, flipping open the long blade with his thumbnail and then slipping the many times honed edge into Linc's nostril. Linc wasn't knocked out enough to not cry out in agony when the blade sliced through one side of his nose, leavin' it soundin' like horse lips flappin' this way and that with each pantin' breath that Linc took. Chafin then stood up, went to the back room, and got the hood of Linc's Grand Titan robe that was hangin' on a hook behind the door. He carried out the hood, pulled it over Linc's head, stood up, and in just about as a defilin' of a way as can be defilin', Chafin began pissin' on Linc and all he stood for. Linc, bein' in no shape to do much about anything, laid there, being drenched in his debasement.

Chafin made his way on over to Hager Hill, hopped on the Dawkins Line, and then hopped off thirty miles or so down around Royalton, there in Magoffin County, when the train was slowin' comin' into the yard. He meandered this way and that and got him a room for a few nights at Annie Barded's Boarding House, who was known in those parts for servin' up just about the finest chicken and dumplins that hungry lips had ever had the pleasure of passin' over them. Then in a few days Chafin left to be on his way. As far as anyone ever knew, Chafin was never known around those parts again.

Chapter 113

ROBERT LEWIS WAS TRANSFERRED from the Paintsville Jail to Eddyville to sit on death row while Eleanor filed appeals on his behalf. The appeals process made its way up to this and that judge until it reached the Kentucky Supreme Court. The final and conclusive opinion of the court read:

"*One of the principal reasons why the death penalty is different is because it is irreversible; an executed defendant cannot be brought back to life. This aspect of the difference between death and other penalties would undoubtedly support statutory provisions for especially careful review of the fairness of the trial, the accuracy of the fact finding process, and the fairness of the sentencing procedure where the death penalty is imposed. But none of those aspects of the death sentence is at issue here. The petitioner, per his counsel of record Miss Eleanor Kitchen, Esq., was found guilty of two counts of the crime of first-degree murder in a trial the constitutional validity of which is unquestioned here. And since the punishment of death is conceded by the collective plurality not to be a cruel and unusual punishment for such a crime, the irreversible aspect of the death penalty has no connection what-so-ever with any requirement for individualized consideration of the sentence. The second aspect of the death penalty which makes it 'different' from other penalties is the fact that it is indeed an ultimate penalty, which ends a human life, rather than simply requiring that a living human being be confined for a given period of time in a penal institution. This aspect of the difference may enter into the decision of whether or not it is a 'cruel and unusual' penalty for a given offense. But since, in this case, the offense was two counts of first-degree murder with premeditation on both counts that particular inquiry need proceed no further. The plurality's insistence on individualized consideration of the sentencing, therefore, does not depend upon any traditional application of the prohibition against cruel and unusual punishment contained in the Eighth Amendment. The punishment here is concededly not cruel and unusual, and that determination has traditionally ended judicial inquiry in our cases construing any and all aspects of the* Cruel and Unusual Punishments Clause. *It is therefore the conclusion of the collective plurality, that death is not a cruel and unusual punishment for the offense of which said petitioner was convicted. Since no member of the Court suggests that the trial which led to those convictions in any way fell short of the standards mandated by the Constitution, the judgments of conviction should be affirmed."*

Robert Lewis was going to die.

Chapter 114

After the final decision came down from the Kentucky Supreme Court, Edwin and Hetty were permitted one last visit with their son before the execution was to be carried out. He had sat for months on end with his only visitor being Eleanor, who tried as best she could to let him know that she was doing her best to undo the wrong that had been done to him, but she had told Edwin and Hetty that the likelihood of undoing that wrong was remote at best. "You're goin' to meet Jesus," Edwin told Robert Lewis. "And, just like Jesus'd been beaten like they up and done to you, Jesus knows what they done did and is goin' reach down and take you in His mighty hands, take you under His breast and bring you on up to Heaven."

"Why you cryin', Momma?" Robert Lewis asked Hetty.

"I gonna miss you son. And because you're so big and strong you're goin' on ahead of us so you can meet us when we depart this earth."

"Is it gonna hurt, Daddy?" Robert Lewis asked.

"No son, you won't be feelin' nothin," Edwin said with a sense of assurance that those listening in didn't understand. It was on that that Edwin and Hetty had spent their allotted time with him and were told they needed to be on their way as the jailer took their son by the arm and walked him back to his death cell. Eleanor had waited, giving Edwin and Hetty time alone with him. It would be the last time they laid eyes on Robert Lewis before the execution.

Chapter 115

IT WAS A BIG day at the Castle on the Cumberland, just about any-body who was somebody was there, shakin' hands for bringin' about another exposition of righteousness. Folks were being seated in chairs setup for viewing the execution of the double murderer.

Rudolph Sword, leanin' over to Deputy Duffy Deeter and the boy Boyd, said in no whisperin' of a tone, "Y'all know this will be the second proudest time I've sat right here and witnessed justice being served," and then he went on to pull the brittle article from the *Madera Tribune* from his suit pocket, clenched his lip to one side, and began reading the circumstances of his first proudest mo-ment. After the district attorney finished his many times told tale he said, "I am about as proud as a man can be to have spent my life working in the shadow of the great warden of this very institution, John B. Chilton, standing upon the tall rock of the law." Deputy Duffy Deeter and the boy Boyd nodded in about as agreeing of a way that a man can nod and make himself clear. A few minutes later Judge Herbert Van Hoose was escorted to a seat with the reverence that he knew himself deservin' of after his many years of servin' as the eyes for Lady Justice herself for the good people of the State of Kentucky. Rudolph Sword rightfully raised himself up from his seat and walked over to Judge Herbert Van Hoose, extended his hand to thank him for being a "lion-hearted purveyor of justice!" Judge Herbert Van Hoose spoke no words but simply nodded in agreement of his courageousness. Other folks of this persuasion and that came in, sat down, most lighting a cigarette until the view of the death chair was obscured by a thick cloud of blue haze.

Eleanor and Spencer Duty, Jr. walked in behind Edwin and Hetty,

369

none of the attending jailers bothered to seat them. They located chairs at the back of the room. Once Hetty sat down she began looking around this way and that. Edwin held Hetty's hand in his, unsure as to who was doin' the most holdin'. When all were seated the door to the death room closed. A guard stood by the door, no one would be allowed to leave until Robert Lewis was declared dead. And, but for a moment, Hetty began to fret in dismay, when, in just as equal of a moment, she felt herself gather up her agitation for suddenly sitting beside her was Sarafina, who reached out and took Hetty's other hand. Neither Eleanor nor Spencer Duty, Jr. had seen Sarafina come through the door or for that matter take a seat beside Hetty.

After the door had been closed Warden Jess Buchannan strode up to speak before the witnesses to the execution. "You are here to provide witness to the lawful execution of one Robert Lewis Rosskam who was convicted of two counts of premeditated murder, one of the victims being a duly-sworn officer of the peace and the other a Negro child. The prisoner will be escorted from the death cell and strapped into the execution machine, where two-thousand volts of electricity will terminate his life. May God have mercy on his soul."

And on that a deafening veil of silence took hold of the room for but a few seconds, as a shackled Robert Lewis scooted his feet, back and forth, stopped within the short stride of the manacles, foiling the silence as the chains clattered against the battleship grey concrete floor. His wrists were handcuffed behind his back and the crown of his head had been shaved. His legs were unnaturally pushed apart from where the jailers, in preparing him for his execution, had stuffed cotton up his ass so when he lost his bowels as the electricity purged through his body, he wouldn't defile the visitor's sense of dignity with an overwhelming stench of burnt shit.

He was directed to the front of the chair, where a jailer pushed his shoulder to turn him around to face the witnesses. Robert Lewis stared ahead glassy-eyed. Later Eleanor heard Rudolph Sword say that they'd given him 200mgs of Phenobarbital to make sure he didn't get out of hand. It was also later as they were leaving the death chamber that she heard Rudolph Sword tell the boy Boyd, "Y'all know what the last thing that nigger wanted to eat? A goddamn onion and a stick of butter."

The handcuffs were taken off and Robert Lewis was pushed down onto the oak seat of the electric chair. A salt-soaked sponge was set atop the part of his head that had been shaved while a steel skull cap was pressed down over top the sponge and secured by a strap under his chin. His wrists were bound to the arms of the death chair by thick leather straps that had been stretched out of shape by other prisoners whose muscles were contorted when hit by the surging current. Robert Lewis' legs were strapped to the legs of the chair so tight that it seemed like they became one. Then a leather strap was wrapped around his chest. Warden Jess Buchannan stood beside Robert Lewis and looked down at him and asked if he had any final words or "expressions of remorse." Robert Lewis' head lolled this way and that but no words came across his lips. The warden ordered the black hood be slipped over his head. In the past, when the shroud had been placed over the heads of the men who were about to die, they could be heard raisin' hell about the vomit stench that wreaked inside the hood.

Warden Jess Buchannan then stepped back and said, "Let the duly adjudicated execution commence," and on that Edwin and Hetty began to weep. Eleanor grabbed the hand of Spencer Duty, Jr., who as best he could pulled her against him. To the right side of the execution machine was a dulled-green electrical panel with two arm switches connected by a 'T' that allowed both switches to be thrown together, so the two-thousand volts of electricity could cause the entire nervous system to explode inside the man strapped in the chair, where many a men before Robert Lewis had sat their last. As a matter-a-fact the executioner, who stood with a black-eye-slitted hood over his face, had already added Robert Lewis to the tally of '78 White' and '84 Negro' slash marks that'd been etched into the green panel. The executioner put his hand on the 'T' and just as he was ready to throw the switch, Robert Lewis let out a loud gasp and as best his body could slumped over dead. And, in but another moment, Hetty's sweating hand that had been held in the warmth of Sarafina's was empty, and Sarafina in an unexplainable occurrence was simply no longer there.

The prison doctor who was going to declare Robert Lewis dead after he'd been electrocuted waved for the executioner to wait to throw the switch until he'd had his say. Doctor Jimmy Grace, who'd been known for longer than longer can be, not just for his doctorin' those who worked at the Castle but also for his Bible readin'. Mind you Doctor Grace *wasn't* no preacher, but he was as a devouted a man as a man had ever been and there were times when he'd be so filled up with the Holy Spirit that it seemed like the Good Book just exploded from inside him. He always carried his Bible with him in case the Good Book took hold of him, then he'd just begin readin' nonstop as loud as loud could be, not carin' for a damn minute who'd be listenin' and who wouldn't. Then just as quick as the Holy Spirit had filled him up it'd just as quick take leave, whereby Dr. Grace'd collapse to the floor like a string toy that'd been fingered.

The good Doctor Grace pulled the hood from the head of Robert Lewis, lifted his right eyelid, and right there pronounced him dead.

"Goddamnit!" Rudolph Sword could be heard swearin' right as Warden Jess Buchannan demanded that Doctor Grace be as sure as sure can be before he made such a pronouncement.

"There ain't no arguin' with bein' dead," Doctor Grace retorted and said again assuredly that Robert Lewis *was* dead. Edwin pulled Hetty close as they silently remembered being visited by Sarafina right after the final ruling that Robert Lewis was to be executed. Sarafina said her time here, after bein' here for longer than she could remember, was assuredly comin' to the end, but before she was called to pass on Sarafina said she had to deliver Robert Lewis to the Lord Almighty Himself, who would raise him, so that he would suffer no more at the hands of unjust men.

Rudolph Sword, the boy Boyd, and Deputy Duffy Deeter shoved past everyone, with Rudolph Sword sayin' that the hangman'd been cheated and justice thwarted.

With no one payin' too much attention to what else was goin' on, no one seemed to notice that Judge Herbert Van Hoose was sittin' just about as stiff backed as he'd ever been known to sit, with his eyes about as open as open could be, and about as dead as dead could be. The good Doctor Grace figured that his heart for some reason or other had just given out and he died just about the same time that Robert Lewis had expired. The state of Kentucky buried Robert Lewis in a pauper's grave with no head marker. Eleanor and Spencer Duty, Jr. watched the grave diggers swinging their mattocks and shoveling their shovels readying the hole for him. Eleanor quietly said to herself, "How brief the moment between discovery and loss."

Then she and Spencer Duty, Jr. walked away. And, like so many others, Edwin and Hetty went on their way too, looking for another beginning somewhere else.

Pinky Jones drove the hearse himself to pick up Judge Herbert Van Hoose's body and reverentially prepared him for presentation for burial. And, like Robert Lewis, Judge Herbert Van Hoose's ass'd been packed to prevent any defilement, but unlike Robert Lewis, the judge had been laid out in his Honors robe, his lips had been sewed together, along with his eyelids, and he'd been embalmed to make sure he remained lookin' like he looked when he was sittin' atop the bench or at least until the water'd seep into his casket and soil what'd been done to preserve his upstandedness. He laid in state in the Paintsville courthouse for upwards of three days, with folks filing by to pay their respects until the sun had well gone down on the third day. Deputy Duffy Deeter himself stood reverentially for the entire three days beside the coffin, standing at attention, holding the very M1 Garand that Judge Herbert Van Hoose'd used to kill Japs at The Battle of Okinawa. And, Deputy Duffy Deeter let it be known, that "*anyone* who'd so dishonor the great man by creatin' any commotion'd better go ahead an up and leave the county" before he caught up with him, for "there'd be the Devil to pay."

It wasn't long after Robert Lewis had died that Eleanor heard Sarafina had gone on back to Packard, and not long after that had passed on herself. It was said that the moored souls that'd been servin' Sarafina heard the sound of the Archangel Gabriel's trumpet and were unmoored, gathered together, and welcomed by St. Peter into the grandeur of Heaven.

Chapter 116

ELEANOR TOLD SPENCER DUTY, Jr. that she'd decided to move on. It was likely she'd be going on back up to Butte, having been offered a partnership in Corette, Corette and Kitchen, Moses' old law firm. Eleanor never likened herself to being defeated, it was just that she didn't belong in Paintsville. She'd been trying to do something that at least for right now couldn't be done. There simply hadn't been enough dying off of the old to bring much of anything about of the new. Johnny Pelphrey'd now been elected judge and was trying cases just the same way that Judge Herbert Van Hoose'd done, and for that matter he even kept Judge Herbert Van Hoose's revered Stars and Bars hung in its "rightful respected place," as Judge Johnny'd say, right before each preceding. Rudolph Sword knew that if he took a case before Judge Johnny that he'd likely be walkin' out of the courthouse with another victory, ensuring over and over again his reelection to county attorney. Eleanor also knew that any case she took before Judge Johnny, regardless of the circumstances, her client would walk out in defeat or be sentenced to prison.

Chapter 117

SPENCER DUTY, JR. WAS brokenhearted. He had been in love with Eleanor since they'd first known about each other through their momma and daddie's letters and pictures of the "youngins doin' this and that" and always figured they'd someday be together. When Eleanor came to Paintsville it was for Spencer Duty, Jr. a homecomin'. For Eleanor, having come from Cambridge not long after law school, it was like a step back in time where Negros were disparaged as subhuman and miners were enslaved by the coal companies. In dozens of cases that she'd brought before Judge Herbert Van Hoose trying to make the coal companies responsible for the suffering, horrid working conditions, and 'the black lung,' not one case resulted in a conviction or settlement. "Goddamn," Eleanor would say, when the UMW wouldn't even send a union representative to testify on a miner's behalf. But, many of the miners themselves didn't want to stir things up. There was little work besides minin' and many of the folks didn't have much education beyond grade school. So if the mines brought back thugs like the enforcers from Baldwin-Felts, well no one wanted that. So even the juries'd turn on their own, in one way or another.

"When are you leaving?" Spencer Duty, Jr. solemnly asked. A simple "soon," was Eleanor's reply. Eleanor didn't have much to pack up. But on the day before she left, Eleanor made her way up to what was left of Moses' tin shack, high atop the sugar maple grove. It'd been battered by many years of notorious Kentucky storms, but the walls were still standing and the door rattled loose on a hinge, refusing to be broken. What was left of the inside was in shambles. There were still a few stove darkened pots and pans scattered here and there. When she lifted a well-posed tin cup sitting atop a knife-hewed shelf, there lay underneath a one-cent coal scrip with a heart shape punched through it, from the Consolidated Coal Company out of Van Lear. Eleanor picked it up and slipped it into her pocket, figuring it had belonged to Moses. Maybe he had left it for a passerby or for some poor soul to find. On the wall was a brittle and barely readable flyer from the 1930s or thereabouts talkin' about the old miners uprisin' in Harlan County, when it was against the law to give food to starvin' children.

Chapter 118

WHEN THE SUN WENT down Eleanor knocked at Spencer Duty, Jr.'s door. They stood on the stoop looking at each other through the screen door unsure what to say to the other. Pulling open the door, Eleanor stepped inside. They said not a word as Eleanor unbuttoned the front of her dress and let it fall to the floor. It was the first time they had kissed and certainly the first time Spencer Duty, Jr. had seen a woman unclothed. "You must know I love you." he said softly. She answered by taking his hand and placing it over her breast.

Naked, side by side they lay, kissing softly, knowing the night was still ahead of them and at the same time knowing they would never again spend another night together. They made love through the early morning, Eleanor surprised at Spencer Duty Jr's passion and he surprised at Eleanor's sensuality and long, seemingly unending breathlessness. Playfully she teased him about having plucked buckshot from his butt and how "this is much better," saying that he had healed up nicely. A storm had come in overnight, shaking the frame house to its nails with each clap of thunder.

Spencer Duty, Jr. knew he couldn't go. He also knew Eleanor had not asked him to. Tonight though had been an initiation as well as a goodbye. "Spencer, will you take me to the train station?" Eleanor asked. He nodded as she turned to walk out the door. A few hours later he picked her up at Wanda C. Music's boarding house, lifting her bag into the back of his car.

Wanda C. Music said her polite goodbye and as Eleanor walked down the steps, the landlady whispered to another boarder that she wasn't sorry to see her go. "Folks'd been right in sayin' that she was nothin' more than a harlotan, she didn't even come back to her room last night. Not to mention me havin' to put up with folks sniggerin' about how I, Wanda C. Music, been rented a room to the woman who'd defended the nigger who'd murdered one of his own kind and then killed poor Thaddeus. But, Wanda C. Music'd been takin' her famous biscuits all over Paintsville, makin' up for the wrong she'd done."

Eleanor stepped up onto the platform of the train that would take her by way of Cincinnati to Chicago to Butte. Spencer Duty, Jr. lifted her bag onto the platform beside her, their eyes meeting one last time, and on that the lawyer picked up her bag and walked into the car, slightly pursing her lips and wiping tears from her eyes as she nodded goodbye. Spencer Duty, Jr. stood at the station until the train departed. Then he stepped onto the tracks and watched, and then waved until the back of the train disappeared.

Chapter 119

IT'D BEEN A LONG while now since the goings-on had happened while Eleanor'd been in Paintsville. But the things that happened now went on quieter since there weren't no one to be causin' any commotions about those goings-on.

Lacy A. Hobbs herself'd been just about as prosperous a soul as anyone in those parts could remember a soul being. She'd even opened up a Hobbs' Five and Dime over in Prestonsburg, drawin' on folks who'd be comin' to visit Jenny Wiley's grave. There was even a special aisle in the store dedicated to nothing but bows, arrows, and tomahawks for youngins to pester their momma and daddies about. A big sign hangin' above the aisle said how boys and girls "love nothing better than to play that there the injuns' takin' Jenny Wiley's scalp," even though she'd got away a little while after she was captured in real life, but that didn't make not one bit of difference to the store clerk who was doin' their darndest to sell bows and arrows. And... "their ain't no better way to play *scalpum* than with a set of bow, arrows, and tomahawks from Hobbs' Five and Dime." It was always a delightful sight when Lacy A. Hobbs herself'd see those boys and girls hootin' and hollerin' for their mommies and daddies to buy them this and that.

Lacy A. Hobbs herself being as successful as she was bought herself a brand new car each and every year now and drove the road between Paintsville and Prestonsburg day in and day out to make sure her help was handlin' the money right and no one was "Jewin' me out of one red cent that I'm due," she would say.

It was on one of those back and forth trips that for some reason or other, on a perfectly clear day, Lacy A. Hobbs herself ran her car right off the road, flipped it upside down about more times than anyone'd ever figured, and on one of those flips her neck snapped, leavin' her not so much as being able to move a finger but somehow or other and likely by God's good graces she was still, more or less and without too much wheezing, able to breathe by herself, not havin' to be put in an iron lung.

The boy Boyd had prayer service after prayer service and kissed about as many a snakes as a man can kiss in his lifetime and still, for another reason or other, was never able to get the top-half of his momma's body reconnected up to the bottom-half. When Lacy A. Hobbs herself talked now it was like she was blowin' her words out of her mouth. One word would come out then she'd rock her head back and throw her neck forward until another word would come out and so on and so on, until it seemed like it'd take forever and a day for her to say "…one goddamn thing," the boy Boyd'd say, gettin' about as pissed off as a man can get and not be chokin' someone himself. Lacy A. Hobbs herself'd always want to know if the boy Boyd was makin' sure she wasn't being gypped.

"…The____gotdamn____help____'ll____take____me____for____ every____last____cent…" and so she'd say, seemin' like she'd never shut her goddamn mouth.

Until one day, in the presence of her relentless demandin', the boy Boyd'd had enough. He'd already spoken to Judge Johnny that this day was comin' and in his chambers and with Rudolph Sword as a witness, the Honorable Judge Johnny Pelphrey declared Lacy A. Hobbs herself "incompetent" to not only care for herself but also that she was unable to speak to the best interest of Hobbs' Five and Dime, and that her only heir, namely "…the boy Boyd would now be considered the custodian of her affairs." That very next day the boy Boyd had Lacy A. Hobbs herself taken on over to the Louisa Rest and Care Center. When the boy Boyd got her there, her bowels were in such an uproar that she had to be given something for her nerves, with the folks at the Rest and Care Center figurin' that she may bring harm to herself with her conniption fit.

One solid year in advance was paid by the boy Boyd, with him then sayin' that he'd be payin' for each year thereafter, as long as she was livin' "…mind you,". Lacy A. Hobbs herself had *never* been more beside herself and not able to do one damn thing about it. The boy

Boyd'd get on back over to visit his momma once or twice a year and each time she was gettin' worse off and worse off, not makin' much sense, even when somebody did bother to take the time to listen to her "word puffin'" as one of the help called it.

The boy Boyd'd moved on into Lacy A. Hobbs' homeplace and figurin' he'd likely be there for a while had a temple built in his name. He named it The Holy Hill Cathedral.

He even started preachin' the Holy Gospel on the radio, callin' his show the *Christ is Rising Hour*. Folks were being saved right and left through the radio. "Jesus is risin' up right from my mouth, jumpin' onto the electricity runnin' through these wires and comin' right through your radio, spinnin' His love around you like a savin' salve." It was shortly after the boy Boyd began deliverin' his healin' message through his radio show that he got the idea, which later he would say had been delivered up to him by Jesus, that he sell his own radio. One where the frequency of his *Christ is Rising Hour* was the *only* station that the radio picked up and that the radio station, which he now owned part of, could play back his healin' services all day and all night. "Lord God Almighty," the healin' that'd be goin' on, folks'd never want to be movin' from in front of their radios. There were 'prayer calls' too, where folks could send in money to be mentioned in a special prayer that the boy Boyd delivered up at the end of each broadcast. The serpent services held in The Holy Hill Cathedral would draw hundreds of folks from all over for its healin' power and to see the boy Boyd commandin' Satan's messengers on earth. Sin was "*ordered*" not to cross the threshold of the temple... And when peccability tried to debase the piety of the Cathedral, the very head of the snake was severed from its sinuous body by an axe and cast into a crucible of burning coals. On these occasions, folks with crutches would throw their walkin' implements onto the hot coals too, with the boy Boyd declarin' them healed from their afflictions, many of those being burdened with the jake walk, and those who could not see and were seeking sight were healed when the boy Boyd's hand passed over their eyes that'd been ruined from bein' witness to too much sinfulness and those dying were granted eternal life from Jesus Christ who'd speak right then and there through the boy Boyd.

It was several years later while Lacy A. Hobbs herself was listenin' to one of the boy Boyd's healin' prayer services where he *always* proclaimed his "love and devotion to my blessed momma" at the end of each radio show that Lacy A. Hobbs was overcome with such consternation as the boy Boyd went *on* and *on* about his devotedness that Lacy A. Hobbs herself's words seemed to get twisted all around the air comin' up out of her lungs and she began gaspin' somethin' awful. Folks began slapping her on the back and shaken her tryin' their best to untangle her words from her breath. Then she started vomitin' blood making the floor slick and coverin' the folks who'd been doin' their best to help her. Suddenly she threw her head back and rolled up her eyes to heaven. In that moment, Lacy A. Hobbs died.

The boy Boyd the very next week had a special prayer hour for his momma, proclaiming her "the most devout woman that the Lord God had ever made from the rib of Adam." It was comfortin', he said, knowin' that every time he mentioned Lacy A. Hobbs herself and holding up her name to Jesus Christ, that in countless homes an "Amen," was being said in praise.

Chapter 120

IT WAS ONLY A couple of months or so after standing guard over the remains of Judge Herbert Van Hoose that Deputy Duffy Deeter got a call that Jackie Booth and Walt Osborne'd been shootin' at each other up around Turkey Knob. He'd just about had it with those goin'-ons havin' he himself been up atop Turkey Knob more times than he had fingers and toes arrestin' and rearrestin' Jackie Booth and Walt Osborne. Those two men had known each other since they were youngins and'd been bickerin' for just about as long. As a matter-of-fact, Jackie'd held Walt's head under water when they was about three or so until Walt turned blue. Said it was, when his momma'd be relatin' the story, she'd say that if she hadn't caught him when she did, that Jackie would have drowned Walt for sure. Jackie, just about the time that he and Walt'd quit school to help their mommas and daddies make ends meet, had stabbed Walt in the left eye with his jigged-handled jack knife, carvin' that eye right out of his head, leavin' him with only one good eye to see what he was doin'. That's was why Walt always walked leanin' to the right and all, not bein' able to see what was goin' on to his left. It'd been some kind of squabblin' like that their whole lives.

A month or so before this last time, when Deputy Duffy Deeter had been called on another ruckus that the two were creatin', he'd beat Jackie and Walt just about to death with that goddamn shot-filled leather blackjack he carried in his hind-end pocket. Deputy Duffy Deeter just about tore out Walt's good eye that day and broke poor Jackie's jaw in so many places that he'd be wearin' wire in his mouth for the rest of his natural life.

On this day though, Deputy Duffy Deeter swore as he was makin' his way atop Turkey Knob that'd be his last time toleratin' what he been toleratin' for far too long and'd decided he was going to shoot Jackie and Walt dead as soon as he laid eyes on them. Jackie and Walt figured that'd be what Deputy Duffy Deeter'd be figurin'. So, right as he pulled his patrol car around the bend that led to Jackie and Walt's shacks, which sat a stone's throw from each other, there was Jackie standin' to the right and Walt standin' to the left of a wolf tree. When they'd heard Deputy Duffy Deeter comin' around the bend they cocked their rifles, stepped out from behind the trunk of the tree, and shot Deputy Duffy Deeter full of holes. One bullet'd hit him and knocked him one way and then another bullet'd hit him and knocked him the other. As much as Jackie and Walt could with their shootin' they shot him in the chest and alike, for sure not wantin' to kill him too fast. But, for more than sure, they wanted Deputy Duffy Deeter to know who was sendin' him on his way to hell.

After the shootin' was done and the sun went down, Jackie and Walt drove the patrol car with Deputy Duffy Deeter stuffed in the trunk down to the swollen waters of the Levisa Fork and pushed it in. The car sank slowly with the two men standing on the bank sayin' to themselves that they figured that Deputy Duffy Deeter was "floatin' right about now."

It took a good number of years for the Levisa Fork to go down enough before the red light atop the rusted out patrol car was seen by Lando Daniels and Hazel Wells when they were foolin' around down by the bank, right where Jackie and Walt had pushed it in in so many years ago.

Chapter 121

IN THE INTERVENING YEARS Rudolph Sword lost his mind. It started not long after he walked out of the death chamber. Some folks'd say it was like he got infected with something or maybe it was that he never stopped shatting blood and he just couldn't take the strain, but no one knew, that was for sure, they'd say.

It was during the prosecution of Quillen Smith, who on the night of January fourth, it was read in court, during a blizzard, that he'd gotten into a disagreement with Lat Lavis about the woman, Juanita Buzzard, who'd been known to be friendly with Quillen Smith but who'd been seen making eyes at Lat Lavis during the Pie Social up at Salt Lick Crick just a few miles west of Hueyville. Said it was in court that day that Quillen Smith called Juanita Buzzard a vile name and Lat Lavis having none of that stepped forward to protect her honor by pulling his pistol. According to those folks witnessing the goings-on, Quillen Smith dropped to his knees and began begging for his life, sayin' that he'd done wrong in his disparagin' of Juanita Buzzard. Well, Lat Lavis took pity on a man who would be beggin' for his life in front of so many folks and reached out his hand to lift Quillen Smith from the ground. When both men were eye to eye, they nodded and Lat Lavis turned to be on his way. And, when Lat Lavis' fully turned away, Quillen Smith pulled his pistol and fired three times. Each bullet took effect in the back of Lat Lavis' head. Juanita Buzzard was beside herself and would spend the rest of her life tellin' whoever'd listen about the goings-on of that day. And when she did, Juanita Buzzard'd be shakin' so hard folks'd become afraid that her teeth would crack and just start fallin' out of her mouth.

It took a while before Quillen Smith'd been brought to justice.

But on this day, Rudolph Sword, as he was relatin' the dastardliness of Quillen Smith's crime to the jury, suddenly began dancing. He was spinnin' and twirlin' and then stopped suddenly, looked up at the bench at Judge Johnny, and said, "Well if you ain't gonna call them I'm not goin' keep dancin'." Judge Johnny was so a taken back that he couldn't even say that Rudolph Sword was out of order. Then Rudolph Sword twirled and whirled out of the courtroom. Juanita Buzzard in that moment lost all hope of justice as she watched the spectacle, rubbin' her swollen belly, tryin' to calm down the endless kickin' that was comin' from within, which she figured was God's punishment for her vileness with Lat Lavis that'd consequenced in Quillen Smith shootin' him in the head.

Later, Judge Johnny called on Rudolph Sword to explain himself. But, having no explanation, Judge Johnny allowed him to be on his way until the very next week when Rudolph Sword began rattlin' off nonsense in Judge Johnny's court, but at least he wasn't dancin', Judge Johnny 'd later say. It wasn't long after that when Judge Johnny declared that Rudolph Sword had lost his mind and sent him to the Kentucky Home for the Feeble-Minded. There he took up residence in a chair that overlooked the cemetery, where there were more than five hundred unmarked graves. It was as though Rudolph Sword was melting. He just seemed to keep shrinking into himself, one of the doctors even said it looked like he was melting. A doctor from elsewhere, who hardly spoke English, said he thought he was suffering from "extreme debility of mind due to syphilis," and decided to give him high doses of iodine of potash instead of penicillin, which, and may God have mercy on his soul, caused him to begin havin' the most severe itchin' that any man of this earth'd ever had, completely losin' control of his bowels, and finally, throw open his eyes like he'd just come face to face with Satan himself, take not much of one last breath, and then die. His widow, Mrs. Sword, who folks'd rarely seen and who Rudolph Sword didn't like to leave their homeplace without his permission, got seventy-five dollars a month for life from the Kentucky Pauper and Idiots Pension Fund.

Chapter 122

ELEANOR HAD MADE A good life for herself and her son, who had come along nine months after she left Paintsville. She told folks in Butte that her husband had died, which was what she also told her boy. She had never married. They lived in a well-tended home in uptown and Eleanor gained a reputation as not only a good attorney but also a legal scholar. She also taught a course in ethics at the law school over in Missoula.

Spencer Duty, Jr. and Eleanor wrote back and forth about twice a month or so but they never laid their eyes on each other again. He'd never gotten married either and so some folks around Paintsville thought there was something wrong with him, maybe even being queer, some would whisper. But Eleanor had been the woman he had fallen in love with, so he figured that if he married someone else that he'd also have a flame burin' somewhere else for Eleanor and that just wouldn't be right to that wife and family.

It was just about the time that Spencer was readying to go to college that the bleeding'd started. Eleanor had gone through the change a while ago now and so blood shouldn't be coming from where it wasn't suppose to be coming from. The doctor said they could do this and that but there really wasn't anything that would stop the cancer from growing and going hither to yon. Eleanor had decided long ago that when this day came she would set something right before she passed on.

Chapter 123

THE BOY BOYD'S PICTURE on the front page of the *Paintsville Herald* was of him leanin' his head back in rapture with a timber rattler draped around the front of his face. His eyes were rolled back in his head and he was shown to be in full command of the serpent. It was not only his rapture that was indisputable but also his authority. The boy Boyd went everywhere in the state of Kentucky, there was even a Holy Hill Cathedral over in Bright, Indiana, just up the road a bit from Louisville. He was drawin' folks from south and north to his healin' services, curin' the sick of their afflictions. And folks showin' their appreciation for the boy Boyd devouring the very bane of their ills would deed their farms and land to the Holy Hill Cathedral offering up all they had in the world. The boy Boyd, being a generous man, would often let them pay him and continue to live there and tend to the farm, unless someone'd made him an offer for the land, then of course they'd have to up and move on. Every few months it seemed like wherever the boy Boyd went to preach, young Negro girls'd go missing, some'd be found, others just never turned up. But whenever the boy Boyd heard about the unfortunate disappearances or outright murders, he'd always offer up a special prayer, hoping that Jesus'd raise the Negro up to where they didn't need so much tendin' and could take better care of their youngins. "Amen, Amen, Amen," was heard when the boy Boyd offered up one of his favorite Bible verses, *Galatians 2:20*, "*I am crucified with Christ: nevertheless I live; yet not I, but Christ liveth in me*," while holdin' a rattler to his lips, whisperin' his goadin'.

But on this particular night the snakes seemed unsettled, slitherin' around each other in the same coffee cans that the boy Boyd had for goin' on thirty years now. Pullin' them out, one by one, they would attempt to strike, no matter what he did, they came after him, hissing and shakin' their rattles. In front of a hundred or more folks the boy Boyd threw a rattler across the stage right before it struck him in the eye. In his declaration the boy Boyd said there was an evil presence in the Cathedral, an evil of the likes he'd never encountered. An evil that was "…rattlin' even the rattlers," he said. And on that the boy Boyd ended the service.

Chapter 124

IT WAS ABOUT TWO or so in the mornin' when the knock came to the door. Lightenin' was streakin' sideways across the sky, illuminatin' the thick and black rain-rich clouds that hid in the darkness of the night. The boy Boyd heard the knock, which was becomin' more insistent. The house looked the same as when he'd moved in and Lacy A. Hobbs herself'd been moved out. A wet figure with its chin to its chest could barely be seen standing on the porch. Opening the door the boy Boyd, being an irritable, ungenerous soul after bein' vexed by a night of a defyin' venomous malevolence that had dared to cross the threshold of The Holy Hill Cathedral, angrily demanded "what the goddamn hell do you want!" Then the figure raised its head. A stunned boy Boyd said, "You!" And in that moment the boy Boyd felt the barrels of Moses Kitchen's L.C. Smith stub twist coach gun pressing against his chest.

Eleanor, now gray and grail, looked grievously into the boy Boyd's eyes and said, "*The Spirit says that in later times some will depart from the faith, giving heed to deceiving spirits and doctrines, speaking lies in hypocrisy, having their own conscience seared with a hot iron.* This is for Robert Lewis," then she pulled back the hammers and fired both barrels. The blast sent the boy Boyd reeling backwards as the buckshot blew out what little heart he had. Then she poured gas around the pillars of the archway and set the house on fire. The flames of the inferno leapt like a deer to the Holy Hill Cathedral, incinerating it to but a smoldering mound of ash.

With what she imagined as the fires of hell blazing at her back Eleanor walked away, reached into her pocket, and rubbed the one-cent heart punched coal scrip that she'd found in Moses' cabin up in the sugar maple grove, now so many years ago. She also heard her Mary Mary's voice telling her how Moses and Spencer Duty had burned down the big white house of Harold LaViers before chasing him and his family off into the night woods. She pulled the shotgun back under her black long canvas coat and made her way back to the station, catching the train that would take her to Louisville, Chicago, and then on back to Montana.

Chapter 125
The Last Days

WHEN ELEANOR ARRIVED BACK in Butte she could barely walk, she'd been taking morphine but it had now reached a point where it was doing little good. Her son met her at the station and took her directly to the hospital. It was then that she told him the truth.

"Your father didn't die," she said. "He is alive, but he never knew that you were born. It is not something that you should hold against him, I kept my pregnancy from him. So you know, he is the best man I ever knew, I just for some reason never felt like I could marry him, it wasn't him and the reason will die with me. His is name is Spencer Duty, Jr. and he lives in Paintsville, Kentucky. I mailed him a letter from Chicago so he will know that he has a son *and* that he has a good son." Eleanor's words were breathy and filled with dying. "You will have to want for nothing, everything I have is left to you. Your father also knows that I am dying. It is up to you to get in touch with him. I hope you choose to and that you don't wait too long, he is getting up in years.

"You have been the greatest joy I have ever known and I am forever proud of you. Live a good life, a life that when you look back on at the end you can be proud of."

And on that, Eleanor closed her eyes for the long sleep.

Chapter 126

Dearest Spencer,

By the time you read this I will be dead. The cancer is very aggressive and has spread so many places there isn't anywhere else left for it to go. You may have figured it out already but I am the one who shot the boy Boyd and burned his house and The Holy Hill Cathedral to the ground, my only regret is that he died too quickly and didn't suffer enough, but time was short and hopefully in his case there really is a hell. That's not why I am writing you this last letter.

I became pregnant after we were together on my last night in Paintsville. I can't say completely why I didn't tell you, I know you would have wanted to know, but I just couldn't bring myself to. I named our son after a man you and I both respect.

His name is Moses Kitchen, II. Spencer, Moses has your integrity and intelligence and I believe you will find him to be a good man. His lifelong dream was to become a doctor, which, as my life comes to an end, I was able to see his dream fulfilled. I will tell him the truth right before I die and hope that he will get in touch with you. I've never said it to you but I have *always* loved you. I think that I was afraid that if we had been married that I would somehow destroy that. And *that* I couldn't bear so I decided to leave things as they were. I know you love me and I have carried your love with me now for these many years and will take it with me when I die. I leave you our son and hope that the two of you will grow to know each other and forgive me for keeping you apart.

All my love,
Forever and always
Eleanor